Praise for *God's Pocket*

"Dexter [knows] the American language inside out and [uses] it to compose this artful hymn to the dark underside of modern urban life . . . *God's Pocket* is a feat: funny, harsh, musical, tough-minded—an impressive debut." —*New York Newsday*

"A darkly amusing look at life [by] a marvelous storyteller . . . Dexter is able to make wonderful sense out of the nonsense that is intrinsic to *God's Pocket*." —*Atlanta Journal-Constitution*

"Striking . . . The plot strings together one catastrophe after another in a black-comedic manner reminiscent of an episode from *Hill Street Blues*. . . . [Dexter] manages to capture both the despair and the essential dignity of his characters—not only in what they say, but in the rhythms they use to say it." —*Booklist*

"Dexter has a bone-deep feel for the street and an ear for the voices you hear there . . . Despite his popular column in the *Philadelphia Daily News*, Dexter is one of the best-kept secrets on the literary scene. *God's Pocket* should blow his cover." —*Playboy*

"Dexter's sense of place, believable characters and raw dialogue create memorable moments while drawing a social portrait that takes the reader to some frightening places. . . . His story puts the reader right in the street among some of the toughest and bleakest characters ever to grace the literary page." —*Richmond Times-Dispatch*

"*God's Pocket* is a strong, vibrant first novel. Dexter's debut offers a variety of gifted sequences along the way: sharp character-sketches, neighborhood atmosphere, raw dialogue, comic/dreadful moments—and, at its best, a sense of soldiering on down dead-end streets." —*Kirkus Reviews*

PENGUIN BOOKS

GOD'S POCKET

Pete Dexter lives in Clinton, Washington, with his wife, Dian, and his daughter, Casey. He was born in Michigan and raised in Georgia, Illlinois, and eastern South Dakota. He is the author of *Deadwood*, *Brotherly Love*, and the 1988 National Book Award-winner *Paris Trout*, as well as many screenplays. A fifth novel, *The Paperboy*, will be published in 1995.

GOD'S POCKET

Pete Dexter

PENGUIN BOOKS

PENGUIN BOOKS
Published by the Penguin Group
Penguin Books USA Inc., 375 Hudson Street, New York, New York 10014, U.S.A.
Penguin Books Ltd, 27 Wrights Lane, London W8 5TZ, England
Penguin Books Australia Ltd, Ringwood, Victoria, Australia
Penguin Books Canada Ltd, 10 Alcorn Avenue, Toronto, Ontario, Canada M4V 3B2
Penguin Books (N.Z.) Ltd, 182–190 Wairau Road, Auckland 10, New Zealand

Penguin Books Ltd, Registered Offices: Harmondsworth, Middlesex, England

First published in the United States of America by Random House, Inc., 1983
Reprinted by arrangement with Random House, Inc.
Published in Penguin Books 1995

1 3 5 7 9 10 8 6 4 2

PUBLISHER'S NOTE
This is a work of fiction. Names, characters, places, and incidents either are the
product of the author's imagination or are used fictitiously, and any resemblance to
actual persons, living or dead, events, or locales is entirely coincidental.

THE LIBRARY OF CONGRESS HAS CATALOGUED THE HARDCOVER AS FOLLOWS:
Dexter, Pete, 1943–
God's pocket/Pete Dexter.
p.   cm.
ISBN 0-394-53057-8 (hc.)
ISBN 0 14 02.4627 4 (pbk.)
I. Title.
PS3554.E95G6   1984
813'.54—dc20   83–42768

Printed in the United States of America
Set in Times Roman

For T. C. Tollefson
(1917–1978)

Now there was a teacher . . .

GOD'S POCKET

COMMON
LABOR

Leon Hubbard died ten minutes into lunch break on the first Monday in May, on the construction site of the new one-story trauma wing at Holy Redeemer Hospital in South Philadelphia. One way or the other, he was going to lose the job.

The foreman was a 270-pound ex-Georgia Baptist named Coleman Peets, who'd had to fight men twelve or fourteen times in twenty years of bossing crews, who'd had to kill a man once on a shopping-center job in Florida, but had never actually had to fire anybody before. Before, they'd always known when to leave.

Peets had a policy about bossing, and that was you never gave anything away that they could use against you.

The best man he had was an old shine who talked to himself named Lucien Edwards, Jr. Everybody called him Old Lucy, and as a rule he didn't answer. He had the same work policy as Coleman Peets, and after eleven years together, on and off, either one of them would have been surprised to find out the other one was married. And that suited them both.

Old Lucy came to work on time. He shaved every day of his life and carried the same lunch box he'd had the first day Peets saw him. You could leave him alone a week, he'd do a week's work. And now Peets had to watch this $17.40-an-hour *bricklayer* they'd sent over from the union office, who couldn't lay a straight line of piss, going after Old Lucy too.

Leon Hubbard had worried most everybody on the crew at one time or another, he'd even touched something in Peets. It wasn't the razor—Peets had taken razors away from people, that was as simple as understanding you were going to get cut—it was something in the kid you didn't want to listen to. The truth was, he didn't believe the kid's stepfather was connected. That was more bullshit, the same way the razor was. He kept it in his back pocket and brought it out twenty, thirty times a day. He used it to cut lunch meat and tell stories and shape his fingernails. There was a neatness connected to it. Once they'd found a bat inside a cinder block and he'd used the razor to cut its head off. Then he'd wrung everything out of the body and said, "I seen that happen to a nun once."

There was another boy Leon's age on the crew. Gary Sample. Leon's age or he could of been a couple years younger. He'd said, "I got a nun I'd like to do like that. Sister Mary Theresa at St. Anthony's." Only he'd said it slower than that, because he stuttered. "P . . . p . . . p . . . pull-ed my ears e . . . e . . . ev-ry day." And that did not sit well with Coleman Peets. The others smiled, and they were worried.

The next time Leon Hubbard pulled his razor out Peets had said, "Boy, you 'bout to figure out a way to wipe your ass with that thing, ain't you?" And they'd smiled at that too, and then Leon Hubbard had stepped in front of him, holding the razor behind his leg, and they'd looked at each other until Peets had given way.

4

He couldn't of weighed 130 pounds, and he took the afternoon off to polish the blade.

Peets never told his wife about that, he never told her the kid was supposed to be connected either. "You ever climbed out on a roof," he asked her that morning, "and looked down, and for just a breath somethin' inside you said, 'Jump'?"

She was in the bathroom, brushing her teeth for work. She opened the door to look at him, the toothbrush was still in her mouth. He said, "Leon Hubbard is what the voice looks like."

She turned back to the sink and rinsed out her mouth. "You're scared to fire him, Peets," she said.

He said, "I do wisht he'd leave." He looked at himself in the bedroom mirror, muscle and belly and scars—there were places he'd of forgot he'd been except for the scars—and wondered how much he'd have to say to get rid of him.

His wife came back out of the bathroom and he watched her dress in the mirror.

"Old Lucy, he won't talk to the boy," he said. "Got half the damn crew standin' around now, watchin' him, looks like we work for the fuckin' city, and then he gets a bug up his ass for Old Lucy, 'cause he's the only one wants to do his work."

She said, "He got a bug up his ass for you too?" Peets shrugged. She stood next to him and pulled her white panty hose up, bunching the uniform around her waist. She was thirty-seven years old, supervising nurse in the emergency room at Hahnemann Hospital, where Saturday nights they brought in bodies like the moving company—"Where do you want this?"—and as far as Peets knew, the idea that he could be hurt too had never occurred to her. He thought she loved him for that, so he never messed with it.

"It's simple," she said. "You go up to him and stand there pissed off, pretend you found me asleep on your side of the bed, and pretty soon he'll move."

Peets said, "Leon's immune. The more you don't like him, the more he likes bein' around. I never run into a case like it."

She said, "I've seen potatoes move because you thought

they were on the wrong side of the plate, Peets." She pulled her skirt down, smoothed it in front and back. Watching her dress always worked on him the way watching her undress was supposed to. He reached out and helped smooth her behind, and they looked at each other in the mirror. She pushed back into his hand, just a shade.

"I used to believe you didn't know what you was up to," he said.

She ignored that and sat down on the bed to tie her shoes. "If standing there looking doesn't do it," she said, "then talk to him. Tell him, 'You're fired, and I'm not going to pay you anymore.'" Peets made a face. "It'll work," she said. "It's a whole new generation out there that won't come to work if you don't pay them. It must of been the rock-'n'-roll." Peets had been brought up strict. He'd gotten over being a Baptist—he had to, to end up with Sarah—but the idea you had to work went deeper. Firing somebody was more of a judgment than he felt comfortable to make on a human being.

"If he'd just leave the rest of them alone, I wouldn't care," he said. "But I see him over there jackin' up Old Lucy, and it ain't going to end. I know that much, it ain't going to end by itself."

His wife put on a raincoat and bent over to kiss him goodbye. She stuck her tongue square in his mouth, so it was showing how worried he was. "It'll work itself out," she said. "It always does."

He watched her from the window until she got to the car, then sat back down on the bed to think. He couldn't do that with her in the house. Five minutes later he stood up and went into the bathroom to shave, and he knew what it was bothering him. He and the old shine had an understanding. And it tortured Peets to think of Old Lucy having to ask him for help.

"Oh, Mickey," she said, "your balls, your cock, oh, Mickey . . ." Mickey was her husband, and he liked her to name the parts of his body while they made love. She didn't mind.

6

Jeanie Hubbard Scarpato was Leon Hubbard's mother, and her life had more sorry chapters than the Old Testament. She had buried one husband in the ground, a couple of possible replacements had gotten lost in her reflections of that event. Neither of her sisters had lost a husband, so they couldn't understand. She was in the habit of reminding them of that. They would say thank God for her police widow's benefits, which had kept her more comfortable than some people they could think of.

Jeanie had been born prettier and more talented than either of her sisters. When she was young, she had gone to dance school in New York and been badly treated there by a man the same age as her father. He was a patron of the arts, but he made her promises he never intended to keep, and in the end he had punched her in the eye in the gentlemen's room on the balcony level of the Lunt-Fontanne Theatre. His name was Rex.

She could still get moody over that night. He was her first real happiness, her first real tragedy. It was a long time since those were separate things. Rex had manners, especially when he wasn't drinking, and he understood the arts. He had taken her to the Met, to restaurants other people couldn't get into and, of course, to the Lunt-Fontanne Theatre. He respected her and asked her opinions. "What do you think of that wonderful contralto?" He had opened the gentlemen's room door for her that evening. "I don't go down on anybody," she had said. He hadn't respected her for that as much as she'd thought he would.

Mickey was getting close. In a minute he would grab her neck in his mouth and breathe hard through his nose, close up to her ear, where she could hear every little thing in there that didn't belong. She settled her chin against her shoulder to wait it out.

There was a hedge of black hair on his shoulders. It grew from there down his back in two wide stripes. On his back, at least, it all grew in the same direction. It looked combed.

It was funny. In the beginning, she'd thought he was an animal. He'd sat in the corner at a party, not talking to anybody. On the street they said he was a man who had made his bones, and when she found him staring at her later, she saw he probably was. He had eyes like he was, anyway. Little ones. And he was the best friend of Arthur "Bird" Capezio, who had the hot meat business for all of South Philadelphia, right out of his warehouse in God's Pocket. Arthur worked for Vinnie the Italian, who had Angelo Bruno's ear. This was before somebody put a shotgun in his ear one night, of course, and changed the way things worked.

She'd sat next to him in the corner. The house belonged to a traffic court judge, on the way to Holmesburg Prison to do one-to-three for bribery, theft, embezzlement. It was sort of a going-away party, and everybody was happy. The rumor was that even if he did ten months, it still came to $10,000 a week. There wasn't a kid over five years old in God's Pocket who didn't know he'd beat the city for $400,000.

Mickey said, "You married?"

"Widowed," she said, and waited. Nothing. "How about you?" He shook his head, and didn't say anything else until Jeanie asked him what he did for a living.

"The meat business," he said. The way he said that ran a chill straight through to her ass. "I work for Bird." She'd noticed his hands then. They were thick hands, hair clear down into the knuckles. She pictured them gripping herself and other victims. When she'd looked up he was smiling at her. She took him home, got him a Schmidt's, and sat next to him on the couch. "This is good beer," he said.

An hour later she gave up hope of being abused and led him by the hand up the stairs to her bedroom. He wasn't quite rough and he wasn't quite tender, and then in the end he took her neck in his mouth and breathed hard through his nose until he'd finished.

Jeanie liked the way the neighborhood women looked at her in the morning, though. She was not the kind to feed gossip, but this much did slip out once or twice during the day: "A jack-hammer," she'd said.

He put his mouth on her neck now and came at her faster. It wasn't a jackhammer, it was more like, well, a dick. Something real hungry with a little-bitty mouth. Like a guppy . . .

And that is how she would remember it. On the day her only child would die, Jeanie Scarpato satisfied her husband at seven-fifteen in the morning, thinking of tropical fish. It was the kind of life she had been given to lead.

Mickey Scarpato was forty-five years old and did not understand women. It wasn't the way bartenders or comedians didn't understand women, it was the way poor people didn't understand the economy. You could stand outside the Girard Bank Building every day of your life and never guess anything about what went on in there. That's why, in their hearts, they'd always rather stick up a 7-Eleven.

And why Mickey, married three years, would still rather be with Bird or McKenna than with Jeanie. It was the strain.

Being in the meat business, Mickey spent his share of time with bartenders. The one who complained the most about women was probably McKenna, at the Hollywood. He delivered there Mondays—it was right across the street from his house—and once in a while if he finished early and Leon wasn't sitting in there buying drinks and flashing his bricklayer money, he'd stay for a couple of beers. Mickey didn't like his stepson to buy him a beer.

McKenna always had a story about his old lady, and when Mickey came in McKenna would bring him into it. Like, "Last Saturday night, I was out all night fuckin' around, you know how you do sometimes. Mickey'll understand this—see, I'm out till eight o'clock in the morning, and when I come toolin' in, the old lady's pissed six ways they ain't invented yet.

"So I know I got to make up a lie, and she knows I got to make up a lie. I been doin' pretty good lately, so I come into the bedroom and says, 'Hey, baby, I been in a game. I won five bills.' I take all the money out of my pocket and show her. I says, 'Here is a couple hundret for you.' She puts her robe on and walks past

9

me into the bathroom. She says, 'I'm very happy for you.' Just like that. Cold.

"She goes in there and locks the door. 'I'm very happy for you.' She don't even give you the satisfaction of sayin' you're full of shit. And she takes the money. Right, Mick? Two hundret dollars, and she don't talk to you anyway."

Mickey only liked McKenna's stories when Leon wasn't around to look at him. He didn't mind being brought into them—it made him less of an outsider—but not with Leon sitting there grinning at him like they were two buddies, just fucked the same whore.

Mickey had only lived in the Pocket since he'd been married. Most of the neighborhood was nice to him because they were afraid of him, but McKenna liked him from the day they met. He thought it could of been because they were about the same age, or it could of been because Jeanie still had her looks. She could dress up and fix her hair so beautiful it still surprised him that she wanted him around.

The truth was, he was forty-five years old and Jeanie was the only woman who had wanted him around, unless it was for money, or doing somebody else a favor.

That night she'd taken him home from Judge Lourdy's party, he'd made her happy. She'd moaned and perspired and said "cock" and "balls" and "dick" into his ear. And she was a biter. She'd said, "Oh, you're so good." He'd lived forty-one years to that point, in Fort Lauderdale, Florida, and everywhere else, and nobody ever said anything like that to him before.

As he'd started to come, he almost bit her too. He'd gotten scared, though, and put his lips over his teeth and closed his mouth over the skin on her neck. He'd been afraid of leaving marks, and she'd know he didn't belong there.

She'd come then. Closed her eyes and tightened and hissed and pulled the hair on his back. So she'd noticed it. Once a whore in Hollywood, Florida, had called him an ape.

Afterward, he pulled back a few inches to look at Jeanie's face. He wanted to see for himself that it wasn't a trick. She was quiet and smiling, except there was something going on. And neither of them moved for what seemed like half an hour, and by the time he'd looked away, Mickey Scarpato understood he didn't even have a guess what it was, and never would.

He rolled away from Jeanie now and looked at the clock. Seven-twenty. "Leon goin' to work today?" he said.

She seemed to come back from somewhere else. "I didn't hear him come in last night," she said. She sat up and put on the black robe with the map of Vietnam on the back. Leon had given her that for Christmas, bought it from some colored vendor on Chestnut Street. It was so thin you could see her nipples through it. He'd given it to her and winked at Mickey when she'd taken it out of the box. He'd got the box at Bamberger's.

The house was narrow and cold. Two bedrooms, one bath, four Touch Tone Princess telephones. She closed the bathroom door behind her, and he heard water running. Then he heard her knock on the door to Leon's room. The bathroom separated the bedrooms and had doors leading into both of them, and another door leading into the hall. Leon had taken all the locks off when he was eleven. Jeanie told that story like he'd taught himself to read.

"Leon," she said, "it's time for work, honey." She sounded tired, he didn't make any sound at all. She knocked on the door again, and a few seconds later she came back into the bedroom with Mickey. He stood up into his pants. She said, "He must of been out late."

He said, "I got to be down to Bird's by eight o'clock, if he wants a ride." She went back and knocked harder. She didn't want Leon to lose another job. On the average, it took three years to get him another one.

In the series of misfortunes that had been Jeanie Scarpato's life, the greatest tragedy had been Tom Hubbard. She had married him after she quit New York. He was the opposite of dance school. She'd married him and lost him, all in eleven months. Shot dead outside a regular Thursday-night crap game in South Philadelphia. Leon Hubbard was the issue of that marriage. He was what Tom Hubbard had left her. Leon and the house and a little over $44,000 she found, mostly in hundreds, in a shoe box out in the garage. Her sisters knew she had something—always remarking about her widow's pension—but she never told them what.

She could close her eyes and still see the way she had looked at the cemetery, holding the folded flag off Tom's coffin, crying, her soft blond hair moving against the front of the black dress. The wind was perfect.

She pounded on the door again and heard him move. "Mickey's got to be to Bird's place by eight, if you want a ride," she said. She listened, he moved again. "Honey?"

Leon Hubbard hated to be told anything. There was something about it that didn't take him into account. He woke up with a hangover and a torn dick, smelling like Fat Pat's bedroom, Jeanie kicking down the door *telling* him where Mickey had to be by what time. "All right," he said.

"Honey?"

"I said all right." He lifted the sheet to look at his dick. The tear ran half an inch, from the foreskin to the center of the mouth, and resembled a harelip. *"Don't ever pick up a cat like that,"* she'd said. *"He was just telling you the only way he could. . . ."*

Fat Pat lived over a little hoagie shop on Twenty-seventh Street in a two-room apartment. Anywhere from fourteen to twenty cats lived there too. "How come you don't have these fuckers fixed, at least?" he'd said, more than once. Three of them were pregnant, and there had to be seven or eight males walking around all day, spraying every inch of the floors and the furniture, trying to stake out their territory over the scent of everybody else who'd sprayed there. She never let the cats out because they were wild and wouldn't come back.

It was a little God's Pocket right inside her apartment.

Fat Pat worked the Hunt Room of the Bellevue-Stratford, waiting tables. Nights she hung out at the Hollywood or the uptown, drinking vodka and 7-Up with cherries in it, waiting for Leon. She never ate the cherries, but she accumulated them in her glass to keep track of how many drinks she'd had, and late at night they got soft and petaled, and looked like an old corsage.

Pat sat at the far end of the bar from Leon and never bothered him when he came by. She didn't even speak to him unless he said something first. That's the way Leon liked it.

Sometimes, mostly on Fridays, he took her home. Not from the bar, though. He always met her outside. "I don't need people knowin' about my personal business," he'd said once. "It's the same principle as changin' your patterns every day."

She'd heard him talking about her, though. At the Hollywood and the Uptown both.

At her apartment, they'd go into the bedroom right away, because there weren't as many cats in there. He'd take his clothes off, fold them and put them in the closet. Leon always took care of his clothes. Then he'd lie sideways across the bed, his head against the wall, and watch her blow him.

Last night, one of the cats was watching too. Sitting on a little table with the pictures of Fat Pat's dead brother Monte in a Navy uniform, half a foot out of reach, blinking the way cats do, like they're changing lenses back there. It was on the table about five minutes, and then Leon felt a soft concussion and it was next to him on the bed. He picked the cat up by the tail, and then three or four things happened, he couldn't say in exactly what order.

The cat screamed. He saw the look of Fat Pat's face and said, "No cat is comin' near this dick." Fat Pat had taken his penis out of her mouth to beg for the cat, and the cat had ripped a coma in the head of Leon's dick.

It hurt too bad to even look for his razor to cut the cat's head off. He grabbed himself and rocked, back and forth, hissing, while Fat Pat told him that it was the only way the cat had to tell people not to pick it up by the tail. A couple minutes later he realized he still had his hard-on.

13

There was nothing in his history to suggest the problem would ever develop, but there it was. Torn and bleeding, it would not fall. "We got to get it down to make it stop bleeding," he said.

Fat Pat said, "Try thinking about something else. Multiplication tables." In the end, he had forced it inside his forty-five-dollar blue jeans and walked home with it pushing into his pants leg. It hurt him everywhere. It hurt so bad at home he didn't even wash off the smell of Fat Pat's bedroom. He took a couple of Percodan and got into bed, and gradually the pain drained back from his eyes and his chest and his stomach and gathered itself in the head of his penis, where it seemed to go to sleep with him.

He got out of bed carefully now, not wanting to wake it up all at once.

Downstairs, Mickey was sitting at the kitchen table with a cup of coffee. Jeanie was sitting on the other side of the table, eating chocolate donuts and reading Richard Shellburn's column in the newspaper. "Listen to this, Mickey. 'The old man had eyes as sad as the dog's. He looked into the empty rooms where he and his wife had lived their lives, quiet lives, and wondered what had happened to his neighborhood, that children would come into the house and beat up an old man for his money. "At least they didn't hurt Hoppy," he said.' Isn't that sad?"

Mickey watched her pour sugar into her coffee and use that to wash down a donut. "I don't know how you eat that shit," he said. "You get sugar diabetes, they're going to cut off your feet."

"You're sweet," she said. "You ought to eat something too. You can't go to work with nothing in your stomach."

He shook his head. He could never eat on a day he had to steal a truck, not until after it was done. He looked at his watch. Seven-thirty. "Is Leon going to get out of bed, or what?"

"I heard him moving," she said. "He'll be down."

He looked at his watch again, but he didn't say anything else. He didn't know much about women, but he knew enough to stay out of the line between Jeanie and her son. The kid was there first, and that counted. No matter what Leon did, Mickey didn't have any opinion on it.

Before they'd gotten married, Jeanie had mentioned from time to time that Leon had been his whole life without a father figure, and she was glad there would be somebody now to show him how to be strong. Leon had been to Byberry twice Mickey knew of, for observation. She would somehow drop his emotional problems into a conversation, and Mickey would somehow ignore it.

A month or two into the marriage, Jeanie gave up on it and settled for Mickey getting him a job. Which looked easier than being a father figure. He asked around and found him a spot bartending four nights a week on Two Street. Leon lasted three weeks. Mickey went down to try to straighten it out.

"Listen," the man said, "I expect him to steal. Everybody steals, that's what a job is for, but he don't have enough respect to keep it reasonable. He comes in the first night and grabs thirty. I got people workin' for me for five years don't take thirty. Plus, I come into my own place and he stands there lookin' at me like he wants to cut my head off."

When Mickey got home he told Jeanie he didn't know what had gone wrong. And after that, when she asked him to find Leon another job, he'd always tell her nobody was hiring. He'd tell her it was the economy.

Which was all right with Leon. At least it had been for three years. Jeanie gave him money for clothes and a place to stay and let him use the Monte Carlo when he had a date. Her insurance was fourteen hundred dollars, letting him use the Monte Carlo. "A nice girl will be good for him," she said.

But they never saw his dates, even Cheryl. Leon said Cheryl was a flight attendant for U.S. Air and lived in the Northeast, which Mickey recognized for the classiest thing Leon could make up. But he never said it, and Jeanie kept giving the kid forty, fifty every Friday night to take her out, and Mickey never said a word.

Then, about six weeks ago, Leon had decided he wanted a

job again. "Not some bar," he'd said, "a real job. You know, a trade or somethin'." He'd told that to Jeanie.

She'd gone to Mickey like this: "It was him, this time. It wasn't me, it was him. Can't you talk to somebody downtown? Please, Mickey, talk to somebody for him." She went through it again, how the kid had grown up without a father figure, and finally time and maturity must have turned him around.

Mickey knew it was something else, but he didn't know what. He did know by then that nothing would turn the kid around but a chance to run over you twice.

"He's always been good with his hands," she said. "You know how old he was when he took the locks off upstairs. . . ." And he'd given in. The next time he'd seen Bird down at the flower shop he asked if he could find something for the kid. Bird was eating a cold cheese steak.

He'd known Bird a long time, since he was still hauling poison for Dow Chemical. They'd drunk beer together and bet the ponies together, and they were friends except for business, which Bird kept separate. Mickey bought his meat from Bird, and once in a while he took a truck for him. But even when he did that—it was never more than two or three a year—it was straight cash, never a percentage.

When he'd asked about Leon, Bird had stopped eating, a piece of onion hanging from the corner of his mouth where he had to know it was there, and looked at him like it was somebody else. "You sure you want to ask that?"

Bird had a famous temper and balanced that against a melancholy that left him weighing his life against his expectations, to measure what he was against a standard that would change with how bad he felt at the time. Any kind of crisis would set him off—a flat tire, a bad day at Keystone, money moving some direction it wasn't supposed to—and it always ended the same way. He'd go from mad to sad, and decide he'd wasted his potential. Bird had to stay pissed off to keep from being weak.

"If it was just me, Mick," he said, "I'd just fuckin' do it. I'd pick up the phone just because I know you, that's how much I think of you. You got a nice thing here the way it is, you know? A nice truck, a nice business, you don't got to ask anybody for nothin'. A lot of these assholes around here don't appreciate what a blessing that is. A lot of these assholes don't appreciate when you start askin' for shit you don't have, you start givin' away the shit you got."

He was still looking at Mickey like there was something about him left to figure out. "I know what I'm talkin' about," he said. "I got shit goin' down right now, I can't even find out where it's comin' from."

Mickey said, "Yeah, well, I didn't mean to put you into awkward positions."

Bird held up his hands. A piece of meat slipped out of the roll. "Nothin's awkward. Like I said, if it was just me, I'd do it. But for somethin' like this, I got to ask somebody to make a phone call. For somethin' like this, they're going to say, 'For what?' You unnerstand? Nothin' is for nothin'."

Mickey nodded.

"You still want me to do somethin'?"

He thought of Jeanie, he put the kid out of his mind. "Yeah, see what you can do." Bird finished the sandwich, blew his nose in the wax paper, and a couple of days later they'd called from the union hall for Leon to go down there and sign the papers to be a bricklayer, first class.

He'd sold something for that, and he didn't even know what it was yet, and the second week the kid was already showing up late for work, telling Jeanie some shit about changing routines. Now he was holding up Mickey's work too. Mickey heard the shower go on upstairs. It was twenty minutes to eight. Jeanie said, "You ought to eat something," and then they heard him scream.

The shower went off and it was quiet. "Did you use all the hot water?" she said.

Leon stood in the shower, holding his mouth and his dick. When he could trust himself, he let go of his mouth. Then he opened the other hand, a crease at a time, making a little stretcher for it. He caught a reflection of himself in the mirror then. He could have been looking through his change for a dime.

The tear didn't look as bad as it was, and for once he was glad. Usually he didn't mind looking bad, like after a fight. But this nobody else was going to see. Nobody is scared of you because you got a torn dick anyway.

He got out of the shower, dressed and took another Percodan. He thought it over and took two black beauties too, to keep his edge. He got dressed and began to feel the black ones right away. He dropped six more of them into his back pocket, with the razor. He smiled. There was nothing he carried in there that was good for anybody else.

He pulled the razor out, smooth and fast and quiet, and held it open-bladed in the empty room. He wished there was a way for them to see into his pocket, they'd see what he was and call all this shit off. He folded the razor and put it on the window ledge while he checked the street, and then he went downstairs.

Mickey was already outside, sitting in the truck. Jeanie was standing at the bottom of the stairs with that look she had. She was his mother, so he loved her, but if he ever got sick enough to do one of those family jobs you read about out in Kansas or Michigan, she was the first one to go. She didn't know that, though. She was always looking up into his eyes like she was now, trying to find something out. She thought she could push in there with him and sometimes, in a way, she could.

But what she didn't know was that he could hide things from her, and that he could look into her too. He did that now and saw she'd been fucking Mickey again. If she was supposed to be his mother, what was she doing fucking Mickey in the next room?

"The shower turn cold, hon?"

He couldn't remember a time when she didn't make everything that went on in the bathroom her business. She'd caught him in there once with a pair of her panties, and the next day she'd taken all the locks off the doors. Never said a word, just backed out of the bathroom and the next day the locks were gone.

A long time later, he'd caught her telling her sister Joyce about the locks, saying he was the one who took them off. She'd winked at him, like it was something they'd agreed on. And she'd told that story to so many people he finally saw she was telling it to him. That's what they did to you when you let them make agreements you never agreed to.

Fuck it. He tried to walk past her but she caught his arm. "Leon? You want something to eat in the truck? You can't go to work with nothing in your stomach, hon."

He pulled away when she tried to kiss him. He didn't want to smell Mickey on her, he didn't want her to smell Fat Pat's bedroom on him. "Well," she said, "you certainly got up on the right side of the bed." He looked at her a minute, trying to see what she meant by that.

He reached the front door and turned the handle. He felt her touch his arm again. "What's the matter, baby?" she said, flirting now. "Cat got your tongue?" He pulled the door open just as the sun broke through the clouds, and for one second he went blind in the sun and thought he'd been shot.

He was halfway to the truck before what she'd said sunk in. *"Cat got your tongue?"* What the fuck had she meant by that? He was so pissed off, they were nearly at Holy Redeemer before he noticed he'd left the razor at home.

Lucien Edwards, Jr., was married to a religious woman. She kept a Bible in her kitchen and prayed while she cooked and cleaned for the destruction of the white race.

She was a good wife and a good cook, and sometimes she'd start dinner in the middle of the morning. Lucien would walk through her kitchen on Saturday or Sunday and find her bent over her work, sweating, reminding God how, when things had got out of hand, he'd smote the oldest-born child in every house in Egypt.

"They makin' prisoners and slaves of your people again,

Lord." She would say that like she knew she was nagging and she was sorry it had to be done. "You warned them, time and again, to let your people alone, but ain't no white people payin' attention to nothin' but Pres'dent Riggin. I know what you got in mind for him, Lord. Oh, you know they need a lesson. . . ."

Her name was Minnie Devine Johnson Edwards, and she told God she loved him night and day, and never spoke that way to her husband. She expected he ought to know by now.

She got up every morning at six o'clock to fix Lucien his lunch. Two sandwiches, an apple, a piece of homemade candy. She laid them out in a symmetrical way in his lunch box, snug, so nothing moved. Then she would close the box and open it once, to see that nothing was creased. She didn't want him looking at no unmade bed of a lunch after he'd been starin' into Satan's eyes all morning.

"Thou preparest a table before me in the presence of mine enemies. . . . Surely goodness and mercy shall follow me all the days of my life."

She handed him his lunch at the door and watched him walk down Lehigh Avenue toward Broad, where he caught the C bus for work. From behind, if he had his hat on like he did this morning, you would of thought he was thirty-five years old. In fact, he was nearly twice that, but there was nothing lame or old in his step.

Lucien had gone bald early, but she hadn't cared. His body was still hard, like a young man. She wondered at the way time seemed to pass him by. He never even wore out his shoes like other people did, and there wasn't a day of his life he went to work against his will.

Lucien crossed Fifteenth Street, nodded to an old Korean he knew who slept in a doorway there, ignored the Muslims that had taken the Korean's newsstand away half a year ago.

The Korean was there six years when the Muslims decided to take the corner. They'd warned him and cussed him, and finally they'd burned him out. At eleven o'clock on a warm Sunday morning in November, two of them got out of a customized black van with a red fist holding a lightning bolt painted on the side, poured a gallon of gasoline over the little wood building, and lit it with a match. The heat melted the custom paint job.

Three hours later, two different Muslims came by and swept up the ashes, and by Monday afternoon they'd built their own stand, and there wasn't nothing to put into yourself that you couldn't buy there but pork.

Botany 500 had its plant on the corner, so twelve hours a day there were cops around to protect the workers from the neighborhood. The Koreans showed up in the morning right after the cops. They sold Bibles or umbrellas or soft pretzels, and they were gone at night before the police left, and after the fire they never talked to the one who'd moved into the doorway.

The Muslims let it out they did not want the motherfuckers in their neighborhood—the ones who said that were sometimes from Newark—and Lucien knew what they wanted from the neighborhood wasn't just money. They wanted to bleed it. They called out to him, "Hey, old brother . . ." They called him that bullshit, but he knew what they were.

The old Korean who slept in the doorway had sent his family away when the Muslims burned him out. He'd moved out of his house, left everything his wife and children hadn't taken, and put himself in the doorway of a boarded-up house, forty feet from the Muslims, where he intended to stay until they killed him. He'd worked the stand six days a week, cleared twenty-five, thirty dollars a day. He'd come to work afraid and left afraid, and even with the cops there he was afraid all the time in between. That was how Koreans was.

When they'd burned him out, though, they lost what they had over him. They called him a crazy motherfucker now. They said it in front of him, they laughed about it, and before long, Lucien knew, they would kill him.

And he knew the Korean didn't have no plan for the way it would be. That was the part Lucien didn't understand. In some little place in the back of their thoughts, the Muslims was scared of the old Korean too, but he wasn't using it for nothing. He'd given up his family, and some morning they was going to find him laying in his doorway with a bullet in his head. It might be the middle of the morning before somebody noticed he wasn't asleep.

And by afternoon it would be like he was never there at all.

Lucien got on the bus and found a window on the left side, where he could see the campus of Temple University. He liked watching girls on their way to college. He wondered what they must be teachin' them in there. On the other side of the bus, you could see what had been some of the finest homes in the city. Somebody had done a lot of good work in North Philadelphia once. Minnie Devine said it was part of a white man's plan to get all the city Negroes in one place, where they'd be handy for scientific experiments. He smiled at her, that she could keep it up so long.

Lucien never argued with Minnie Devine, but he knew nobody had built houses like those for anything but the houses themself. You couldn't do that kind of work for hate. Twenty minutes later, though, at Washington Avenue, he could look east and see the Southwark Homes projects. Eight thousand people in fourteen stories. She was right that there was a plan—Southwark Homes couldn't be no accident—but it wasn't sneaky the way she thought. Most of the time, things was the way they looked. But Lucien never argued with Minnie Devine.

He got to the hospital a little after seven-thirty and squatted next to the cherry picker to wait for the boss. The ground was wet, but he wouldn't of sat down anyway. Not before work. The cherry picker was a small crane they used to move steel rods or cement blocks, or anything else wasn't in the right place. The more youngsters you had on a job, the more things wasn't where you could use them. Lucien expected they would need two cherry pickers soon. Shit, the new boy with the razor could use one all to hisself.

Lucien never wanted to be boss, and sometimes he looked at Peets and wondered how he put up with somebody always gettin' in the way of what he was tryin' to leave behind. He thought

22

work must be different for Peets, not as personal. For the youngsters, it wasn't nothing at all.

The boom on the cherry picker was fifteen feet high. A steel cable dropped from both sides of the pulley and connected at the bottom at an eight-pound U-bolt. The bolt was tied to the boom with a thinner cable to keep it out of the way. Lucien had seen one like it swing into a man once, not even hard, and break his chest. You could walk into one and knock yourself out.

The foundation for the new wing ran east from the cherry picker eighty feet, then another sixty feet south, back to the main building. Lucien was laying cinder block when they quit Friday. He saw where he'd left off, and the work was as level as you could draw it. Things was what they looked like, good work looked like good work. There were a dozen empty beer bottles on the ground near the wall, and he'd picked them up by the time Peets climbed out of his pickup.

The ground was softer where he parked, and the old man heard Peets' boots sinking into the mud and then sucking up what was underneath. He was naturally messy.

"Mornin', Lucy," Peets said.

"Peets." He didn't move, and Peets squatted down beside him. The old man could feel the heat from his body and hear his hinges creak. A couple of minutes passed and Peets looked at his watch. "Damn, it's nobody wants to work today," he said. There were nine men on the crew, and as of eight o'clock, seven of them were late. "It ain't turned to daylight savings time again, has it?"

Lucien looked at him and smiled. Minnie Devine called it Daylights Scaring Time, and thought it was something a white man had invented to keep city Negroes lazy. She said they had no such thing in the country.

Peets said, "Could be it's just us today."

Lucien said, "Could be we get somethin' done." They stood up together and walked over to pull the plastic cover off the cement. The sacks were eighty pounds, and the old man handled them like nothing. Peets primed the Wisconsin that ran the mixer, and it caught on the third try. It was whisperized, according to the law. Peets missed the old noise, but times changed, and being the job was next to a hospital, it was probably to the best.

The old man tore open a cement bag and poured it into a wheelbarrow. Peets shoveled. Lucien had worked for bosses who cheated, even on little jobs, or were lazy, which came to the same thing. Some of them mixed it two to one. He'd also worked for bosses that didn't use half the steel they was supposed to. Peets kept it honest. Three sand, two cement, one lime. He wouldn't be coming past in no Mark VI in five years, but he wouldn't have to wonder if his wall was still there either. Lucien didn't believe in leaving things unsettled. If you did, they never let you rest.

Lucien got the hose and watered the mix. He added by eye, but it was never soupy and it was never hard. When his cement came out the mixer, it would stand up three inches on a trowel.

The sun was up, and Peets and the old man worked fifteen minutes before a caved-in station wagon with five men from the crew stopped on the sidewalk and emptied out. Peets didn't say so, but he was sorry to see them come. The job was twenty days behind now, and there'd be more wet weather next month, but working alone with the old shine, he was happy. He would of been glad to haul blocks and mix cement for him all day. With just him and Old Lucy, he didn't have to tell nobody to leave the damn nurses alone, or argue over some damn union rule he never heard of. He didn't have to think any way but practical.

He gave his shovel to the boy Gary Sample and put Old Lucy back on the wall where he was laying block Friday.

Mickey was two blocks from Holy Redeemer when the kid said he had to go back. He told him, "Leon, I got to be somewhere. You got me ten minutes late already."

"Listen," he said, "I forgot my medicine."

"What medicine?"

"The medicine the doctor gave me. I can't go to work without that shit, Mickey. If you can't go back, let me out here and I'll walk." He looked over and the kid was sweating.

"What the fuck is wrong with you?"

"Nothin'," he said. "I just can't go to work without my medicine. Jeanie didn't tell you about that?"

Jeanie. Mickey pulled the truck into an alley, found a cross street and took the kid home. Then at the house the kid said, "Not here, drive up half a block."

He stopped half a block from the house. Leon dropped out of the truck. He hit the sidewalk crouched, looking all around him, and then ran to the house, zigzagging in and out of garbage cans. Monday was garbage day on Twenty-fifth Street. Mickey didn't let himself think about what Leon must be like at work, or what kind of an asshole that made him with Bird.

Seven seconds after he'd gone through the front door, Leon was in the window on the second floor, checking the street. Then he was back out on the sidewalk running toward the truck. Jeanie's head came out the door and watched him all the way back. Mickey waved, but she must not have seen it.

The kid got in and slammed the door. "See? I told you I'd run." Mickey thought there must be some conversation going on all the time in Leon's head that he thought he was having out loud. "Didn't take no time at all," he said.

It had taken long enough, though, so a City of Philadelphia sanitation truck had turned left off Lombard and got in front of them and was moving half a mile an hour down Twenty-fifth now while three democrats strolled back and forth across the street, picking up garbage cans, dumping half the shit inside into the truck, the other half into the street. At the end of the block, the driver got out, and all four of them went into the Uptown to shake the place down for a ten and a drink.

There was a half a block of cars lined up behind Mickey by then, most of them blowing their horns or shouting, but none of it had much conviction. Nobody hurries the City of Philadelphia. Mickey looked at his watch. "Eight-fifteen in the morning," he said. "They ought to be ashamed of themself."

"I seen a guy get thrown into the back of one of them once," Leon said, to pass the time. Mickey looked over and the kid was smiling in a way that Mickey almost believed him. That was the

25

trouble with Leon. You could never be sure he was completely full of shit. There was a way he *committed* himself to it. "You ever seen that, Mickey? They throw the guy in the back and then mash him into all the other shit back there."

Mickey didn't say a word, and Leon didn't read nothing into it. "I knew the guy they did that to," he said. Mickey checked his watch. They'd been inside the Uptown four minutes. The kid had been sweating out his eyeballs fifteen minutes ago, now he was cold.

"He was cute," Leon said. "Asshole bet K.C. against the Phillies the whole series. A grand, a grand, two grand. The series ended, he owed five, and he didn't have no idea where he was going to get his hands on something like that.

"That's what he told Skully. You know Skully, what a nice guy he is, but the people he works for ain't nice. And a couple nights after the parade they had for the team, a couple guys come by and take this guy right out in the street, in front of his family and everybody. Just then a garbage truck was comin' by, and they just threw him in there instead of breakin' his legs themselves. It was sort of like progress. Like computers, they throw this guy in back so they don't have to do all the work. Wasn't as noisy, either. One of them gets in the cab, the niggers go into a bar. But the guy had claustrophobia, see, and nobody knew it. So when they pulled him out of there, he wasn't just broke up a little bit, you know what I mean? He was suffocated."

The garbage men came out of the Uptown and started down Twenty-fifth Street. Mickey made a left through an alley. "He panicked," Leon said, "or he'd of been all right. You panic sometimes, that's all she wrote."

"How come you're always talkin' that shit, Leon?" Mickey said. He looked over at him again and wished he'd kept his mouth shut. "I mean, it's the first thing in the morning. . . ."

"You think it's shit?" the kid said. "You think it's shit? Say it, you think it's shit."

Mickey stopped the truck and waited. "Leon, I don't need this now." If it came to that, he'd decided to choke him enough to change the amount of air his brain was getting and figure out a way later to explain it to Jeanie without saying Leon was crazy. Then, while he watched, it changed again. Leon smiled at him, began to nod.

"I know you done your share, Mickey," he said. "I know you been there." They rode the rest of the way to Holy Redeemer without talking. Then the kid climbed out of the truck and said, "Thanks, Mickey. Hey, I really appreciate everything," and slammed the door.

Mickey drove back into the Pocket, thinking what a crazy fuck the kid was and how someway Jeanie would eventually tie him into that, turned left for seven blocks thinking the same thing, and then he saw Bird sitting in a new yellow Cadillac outside the flower shop. Mickey liked the color. There was another man in the front seat Mickey had never seen before, and the life and times of Leon Hubbard was old business.

He left his truck running in back of the Cadillac and walked up to Bird's window. It was twenty minutes to nine. "Another five minutes, we was going to leave without you, Mick," he said.

Mickey said, "Lemme put the truck in back. I still got meat back there."

"You can put it in there, but it ain't going to do nothin' for your meat," Bird said. "We ain't had electric since six o'clock last night." Mickey looked around the street. All the ladies were sitting on their steps instead of watching Phil Donahue. The man he hadn't seen before didn't say anything.

"Then what you going to do with the load?" Mickey said.

"What the fuck you think we're doin' in here, Mick?" Bird said. "Talkin' about the power windows?" There was an edge to Bird that wasn't his natural edge. It was like he was afraid to get mad. Mickey didn't know if it was because he was late, or if it was the man in the front seat. There wasn't no reason it took three people to steal a truck. Either way, he'd explain later, when it didn't make him look weak.

He took the truck around the block and pulled into the garage behind the flower shop, which had two stalls, both of them with twenty-foot clearances. He shut the door on the truck and himself, then got a flashlight from under the front seat and walked through the cooler. The place had once been a warehouse for the school district.

From what he could see, it was about half full. The light and the sides of beef made changing shadows—dog heads, monsters, nightmare shit—always changing, always moving. He had the sudden thought that something must be walking around inside Leon's head with a flashlight.

Bird kept the meat from Argentina and Australia separate from the Kansas Beef Association stuff, which was for the best people he knew. Bird's thinking was that the only steak in the world better than Kansas Beef Association was from Japan, and nobody knew about it. "The way the Japs do business," he said, "they got a lot of cars, you know about their cars. They got a lot of cameras, you know about their cameras. They got maybe twelve acres in the whole country that ain't got no cities on it, though, so you don't know that they got beef. They know what they're runnin' over there."

The cooler felt warmer than it usually did, but the way you'd notice the electricity was off was the dampness in the air. Nothing cold could get warm without getting sloppy. Not meat, not air, not anybody you know. The cooler seemed bigger without the lights. At the far end were two band saws, where the cutters and boners usually worked, and beyond them was a door that led into a smaller cooler, where they kept the flowers. If it was Mickey's, he'd just as soon been in the flower business. For one thing, with flowers you didn't have all those fucking hooks hanging out of the ceiling.

He stepped out of the flower cooler and said hello to Mrs. Capezio, who ran the shop and was Bird's mother's sister. The name was the same because the sisters had married cousins. "Everybody look so worried this morning, Mickey," she said. "I tell Arthur he got to relax. What's going to happen is going to happen, it's planned a long time ago. All you can do is have faith in the electric company, right? He don't listen to me, though. You talk to him when you see him, Mickey, he listens to you."

She picked a pink carnation off a funeral arrangement sitting on the counter, broke the stem and pinned it to the outside of his jacket. Her old hands shook, and it took a long time. "Ever since all the terrible business with Mr. Bruno," she said, "Arthur don't know what's going on no more."

He walked outside and got into the back seat of the Cadillac, behind the man he didn't know. Bird was saying, "I think sometimes I got a prick for a brain and a brain for a prick. I mean, I could of got into a nice, comfortable little bar twenty-four years ago, had it paid off by now. I could of got into the movin' business with my brother Tommy. I tell him, 'I wisht I was in a business where the worst thing can happen is a hernia.' Sometimes I think I might still do that. . . ."

He was asking the man something, the man wasn't hearing it. "My brother Tommy," Bird said, "he looks at me like I'm crazy. He says, 'Lookit all the money you're makin'. Lookit all the pussy.' He don't know. I tell him, 'Sure, there's pussy in the meat business, but anybody goes into a business for the fuckin' don't enjoy it. It's like you lost your taste buds but you still get hungry. How is that worth it?' "

Bird looked into the rearview mirror. Mickey hoped it wasn't for an answer. "My aunt give you that flower? What'd she tell you?"

"She said you had to have faith in the electric company," he said.

The man next to Bird looked at his watch. "C'mon, let's go," he said. Bird started the Cadillac and drove north on Twenty-fourth Street.

Bird was smiling. "That old woman is somethin', ain't she, Mick?"

"A very nice woman," he said.

"She don't look like it," Bird said, "but she knows what she's runnin' there. Did you know that flower shop's makin' money? She don't have to do nothin' but sit on her ass like

29

everybody else, watch 'All My Children' all fuckin' day, but she keeps it runnin'. She's in there right now, worryin' what the electric's doin' to her flowers."

"What happened to it?" Mickey said.

Bird shrugged. "They don't know," he said. "I noticed it always happens right after the democrats get their welfare checks, though." Bird always called them democrats. "They get the juice runnin', Jesus knows what they can think of to fuck things up. They come down in civil rights buses from North Philly to do it. . . ." Bird took a right on Race Street and took it all the way to the Ben Franklin Bridge. The right-hand lane was closed down because they were painting that side of the bridge.

Bird said, "I heard they never stop paintin' this fucker. You heard of that, Sally?" The man next to him didn't answer. "They start at one end, and the air in Camden is so bad, and it takes so fuckin' long to get to the other end, that by then it's all peelin' and they got to go back and start all over again."

Mickey saw that Bird was scared to death of the man in the front seat. "The meat business is like that," Bird said. "I mean, lookit. Here we go, drivin' to Jersey to take a truck, right? Someplace in Kansas, a young calf is just learnin' the ropes. You know—eat, shit; eat, shit . . ."

The man in the front seat gave him a look, which Bird took for interest. "The guy drivin' the truck knows what we're going to do. In fact, right now he's wonderin' where the fuck we are. Am I right or wrong?

"The guy shippin' the load knows we're going to take it. He sends us a set of keys. The guy s'posed to be waitin' for the load knows somebody's going to take it. He's got a receipt for State Farm says he paid eight thousand more than he's got in it."

He stopped beside the tollbooth and threw in three quarters. "Now what happens," he said, "if we don't show up? We got all this business dependin' on us to take the truck, and there's cows comin' up right now in Kansas, and without us there's no place to put them. Without us, nobody's got nothin' to do."

Bird took Admiral Wilson Boulevard to 70, then 70 to the

Turnpike. He said, "Sometimes, you wish you didn't have so many people dependin' on you," and then he shut up. Mickey settled back into his seat and looked at New Jersey. It was pretty. He'd never say that out loud, but this part, shit, it could be Iowa.

They drove north about twenty minutes, to Exit 7. The truck stop was a twenty-booth restaurant with showers and bunks in back, a couple of Pac-Man games and a parking lot a quarter-mile square, which was full. The man in the front seat turned to Bird and said, "Which one?"

Not, *"Holy shit, look at all of them trucks"* or, *"What the fuck?"* but, *"Which one?"* So it was all in Bird's lap, any problem they had. Mickey watched it work on him.

"It's a silver truck," Bird said. "Here, I got a plate. . . ." He went into his shirt pocket and came out with a piece of paper.

"They're all silver," the man said, "and it's going to take half a fuckin' hour to read all the plates just on that one." He pointed at the first truck in the first row. Fourteen plates, half of them covered with mud. Then he said, "Hey, it's runnin'. . . ."

Mickey saw Bird looking for him in the rearview mirror. "That ain't it," Mickey said. "We're lookin' for a reefer." The man in the front seat turned around to look at him. "A refrigerated truck," Mickey said, "you know? So the meat don't cook on the way to Vermont?"

The man turned back in his seat without saying anything else, but he was looking at the truck again. "They don't turn them off," Mickey said, "they're diesels. They leave them goin' a week at a time."

The man in the front seat said, "That's very interesting, the history of the trucking industry." So Mickey shut up and Bird drove the Cadillac up and down the rows of trucks, stopping when he came to a reefer to check the plate numbers. Then he almost ran over a whore, coming out from between trucks. Bird hit the brakes, then gave her a little wave and a smile. She gave him the finger.

"Truck whores won't have nothin' to do with nobody but truckers," Mickey said.

Bird looked concerned. "Is that so?"

"That's a fact," Mickey said. The man in the front seat looked straight ahead. Mickey wondered what kind of trouble Bird was in that they'd pick a hard dick who wouldn't know the difference if they stole a load of live chickens to keep an eye on the job. Before, it was always just him and Bird.

"Pull up here," the man said. "I got to piss." Bird stopped the Cadillac and the man walked between two trucks.

"Who is that?" Mickey said. Bird shrugged. "He don't seem to know a hell of a lot."

Bird said, "He knows what he knows, and he don't give a shit about the rest."

"I can see that," Mickey said. "But what's he doin' here with us? I don't like none of this."

"It's nothin' to do with you," Bird said.

"A guy like that, I seen them do things," Mickey said. "I mean, he don't know somethin', that's fine until you know he don't know. Like right now, he's standin' there pissin' on his shoes. The wind's comin' from under the trailer, but he don't notice it because of all the noise, which he ain't used to. But if you were to go out there and tell him he's pissin' on his feet, he might shoot you, just to show you he knows what he's doin'."

Bird said, "That's why God gave you and me brains, not to go out there and tell him he's pissin' on his feet."

They found the truck in the last row, a new Peterbilt. The driver was a skinny kid with a beard and a Cleveland Indians baseball cap. Bird stopped the car in front of him, and the kid watched the three men get out. He was sitting sideways in the cab with his feet up on the other side, listening to some shit wasn't even music. You could hear it even with the windows closed and the engine on. He was a dirty kind of kid, you could see that. If the truck was his, Mickey wouldn't let somebody like that put air in the tires. The kid looked down at the three of them awhile, then he turned around slowly in his seat and rolled down the window. He said, "Yeah?"

The man with piss on his shoes turned to Bird. "You notice," he said, "the fuckin' world's got an attitude anymore." He glanced at Mickey, to include him, and then he stared up into the cab. The kid shrugged, turned off the tape and climbed down.

Bird handed him an envelope and said, "Go on in there and have some breakfast, pal. Take an hour, unnerstand? An hour before you come out here lookin' for your outfit."

The kid smiled. "Who's driving?" he said. He looked them over one at a time, still smiling. Some private joke. The man with piss on his shoes was left-handed. He turned halfway around, like he was walking away, and then he came back. The fist drove up under the ribs, toward the liver. The kid's face all came together in the middle, and he dropped.

He lay where he fell, afraid to move anything that might make it worse. The man watched him, nodding as the kid improved. "All of a sudden," he said, "the world don't have no attitude no more." He sat down on the hood of the Cadillac and waited.

Bird bent over the kid and started talking. "Lookit," he said, "it's none of your business who's drivin', am I right?" The kid held himself, waiting for things to come back together. "Lookit, you all right, pal? You run your business, we run ours. We give you the trump, your business is over. Now go on into the restaurant like I said, eat a nice breakfast, all right? Nothin' happens. I mean, it was lucky you wasn't hurt, pally. . . ."

Bird was sweating. Mickey saw things were getting away from him. He didn't like the job at all. He didn't like what had happened to the kid, but more than that he didn't like it that nobody was under control. The next you knew, the kid would be crying.

The man was looking at him now. "Business is business," he said. The kid sat up in the dirt, still holding his side.

"An hour," Bird said, "all right? You go have a nice breakfast, you feel a lot better, then you come out lookin' for the truck."

The kid stood up, Bird holding his arm. "Take a couple deep breaths," he said. The kid took a couple of deep breaths, so his ribs weren't broke. Bird picked up the Cleveland Indians hat and dusted it off, then put it on the kid's head. "Am I right or wrong?" he said.

The cab of the truck smelled like a Chestnut Street double feature. There were a couple dozen roaches in the ashtray, smoked down to raggedy little squares. The kid had left orange peels and banana peels and empty cartons of Wendy's chili all over the floor. Mickey wondered how people could live like that. You did live in a truck.

He pulled the rig out of the lot, getting used to the throw of the gears, fixing the mirrors. The Cadillac came out behind him, Bird was alone with the man again. Mickey looked over the tapes. Plasmatics, AC/DC, the Sex Pistols. Sex Pistols? He remembered the look on the kid's face before the man with Bird hit him. Queers always thought they were smarter than anybody wasn't in their club.

He drove away from the Turnpike, up over a little hill, and pulled onto 295 South. The truck was new and tight and strong, ten forward gears, and his hands and eyes fell into old patterns, and there was something simple and comfortable about it that he didn't have anymore.

He'd driven trucks since he was fourteen years old. He'd made the run from Miami to Atlanta with the old man a hundred times before that. The old man didn't care if he went to school, as a matter of fact he felt better if Mickey was with him because there wasn't nobody to watch him at home, and when he'd died Mickey had taken the truck and made the runs for him. He was sixteen, and that's what it felt like he was doing.

Daniel had taught him the driving end and he'd taught him the business end. He didn't talk about much else. Once, coming down old 441 through Georgia, Mickey had said the sunset was pretty behind the pines. The old man had said, "If it is, you can't make it no better, sayin' it."

And when he'd died—the old man thought he had hemorrhoids for two years, truck drivers always had hemorrhoids, and by the time the doctors went in there it was in everything—when he'd died, Mickey had taken the rig and made the runs and kept his feelings in order, and to himself.

He looked in the mirror and caught the yellow Cadillac a quarter mile behind him.

The old man had never taught him anything about women, of course, or drinking or the ponies. When Mickey got older, he sometimes wondered if it was because the old man didn't know anything about it.

He found the ponies for himself. First at Hialeah, then Gulfstream and Sunshine. He'd lost the rig to the ponies when he was eighteen. He kept coming back. He didn't cry the blues when he lost, he didn't kiss strangers when he won. And there'd been days when he won as much as the old man had made in half a year.

Mickey knew he didn't have hold of it, it had hold of him. It made him feel weak, and a couple of times he quit. And he kept coming back.

He'd took a job with Peabody Movers and went all over the South. His favorite track was the Fair Grounds in New Orleans. It was a dignified old track, you walked in there and you could see it was built with that in mind. He always did all right at the Fair Grounds.

Peabody had died—he heard that at the garage and it surprised him to hear there was actually somebody named that—and the company folded in four months. He'd gone back to Florida for a while, pulling double-size mobile homes, but with the winds and the narrow roads then, it was about as peaceful as hauling leaky dynamite. And by then he didn't like the way the mobile home business was doing Florida anyway. There was nothing safe from them but the ocean.

He'd gone to Chicago then, and hauled cattle in from Iowa and Nebraska. In the winter, you'd have to stop every hundred miles to see that none of them were down. The driver was responsible for that. They gave you a hollow metal pole, and when one of the cattle went down you slid the pole in through the slats and poked it in the eye.

35

A cow didn't lie down back there for nothing, and when it was cold that's all you could do to get them up. When it was cold enough, they didn't care what you did.

Sportsman Park and Arlington didn't fit him at all. In Chicago, it was like nobody gave a shit who they were when they got around money, and he went east and got a job with Dow Chemical, hauling poison. Mostly to Florida. They needed a lot of poison in Florida.

He'd met Bird at Garden State, sitting in the reserved seats in the clubhouse. Bird had been to every track in the East, and he was interested in Mickey's work. "Listen," he'd said once, "they give you a mask or somethin', handlin' all that shit?" Mickey hadn't thought of that. It was always something.

Garden State was a good track, old and comfortable, and he and Bird were there the day it burned down. They stood in the parking lot and watched it go. Four hours later, in a bar across the highway from the track, Bird told him about the meat business. They had the place to themselves because it was full of smoke.

The Cadillac had moved up and was sitting on his ass now, close enough so he could see the faces in the front seat. Bird was still talking, the other man looked straight ahead.

They went by the state trooper at sixty-two miles an hour, which should of been safe. He came out behind them though, and Mickey felt himself go weak. His hands were shaking and the cop was coming. So the kid had gone inside and made a call. Well, he was a kid. The man with Bird had hit him, and he'd called the cops. He was a kid. The Cadillac pulled into the passing lane and went around him. Mickey touched his brakes and looked over into the car, but the man with Bird didn't look back.

Seven hundred dollars, that was his end. Half a day's work, and some fuck who pissed on his own feet had decided the world had an attitude. He was probably up there now, getting his story together with Bird, how nothing had happened at the truck stop.

Mickey eased the truck down to fifty-five. The cop was two hundred yards and coming. Mickey thought about the kid. Whatever kind of shit this was, the kid was in worse. The man in the car with Bird turned around to watch, and at that moment the cop pulled into the passing lane, went around the truck, and stopped the Cadillac.

It turned out they got a ticket for following too close.

He got off 295 and headed over to 130, the old truck route. There were lights and some traffic, but on 130 he wasn't as worried about what the kid back at the truck stop might do. He still got back to the flower shop twenty minutes ahead of Bird. He pulled the truck around to the back, opened one side of the garage and drove in, and left it there next to his own truck.

The sun was working, and the place was warmer than it had been that morning. Mickey walked around the outside of the building, and then went into the flower shop and talked with Mrs. Capezio. She was worried that Bird was working too hard. "Arthur's nerves ain't what they was," she said. "He went to the doctor, they said his pressure's too high. I don't know, I tell him to have faith in God but he don't seem to think things is going to work out." The old woman shook her head. "This is bad business, started with poor Mr. Bruno. Arthur's thinkin' all the time, and you know that ain't good for him, Mickey. . . ."

Fifteen minutes later Bird parked the car on the sidewalk in front of the shop. The man with piss on his shoes was gone. Bird came in and kissed his aunt on the cheek. "They didn't get the electric back on, Sophie?"

"They say very soon, Arthur," she said. "They say not to worry, have confidence in your electric company."

Mickey followed Bird through the flower cooler and the meat cooler, all the way back to the truck. There were windows back there, covered with shades, about twelve feet up the walls, so you could see without a flashlight. Bird wasn't talking, which wasn't like him. "You got a problem with somebody?" Mickey asked.

"Sally? No, he's out of it. He was only along, you know. To see it all went down." He ran his hands through his hair. "We got a little business to talk over, Mick."

Mickey did not like the way that sounded.

"See, I got a problem. I didn't especially even want to do the job today, even before the fuckin' electric went out, and I got a cooler full of meat that's been in there a week already. Even before that, I didn't want it because of a problem I'm havin'."

Mickey noticed again that Bird was scared. "You don't have the seven hundred?" he said. Bird held out his arms. Embarrassed and scared, trying to hold it together.

"Somethin' is goin' on," he said. "They hit Angelo, all right. He was a nice old man, but they want A.C. Then they hit Chicken Man. He gives them A.C., brings in shit the old man wouldn't allow, I mean he's bringin' it in in suitcases, and they hit him too. And Frank and Chickie and fourteen other guys, some of them don't even make sense. Nobodies. And it's changin' things all over. Business . . ."

Mickey said, "Forget it. I'm doin' all right." His lies always sounded like lies. "When you got it, you can give it to me then."

"Take some of the meat," Bird said. He took a set of keys out of his shirt pocket and opened the locks on the reefer. He opened one of the doors. The meat had been loaded in a hurry, 150-pound sides thrown in there any way they landed. Each side had been put into a gauze envelope for shipping. With arrows, it could of been a hundred-year-old massacre.

"I can't do nothin' with that," Mickey said. "It ain't even cut." Bird was staring into the reefer.

"What the fuck, Mick? What the fuck are they tryin' to tell me here?"

"I don't know these people, Bird," he said. "I never dealt with them, so I don't know. " Bird was still staring into the truck. "Lemme help you get it in the cooler."

Mickey took off his shirt, and he and Bird picked up one of the sides of beef. It kept slipping out of Bird's hands, but they got it into the cooler, stumbling in the dark, and put it on a hook.

They went back and looked into the truck again. Bird couldn't stand it. "Fuck it," he said, "we'll leave it in the truck."

"We ain't going to take the truck to Delaware?" Mickey

said. They always took the empties to a shopping center in Delaware. "These people are going to want their truck back, Bird."

"Fuck them," he said. He seemed healthier, now he was pissed. "Let's get some of this shit in your truck, Mick."

Mickey said, "I can't use it like this. I got nowhere to cut it up." He saw Bird wasn't listening. "Bird?"

Bird jerked a side of beef down and Mickey helped him get it out and carry it to his truck, and helped him put it in. They stacked eight sides of beef, four on the left, four on the right, putting most of the weight over the axle. Bird was out of breath when they finished. "You sure you don't want a couple more?" he said.

"This is enough," Mickey said. "It only keeps a week in there anyway." Bird went back over to the truck and closed the door on the meat. It seemed to make him feel better, not to be looking at it.

"Look," he said, "we'll get the electric back on. Come back tomorrow and I'll get somebody to cut it up for you." He put a long, thin arm around Mickey's shoulders and walked him to his truck. He couldn't get him out of there soon enough. Bird pulled the garage door up and waved as Mickey backed out. Then he pulled on the rope to get the door started back down again. The door was weighted, and hit bottom hard. It shut while Bird was still looking out, before he expected it. It closed down like bad weather.

It was two o'clock in the afternoon when Mickey got home. He put his truck in the garage, plugged in the cooling unit, and checked his load. It was still where he'd put it. Twelve hundred pounds of beef he couldn't sell to anybody. For transporting a stolen truck across state lines. For getting the piss scared out of him, for watching the kid with the Cleveland Indians baseball hat turn inside out when the man with Bird hit him. Business.

He'd sweated all the way from the truck stop, right from what had happened with the kid. Then he'd lifted the eight sides of beef—it would of been easier without Bird helping, but how do you say that?—and that was a different kind of sweat, but he could still smell the nervous kind in his shirt. He thought about having a beer down at the Hollywood before he went in the house. He didn't want to talk about Leon now. He did want to wash off the scared smell, though.

The front door was unlocked, but he didn't hear the radio. Jeanie listened to call-in shows all afternoon. He walked in, and something was different. The house seemed still. "Jeanie?" Nothing. "Jeanie, you here?"

He found her upstairs, lying on the bed, holding a pale blue Princess telephone against her stomach. Her eyes followed him, across the room and then as he sat down next to her on the bed. "What is it?" he said. He didn't try to touch her.

"Leon's dead," she said.

All morning long, the kid had been crazy. Crazy even for him. One minute he was working nice as could be, keeping Old Lucy in blocks and mortar, the next minute he was putting everything on the wrong side, and a minute after that he was screaming about working for a nigger. Threatening to file a complaint with the union.

Old Lucy never paid him any notice.

Peets thought for a while that Leon would quit. The first time he screamed about doing yard work for the nigger, that looked promising, but after that he picked up the blocks he'd dropped to make the announcement, and then he took them to Old Lucy and put them down on the right side. He said something to him too, like it wasn't nothing personal, and he'd smiled.

Old Lucy acted like he didn't hear, and for fifteen, twenty minutes the kid kept with him. By eleven o'clock he'd walked by Peets ten times, carrying blocks or mortar, and every time there was something different in his eyes. One minute they were laughing, the next minute they were mad. And he was talking to himself the whole time. Not singsong like Old Lucy, but like there was somebody else there. "Don't ever tell anybody where I'll be," he said once. And another time, "Oh, sure. Right, anything you say. . . ."

And once he'd seen the boy take a black pill out of his back pocket and center it on his tongue. Peets wished they were doing high work, maybe a second story. Where the fall wouldn't necessarily kill him.

And all morning long, of course, the kid was bringing out the razor. Telling some story about him and a cat that got worse for the cat every time he told it. And whatever the black pills was, it wasn't making him any slower. That razor came out like an idea in the boy's head, and disappeared just as fast. It was like there was a name he couldn't remember, and every ten minutes or so he'd think he had it, but it was always the same name he brought out, and it was always wrong. He'd smile and put the razor back, and the crew would go back to work.

Peets' morning went by a minute at a time. He was watching the kid and couldn't do anything useful. From what he'd seen, the reason people wanted to be supervisors was so they wouldn't have to do what they did to get there. Not just construction, everywhere. Nobody wanted to do the real work, they all wanted to control it. Peets wasn't like that, he was the opposite.

"I grabbed that fucker by the tail," the kid was saying, "you know, they hate that. I grabbed him, and held him upside down, and this flight attendant was screamin' to let him alone, and I says, 'I'll leave him alone, all right . . .'" The razor was out again. "And I cut him from the middle out, so he'd know what I was doin'."

Peets looked at his watch. Eleven-fifteen. He'd been looking at his watch all morning. It was like a circle. The kid was telling himself the same story over and over, only it was never quite right. And every time he got to the part about the cat he'd stop work to tell it to the whole crew, and thirty-five minutes later he'd be at that same part again.

Once, coming past him with cinder blocks in both hands, the kid said, "Yeah, I got somethin' for you too, Peets."

Peets said, "What?" but the boy didn't hear him. He was in some different part of the story, dealing with Peets. The kid came back to him now. "You say somethin', Leon?"

The kid dropped the blocks and put his hand in his back

pocket. "I didn't say a fuckin' word," he said. "I ain't said nothin' all morning." And a few minutes later, "I'd like to know what a white man is doin', haulin' block for some nigger's not even a bricklayer."

Peets said, "He's the only one we got today, boy." The kid didn't hear him, but the rest of them did, and they went back to work. And Old Lucy just kept working, the same pace, the same rhythm. When the blocks weren't there, he never turned around to look for them. He just waited till they came. Then the kid would take another pill and five minutes later he was bringing them four and five at a time, as fast as he could walk, the corners of the blocks pinching his hands, putting little cuts in his fingers. Leon had worked six weeks and his hands was still like a baby's ass. And Lucy just let the blocks pile up, and used them as he needed them, and didn't hurry or slow down for anybody.

And talked to himself in that singsong way that he probably didn't even know was out loud.

Peets called lunch break twenty minutes before noon. He walked away from the crew and sat down in the cherry picker to eat some Kentucky Fried Chicken he'd bought on the way home from work Friday, sat up there to eat so he wouldn't have to look at anybody else while he did it. It was testing him today.

The kid, of course, wasn't hungry. The rest of the crew—everybody but Old Lucy—sat on the cement sacks talking about an El Camino pickup one of them just bought. Peets listened, because there wasn't no choice, and it turned out what they were talking about was the sound system in the El Camino pickup one of them just bought.

Old Lucy got his lunch box and walked up the wall to where he'd been working to eat. He sat on the ground with his back against the wall and looked at where he'd come from that morning. Peets watched him, thinking the old shine was the only one he had who cared that they were supposed to of done something when they'd finished for the day. There was others who would do what you told them, but Lucy was the only one wasn't just putting in the hours. Peets expected it wasn't their fault. No, what they was talking about was how the sound system in the El Camino pickup got somebody some pussy off a little hippy girl he'd found up on South Street.

Then Leon was cutting the air with the razor again. This time he said he'd almost cut the flight attendant's tits off after he took care of her cat. "I seen that happen to a girl once," he said.

The kid Gary Sample stuttered, "Shit." The older men ignored it. Leon moved closer to Gary Sample, like he hadn't heard him. Peets stayed where he was. The kid who said that smiled to show he hadn't meant anything by it. "Really?"

Leon stopped and saw some of the others were beginning to get away from him. He put the razor back in his pocket and backed off the story. "The truth is," he said, "I didn't get to see it happen. I seen the tits afterward, though."

The way the rest of them looked at it, Leon said some things that were full of shit, but they did send him over from the union as a bricklayer, first class, and Jesus knows he had to be connected to get that. He said it was his stepfather, so it probably was. It had to be something, he didn't know nothing about work. And it didn't make a shit one way or the other anyway. The way the rest of them looked at it, Peets was scared of him and that was good enough for them.

Peets sat in the cherry picker, holding a piece of cool gray chicken until he decided he didn't want to eat it. "At the end of the day," he said, "he's gone. One way or the other." Peets only talked to himself to make promises.

He dropped the chicken leg back into the box and carefully closed the lid. He hated to see food wasted, it was the way he was brought up. While he was closing the box, Leon had moved over in front of Old Lucy.

"I heard you talkin' about me," he said. "I don't give a shit personally, but I don't like a nigger talkin' about my business." Old Lucy chewed his sandwich, slow and all the way through. He never even acknowledged there was something standing in his light.

"You want part of me, old man?" Leon said. "You and Peets, standin' there, tellin' me, lookin' at me behind my back . . ."

Peets stayed where he was. Old Lucy didn't say nothing, he

just ate his lunch. It was like some people Peets knew at home, they'd fish all afternoon out on Hard Labor Creek, and the mosquitoes never bothered them. They'd get bit once in a while, but they never got bothered. Peets would slap himself silly, killing mosquitoes, and the Hard Labor Creek never ran out.

Leon looked back to the rest of the crew. "This old nigger has been talkin' about me all morning," he said. "I heard him, but you know, it's never out loud so you know what he's sayin'." Gary Sample laughed.

Leon pulled the razor out, almost without thinking about it, and put the blade under Old Lucy's chin. The razor brought the chin up, and the old man's eyes came with it. Leon didn't recognize what he saw there. "You hear me now, don't you?" he said. Old Lucy didn't move or speak. The kid pulled the razor away, and a thin pink line marked the place it had been.

The line darkened, puddled, and a tear of blood ran down the old man's neck into his shirt. Leon felt the weight of his eyes and began to laugh. He didn't mean to, he couldn't help himself. "Hey," he said. "I didn't mean to cut you, Lucy. . . ."

Peets stayed in the cherry picker. "Hey, go get a Band-Aid," Leon said, "it's a hospital right here." He pointed at the hospital, and he couldn't say more than two words without this strange laugh coming up out of him. He looked at the men sitting on the cement sacks, dead still, and they were laughing too. But not out loud, like he was. The sun was warm on the top of his head, he felt that, and he felt the weight of the old man's eyes, and he started to say something to the men sitting on the cement. But there was a cracking noise and he couldn't remember what it was, and somehow they couldn't hear him anyway. And for a long second he looked up into the sun and went blind in the light.

It developed before Peets could move. No, that wasn't exactly true. It developed without a place where he could interrupt it. The old shine had never asked him for help, and then the razor was sitting under his chin where Jesus knew what Leon had

44

in mind, and then he'd taken it away and Peets had started out after him.

The kid had turned to the others, and Old Lucy had put his sandwich down and stood up with a piece of half-inch pipe in his hand and brought it down on the back of Leon's head.

The old man only hit him once. Leon reeled in the air and dropped on his side and slowly curled into himself in the dirt. Old Lucy watched a minute, then he sat down where he had been. He wiped blood off his chin and put the pipe next to him on the ground and then, because there was no way not to, he stared at the body. He didn't try to get away from it, it was his.

Peets was out of the cherry picker. He didn't hurry, he'd heard the sound when the pipe hit Leon's head. It was like dropping it into mud. By the time Peets leaned over him, Leon Hubbard had already begun to shake. Spasms in the legs and hands. There was no blood Peets could see, but the back of his head was ruined.

He stood up, avoiding Old Lucy's eyes, and called Gary Sample over from the sacks. "You better get somebody from the hospital," he said. The kid half-ran, half-walked to the front of the building. He didn't know what was appropriate.

Old Lucy dabbed at the blood on his chin again, the rest of the crew gradually fell into half a circle around Peets and the body and the old man. "He's barely breathing," one of them said. Little pieces of dust were blowing up in front of his mouth. His eyes were open, but it was like they were looking in instead of out.

And a minute after that, the dust settled. Peets was feeling the side of the boy's neck, and while his fingers were there the pulse stopped. All the tanglements to it were over, then.

Peets was relieved.

Gary Sample came back with a couple of nurses and a doctor, and they pounded on Leon's chest and held his nose shut while they blew into his mouth, but the tanglements were over. One of the nurses, a young one, was crying. She looked at Peets and said, "Don't any of you ever learn?" like it was the fifth one they'd killed that month.

Old Lucy sat still and watched. The doctor and nurses tried for a few minutes, and then two men came out of the hospital pulling a stretcher. "He's so young," said the nurse who was crying. Peets thought she probably wasn't much use in an emergency room.

They moved Leon onto the stretcher, and carried him inside. His razor was still lying in the dirt, and a few feet from that was a small spot of blood that had dripped from his ear.

Peets picked up the razor and kicked dirt over the spot of blood, and all the tanglements to it were over.

The police came five minutes later. There were two of them. One limped and looked out of place in his uniform, the other one was little and cold. He did the talking. He took out a note pad and a pencil and wrote down Peets' name, a letter at a time, like he was carving it in wood. In Peets' experience, there were some cops who got used to writing things down and there were others who never stopped resenting it. It's what made them cold.

The little cop finished writing his name and said, "All right, what happened here?" The question was for anybody. Nobody answered.

And then Peets did something against his policy, and mortgaged himself forever to everybody there. He said, "It was the cherry picker."

They all looked at him, he looked at the little cop. "The U-bolt come loose," he said. He moved over to the boom and lifted the U-bolt. The cable bowed. The bolt didn't look as heavy as it was, and he handed it to the little cop the way the cop might of handed his gun over to his boy, so he could feel the weight and see it was serious.

"Usually," Peets said, "the cable and the bolt are tied to the boom when we're not usin' it." He picked up the smaller cable they used to tie the cable to the boom and handed it to the cop too. "The tie must of come loose, the cable swung out, and the U-bolt hit the boy right in the back of the head."

The cop looked at the U-bolt, the boom, the cable in his hand, trying to see it. One of the men on the crew was nodding. "That's what happened," he said. "I seen the whole thing. The kid never knew what hit him."

The cop turned to look at him, then he looked at the rest of them. "Anybody else?"

Peets waited, and then somebody else said he'd seen it too, and then a couple of the others said they *almost* seen it. Gary Sample had eyes to say something different, but he didn't. Old Lucy just sat in the dirt, the pipe right there by his side and, as far as Peets could tell, he didn't hear any of it.

The little cop walked from the cherry picker to the spot where the body fell, counting his steps. He estimated heights and distances and asked questions about Leon's job. "He was a brick-layer," Peets said. Shit, he might as well lie all the way.

The little cop moved here and there, satisfying himself. His partner stood in one place, watching Peets, studying the rest of them too. The little cop turned to him. "Let's go get the groceries," he said.

His partner's name tag said EISENHOWER. The little cop walked toward the hospital entrance, Eisenhower stayed back. He had been watching Peets about fifteen minutes, and he moved closer to him now and spoke into his chest so only Peets could hear. "That kid," he said, nodding toward Gary Sample, "is about to make you some problems."

Then he stepped around Peets and followed the little cop into the hospital.

THE
POCKET

There wasn't a man on any shift in Central Detectives who didn't admire Calamity Eisenhower. Even the captain who brought him up on charges admired him, although he didn't miss him now he was gone, the way the detectives did.

Calamity's brother How-Awful! had been lost at a police convention in Phoenix, Arizona, one year to the day before Calamity broke his hip falling down the stairs at South Detectives. How-Awful! had climbed out on the roof of a Holiday Inn at three o'clock in the morning and jumped into a swimming pool that had been drained for painting. At the time, it seemed to settle the question every cop in every corner of the city lived with every day of his life. How-Awful! was crazier than Calamity.

But then Calamity had been found, broken-hipped and

dressed in a rabbit suit, at the bottom of the stairs at South Detectives, and it was an open case again.

There had been six detectives with him, all dressed in rabbit suits they'd rented from three different costume shops in three different cities—let internal affairs find that. They'd gone into South Detectives at high noon on a Wednesday a couple of days after South Detectives had beaten Central Detectives 22–2 in a game of slow-pitch softball, and shot the place up. They blew out the lights and put holes in the ceiling just to watch cops dive under desks.

You do not steal home against Calamity Eisenhower with a twenty-run lead and hope it will be forgotten.

They'd shot the place up and then run down the stairs and out the door, and Calamity, who was last to leave, who could not get enough of the way it looked, Calamity had tripped on his own rabbit's foot and rolled all the way down.

The captain at South Detectives found him there fifteen minutes later. The detectives from Central were back at Sixth District before they noticed somebody was missing.

They'd suspended Calamity for thirty days without pay and then assigned him to the radio room until his hip mended. When he could walk without a cane they stuck him in AID, where he spent his time sorting out how some kid got drunk and drowned trying to drive his car across a city reservoir.

It was a shameful misuse of talent, and the partner they'd given him, Chuck Arbuckle, was simply a mistake in conception. Eisenhower wondered sometimes how a sperm could swim all that way knowing that's what he was going to turn into. They were taking the body from Holy Redeemer to the medical examiner's office at Thirty-fourth and Civic Center, and Arbuckle was going over it again.

"It must of been the ape," he said, meaning Peets. "He probably never tied that thing up like it was supposed to. The kid comes walking through, thinking of all the money he's making, the thing moves and splat. We got to spend half the fuckin' day cleaning up the mess." Chuck Arbuckle did not like anybody under forty making more money than he did. He hated any doctor without gray hair.

Eisenhower looked across the van at him. Arbuckle said, "I ain't saying it was his own fault, but you work around sloppy fuckers, you got to take it into consideration. You got to be aware of where trouble is coming from. Anything you do, the first rule is know where the problem is going to come from."

Arbuckle was thirty-five years old. He'd investigated ninety-four fatal accidents in the last eighteen months, at great personal inconvenience. He got his name in the *Daily Times* once every two weeks. Eisenhower had been given Arbuckle in February, and in that time he'd noticed that Arbuckle never came away from a fatal accident without finding a lesson in it. It was Arbuckle's order of things that people deserved what they got, and his job was to figure out why, after they got it.

Arbuckle thought that protected him.

Of course, if he wasn't the way he was, Eisenhower thought, he'd of seen the foreman was lying. A fifteen-year-old kid would have seen that. In Eisenhower's experience, when everybody lied it was usually best to leave it alone. Shit, it's how religions got started. You could tell good people from the lies they told, and he'd liked Peets right away.

Arbuckle turned left off Market Street and went into the University of Pennsylvania area, then around to the back of the M.E.'s building where they accepted deliveries. A kid in hospital clothes was waiting at the door, smoking a cigarette. Arbuckle backed the van up and got out. The body was zipped into a plastic bag, and the kid unzipped it while Arbuckle read to him from the hospital's certificate of death. "Male Caucasian, twenty-four years old, massive cerebral hemorrhaging ..."

When he'd finished that, Arbuckle told him what happened. "The kid was walking by this crane and it came loose or something, and hit him in the back of the head."

The kid said, "Yeah, well all I do is accept the body."

Arbuckle shrugged. "It don't matter to me, pal. Sometimes they like to know." Another kid in hospital clothes came out of the building, and he and the first kid put Leon Hubbard's body on a stretcher and wheeled him inside. The doors opened on weight, like at the Acme.

Arbuckle drove the van back to Center City over the Walnut Street Bridge and stopped at a phone booth outside Cavanaugh's Bar. "You got that woman's phone number?" he said.

Eisenhower looked through the papers until he found the number Peets had given them for the kid's parents. "I thought somebody there was going to take care of it," he said.

Arbuckle shook his head. "Naw, I said we'd do it." He looked at his watch. It was ten minutes to two. "This won't take a second," he said. Eisenhower sat in the van and listened. "Mrs. Hubbard? . . . Oh, I see, but you are the mother of Leon Hubbard, who worked on the construction crew at Holy Redeemer? . . . No, he's not exactly in trouble, Mrs. Hubbard . . ."

Eisenhower cringed. There wasn't another cop he knew of who liked talking to the relatives. Arbuckle told her about the crane, Eisenhower closed his eyes. He didn't even know what Arbuckle was talking about, and he'd been there. "No," Arbuckle was saying, "you're not listening, ma'am. It didn't fall on him, the thing on the end hit him in the head. No, I already told you . . ."

Five minutes later Arbuckle hung up and got back in the van. "That's it," he said.

Eisenhower said, "Well, Chuck, you never know."

Mickey sat on the bed with her until the sisters came. She watched him awhile, crying that way that didn't make any noise, then she stared at the ceiling, and the tears ran sideways into her hair. He never touched her, something told him not to touch her.

Three years in Jeanie's house, in her neighborhood. It wasn't long enough to touch her now. It wasn't long enough to be part of this. The sisters came together. There were two of them, but it seemed like more. All lipsticked and dressed. One of them had five kids, the other one had a job at Pathmark. He could never remember which was which.

He let them in the front door, and walked behind Joyce up the stairs to Jeanie's room. Joanie went into the kitchen to fix

51

coffee. Joyce was ten years older than Jeanie and looked like she could have been her mother. Joyce and Joanie both. She sat down where Mickey had been on the bed and Jeanie moved toward her, and they put their arms around each other and rocked back and forth.

Mickey stood in the doorway, feeling like he shouldn't be watching. He remembered now, Joyce had the job at Pathmark. Her husband was a pressman at the *Inquirer*. She came over once a month to look at everything in the house and comment on how nice Jeanie's things were. How even with two incomes, they couldn't afford a Betamax. And Jeanie would ask if they were going to their place at the shore this summer, and Joyce would remind her it was only a house trailer, and they'd go at it like that for three hours, every month. Then Joyce would leave, and Jeanie would smile at him and shake her head, and say something about how it wasn't easy being the talented sister. He didn't know why, but after Joyce left, Mickey always got laid, so you could say Joyce was his favorite sister-in-law.

Joanie brushed past him and came into the bedroom with a tray. A coffeepot, three cups and saucers, a sugar bowl, the box of donuts. She sat in the chair by the window and settled the tray at the foot of the bed. Joyce propped Jeanie up with pillows and got her to try the coffee. Jeanie shook off the donuts, but the sisters insisted. "You got to eat something," Joanie said.

"She probably just ate lunch," Mickey said. Jeanie ate about two most afternoons. Nobody in the room seemed to hear him. Joanie held a napkin under the pastry and moved them together toward Jeanie's mouth. Jeanie took a small bite and began crying, real crying now. The kind you could hear out on the street.

"He was only a baby," she said. "They said something fell on him. . . ." The sisters put down their coffee and held her again. Joyce looked over Jeanie's shoulder and caught Mickey's eye. He would have been just as welcome down in Society Hill knocking on doors asking to use the bathroom.

The phone rang. Mickey picked it up and moved out of the

room to talk. The cord on it, you could take it to the john, except there was already one in there. "Mr. Hubbard?" It was the medical examiner's office, saying they needed somebody to come over and look at Leon. He told the sisters he had to go, and what he had to do. He didn't know how to say it, so he just said it. That brought Jeanie around, and she wanted to come too.

"You don't want to see him now," Mickey said. And she didn't. And neither did he.

A lot of it, he figured, depended on what had fallen on him. He took the Monte Carlo over the South Street Bridge, looking at the Schuylkill River, the trees, kids on bicycles. He was in no hurry to get to Leon, no hurry to get home. If it was a hammer, Leon probably wouldn't look too bad. That's what he was hoping for, a hammer, so it wouldn't look bad. Christ, don't let it be one of those radios. . . .

Jeanie would want to know what he looked like, she would want to hold on.

He parked in a lot and walked a block to the M.E.'s office. A doctor took Mickey back into the building to a window cut into a wall. The window was two-foot square, it could of been the complaint department at Sears, except it wasn't bulletproof. On the other side of the window was an empty stretcher with a pillow at one end. The imprint of somebody's head was still in the pillow. The doctor shrugged and picked up the telephone.

"Could we have the, uh . . ."—he looked at his clipboard— "the L. Hubbard crypt please?" There was an impatience in that voice that had taken a while to build, but when the doctor hung up he was calm and easygoing. He took Mickey by the arm and turned him away from the window. "It'll be just a moment, Mr. Hubbard," he said.

"Scarpato," Mickey said. "I'm the stepfather." When the doctor turned him back around, Leon was there. It took Mickey a second to be sure—it was the first time he'd ever seen him relaxed—but it was Leon. They'd propped his head up to make him look comfortable, and they'd put a blue curtain over his body, so all you could see was the head and part of the chest.

53

A circle of blood had crusted inside the ear, and some hair was gone from the back of his head, but he looked good.

"It don't look like he's even hurt," Mickey said.

The doctor looked at his clipboard. "The fracture is in back of the head," he said. He patted himself on the back of the head, to show Mickey where that was. Mickey looked at Leon again. Leon without all that crazy shit floating around in his head, it was just a kid, a skinny kid. Dark hair, skinny neck. It didn't look very substantial to already be a whole life.

His nose was straight and rounded at the end, just like Jeanie's. And he had her cheekbones. There wasn't anything complicated about it now. The shoulders were hollowed out, no muscle to speak of. Women's shoulders, bird wings. That was what it was. Without all that crazy shit floating around in his head, he looked like an angel.

Mickey saw that that was what Leon must of looked like to Jeanie every day of his life.

"Mr. Hubbard?"

"Scarpato," he said. He wanted that straight. "I'm not a blood relation." Mickey signed the papers out in front.

"We can release the body anytime after ten tomorrow morning," the doctor said. "There hasn't been any request for a postmortem, unless the family . . ." Mickey thought about it, shook his head.

"I don't think so," he said. "I don't think they'd want anybody cutting up the body." He walked back out into fresh air and didn't know where to go. He bought a hot dog and a *Daily Times* and sat down on the hood of the Monte Carlo to look at the entries at Keystone. He studied them a minute, then turned to the back of the paper. They ran horses at Keystone in worse shape than Leon. There were worse tracks as far as horses went, but he'd never been to a worse track. Keystone reminded you of pre-fab housing. He checked the Phillies score, which he didn't care about, and then he checked Richard Shellburn. *"Thomas Haskin lived a quiet life, in a quiet neighborhood. He and his wife and his dog, Hoppy. The wife is gone now, perhaps the neighborhood is too. . . ."* Jeanie loved that shit. Everybody did.

Richard Shellburn was the most famous newspaper columnist in Philadelphia. He was famous for his drinking and for getting pissed off at the government and for standing up for the little guy. People said he used to be a little guy himself and never forgot where he came from.

And he wrote things that made old women cry and things that made street people laugh. With Richard Shellburn, there was always somebody to get pissed off at. Some mornings, Mickey would be delivering and every bar he went into they'd ask him did he read Richard Shellburn yet. When he hadn't, they'd stick the *Daily Times* in his face and tell him what Richard Shellburn had said while he read it. "That's exactly what everybody's thinkin'," they'd say. "He's the only guy knows what it's like out here."

Mickey didn't know why writing down exactly what everybody was thinking was any better than thinking it in the first place. He never said that, though, to anybody. In the neighborhoods you got along by getting along. You might hate the 76ers and get away with it if you lived in South Philly all your life, but nobody wanted to hear that shit from the outside.

Nobody really wanted to hear from the outside at all. If you didn't like the way things was, that's what they had Delaware County for. Move there.

Center City was different. You could come and go in Center City, but the neighborhoods belonged to the people who lived there. At least the strong ones did. Tasker, Whitman, Fishtown, Two Street, God's Pocket. Outsiders walked around those neighborhoods, they stayed out of their bars.

Mickey had heard the coloreds were the same way, but he doubted it. You could get yourself shot or your head split open in North Philadelphia or anyplace west of the Schuylkill, but out there it wasn't a community project.

There were people in Fishtown and Whitman and the Pocket who never left. Who would as soon get on a bus for Center City as a bus for Cuba, who married each other's sisters and knew each other's business. There weren't many, but they were the hardest cases when an outsider came in.

Jeanie's family had been like that. She'd told him her father had never seen her dance because the dance school wasn't in the Pocket. Her sisters had married boys from the neighborhood and settled into the houses of their parents. Joyce took a bus to Pathmark and a month at the shore every year. Joanie was the oldest and never left.

Or maybe it was the other way around.

Jeanie had married two outsiders—him and Leon's father before him—but she'd never moved out of her house. Only when she was a kid and thought there was something for her in New York, and everybody in the Pocket knew what that had led to. It was a story mothers told to scare their daughters. And as much as her sisters, Jeanie was part of God's Pocket.

Mickey finished the hot dog and wrapped the *Daily Times* around the napkin and threw it all in the trash. He gave the old man running the parking lot a buck tip and headed back across the Schuylkill. Once, he thought about Leon. Eight or ten times, he thought about the sisters in his bedroom. Jeanie's bedroom.

He pulled into the alley that led to the garage in back of the house, looked at the second floor and knew they were still there. He had to see Smilin' Jack about the arrangements, but there was plenty of time for that. Jack would be over to the funeral parlor all night. Either there or at the Uptown. Mickey walked to the end of the alley, and then back up the street to the front door of his house. Then he crossed the street to the Hollywood. Out of habit, he checked in the window for Leon.

McKenna stood up as soon as he came in, walked to the end of the bar and shook Mickey's hand. "We're real sorry, Mick," he said. "Leon was a good boy."

There were six other people in the bar, and they all nodded. Mickey sat down at the end near the window and McKenna gave him a Schmidt's and, out of the occasion, a glass.

The other people in the bar were old, and remembered Leon from a long time ago. They came in at the same time every afternoon, they sat in their same seats, drinking the same drinks. They argued or they kept to themselves, and at suppertime they'd go home and the kids and the working people would take their places.

A woman named Eleanore said, "It don't make sense to me. How come nobody else got kilt, if it was an accident?" The man next to her shut his eyes. "Somebody ought to do somethin'," Eleanore said. "The youth is our hope for the future."

She killed a small glass of beer, stood up and stumbled. She steadied herself and walked to the bathroom. On the way, she dropped a dollar into a five-gallon jug at the other end of the bar. "We're collectin' to bury Leon," McKenna said. Mickey took a long pull off the beer, McKenna leaned closer.

"I keep hearin' different things," he said.

Mickey shook his head. "I don't know. I think somethin' dropped on him at the job. I haven't talked to the cops yet." He sighed. "I suppose I'll have to."

McKenna said, "Well, you know, you're going to have to put Jeanie's mind to rest. You know women. . . ."

He picked a beer out of the cooler and put it in front of Mickey. "You want me to do that for you, Mick? I could call them like as a friend of the family and tell you what they said." Even McKenna wasn't going to leave him alone. Mickey felt like going home and sleeping, except nobody was going to be doing any sleeping in that house for a while.

"Naw, it's all right," he said. "I better do it. I'll do it after I see Smilin' Jack about the arrangements."

"Saturday's best," McKenna said. "Saturday's always a good day for a funeral. You know, more people can come and nobody's got to get up and work the next day." Mickey finished the first beer and half of the second. Eleanore came out of the john and walked past her seat over to Mickey's end of the bar. She shook his hand and said how sorry she was. "He was always such a nice youngster," she said. "Tell Jeanie that for me."

Then she said the same thing eleven more times and McKenna tried to help him out. "Eleanore, go sit down," he said. She ignored him and stood, boozy and sweet, looking into Mickey's face. He saw that she was starting to cry. "For Christ's sake," McKenna said, "you didn't even know him."

She turned on him. "That is a damnable lie. I know all our youngsters. . . ." She looked back at Mickey. "I knew him," she said. "And he was a nice youngster. He never broke into nobody's house in the neighborhood."

McKenna said, "Eleanore, you going to sit down, or do I pour out your drink?" She looked at him, still holding onto Mickey's hand. Tears began to run down her old, cracked cheeks. "This is important," she said.

McKenna said, "I mean it today, Eleanore, I'm throwin' your drink out and flaggin' you for the rest of the week."

"There's something I need to tell Mickey," she said. McKenna looked at the ceiling. She fastened in on Mickey's eyes and squeezed his hand. "He was a nice youngster," she said.

McKenna said, "All right, you told him. Now go back to your seat and drink your drink or I'm cuttin' you off."

She looked at McKenna and said, "You can't cut off the truth." And then she went back to her seat.

McKenna shook his head. "This neighborhood," he said, "even the old ladies are hard dicks. You want another one?"

"Yes," Mickey said.

McKenna said, "That's the spirit. You sure you don't want me to call the cops for you?"

Mickey drank a six-pack at the Hollywood, and on the way home he saw Dr. Booras going into his house. He followed him through the open door and ran into Joanie, who had a no-account husband of her own and knew what he'd been up to. She stood in the path to the stairs, folded arms under folded breasts. "The doctor's going to give her a shot," she said. "He said it would be best if she got some rest."

Something was cooking in the kitchen, maybe ham. He tried to walk around her, but Joanie moved in his way. "The doctor thinks she should rest," she said.

"I'll just use the bathroom," he said, and she let him past. While he was up there, he heard Joyce talking to Dr. Booras. "My sister and me will stay a couple of days," she said. "She'll need support."

Dr. Booras said that was a good idea. "It never hurts to have the extra support," he said. "This is the worst kind of shock a woman can have."

Mickey wondered if Jeanie was lying on the bed listening or if she was already asleep. He went back downstairs without looking in. Joanie had put herself by the door and was accepting a macaroni salad from one of the neighbor women. The phone rang and she picked that up and handed the macaroni salad to him. "Who?"

She retrieved the salad and gave him the phone, and a warning look. Then she went into the kitchen, but there wasn't a sound in there, so she was listening.

"Mick? It's Bird."

"Yeah. You get your electricity back?"

"Right, right. It come on right after you left. Is somethin' wrong? Jeanie don't sound good."

"That was her sister," Mickey said. "We had an accident with Leon."

"What, he got his dick caught in somebody's cash register?" Mickey had told him about the job at the bar before he asked for the one laying brick.

"No, the real thing," he said. Joanie came out of the kitchen and sat down on the sofa. Mickey moved a few steps away from her, up the stairs. "Somethin' happened at work, some kind of accident, and he's dead."

Bird said, "No shit. What was it?"

"I don't know yet. Somethin' . . ."

"You want me to find out? I could do that for you, Mick."

"No, let's just see what happens."

Bird said, "Some strange shit's goin' around. Everywhere. I ask but, you know, it ain't on my level or somethin'. This, though, I could find out about this."

"Let me talk to the cops first," Mickey said. "Just see what happens, if it settles down." He didn't want any more obligations on account of Leon, even if he was dead. "Bird?" The line had gone quiet.

"Right, right. I was just thinkin'. Anyway, what I was callin' you about Mick, I don't know if it's the appropriate time, but it's Turned Leaf. They got her in a $15,000 claimer Wednesday at Keystone. I'm scarin' up everything I got out, and I figured you'd want to know."

Mickey looked at Joanie. "Right," he said, "thanks. I'll tell Jeanie what you said. . . ." He hung up and smiled at her. "I got to take care of the arrangements," he said.

The first place Mickey had seen Turned Leaf was New York, at Aqueduct. She'd run six furlongs in 1:09.2, and he'd seen her gather herself at the top of the stretch and then run down two of the best three-year-old fillies in the country, and win by two.

He'd looked at the board, and she'd run the last quarter in 23.5, and he knew somewhere, sometime, she was going to make him some money.

And three months later, here she was running a claiming race at Keystone. He'd seen her name in the entries again at Aqueduct, and he and Bird had driven up to bet her. She'd broke on top, stayed on top all the way around, and then, with a furlong to go, she'd quit. Quit so bad that for a minute he thought she'd broke down.

He'd turned to Bird, who was flipping fifty-dollar win tickets into a line of empty plastic beer cups in front of his seat, and said, "There's somethin' wrong with that horse."

"Whatever it is, it ain't enough," he'd said. Bird was a fair handicapper, but he got too personally involved with the animals. He got the idea that some of them owed him money. An honest horse, Bird could forgive. But when he saw one quit in the stretch, the way Turned Leaf had, he never forgave and he never forgot.

"I'm tellin' you," Mickey had said, "there's somethin' wrong. I seen it a lot down in Florida, where it's hotter. Some beautiful little filly would hit the stretch and just back up. It would turn out they'd sucked air. You know, vaginally."

"Are you tryin' to tell me," Bird had said, "that this horse's got somethin' wrong with her pussy, makes her quit three hundred yards from the finish?" They'd been sitting in the restaurant at the clubhouse, and a few people began to turn around. "That's beautiful," he'd said.

"It happens all the time. Her vagina opens up while she runs"—people began moving away now—"and a couple gallons of air gets trapped in there. It cramps them all up, and they can't run."

Bird said, "Like runnin' while you're tryin' to take a shit," and they had that part of the restaurant to themselves. He'd sat there with Mickey five minutes, then he'd gotten up and gone into the trainers' room. Technically, Bird was a trainer. He'd paid for a license in New York the day after a horse name Pete's Delight went off at three to two, with a couple grand of Bird's money on him, and then broke last and stayed last all the way around, behind a field that had to improve to suck. Bird had intended to claim Pete's Delight the next time he ran and shoot him. To do that he had to be a trainer. That, of course, was before he had money problems.

Mickey walked from the house to Twenty-seventh Street, thinking about Turned Leaf and Bird. He could always lose himself in the ponies. They told you enough, if you paid attention, to get close to what they would do. Of course, you could never get all the way back to the magic. Sometimes you thought you could, though, when you could do your handicapping and then just look at the horse and feel something going on inside it.

The trouble was, you couldn't be sure if you felt it, or you just wanted to feel it.

Mickey'd had a streak once, back at Hialeah, that ran fifteen days. At the end he was $40,000 to the good, more money than he'd ever made in a year. It was still more money than he'd ever made in a year, and it was damn sure more money than he'd ever lost in nine days, which is what he'd done with it.

Smilin' Jack's was on the corner. He had a green neon sign in the window, written in script. Moran's Funeral Home. There were half a dozen stands in the street that said NO PARKING, FUNERAL. Jack had moved two of them to park his pickup, which he always claimed belonged to his cousin. He'd told Mickey once that when people know an undertaker's got a truck, they start wondering what he does with it.

Jack Moran was born to his job. His father, Digger, had the only funeral home in the Pocket, and when he'd seen it was time to retire—the little mistakes can kill you in the funeral business—he handed the whole operation over to Jack, his only son. The old man had married late, and was fifty the year Jack was born. He was eighty-eight now, and nobody but Jack and their housekeeper had seen him since the stroke six years ago. He just sat up there on the third floor refusing to die. You had to wonder what he knew.

Jack was short and famous for his temper, and since the day he had taken over, he had tried to separate his job from his personal life. He'd told everybody in the Pocket about the arguments with his father. "You don't gotta stay in all night because you work for the city," he'd said. "You don't gotta stay out of clubs even if you're a teacher. What you do with your own time, that's your own business, and it ain't got nothin' to do with work. It's in the Constitution."

His father's argument was that Jack ought to go out of the neighborhood to drink. Everybody agreed the old man must of gone senile. Nobody went out of the neighborhood to drink, except for a month every year at North Wildwood. Everybody in the Pocket who went to the shore had places in the same part of North Wildwood.

Mostly, Jack would go to the Uptown or the Hollywood three or four times a week, sit around and argue about the Eagles or the Flyers or the niggers, and once a month he'd get into a fight. It was a queer thing how all the arguments were over the things everybody agreed on.

Jack had been the way he was since he was a kid, because he was always small. Every time a nun lined up the class according to height, that was somebody who got sucker-punched twenty years later. And even though Jack Moran wasn't much of a fighter, he was dangerous in a fight. It was nothing for him to pick up a beer bottle.

Mickey walked through the little white gate Jack had put up and into the front room of the funeral parlor. It was dark and quiet, and you could just see the neon sign through the curtain. Someplace in back a buzzer went off.

Smilin' Jack came through a pair of green velvet curtains, wearing a dark suit. His hair was slick and close to his head, and he took Mickey's hand in both of his. "We are so sorry to hear about Leon," he said. "You wonder sometimes about God's plan. . . ."

Jack had a black eye, which he'd almost covered with makeup, and he'd dropped his voice about six feet. "I was thinkin' of something that would make Jeanie feel better," Mickey said.

Jack nodded and smiled the exact smile he smiled before he sucker-punched Mole Ferrell at the Hollywood last February. Mickey had seen that. He wondered if the smile had started with sucker-punching or with grieving relatives, and how Jack had put it together that it worked both ways. Maybe for smiles it was all he had. Jack said, "Let me show you what we got, Mick."

He held the curtain for Mickey and then led him past the viewing room, through a door to a room of caskets. They were all open, linings like the sport coats at Jacob Reed. It looked like a room full of traps. Jack closed the door behind them. The prices were printed on folded cards, sitting on top of each unit. That's what Jack called them, units.

The figures were broken down into total funeral services, and then a price for only the box, in case you just wanted to have one around. Jack put his hand on a dark mahogany unit. It had a real serious look. "Of course, you know Jeanie best," he said, "but you know, she ain't going to want some piece of junk. You know, she likes things to look good."

The price for the mahogany casket, by itself, was $2,700. If you wanted a funeral with it, and an embalmed body and a vault, it was $5,995. Mickey felt the wood, which was smooth, and looked at his reflection in it. It distorted his face, the way the toaster did. "Of course," Jack said—he didn't say "of course" much at the Hollywood—"there are some people who prefer bronze. The sealing's better, and it's airtight." Mickey looked up and Jack had moved to the bronze casket, which was $5,995 all by itself. Mickey noticed how graceful Jack was around caskets. "It's all up to the family, of course," he said.

Mickey thought of the box they'd buried his father in. It wasn't what he had in mind for Jeanie to be looking at Saturday morning, but it was what he could afford. Smilin' Jack assumed he had money that he didn't have. Everybody in the Pocket did. They assumed he was connected too. There was nobody but Bird that knew anything about it, and that included Jeanie.

With Jeanie, it was always kind of an *expectation* of what he was, and he saw right away that's as close as she wanted it. If all he did was deliver hot meat in ten- and twenty-pound pack-ages—if he was no better than the rest of the Pocket—she didn't want to know. She kept her accounts and he kept his, and it seemed like a funny way to be married, but she kept a distance from everything. He guessed it was her way of seeing things.

"I tell you what," Mickey said, "I got to think this over, maybe talk to Jeanie. I don't want to do nothin' that she ain't gonna like. . . ."

Smilin' Jack smiled the smile that sucker-punched Mole Ferrell. "There's no hurry," he said. "The important thing is to be sure."

Mickey said, "There's a lot ridin' on this," and Jack led him past the viewing room to the front door, and gave him another one of those handshakes like he was making a snowball. "Maybe I'll drop over tomorrow morning," Jack said. "It might be easier for her to talk about it in familiar surroundings."

Mickey started down the street and Jack stopped him, not quite yelling. "Yo, Mick," he said, "was the body messed up?"

Mickey shook his head. "No, the body's all right. It's just the back of his head."

"That's no problem at all," Jack said. "The back of the head takes care of itself." Mickey walked back toward his house, and for the second time that afternoon he didn't know where to go. He didn't think he ought to get drunk, the sisters were guarding

Jeanie. It felt like everything was moving but him. He had eight hundred dollars and the truck, and he couldn't sell the truck. He thought of asking Bird for the seven hundred again, but if he'd had it, he'd of given it to him.

In Jeanie's mind, he'd fucked it up with Leon. She'd expected something—he didn't know what—and the kid was dead. She would expect something now too. She would expect him to make things different than they was.

Mickey got into the Monte Carlo and drove into Center City. They were showing a double feature at the Budco. *Halloween* and *The Texas Chain Saw Massacre*. He put the car in a lot, bought himself a ticket, and went to sleep in a seat three rows from the front and all the way to the wall. Away from the damn marijuana.

He went to sleep and dreamed of Turned Leaf.

Monday afternoon, Shellburn went to court.

"And then me and the defendant went into the office where he was and, you know, capped him. . . ."

The prosecutor said, "What exactly did you do when you capped him, Charlie?"

Charlie Piscoli was nineteen or twenty years old, a night-shift waiter at Bookbinders Restaurant. "Well, me and Eddie—the defendant—we went in there, and I talked to him, said, you know, that he'd been takin' a quarter off the top, everything he was supposed to be cuttin', and he says, 'The fuck I have, you think I'm crazy?' And while I'm talkin' to him, Eddie caps him."

The prosecutor looked back over to the table where a man a few years older than Charlie Piscoli was sitting in a suit that did not fit him, considering his fingernails. Eddie Allen sold souvenir Liberty Bells on the street, across from Independence Hall. "Eddie being Edward Allen," the prosecutor said.

"Yessir, the defendant."

"And exactly how did he *cap* him?"

"Well, first he shot him in the head, but it didn't seem to do nothing. I mean he stood up and started sayin' something. . . ."

"What did he say?"

"Uh, I believe he called us motherfuckers."

"All right, go ahead."

"Well, like I said, the bullet didn't seem to do nothin', so Eddie shot him again, in the side I think, and he grabbed himself there, and tries to get the gun. That's when he got his finger shot off. By then I see it's trouble, because his old lady's comin' down the stairs. You know, the office was in the house."

Richard Shellburn was sitting at the end of the bench reserved for the press. He was fifty-three years old and he'd never been in as much as a fistfight in his life. He leaned forward to hear Charlie Piscoli tell the rest of the story, how the wife had come down the stairs and started screaming, "You're killing him!" By then Charlie was holding him from behind and Eddie was sticking him in the eyes with a screwdriver, and the victim—a fifty-year-old hood named Pirate John Bonalini—was still calling them motherfuckers.

"And what did you do then?" the prosecutor asked.

Charlie Piscoli shrugged. "I told the lady we was tryin' our best," he said. Shellburn heard some of the people on Eddie Allen's side of the courtroom laugh. Up on the bench, Judge Kalquist pounded for quiet, issued the familiar warnings. Shellburn watched as the judge and the witness looked at each other. He wondered what things had come to, that the people who ran things had taken to using lowlifes like Charlie Piscoli and Eddie Allen to do their killing.

Screwdrivers, fingers on the coffee table, wives running down the stairs.

And of course, the cops caught one of them coming out. Charlie had run into the side of the police car, and he gave them Eddie, and everybody else he knew, and before the district attorney and the federal prosecutor got him a new driver's license and a room somewhere in Phoenix, he would testify against everybody he'd ever met.

"Thank you," the kid told the judge.

Kalquist covered his eyes. The judge was protecting Charlie

Piscoli as much as the government was. Four weeks ago, before he declared a mistrial and separated the defendants, Kalquist had lectured the courtroom on the serious nature of the matter being tried, and to end the lecture he had looked down at the bench where Shellburn was sitting and said, "It is not funny, and it is not romantic, except to the most adolescent of minds."

The day before this lecture, Shellburn had written a column comparing the coming of New Journalism to the coming of the Charlie Piscolis to organized crime, wondering if there were any standards left. He had written about the way newspapers used to be, and the way organized crime in Philadelphia used to be, before somebody put a shotgun in Angelo Bruno's ear and blew away all the order and dignity and discipline organized crime had. That was when the drugs came into it—the old man never allowed that—and the next thing you knew, motorcycle gangs and guys like Charlie Piscoli were doing family business.

The day Judge Kalquist looked at Shellburn and made his remark about adolescent was the day Shellburn started his investigation of Kalquist. He put his man Billy on it, looking through Kalquist's trial records. Billy had said, "What is it we're looking for again?"

"Anything," he'd said.

"How do we know there's anything there?"

Richard Shellburn had said, "Judges are lawyers, Billy." Sitting in the courtroom now, Shellburn knew what Kalquist's house cost, where his daughters went to college, sentences he'd given everybody with money who ever got convicted in his court. That wasn't why Shellburn was there, though. Billy would take care of that. Shellburn wanted to know how it was when Pirate John Bonalini got shot in the head. He was fifty-three years old and had never been in a fistfight in his life, but violence held something for Richard Shellburn.

"What happened," the prosecutor asked, "when his wife got down the stairs?"

"By then, the Pirate was gettin' heavier, you know? Like when I grabbed him, he was sort of stunned but he was still standin' up, talkin', but as she come down the stairs he got heavier to hold. He got so heavy that finally I let him go, and he sunk to the floor."

"He sunk to the floor," the prosecutor said.

"Yessir."

"And what did his wife do?"

"She sunk to the floor also," he said. "She was, you know, real upset. And me and Eddie ran out, he went one way up the street, I went the other, and I run into the cop car. Oh, yeah, Eddie wanted to cap her too, but I just wanted to get out of there. . . ."

Shellburn had almost died once, three years ago driving home from a lecture he'd given to a bunch of women for $1,200. First he'd thrown up, and then it grabbed the middle of his chest, like everything there had seized up, and then it shot into his jaw. He'd stopped his car and opened his door, and somebody had found him there, half in and half out, and they'd called an ambulance.

He woke up in Jefferson Hospital, and the doctor told him he'd almost died. "I remember," he'd said.

But there was something else too, that he couldn't remember. For a while that night he couldn't breathe, and once he'd stopped fighting, it wasn't so bad. It was like boarding up the windows, the things that happened. The house got dark inside, smaller at first, then bigger, and then he seemed to fill it.

And there was something else, the hum of it, that started moving away from him even before he woke up. Away, or back inside.

And then the doctor was telling him he'd almost died, and then his boss from the paper—T. D. Davis—was standing there, and Shellburn was shaking and couldn't talk. There had been something sad in that humming. "Pull yourself together," T. D. Davis had said.

Davis didn't know it, of course, but that's what boarding up all the windows had been about.

Charlie Piscoli said, "No, it wasn't me that capped him. I

never capped nobody in my life. The worst I ever done was scare somebody."

Judge Kalquist looked at his watch, and then at the prosecutor. "Do you anticipate your questioning of this witness is going to take much longer?"

"Yessir," the prosecutor said. "It could go on for quite a while."

The judge considered his watch again, blew some air into his cheeks, held it a minute, and then let it go. "It's three-thirty," he said finally, as if that was something none of them had ever run into before, "and I think I'll stop us here, and we'll get a fresh start early in the morning."

It was all right with Shellburn, he had to go to work anyway.

"I love this city," he said, "not the sights, the city. I loved her last night, and I love her this morning, before she brushes her teeth, knowing she snores." He was forcing his voice so the tape recorder on the seat next to him would pick it up.

"I am used to the feel of her beside me. I know her warmth and her coolness. She has forgiven me, and I have forgiven her, and I am used to the feel of her beside me. . . ."

A carload of Puerto Ricans was sitting next to him at the light on the corner of Fifteenth and Callowhill. By the time Shellburn noticed them, they'd heard it, and the ones at the windows were smiling.

"You right," one of them said. "I think I fuck her last night too." He waited in the window, his chin on his hands, smiling. Shellburn had nothing against Puerto Ricans, some of his best columns came out of their neighborhoods. The cops would go in to settle a domestic argument, the Rican would hit a cop, and then they'd call for backup cops because nobody in his right mind is going to shoot a Rican in a Rican neighborhood without a way out. And maybe the Puerto Rican would have a machete, and before they carried him out of there in a plastic bag, six or seven of the cops would go to the hospital.

And Shellburn would write yes, they were a spirited and

proud people, but surely there was some way for eight grown, trained men to handle one out-of-work, drunk and depressed Puerto Rican without shooting him eleven times. He would write about the Puerto Rican's neighborhood. Burned-out houses, wine bottles, rats, naked children. He would suggest giving Juan Diaz a job instead of shooting him eleven times. Sometimes it won him a Keystone Press Award.

He didn't write about the Puerto Ricans often enough to piss off South Philadelphia, or even often enough to piss off the police. Sometime in the week after they killed the Puerto Rican, the cops would do something right, and he'd do a column about that. Billy would turn something up, or Shellburn, if he had to, could build a column around, say, a cop walking around a wino instead of kicking him. He'd call it "The Loneliest Job" or "Down Any Alley." It worked out because he had a sense of balance.

The Puerto Ricans were still looking at him. "I hope she don't have no type of herpes," the one in the window said. "I am used to the feel of her, you know?"

The light changed and Shellburn turned right. The Puerto Ricans went straight, headed into North Philadelphia, and the one who had talked to him sat in the window with his chin on his hands and watched him until the fence around the newspaper's parking lot took Shellburn out of his view.

He had nothing against Puerto Ricans, but that one deserved it. Shellburn had paid $14,000 for the Continental, and it was the safest place he had in the city.

He turned the tape recorder off and pointed the Continental into the company parking lot. There was a space with R. SHELLBURN printed across the cement curb in front of it, or there should have been.

It was the third parking space from the shack where the guard sat. He checked himself. There was E. V. Davenport's space, and T. D. Davis's space, and then R. Shellburn. Davenport was the owner of the paper and the chain, and came in only on Thursdays for a meeting with his editors. He sat at the head of a long, shiny table and directed a review of the past week's papers. The secretaries served tiny sandwiches and radishes cut to resemble flowers. E. V. was in his eighties and interested in style. Last week, for example, he'd outlawed contractions, and memos to that effect went up all over the building.

T. D. Davis ran the paper day to day and had been editor nine years. His Volvo was parked in its space, but the space next to it, R. Shellburn, was gone. There was a hole where it had been. Six or seven feet wide, at least that deep. Shellburn honked twice and the guard came out of the shack. His name tag said FLOYD. Shellburn couldn't remember if he knew him or not.

"Somebody stole my parking place," Shellburn said. Floyd looked at it a minute and shook his head.

"I sure didn't see nobody come in, Mr. Shellburn," he said. "I had to go up to the garage 'bout twenty minutes ago, they must of come in then."

Shellburn said, "What are they going to put in there?"

The old guard looked again, shook his head. "Maybe you best park over in Mr. Davenport's place," he said. "Mr. Davenport don't come in on Mondays."

"It looks like a fucking grave," Shellburn said.

"Yessir," the guard said. "Probably somebody who don't know no better."

Shellburn sighed. "I'll tell you, Floyd, it's harder than that to get rid of us. They keep bringing in the replacements, the New Journalists, waves of them, kids out of every dip-shit little paper in the chain, and they come in with their own rules, and they wash in and they wash out, and you and I are still here." He'd decided he knew the guard.

Floyd shook his head. "We sure as hell still here, Mr. Shellburn," he said.

Shellburn got out of the Continental and looked in the hole. "What if somebody stepped into that in the night?"

Floyd looked in the hole with him. "T. D. Davis hisself could of got out his car and broke his ass," he said.

Shellburn thought it over. "I guess it isn't hurting anything there," he said.

Shellburn's office was a desk, a chair, a phone and a typewriter. Four hundred square feet with a view of City Hall. He could look out his window and see an oxidized statue of William Penn, anytime he wanted to. There was no carpet on the floor, no pictures, no awards or plaques in gratitude from the Fraternal Order of Police. When it came up, he would say that the only picture he needed was the one out his window.

William Penn stood on top of City Hall—by law the tallest building in the city—and beyond that was Center City, and beyond that South Philadelphia. History aside, it seemed to him South Philadelphia was where the city started. When he looked at a map, he could see how something must have tipped over there and spilled out in two giant stains, the northeast and northwest parts of the city. The source was South Philly. When it came up, he would say he could look out his window and see the people he wrote for.

It didn't come up much, because Shellburn didn't encourage casual visitors. In his office or his home, for the same reason.

He sat down in front of a small pile of letters, and began throwing them away. He threw away all the press releases, without opening them. He threw away the Guild notices, the interoffice communications about changes in the VDT system. He threw away letters from Golda and Irene and Henry and Dora, which he recognized from the handwriting. Arthritic, jagged script, it looked like cracked glass. He threw away their letters because he knew what they would say, not because he didn't appreciate them. They were proof of what he was in the city.

That left the real mail. Eleven letters, all of them from women, thanking him for some column he'd written in the last couple of weeks, complimenting him on his courage for writing it. People always thought it took courage to write columns. He read the last line or two of each of the letters and tossed them into the wastebasket too.

He remembered a woman in a purple hat with a piece of net hanging from it onto her face. She'd stood up during the question-and-answer period Saturday night—he couldn't remember what group it was, but it was the regular $700—and asked if he really read all his mail. Personally.

"When I stop listening to the people," he'd said, "then they ought to stop listening to me." Richard Shellburn had been writing his column at the *Daily Times* exactly twenty years, and he'd been saying that a long time. Back when he'd started it, it may have even been true.

He was twenty years into it now, and the people hadn't said anything he wanted to listen to for at least half that long. And he hadn't said anything he wanted to listen to in that time either. He picked up the phone and called Billy.

Billy Deebol was his legman. He'd grown up in the Northeast, and he'd grown up wanting to work for the *Daily Times*. Shellburn often told people that he didn't care if Billy never went to Columbia to learn New Journalism, he cared something about the city, which was more than you could say for all the kids they brought in on their way to the Washington *Post* or the New York *Times*. Or on their way to other Davenport newspapers, to be city editors.

If you weren't enough of an asshole for that yet, Philadelphia was where the chain brought you to learn.

Billy answered the phone on the second ring. He always answered on the second ring, he was an absolutely reliable kid. Kid. Billy Deebol was thirty-seven years old and two-thirds bald, and he had a wife and six kids of his own.

Billy had less imagination than the door to the office, but in a strange kind of way he understood what went into Shellburn's writing. He knew what kind of detail worked and what didn't, he knew what would fit into eight hundred words. It was funny he'd never thought of writing a column himself. And he hadn't, Shellburn would have seen it.

When Richard Shellburn wrote about rats and burned-out shells and naked children in North Philadelphia, it was Billy who went out and saw it. And he was the one who talked to grieving widows and mothers, and he was the one who went over the things that had happened every day in the city and told Shellburn what was out there.

And the one who typed Shellburn's copy into the computer system. Shellburn knew he cleaned it up—like when he wrote drunk—but he didn't know how much. Shellburn never read the paper.

And Billy never wanted anything for it except to be paid, and to be allowed to do it again. The thing Shellburn liked best about Billy was that he didn't want anything else. "Billy, my boy," he said, "what's going on in the City of Brotherly Love?"

"It's a funny thing, Richard," he said. "Nothing. Nobody killed in three days, nobody important got mugged. There wasn't even a parade, all weekend long." Shellburn hated parades and often wrote about them.

"Nothing?" Shellburn let himself sound disappointed. There was nobody who wouldn't get lazy if you let them. He didn't tell him he'd already written half a column for Tuesday, on the subject of his twentieth anniversary at the *Daily Times*. The phone was quiet for a few seconds. Shellburn said, "Death takes a holiday, huh?"

"Well," Billy said, "almost. I mean, there was an accident this morning down at Holy Redeemer. Twenty-four-year-old construction worker named Leon Hubbard was hit by a crane or something."

"White or black?"

"From the address, it has to be white," Billy said. "Yeah, it's God's Pocket." He waited while Shellburn thought it over.

"Is it any good?"

Billy said, "Not that I saw. The guy's a union bricklayer, lived with his mother. Unless you want to do something with the hospital end, you know, irony or something."

"No. The mother crippled? Did he support her?"

Billy said, "I could run over there tomorrow and take a look if you want me to. I could go over there tonight if you're hung up for a column. . . ."

Shellburn let the line go quiet again. "No," he said finally, "I'll scare something up. By tomorrow, they'll be something better. Don't worry about it, my boy."

"You sure? I could run over there."

"Don't bother. The mother's probably asleep anyway." He looked at his watch. Quarter to six. "Take the night off."

Billy said, "I'll make another check with the police before I put you in the system. . . ."

Shellburn said, "Whatever you think. I'll be here." He hung up and moved over in front of his typewriter. It was an old Royal that weighed as much as a watermelon. Nothing fancy, nothing electric. It was the same typewriter he'd had for twelve years. The rest of the staff of the *Daily Times* had gone to VDT machines four years ago. The New Journalists sent their words into a computer. Shellburn had refused to learn.

He'd fought with a managing editor over that, gone all the way to Davenport. T. D. Davis had refused to hear the argument, Shellburn being a city institution and the managing editor being the man who was supposed to deal with him then. T. D. Davis had a chain of command, and he lived by it, although eventually he took over Richard Shellburn himself.

Shellburn could still see the look on the managing editor's face. "If Richard Shellburn wants to write with piss in the snow," the old man had said to the M.E., "you keep him in snow. As long as he writes here, you keep him in snow. . . ."

Shellburn began to think of the old man as the only real newspaperman on the staff. He began to think the old man was his friend. He went into his office later that week, though, and Davenport thought he was the air-conditioner repairman.

He put a piece of yellow paper in the typewriter, wrote his name in the corner, straightened the chair. Thinking of piss in the snow, he went in the bathroom and took half a minute in front of the urinal to work up about what you'd get wringing out a sock. Shellburn's kidneys were in worse shape than his liver.

He went back into his office and sat in front of the typewriter again. He rewound the tape recorder, and began to switch it on and off, writing down what he'd said on the way to work. He called it "A Love Affair with the City."

It started out, *"I have written the story of this city for twenty years. Twenty years today . . ."* and was five hundred words deep when the Puerto Rican's voice came up at him from the desk. *"You right. I think I fuck her last night."* It intruded all over again, and Shellburn was almost two hours writing the last three hundred words.

Just before he finished the phone rang. He picked it up and a voice was shouting at him out of a crowded bar. "Mr. Shellburn? No shit? You answer your own phone?"

"What can I do for you, pal?" he said. Usually Billy answered his phone. The man on the other end was telling his friends to shut up, that he was talking to Richard Shellburn.

"Hey look," he said, "I mean, we're not important or nothin', but we thought you ought to know Leon Hubbard was a tragedy, with his mother and all. It's a human interest story. He come from the Pocket, and we thought maybe you could write somethin' about him, how it was a tragedy the way he died."

"How did he die?"

"Well, you know, it was common labor," the man said. "I don't know if it was malfeasance or not, but he wasn't the kind of guy to walk around havin' shit fall on his head, I'll testify to that in court. So will everybody else down here. We thought maybe you could write somethin' up about it. You know, the neighborhood takin' up a collection for his mother and all."

Shellburn said, "I'll see what I can do."

"You're a great man," the man said. "I mean it. I wouldn't just fuckin' say that."

The man thanked him for another five minutes.

Shellburn hung up afterward and looked past William Penn to the city that loved him. Then he finished the column and read it over. Somehow it sounded familiar. But it was finished, and that was what Richard Shellburn asked out of a column.

To be finished, and get him away from the typewriter for another night.

When Mickey woke up, there was a family of Texans cutting the parts off houseguests up on the screen, and five hundred screaming colored people in the audience. He'd been dreaming, but it took a while in the noise to remember what it was about.

Turned Leaf.

She'd come into the stretch all by herself and the crowd was screaming, and then something had happened. He could hear it from the crowd, but he couldn't see what it was, and when he opened his eyes they were cutting up houseguests in Texas.

He wanted to know what had happened to the horse, but the theater had filled up while he'd slept, and it didn't seem like a good place to sleep anymore. Once you started to think about going back after a dream it was too late anyway. That's when it got away, when you were trying to figure out how to get it back.

That's how it all slipped away.

He sat up and stretched. The air in the theater was warm and wet and smelled stale. It was two different smells when people were sitting down in a place and when they were moving around. Movie seats kept something from every ass that sat in them too. He looked around to see how close the colored people were, he checked to make sure his wallet was still in his back pocket. He started to get up, then he thought of the situation with Leon and settled back into the seat. There wasn't anything he wanted to do outside.

He watched *Texas Chain Saw Massacre* all the way through, and then the first part of *Halloween,* which was about a crazy man killing teenage girls. The girls had boyfriends and laughed when they got laid. Mickey had seen a hundred movies where the girls laughed when they got laid. He couldn't imagine it.

He walked out of the theater. It was dark outside, beginning to rain. In his whole life nobody had laughed while he was laying them. Could they have made that up in Hollywood and used it for fifty years if it never happened anyplace else?

An old woman who'd painted her lips half an inch beyond where they stopped watched him from inside the ticket booth. She looked like a baby chicken in an incubator. He wondered who she painted herself up for. He wondered if she'd laughed when she was younger, while she was getting laid. She yawned while he watched her, her mouth turning into a tiny black hole. He could imagine a lizard coming out of there, but not the getting-laid kind of laughing.

He'd asked an old trucker once how it was with his wife. The trucker had been married forty years, and Mickey had been about twenty-two then, and wondered what the man saw when he looked at his wife. It was at a truck stop outside of Canton, Ohio. He'd said, "I mean, does she still look like she did to you? Or does she look older, or . . . ?"

The old trucker had studied him across the table, making sure he wasn't a wiseass, and then he'd told him. "When I look at my wife," he'd said, "I see an old fuckin' bag."

Mickey had smiled, tried to joke, but the old trucker had kept him right there. "You wonder what she sees when she looks at me, right?"

Mickey had said, "No, I was just thinkin' . . ." The old trucker had held up his hand.

"I don't know what she sees," he'd said. "I never asked her. But I don't sit around the house in my undershorts no more, I can tell you that."

The old woman in the ticket booth was staring at him now like she was waiting for him to do something. He knew she would have been afraid to even glance at him on the street, but sitting there behind a pane of glass and a job, she looked at who she wanted. It was funny, the things that made people feel safe.

He found the Monte Carlo in the parking lot and sat down behind the wheel, still tired. There was nothing he could think of to do, but he started the car and turned south on Seventeenth Street, just to see where it would go.

It went to the Hollywood Bar.

It was the most people Mickey had ever seen in the bar on a Monday night, except for the year the Mummers' Parade fell on a Monday. There was a lot of them, but there wasn't much noise. When Mickey walked in the door it got even quieter. He stood still and they stood still, and then Eleanore came from the back and put her old arms around him. "He was a good youngster," she said, and then folded up and fell into his arms. He was surprised at how light she was, there wasn't anything left to her at all. He held her until McKenna came around from behind the bar and took her off. Eleanore's eyes rolled up into her head, and she went off to sleep smiling.

And then everybody in the bar was buying Mickey drinks. Some of them he'd never seen in there before, most of them he'd never talked to. Kids. But they watched him, and who he was talking to, and when it was their turn they came over and brought him a beer and told him Leon was what the neighborhood stood for.

"Leon didn't take no shit," a kid said. "I was a father, that's what I'd want my kid to be like."

"And he was a volunteer," another one said. "He saved some people in a fire. I know that for a fact, he saved a bunch of people."

They said what they'd planned to say and then left as soon as they could, like hospital visits. Mickey shook hands and took the drinks and listened to all the good things people said about Leon and themselves. "All he ever wanted was to work at his job, be let alone," a man told him. "Leon never bothered nobody in his life. He was just like everybody else in here."

Mickey worked his way to the end of the bar where McKenna was standing, trying to settle an argument. "I seen the medals," somebody was saying. "He was decorated for valor for killin' I don't know how many gooks."

A man named Ray, who was fifteen years older than Mickey, shook his head no. Ray had worked in the wire room at the *Bulletin* for thirty years, until it folded, and it was a known fact in God's Pocket that he had a photographic memory and could remember everything that had ever happened. That, and he knew things nobody else knew. If you asked him what time it was the Japs hit Pearl Harbor, he'd close his eyes a minute and then ask what ship you were talking about. Then he'd say, "The *Arizona*? The first bomb hit her at eight-eleven a.m., and she sunk fifty-five minutes later in thirty-two feet of water with forty-six men still on board." How the fuck you going to argue with that?

Nobody ever caught him making a mistake, except about

the Phillies, and ever since that happened Ray wouldn't talk sports. Now he was shaking his head no. "I remember when Leon left," he said. "It was June 26, 1976. They weren't sending anybody to Vietnam in 1976."

"I seen the medals. . . ."

Ray spilled beer on his coat, shook his head no. McKenna held up his hands. "Maybe it was another year," he said. "I think I heard him talk about Vietnam once or twice myself."

Ray was still shaking his head. The man he was arguing with said, "Then where'd he get them medals? They don't just give you medals for nothin' in the Army. You got to see action to get the kind of medals Leon had. . . ."

Mickey slipped past Ray, not wanting to get into it, and found a place at the bar in front of McKenna. "A lot of people been askin' for you, Mick," he said.

Mickey shrugged. "I went to a movie."

McKenna smiled. "I know," he said. "The day my mother died, you know what I did?" Mickey looked at him. "Yeah," McKenna said, "I went out and banged a Locust Street whore, came home at one o'clock in the morning, and they're all there waitin' for me. It was the Christians and lions all over again."

"On the day your mother died?"

McKenna nodded. "Cancer. Everybody thought I'd gone and got drunk out of grief, you know? They were right I felt bad, but that's not why you get drunk and bang a thirty-dollar whore. You do that 'cause you've got to do *somethin'*. . . ." He opened a fresh beer and put it on the bar for Mickey, then poured himself a shot of Ancient Age bourbon, and touched the shot glass to the neck of the beer bottle. "All I'm sayin'," McKenna said, "is that afterward I felt bad, what I'd done. All I'm sayin' is that you ain't the only one ever went to the movies when somethin' happened."

Mickey said, "Yeah, but I went to the movies. . . ."

McKenna smiled at him. "Whatever, Mick. What fuckin' difference does it make anyway?" Mickey saw that was true, and felt like he'd got out from under the load, and when the weight came off he noticed himself getting drunk.

The bar seemed to get drunk with him. Drunk and loud, and then old Ray tried to punch somebody in the face over the dates of America's involvement in Vietnam, and fell down and hurt his back. Everybody walked over him on the way to the bathrooms, and he lay on the floor talking about the lawsuit he could file against the Hollywood if he was that kind of person to do it.

And for a couple of hours everybody shut up about Leon, which suited Mickey, and people threw money into the jar by the window to bury him. Once Mickey glanced over to the other end of the bar and noticed a fat girl sitting over a drink with cherries in it, crying. There were people all around her, but he could see she was alone. When he looked again, just before closing time, she was gone.

He left the car where it was—double-parked in front of the Hollywood— and walked down the street and back up the alley to the garage. The night was dead still, and the sound of the bar was still in his ears, along with the sound of his feet on the cement. He wondered who the fat girl with the cherries in her drink was. It seemed to him that she was the only one that wasn't part of the ceremony.

It seemed to him he was thinking about a lot of spooky shit lately that he wasn't used to thinking about. He made a promise to go back to thinking regular shit tomorrow. He checked the truck before he went into the house. The refrigeration unit was plugged in, the meat was all in place, balanced over the axle. He stood there a minute, wondering where they'd put Leon for the night, and it was the first time since it had happened that he'd felt sorry. Then he closed the truck and the garage, and a light went on in the kitchen.

He went to the back door and began going through his keys, looking for the one to the door. Mickey kept thirty-five or forty keys on a ring that hung off his belt. He didn't know exactly how many there were, but he could look at them and tell you what every one of them was for. There were keys from old cars, old trucks, old apartments. Mickey never threw his keys away. The truth was, he'd always tried to keep things from changing.

He dropped the keys on the steps, picked them up and was going through them again when the door opened. The light washed out over the steps, and one of the sisters was standing in the middle of it, an eclipse. It was hard to see which one it was. He stared up into the light and at the dark and unhappy form in the middle of it. "Hey, Joanie," he said, finally, "what are you doin' up?"

She made a noise and turned back into the house. "Joyce?" He followed her in, locked the door behind him. "It's the dog-damnest thing how I can't remember which one of you is which," he said. She walked to the couch, where there was a blanket and a pillow, and rubbed her eyes. "What time is it?" she said.

"Closing time," Mickey said. "What difference does it make, anyway?"

She looked at him hard, and he saw that he hadn't said that as well as McKenna had. "You been out drinking? Tonight, you been drinking?" She made a face and lay down on the couch, and covered her eyes. The front of her hair was wrapped around three pink curlers the size of a pig's leg. She covered her eyes with her arm, but she didn't go to sleep. Mickey shrugged and headed toward the stairs. "Don't go in Jeanie's room," the sister said. "The doctor had to come twice to give her medicine, and he said she needed a good night's sleep."

He said, "I thought maybe she'd want somebody . . ."

"Joyce is up there with her," the sister said. Mickey looked at her a minute, figuring out who that made her, but she never took her arm off her face. He was straight and sure climbing the stairs, somehow feeling her watching him. He reminded himself to stop thinking of spooky shit tomorrow.

He went into the bathroom and closed the door. He dropped some paper in the toilet to cover the noise and then urinated against the bowl above it. He brushed his teeth, he looked at himself in the mirror. She'd said, "You been drinking, *tonight*?" He wondered how bad that was.

He cracked the door into the bedroom and saw Jeanie's hair on a pillow. Her face was buried into her sister's shoulder, and as he stood in the doorway looking down he suddenly realized this sister was awake too, lying there in the dark watching him. He closed the door an inch at a time, turned the light out in the bathroom, and went into Leon's room to sleep. The bed was narrow and cool, and the springs yawned when he lay down. There was a smell to it too. It took him a minute to figure out what it was. Cats.

T. D. Davis was the handsomest man in the entire Davenport chain of newspapers, he may have been the handsomest man in Philadelphia. He had an affected Southern accent, gray hair and a boy's face and spent seventy minutes a day at the Philadelphia Athletic Club, running on a treadmill. T. D. Davis did not like to jog outside.

No woman on the staff of the *Daily Times* had ever worked for anybody even close to being as handsome as T. D., or as courtly, and it was the nature of T. D. Davis that once a woman had been on the staff a year, she would no longer dream about handsome men. After a year, *cute* was all any of them could go. It was the same thing as a kid who gets sick on vodka or gin, and never likes the taste again.

T. D. came into the office Tuesday morning at eight-fifteen, passing under a five-foot sign that he'd hung at the entrance to the newsroom. It said: THE REPORTER IS THE MOST IMPORTANT PERSON IN THIS ROOM.

It used to say THE REPORTER IS THE MOST IMPORTANT MAN IN THIS ROOM, but T. D. changed it when one of the women reporters complained. Times changed, T. D. changed with them.

He walked under the sign, past the city desk, and said good morning to Brookie Sutherland. Sutherland was an assistant city editor, brought in six months ago from one of the chain's papers in Florida. He smiled at T. D. and asked after his family.

"Ellen's just fine," Davis said. "Y'all have to come out for dinner sometime." T. D. Davis said that a couple of times a month, but Brookie Sutherland never actually got asked out to the Main Line for dinner. Brookie Sutherland thought he was T. D.'s friend.

Davis went into his office and shut the door. He hung his

coat in the closet and sat down behind his desk. There were pictures of his wife and his three children on his desk, a proclamation from the Chamber of Commerce on the wall, thanking him for his service to the business community. There was a picture of T. D. shaking hands with Mayor Bill Green, and a picture of him shaking hands with A. J. Foyt, and pictures with Sammy Snead, Jimmy Hoffa and Lyndon Johnson. Finally, there was a picture of T. D. standing with Jackie Robinson, but it had been torn in half and taped together.

If you looked at the pictures in the right sequence, you couldn't help noticing T. D. was getting handsomer all the time.

A yellow interoffice envelope was sitting in the middle of the desk. Someone had been in there, somebody besides Gertruda, who brought him his mail at nine o'clock every morning. He didn't like anybody in his office but Gertruda, who was seventy-seven years old and didn't care about anything he kept in his desk. The envelope was from Brookie Sutherland. There was a copy of this morning's Shellburn column and a copy of his anniversary column two years before. Brookie Sutherland had used red ink to underline all the places where the columns were the same, then added it up at the bottom.

"T. D.—," the note said, "31 sentences almost the same, six sentences EXACTLY the same, plus similar mood. Staff aware of similarities, as you will recall from memo of last week, when anonymous person or persons went through Shellburn column on dead mummer and underlined the word OLD 52 times, out of 800-word column.

"Have also done some talking, as per your suggestion, on prospects of having Peter Byrne followed, to the purpose of gathering info, cud be used to fire him. Still think that, under circumstances, it is the way we shud go.—Brookie."

Peter Byrne was the *Daily Times'* afternoon-shift police reporter, who liked cops better than editors.

T. D. Davis took off his shoes and put his feet on his desk. He took the two columns that Sutherland had left for him and read them over, but it wasn't time to hit Richard Shellburn. He'd stopped going out into the street years ago, and that skinny kid—Billy somebody?—had been doing all his legwork, probably writing some of his copy, but it wasn't his time yet.

Shellburn was still Shellburn, the man who cared about the common man. He'd spent twenty years getting to be that. Partly writing, mostly just being there on page 2 every day. Brookie Sutherland didn't understand it but Shellburn could go senile tomorrow and write that same column every day for a year and get away with it.

Richard Shellburn was the only man on the staff T. D. Davis couldn't fuck with. At least not yet. T. D. was always thinking about the timing of things.

Before he'd come to Philadelphia, T. D. had worked in New York, where he'd learned what timing could do to you. He was a sports editor there, and he had one reporter named Jimmy White that he bent in this way or that just to see if it was possible.

Jimmy White had a sixteen-year-old daughter who was the kind of retarded you didn't notice until she talked, and somehow that made him scared to death of losing what he had, and scared of being out of town, and anytime T. D. asked for something more out of him, Jimmy White found a way to give it to him.

He'd work late off the clock, he'd come in early, he'd answer phones or take dictation, just to stay in New York, just to stay where he was. Jimmy White didn't have a friend on the paper, although the ladies who knew about his daughter said they felt sorry.

And then his daughter had run away, and showed up in Los Angeles a month later with every kind of venereal disease there was back then. And Jimmy White began to miss work, two and three days every week. And the sports department didn't run right when he was gone.

T. D. threatened him four times, and then he saw it was hopeless—that he wasn't afraid anymore—and he fired him, figuring he might be worth something as an example.

Jimmy White walked out of the office without a word. The Guild went to arbitration to get him his job back, but one afternoon a week later, Jimmy White came back to the office and took his case off the books. T. D.'s secretary—she was one of the ladies who felt sorry about Jimmy White's daughter—had looked up that afternoon and there he was, standing in front of her desk holding what she thought was a cello case.

"Why, Jimmy," she said. "How are you?"

He pointed at the door behind her. "I need to see Mr. Davis," he said.

The secretary smiled. "I'm sorry, Jimmy," she said. He smiled back and put the cello case on her desk. It opened in two places, she remembered that later for the police. Two clicks, and then he pried open the lid and brought out a brand-new eighteen-inch, 3.4-horsepower Craftsman chain saw. He played with the choke a minute, flipped the switch to ON and pulled the starter cord.

The chain saw was freshly turned and sharpened, and caught on the second pull. It made a noise that startled the secretary and hurt her ears, and she wore cotton in them for six months.

T. D. was sitting at his desk when he heard the saw, and without knowing it was a chain saw, he knew it was serious. Then his door opened and Jimmy White came in, holding a bright-red chain saw in front of a pair of two-hundred-mile-an-hour eyes, and T. D. tried to move one way, and then the other way, and both ways Jimmy White moved with him. He pushed himself back in his chair, back away from the desk and the saw, and Jimmy White kept coming, a step at a time, racing the machine, watching him.

Jimmy White brought the chain saw over the desk, pointing it at T. D.'s face, and then, a foot away, he revved it again, dropped the point, and cut the desk exactly in half.

T. D. knew not to try to move. Jimmy White finished the cut and the desk dropped in on itself, the pictures of Ellen and the boys slid onto the floor, along with a photograph of T. D. standing with Jackie Robinson, which was cut in half and irreplaceable. There were also pencils, files and fourteen kinds of vitamins, a couple of bottles of non-aspirin and a little plastic bottle of Man-Tan. The secretary insisted on helping him clean up, and she found that.

Jimmy White finished and turned the chain saw off, still looking into T. D.'s face, and then he walked out, smiled at the secretary while he put the saw back in the case. "Goodbye, Marion," he said.

"Have a nice day," she said.

T. D. heard that from behind his door. As soon as Jimmy White was gone, T. D. called the police, and then he called a meeting of the sports staff to announce that nothing that had happened there that afternoon was to be discussed outside the office, and anybody who discussed it inside the office would be fired too. He didn't understand timing then, that there were things you couldn't force.

The story broke in the *Daily News* the following day, on page 3, along with a picture of Jimmy White and his chain saw, and a paragraph about how T. D. had threatened to fire anybody who talked about it.

The caption under the picture of White was: DESK KILLER: "I'D DO IT AGAIN." After the *Daily News* ran the story, the *Times* ran it, and the *Post*. Then *New York Magazine* got ahold of Jimmy White and got him to talk about his daughter and his job, and then the television stations picked up on the story, and every time Jimmy White was interviewed he got a little better.

And while Jimmy White was becoming a city's hero, T. D. Davis had no comment. A spokesman for the paper would say only that a complaint had been filed with the police, and it was inappropriate to discuss it.

Jimmy White got job offers from the *Post* and the *News,* along with donations, cards and an offer to go into partnership with a chain saw dealer. There also were about a hundred calls from people who wanted to hire him to saw their boss's desk in half.

The man on Channel 11 said, "Jimmy White has somehow touched a chord in this city."

It took half a month for the story to die down, and by then T. D.'s paper had decided not to prosecute Jimmy White. Then it decided to offer him his job back.

And then T. D. came in one morning and his secretary told him that the editor wanted to see him, and fifteen minutes later he was cleaning out his desk.

And nothing had come up since that he didn't consider the timing.

The phone started ringing at eight-thirty. There were six calls from God's Pocket about a two-paragraph story on page 16 that a construction worker had been killed on the job at Holy Redeemer Hospital. T. D. always answered his own phone calls.

"You got it all fucked up," the first one said. "Leon didn't slip on nothin' and fall, they ain't even workin' in the air over there. They're layin' cinder block. Where was there to fall? And you fucked it up how old he was too. He wasn't twenty-two, he was twenty-four, twenty-five years old. I went to school a year behind him. No way he was going to get careless and slip...."

T. D. thanked him and all the others, and promised to look into it. He picked up the paper and read the story again.

"A 22-year-old construction worker was killed yesterday when he apparently slipped and fell to his death at Holy Redeemer Hospital.

"Leon Hubbard, 22, of 25th Street in God's Pocket, was taken to the hospital's emergency room but, according to police, he was dead on arrival."

Between calls, T. D. had Brookie Sutherland find out who'd written the story. "I'll have it for you in two minutes," he said. T. D. looked at his feet and thought about the people who had called. For most of them, it was the only personal contact with the newspaper they'd ever have. They were tough, ignorant people, but he'd heard something in their voices—every one of them—when they'd realized who they were talking to. A long time after Leon Hubbard was forgotten, they'd remember T. D. Davis had spoken to them personally on the telephone.

That's the way neighborhood people were.

Old Satchell, the morning bartender, was in bed with his liver problem, so McKenna was left shorthanded again, and had to open up himself. The Hollywood opened at seven every morning but Sunday, and did half its business before noon. Post-office workers, the night shift at the refineries—oil and sugar—those people came out of work when the sun was coming up. They walked outside, tired, when the rest of the city was just getting started, and it felt like they'd borrowed time against the day, and most of them would never get used to that. Some of them said they liked it, but when they had days off they slept at night like everybody else.

The crowd at the Hollywood had lasted right up to closing time, and McKenna had gone home without sweeping up or washing the glasses. He'd put the jar with the money to bury Leon in the refrigerator with the microwave cheeseburgers that nobody but strangers ever ate, emptied the cash register, and locked the door. McKenna was tired at two-thirty, and he was tired four hours later when he came in to get the place ready.

And it was no shot of sudden energy to see Ray standing outside of the front door in a neck brace and that green sport coat he always wore, waiting for him to open. "Don't you ever sleep, Ray?" he said. "Fuck yes," he said, answering his own question, "you sleep in the bar all the time."

Ray grabbed the side of his neck brace and described the route the pain was taking through his body. He said if he weren't the kind of man he was, he could sue the Hollywood for everything it had.

"Now," McKenna said, "do it now. . . ." He walked past him, through the door, and closed it in Ray's face. "Open at seven," he said, and Ray put his hands and his nose flat against the glass to wait, so every time McKenna looked up he saw Ray stuck there like some kind of homeless bug, and finally he unlocked the door and said Ray could wait inside if he wouldn't talk about his neck while McKenna was trying to count the money.

And while he was holding the door for him, a woman's voice screamed from somewhere across the street.

McKenna said, "What the fuck, at this time in the morning?"

Ray squinted. "It's labor pains," he said. He looked at his pocket watch. "I'd say they had about half an hour to get her to a hospital. . . ."

The drug that the doctor had given Jeanie lasted until six in the morning. She woke up then and pulled away from Joyce, smoothly, not to wake her up, and slipped into the bathroom. Her sister was snoring softly, and she closed the door behind her. The medicine left her heavy-headed, and she brushed her teeth slowly, looking at herself in the mirror, thinking she didn't look old enough to have a twenty-four-year-old son. Wondering if what had happened to him would show on her face. She'd heard of that, women turning old overnight. She didn't think she was that type.

She washed her face, slapping her cheeks to get some color, and then, without thinking about it, she began to put on her makeup. A base, then a little blush in the cheeks. A natural shade of lipstick over a colorless base, eye liner, then shadow over one eye. She was about to dust the other eye when she noticed the door to Leon's room. It was closed, but not all the way. She stepped away from the mirror and pushed, and the door opened a foot, a foot and a half, and she stood still, afraid to go any farther or touch the door again, and then she saw him lying in the bed, and for just a little while she thought it was Leon.

The scream woke Mickey up first. He was closest, and it was aimed at him. She was standing in the doorway to the bathroom, looking at him, screaming. It took him a second or two to figure out where he was.

Then there was a sister behind her, looking scared and angry, and then he heard the other one running up the stairs. She came in out of breath, carrying a tennis racket so old it could have been a snowshoe, looking side to side for somebody to swing at. They turned Jeanie around so she wouldn't have to look at him, and that seemed to calm her down. "It's all right," one of them said, "it's all right now."

Mickey sat up in bed, keeping himself covered with the sheet. The only thing he had on was a pair of shorts, and he didn't want Joyce and Joanie seeing him in his underwear. "It must of been the light," Jeanie said. "I got up and looked in Leon's room, and I thought it was him. I looked in there and I thought it was Leon in his bed. . . ."

The sisters led her out of the doorway. Mickey was still sitting in bed with a floating head and a sheet that smelled like cat shit wrapped around his waist. When they closed the door he got up and put on the pants he had left on the floor.

She couldn't point to a particular time when she began to think that Leon hadn't died the way the police said he did. When the thought came to her organized, though, so she could recognize it, it was half an hour later over breakfast.

Joyce had fixed waffles and opened up a fresh box of powdered donuts, which she and Joanie used to move the pieces of waffle around in half an inch of maple syrup, the way other people use toast to push eggs. Jeanie sat between them, poking at her food, thinking like a slide projector. She'd stare at the sink, hearing everything—Joyce and Joanie were talking, Mickey was moving around in the bathroom upstairs—but she'd stay frozen on the sink until gradually she'd remember Leon there, remember how he'd bent over it one night to eat dinner. And a few minutes later she'd find herself staring at the refrigerator, or the grease spot on the wall where he rested his head. It was like being in the same place at two different times.

She saw him nervous, and in a hurry, and she saw him one day in the street when he'd suddenly dropped behind a car to hide. And then, while she was sitting at the table with her sisters, it came to her, in words, that Leon didn't just let something drop on his head and kill him.

And when it came to her, she realized she'd known it all the time. "What's wrong, honey?" Joyce said. Both of them had stopped eating waffles and were looking at her face.

"Something's happened to Leon," Jeanie said. Joyce put her fork down and covered Jeanie's hands with her own.

"I know, baby, I know."

She shook her head. "I mean something else happened. They didn't tell the truth." The sisters looked at each other across the table.

Joanie said, "Why don't you eat something, hon? You need to eat. . . ."

Mickey was in no hurry to get downstairs. He shaved, showered, brushed his teeth, shaved again. He spent ten minutes in his closet, deciding between three yellow shirts. He dressed slowly, fitting the ball and heel of each foot into the pockets of the socks, tucking in his shirt so it was smooth down the front, hanging his keys from two or three places on his belt to see where they looked best.

Downstairs the sisters were talking in the kitchen. He couldn't make out the words. He looked out the window, and an old one-legged man named Petey Kearns who was dying of cancer was crossing the street, favoring his plastic leg, headed for the Hollywood.

He was two-thirds of the way there when the bus blew past, honking, and when he turned to see what was after him, he fell. Mickey watched him slowly get his legs under him, push up with his hands and arms, and finally, life and death, he stood up.

Downstairs somebody was crying. Petey Kearns, Mickey said to himself, you want to walk good for a couple of days? Be me, I'll be you. . . . He watched Petey Kearns go into the Hollywood, he watched a kid that couldn't light his cigarette, he watched the trucks and the cops and the deliveries until there wasn't anything left to watch, until he realized the sisters would be wondering if he was up there playing with himself.

No hurry to get downstairs at all.

He went to the top of the stairwell and started down. He

thought of the way he'd scared Jeanie that morning and coughed
so they'd know he was there. Nobody can blame you for cough-
ing.

As he reached the bottom, the talk stopped in the kitchen.
He walked in, and the sisters and Jeanie were sitting together at
the table with dirty dishes and an open box of powdered donuts.
"Morning," he said.

The sisters didn't answer. Jeanie said, "Hello," all the color
washed out of her voice. He poured himself a cup of coffee and
drank it over the sink. "Jack Moran said he'd be over this morning," Mickey said. Jeanie just looked at him. "He thought maybe
it'd be easier talking about the arrangements over here. . . ."

At the word "arrangements," Jeanie began to shake. The
sisters moved over her, putting themselves between her and
Mickey. "Maybe you'd feel better in the living room," one of
them said. They left him there, Jeanie keeping out of range as
she went past in case he tried to touch her. For half a minute
Mickey thought he was going to throw up in the sink. He got his
stomach settled and followed them into the other room and sat
down in a chair by the window. The three of them were on the
couch, Jeanie in the middle. It was a tight fit—the couch was
made for two people—and the sisters' butts seemed to be climbing the arms.

He noticed Jeanie had put on her makeup. Her hair was
brushed down and back, and the sun lay in it on her shoulder. It
wasn't his. For a little while, he was back to nothing.

Jack Moran came by forty-five minutes later, wearing a
black suit and black loafers and black socks. At first, Mickey saw
him coming up the sidewalk and thought it was a foreigner.
When he opened the door, Jack Moran's hand was already there,
waiting to be shook. He came in, making nervous bows with his
head, like a foreigner, and then he went to Jeanie and took her in
his arms and held her.

He'd gone to her, but she'd gone to him too. Mickey
watched her holding on to him—shit, she barely knew Jack
Moran—saw how naturally she'd gone to him. He wished they'd

hurry up and let each other go. The day was two hours old and moving along like a tour through the art museum.

"We were so sorry to hear," Jack said to Jeanie. "It was such a waste. . . ." He half let go of her then, held her by her shoulders and looked into her face. "You wonder about God's plan." The makeup over his black eye looked an inch thick. "I've brought some things we can look at," he said. "So you can decide what you'd like. . . ."

So Jeanie and the sisters sat back down on the couch, and Smilin' Jack kneeled in front of them, like he was fitting them for shoes. He opened his briefcase and began showing the pictures of the different units he had available to bury Leon in. The units he had pictures of were mostly topped with some sort of flowers or plants, and there was a cross beyond and behind each one.

It was hard to tell which unit Jeanie liked. She sat on the couch, holding a sister in each hand, and stared at each picture as Jack Moran held it in front of her. He looked up at her for some sign one way or the other. She sat still, almost without blinking, while he went through all the pictures, and she didn't say anything or move anything, and when he had shown her what he had, he smiled, turned around to Mickey and said, "I think she likes the mahogany."

He handed the picture of the mahogany unit to Mickey, who remembered it from the day before, sitting in the display room with a $5,995 price tag on it. That included a funeral, of course.

Then Jeanie was looking at him too, like there was still hope for Leon, and he was holding the picture of the mahogany box, and then he was nodding. "Sure," he said, "sure. If that's what Jeanie wants."

Jack Moran took the picture back, put it in with the others, and fit them all back in the briefcase. "Now," he said, "did you have a particular suit in mind for the service?" Jeanie began to shake again and the sisters threw him looks that promised revenge. Mickey suddenly felt like he'd just got out of the dentist's chair. He took Jack upstairs to Leon's room to look in the closet.

Leon had spent a lot of time getting dressed, but Mickey never noticed that he had more clothes than anybody else. Mickey didn't particularly notice clothes at all, except Jeanie's. The first time he'd looked into her closet he'd got a hard-on. Some of her dresses, they smelled like she was still in them.

He and Jack Moran opened Leon's closet and looked inside. "Jesus," Mickey said. "it looks like the fuckin' men's shop at Strawbridge and Clothier." There were half a dozen suits, ten or twelve sport coats, a yard of pants, arranged dark to light. Eight pairs of shoes. Mickey had never owned anything you couldn't put in a drawer, until he was going out with Jeanie.

Smilin' Jack was professional. He went through the clothes, feeling the material, and pulled out a dark blue suit with white lines so narrow you could hardly see them running up and down. Coat and pants both. "I think this might be best," he said.

He held it up for Mickey to look at, but Mickey couldn't get his eyes out of the closet. "You suppose all this shit is hot?" he said. "I mean, where'd he get the money?"

Smilin' Jack sighed. He said, "Usually, it's best not to question. You learn in my business not to question. When it's gone, it's gone."

He put the suit on Leon's bed, then pulled a pair of black shoes out and put them on the floor under it. He found a white shirt with a starched collar and a dark red tie with blue stripes running kitty-corner all the way down the front. Mickey picked up the shirt and looked it over. It wasn't yellow, but it wasn't bad.

Jack Moran took the shirt and the suit off their hangers and arranged them over his left arm, careful not to wrinkle anything. He picked up the shoes in his right hand. "This should be all we need," he said.

Mickey nodded. "That's all I can think of," he said. They went back down the stairs, through the living room. Jeanie and the sisters were still on the couch. "I'm terribly sorry," Jack said. Jeanie looked up in time to see what he was carrying out.

Mickey opened the door for him because his hands were full

and watched him until he'd gone around the corner. When he went back in, Jeanie seemed improved, like she might know who he was. "Something happened to him," she said to Mickey. "Something happened over at that hospital nobody has told us yet." She looked at him carefully. "They didn't tell you something you didn't tell me, Mickey . . . ?"

It was good to hear her say his name again. "They didn't tell me nothin' but that something dropped and hit him on the skull," he said. He went dry, hearing the word "skull" come out of his mouth. She looked at him, reading him for a lie. "Nothing," he said, "that's the whole thing."

"Something else happened out there," she said. "It did." And then she was quiet again. Mickey waited maybe ten minutes—maybe ten months—and then checked his watch.

"Look," he said, "I got a little work . . ." Nobody said anything, so Mickey stood up. Nobody said anything, so he went to the door. "Be back in a little while," he said.

He opened the door to the garage and checked the meat in the truck. It was nice and cold in there. The refrigeration unit was a new kind, cost an extra $2,000, supposed to operate indefinitely in the extremes of climate. Unit. He didn't like the way that sounded as much as he did when he bought it.

He took the plug out of the wall and started the truck. He let it warm up, feeling it shake, and then he turned on the refrigerator in back—it ran off the generator—and backed out. The alley was one-way. He was watching the direction traffic would come from and almost backed over his sister-in-law Joyce.

The truck was just creeping, but it barked when he stopped, and he could feel the load shift in back. Joyce stood still in the alley—he thought it was Joyce—looking at him in a different way than she'd been looking at him inside. Then she moved, and he finished backing out and then headed over to the flower shop.

He parked in back and tried the garage door. It was locked, and he hit it open-handed. The door was metal. He rattled it, it rattled him back. He tried it again, but nobody came, so he walked around to the front and tried the door there. He rang the door and knocked on the glass. It was nine-thirty, and Bird never slept in.

A light was on in back where the old woman put together her arrangements. He knocked harder, and a minute later Sophie Capezio came out, slowly, checking who it was before she cracked open the door. She'd been counting her money.

"Good morning," he said. She smiled at him but kept the door cracked. "Is Bird in there?"

She shook her head, worried. "Arthur ain't feelin' good today, Mickey," she said. "He's just layin' in bed, got his eyes open, you know? I says, 'Arthur, what you lookin' at on the ceilin'?' He don't answer. It don't smell bad in there, and I know he ain't been drinkin' last night anyway, 'cause he never went out and Arthur don't drink alone."

Mickey said, "Maybe he's got the flu, you know? There's some of that around." She shook her head.

"It's because of this terrible business started with Mr. Bruno," she said. "He don't know what's going on. Arthur don't have no faith, and I blame myself for that. He was up there lookin' at the ceilin' all night, I know." She looked up at Mickey for a minute then. "You want me to get him?" she said. "I'll run across the street and tell him you're here. Take his mind off the ceilin' awhile."

"He'll be down," Mickey said. "I'll come back this afternoon, we'll do it then." She reached out through the opening and touched him. It was an old freckled hand, shaped like a squid, turned halfway blue. She smiled at him and squeezed, and he would think back later, after the shooting, and remember he was surprised at how strong she was.

He got back in the truck and then it dropped on him that he didn't have anywhere to go again. He could go back and sit in the living room with Jeanie's sisters, or he could go watch Smilin' Jack drain Leon and discuss the lessons of the funeral business.

"The thing you learn is not to ask questions. . . ."

Mickey heard it again, thinking of how pitiful it looked when you tried to change who you were.

97

He could have gone to a movie, but he couldn't leave the truck in a lot, not with a load of meat. Especially that meat. He could go to Thirteenth and Market and pick up a racing form, but he wasn't sure he wanted to. He wondered if Leon had somehow died and left him his ambition.

He sat in the driveway a couple more minutes, then put the truck in reverse and, checking both ways for Joyce—Jesus, he had to stop thinking this crazy shit—he backed out. There wasn't anything to do, but that's what bars were for.

By ten o'clock, the Hollywood was half full. Most of the Pocket had taken the day off because Leon had died. Women were making hams and macaroni salads to bring to the house, and men were sitting in bars drinking. When Mickey walked in, there were twelve or fifteen people to shake hands with who hadn't been there the night before. The jar with Leon's money was back on the bar, full of fives and tens. McKenna was standing behind the bar, looking tired, listening to Ray describe the research he'd done into his accident. "The average settlement against a tavern in the Commonwealth of Pennsylvania is $62,475," he said.

Mickey found a seat and McKenna came down to look tired in front of him. "You look worse than I do," McKenna said. Old Petey Kearns was sitting in the next stool, his pants leg rolled up around his knee to show the plastic leg. It was the color of one of those dolls that shit in their pants.

When Petey Kearns drank, his artificial leg got hot. It defied medical science. A couple shots and a couple of beers and he'd have to roll up his pants leg to cool it off. There was a rule on the wall—right below NO CHECKS and WE RESERVE THE RIGHT TO REFUSE SERVICE—that Petey Kearns could not be served if he came in with his pants leg rolled up. If he came in clean, though, he could stay as long as he wanted. If he built his load at the Hollywood, he was the Hollywood's problem.

Petey Kearns was sitting in front of a shot glass and a beer, reading the *Daily Times*. The paper had been folded back to page 16, and passed up and down the bar. He made hen noises and sipped at his beer. Then he looked up from the paper. "We ought to sue the motherfuckers," he said. All up and down the bar people nodded. Even Ray, except he was nodding at the lecture he was about to give.

"There are two basic components to a successful libel suit," he said, straightening. "The first is you have to be able to prove intent. You have to prove they intended to write it. And the second is damage. You have to prove Leon was damaged by the story, unless he was a public figure. If Leon was a public figure, they could write anything they wanted about him."

McKenna looked like he'd just spent Christmas Eve putting a tricycle together and ended up with an extra wheel. "Ray," he said, "it don't mean a fuckin' thing, because Leon wasn't no public figure."

Ray dug in. "It's something everybody ought to know," he said. "It might come in handy next time. . . ." McKenna looked up and down the bar.

"Like if one of us celebrities gets killed, we can sue the motherfuckers."

Ray said, "I'm just telling you the law. You can interpret it any way you want to." Petey Kearns finished the story and pushed the paper away. There wasn't any point in reading more than you needed to, it was asking for trouble. Like answering a pay phone. Mickey picked it up to see what they'd written.

He read the story twice. "You can't sue them, Mick," Ray said. A kid was standing there too. A fat kid named Dick. This was the first thing he ever said to Mickey:

"Don't listen to what this fucker says. He works for the newspapers. They put it like that in the *Daily Times*, everybody in the whole fuckin' city sees it, thinks we're a bunch of jerk-offs down here. Walkin' around fallin' off shit all the time. Then they go and say Leon was twenty-two, it's on the record, and what really happened down here don't count."

McKenna looked at Mickey. "You got time for a beer?" he said.

Mickey said, "I got time to baptize China." Half an hour

later Charlie Kearns came by with another jar of money to bury Leon. Charlie owned the Uptown and was not related to Petey Kearns. It was how he introduced himself, "Charlie Kearns, no relation to Petey...." The jar he was carrying wasn't as big as the one at the end of the bar, but then Leon did most of his drinking at the Hollywood. Charlie bought Mickey a beer and told him the Uptown was sorry for what happened.

McKenna took the jar behind the bar and began to count. "Now in the case of personal injury," Ray said, "it's a different legal question." McKenna looked up.

"I'm countin' money, Ray," he said. "You know I don't like talk while I'm countin'."

Mickey drank the beer and the bar went quiet so McKenna could count. He saw they thought he'd come in for the money. When McKenna finished he put the stack of money on the bar and said, "Five forty-five."

Mickey shook hands with Charlie Kearns. Charlie said, "You comin' by with some meat today, Mick, or you going to take the cash to Florida and retire?"

When Charlie had left, McKenna took the jar off the bar and counted the money in there too. McKenna was a slow counter for somebody in the bar business, and it was quiet for a long time. When he finished, he put the two stacks of money together, and then took a hundred-dollar bill out of his own pocket and put it on top of the stack from the Hollywood. "Fourteen hundred and forty, all together," he said.

McKenna put a rubber band around the money and then dropped it in a paper bag he kept behind the cash register. The bag was where he kept cash overnight, it had been folded and unfolded a hundred times, rolled and unrolled, and it was as soft as a piece of cloth. He always hid it in the same place, everybody in the Pocket knew where.

He handed the sack to Mickey, smiling in a sad way like it was Leon's ashes. Mickey took the sack, but he didn't know how you thank a bar. "Lemme have the bag back sometime," McKenna said. It was heavier than Mickey would have thought, about like a wet hoagie. He took the bag and saw he couldn't stay in the bar, that it was some kind of ceremony, and it was over.

He'd left the truck around the corner, where you couldn't see it from the house. He put the bag of money under his seat, up with the springs, and then drove home. As he was going in, two cops were coming out.

A big one and a little one. Jeanie was thanking the big one—his name tag said EISENHOWER—and he was stumbling all over himself getting out and smiling at her at the same time. Mickey knew why Eisenhower was stumbling, he remembered the way she'd looked to him at first. Still looked to him.

The little cop was younger and didn't seem interested. "We'll be back to talk to you, Mrs. Scarpato," Eisenhower said. Then he noticed Mickey standing on the steps.

Jeanie said, "This is my husband." Eisenhower shook his hand, trying to see how Mickey fit here with her.

"Good," he said finally. Mickey got his hand loose. "We're still investigating the accident," Eisenhower said, "and we'll be back to you when we've finished." He turned for a last look at Jeanie. "We'll be in touch," he said, and she smiled at him in a way he'd think about that night. Mickey knew the smile.

He shut the door on the police and sat down on the chair he always sat on. It was warm from one of the cops. "What'd they say?" One of the sisters appeared from the kitchen—or the ceiling or someplace—and stood next to her.

"They were very nice," Jeanie said. "They said they'd go back and talk to the men at the hospital." He looked at her, she looked at her hands. "Something happened," she said.

"What happened?" Mickey said.

"Something they didn't tell us," she said. And suddenly she was staring right at him, like he was in her way.

"How do you know?"

"I don't know, but I know."

Lucien had been late getting home from work. It didn't spoil supper—she'd fixed him a ham and green pea soup—but when he came in he wasn't hungry.

He'd come to the table, but he didn't eat, not like he'd done no day's work. He pushed the ham and potatoes around his plate, run his spoon through the thick soup, never got none of it in his mouth. He was smiling at her too. He'd sit there runnin' his spoon through his soup like he'd lost a tooth in it, smiling at her with that kind smile.

"Lucien, you comin' down with something?" she said. He'd shook his head.

"I'm healthy, I just ain't hungry." She'd asked him then if he'd ate his lunch, and she could see from his face that he didn't. All he'd said, though, was, "Things was real busy today." And then he'd smiled that way at her again.

The last time she'd saw such a smile his mother just died. She was ninety-seven, and they wasn't nearly enough power left in her motor to make things work all at once, so sometimes she did her thinkin' and sometimes she did her talkin', but it wasn't never at the same time.

Lucien had stayed close to her until the day she died, and it had hurt him bad when she died, and he'd walked around the house for a week giving Minnie Devine those kind, killer smiles.

She was afraid now, like she was then, but she did what she could. She got up half an hour before the sun to make him breakfast. She took the fat off a pork roast and then cut the meat into squares. Then she cut the fat into squares too, and then ran them together through the grinder. She put the skins to soak in a pan, added vinegar to soften them up. She put the bowl of ground meat on one side of the kitchen counter and the bowl of skins on the other, and stood between them reading her Bible.

"Dear Jesus," she said, with her hand touching His picture, "don't let this be nothin', please." She stood at the counter half an hour, but she couldn't find nothing in the book aimed at what was going on this particular morning. She went over the familiar comforts, but she thought there must be something in there closer to what was going on. She couldn't find it.

She added salt to the pork, then black pepper, then a couple of cloves of garlic and some coriander. She measured by eye. Finally she crushed part of a red pepper she found in the icebox and put that in the meat too. She worked the meat through her fingers, talking to Jesus until the muscles in her forearms started to hurt her, and she kept at it, looking at the ceiling now, until her muscles cramped, and when it hurt enough, she knew Jesus was listening.

She ran the meat back through the grinder, a little bit at a time. It went in at the top and came out into the skins she fit over the funnel on the side. She stuffed a couple inches of meat into the skins, careful not to split them or get air pockets, and then twisted them twice—always the same direction—and then ground a couple more inches of meat into them, making links. When she'd finished, there were three long pieces of sausage with six links in each one. She put two of them in the icebox and cut the third one into pieces and put them over a low fire on the stove.

It would be good for Lucien, waking up smelling homemade sausage. "Maybe he was just tired," she said to Jesus. "He's sixty-nine year old, maybe he just get tired like everybody else. . . ." It didn't feel like Jesus was paying attention.

She heard Lucien moving around in the bedroom and put biscuits in the oven. She chopped the potatoes he hadn't ate last night and put them in a pan to fry. She heard him dressing, and when he started down the stairs she put four eggs in with the sausage, shook in a handful of water to make it steam, and then covered the pan.

It seemed to take him a long time to get down the stairs, like he was hurt and leading down with the same foot. "Please, Jesus," she said, "don't let this be nothin'. . . ."

He smiled at her across the kitchen table. He was wearing his robe and slippers, and he kept one hand on the chair and one hand on the table when he'd sat down, like he'd just let go of a walker. There was white whiskers on his chin. She took the eggs off the fire and slid two of them onto a plate, with most of the sausage and potatoes, and four biscuits. She put the plate in front of him, and he smiled at that too.

She fixed a plate for herself. He put a piece of potato in his mouth but he didn't chew it. She said, "How is things at work, Lucien?" He smiled at her, shook his head.

"Real busy," he said.

She said, "You don't look in no hurry to get back at them." He put another piece of potato in his mouth.

"I ain't in no hurry," he said. He felt her looking at him then. "I don't think I'll be goin' in today," he said. Lucien Edwards had missed two days of work in the time Minnie Devine had known him. One for his mother's funeral, one for getting married. There was times there wasn't no work, but he'd never once called in sick when there was.

"What did they do to you?" she said. He smiled at her again. "Lucien, don't look like that to me. Please." So he met her for just a minute, dead in the eye, and let her read what was there. Then he looked back down at his plate. He hated to waste food.

"They didn't do nothin' to me," he said. Then, "I did somethin' to a boy, where I couldn't help it." She sat and waited. "I expect the police will be comin' by."

Her mouth opened, but she didn't know what to ask. Finally, "How long they going to want you, Lucien?" He shook his head. Then he smiled at her—that kind, killer smile—and left the table. He walked slowly to the front room, moved his rocking chair away from the television and the Bible Minnie Devine kept on the table beside it, next to the *TV Guide*. He moved the rocking chair to the window overlooking the street, then he sat down in his robe and waited for them to come get him.

Minnie Devine felt her eyes fill, then there were cool tracks where the tears—one from each eye—had slid down her cheeks. She wiped at her eyes and cleaned the dishes off the table. She looked into the front room, and Lucien was sitting there in the rocker, moving back and forth in the window, just enough so he had to be alive.

He looked a hundred years old.

Peets had told his wife what happened as soon as she'd got home from the hospital. "Old Lucy killed the boy," he'd said. "I lied about it to the police."

She picked up his hand and held it in hers. Dead weight. "How did it happen?" she said.

"The boy cut him," Peets said. "He was fuckin' with that razor again and cut his face, and the next thing I knew Old Lucy had a piece of pipe up the side of his head."

"That doesn't sound too bad," she said.

He shrugged. "I told it was an accident."

She smiled and pushed at his hair, "Peets, that imagination of yours is really something." He didn't smile back. She rubbed his leg up and down, first on top, then the inside, touching him. That was the way she was when there was trouble. He began to get a hard-on he didn't want. "There was nothing you could do, was there?"

"No," he said. "Not really. No." She unzipped his fly. Peets' dick was built something like Peets, only smaller and without the scars. It took things just as serious.

The hard-on disappeared. "The thing is," he said, "I'm not sure I couldn't of got over there in time. It was like when you're watchin' something you don't want to see, but you can't look away. It was like when you don't exactly know where you stand on it."

And later, lying in bed, "I didn't say nothin' to the crew in front of Lucy. I'll have to talk to them tomorrow. . . ." Peets lay in bed, imagining what that would be like. "And I got to talk to Lucy too. Away from the others . . ."

She'd said, "Old Lucy won't be there tomorrow, Peets."

"You don't know him," he said. "He never missed a day's work in his life."

But the next morning when Peets showed up, Lucy wasn't there. It was a cool morning, and there was half a foot of fog on the ground. Peets uncovered the cement by himself, backed the pickup over to the mixer and began to work. A C bus would stop every five minutes, on the other side of Broad Street, and every five minutes Peets would stop what he was doing and watch until everybody that was going to had got off.

He didn't stop waiting for Old Lucy until the rest of the crew had showed up. He knew if Lucy wasn't there ahead of them, he wasn't coming. He wondered how Sarah had known that.

They pulled the old station wagon onto the sidewalk and got

105

out slowly, like they was afraid of him. Nobody was doing much talking or laughing, they didn't even lie about why they was late. They just come over and stood in front of him. The ones in front had folded their hands and was looking down, like he was the minister committing Leon back to the earth.

Peets looked them over. There was something he needed to say, but it still wouldn't come to him exactly what it was. Only the kid Gary Sample looked back. He was the one that wasn't old enough to let the thing go. He was the one that didn't see what happened to Leon wasn't no random drawing.

Peets cleared his throat, but it still came out weak and dry. "It was an accident," he said, "that's all there is to it. The boy was the wrong person at the wrong place, and it fell on him." As he talked, Peets realized what he was saying was the truth, in a way. "You can't say why a person is the way he is. . . ." That fast, he was out of things to say. He'd meant to say thank you, but he didn't know how to do that and still keep it an accident.

So he looked at his watch, then the sun, and then said they'd wasted half the morning already, standing around gabbing. They seemed glad to move, everybody but Gary Sample. "Did the cops get the nigger?" he stuttered.

Peets saw the boy was tougher than he was the day before. It was how you grew up—changing when things happened. He understood that, and he didn't mind. He walked through the others and stood in front of Gary Sample. He put his hand under the boy's jawline and lifted him up off his toes, all the way up out of Peets' shadow. The boy's weight rested on his cheeks, giving him bulldog eyes. He held onto Peets' arm below the wrist, supporting himself more than trying to get loose. By now the boy knew he couldn't get loose.

Peets brought the face closer. "You ain't grown enough to call that old man a nigger," he said. And then he put him down. The kid Gary Sample held his jaw, working it up and down. The fingerprints on his cheeks turned from white to red, and he blinked away the tears that Peets had squeezed out.

Peets put a hand on Gary Sample's shoulder and looked at

106

the rest of them. "Old Lucy'll be back when he's ready," he said. Gary Sample pulled away, and he let him go. He'd got the boy's attention, he didn't want his pride.

It was probably the best they'd worked, but Peets knew it wasn't anything permanent. He wouldn't of wanted it to be. They were scared, and if you couldn't see what you was doing, there wasn't no point. It cheated you to work because you were scared.

Sometime after ten, the police came back. It was the same two, Eisenhower and Arbuckle, and the big one took Peets over by the cherry picker to talk to him again. The little one, Arbuckle, walked around the construction site, touching things, asking what this or that was for. Arbuckle had soft, white-blue hands that he must of kept in mittens. A man got harder hands than that pulling on his wang.

"It's the mother," Eisenhower said to Peets. "The mother thinks something happened."

Peets considered that. "What does she think?"

"She doesn't know," the cop said. "But I met her, and she'll have somebody to find out for her."

Peets said, "She got the police workin' for her?"

Eisenhower smiled. "No. If it was me, you'd know it. I just came out to let you know it ain't settled. Before it's over, she'll get somebody to help her." The cop looked around then, over to where Arbuckle was standing with Gary Sample. The kid was trying to talk.

Peets thought Eisenhower was watching them, but he said, "You missing somebody today besides Leon Hubbard?" The cop counted the men with his finger, twice, and then he said, "There were eight yesterday, not counting Leon Hubbard."

Peets didn't bother to count. Eisenhower closed his eyes, trying to remember. "Seems like there was an old man," he said. "He was sitting over against the wall."

Peets said, "That was Old Lucy. Some days he comes in, some days he don't. Does as much work either way. He's about a hundred years old, sickly. You know . . . weak." Peets was sur-

107

prised how easy that story came out of his mouth. He'd heard of old women, though, who picked up Chevrolet Malibus when they'd fell on their sons in the yard, so you never knew what you could do until you had to do it.

Arbuckle was over by the cement mixer, still waiting on Gary Sample to get what he was trying to say out of his mouth. Peets saw it was out of his hands.

Eisenhower walked underneath the cherry picker and looked up at the beam. Then he looked at the ground, and then at the U-bolt fastened to the beam. He smiled up into the sun. "Days like this," he said, "I got to drive around in that car with Arbuckle or sit in an office, I wish I was something else. I'd just as soon to come out here, for instance, and do my work and watch the nurses come by, not worry about anything. . . ." He looked at Peets. "You must go home and sleep like a baby."

"A baby," Peets said.

"I knew it. I go home and I think about everything that's happened. I go home and wonder if I did my job right." He and Peets were still looking at each other.

"You done your job right," Peets said. He was saying too much, but it was like the kid Gary Sample talking to the other cop. It was out of his hands.

"What I was saying," Eisenhower said, "the mother's got something. She can look at you a certain way and you could just stick a fork in your leg. . . ." They looked around to the construction site again. Arbuckle had given up waiting for the kid to quit stuttering and started back. When he got close, Eisenhower said, "How far down did you say this thing is going to go?" and he left Arbuckle by the cherry picker and walked to the end of the wall Old Lucy had laid.

Left alone, Arbuckle began measuring off distances.

Eisenhower said, "In the neighborhood, they say the guy the mother is married to is connected. Mickey Scarpato, which I never heard of, so he ain't anybody that matters. But if it's true, that's where your problem might come from. The woman's got his balls in the blender, I could see that. You can't tell what anybody'll do with his balls in the blender."

Back at the cherry picker, Arbuckle was standing with his back to Gary Sample, who had followed him over and was still trying to tell him something. "Fuckin' write it down or something," he said, and left him again.

"Is it possible?" Eisenhower said. "That that fuckin' thing could actually kill somebody?" Peets just looked at him. He needed some time to think about Eisenhower. "Because if it is," the cop said, "let's give it a little while and see if it likes Arbuckle."

Mickey sat through lunch, waiting for a sign that she was getting tired of her sisters. They were all eating peanut butter and honey sandwiches, drinking Pepsi-Cola. One of the sisters was standing behind him, by the oven, where she could check on the tollhouse cookies. A bell went off inside the oven, and when the sister opened the door, the heat singed the hair on the back of his neck.

She put the cookie sheet on the table and the other sister put one of the cookies in her mouth whole. Three hundred and seventy-five degrees was nothing to that mouth. "Ummmm," she said. "Jeanie, taste how good . . ." Jeanie took one of the cookies and put an edge in her teeth. "What's that smell?" said the sister with the cookie in her mouth.

She wrinkled her nose and looked around. The other sister wrinkled her nose and looked around too. You could see they were sisters. "It smells like a dead mouse," one said.

While they looked around the kitchen for dead animals, Mickey ran a hand over the back of his head and smelled his fingers. It was a little like a dead mouse, and it was a little like cat shit. They weren't the kind of smells that just washed off.

He drove back over to the flower shop. Bird had come down out of his bedroom and was in back, watching two butchers boning and cutting the load of meat they'd taken in New Jersey. He was dressed in a clean yellow shirt. His neck fit the collar like a hard-on in an innertube. Mickey always wondered if Bird used to be bigger.

"Mickey," he said, "Aunt Sophie said you was over. Should of woke me up, pal. It's the old Bird again." The butchers looked up from their saws, nodded and went back to work. Bird crossed the room and shook Mickey's hand. He was smiling like the old Bird, only there'd never been that kind of old Bird, at least that Mickey knew of. He wished he could see an old picture.

"I thought if the electricity was back, you could cut some of the meat we threw in the truck," Mickey said.

"No problem, Mick. Lissen, I appreciate you helpin' me out, takin' it instead of the trump. We'll get this shit all straightened out, don't worry. . . ." He hugged Mickey's shoulder.

"You talk to your people?" Mickey said. Bird shook his head.

"I didn't talk to nobody," he said. "I ain't going to. Fuck it, I may get out of the business, you know? Fuck, I may get out of the city." He looked down at his sleeve and then pulled Mickey's arm up next to his, so they could compare yellows. "Hey, lookit, queers. You remember when they said you was queer if you wore yellow on Tuesday? Back in school?"

Mickey shook his head. "Queer if you wore *yellow*? That's the most fucked-up thing I heard all day." Bird laughed and hugged him again. It wasn't like him to hug so much.

"I forgot, Mick," he said. "You ain't from around here. You missed a lot of great shit."

Mickey said, "You really thinkin' about gettin' out?"

Bird winked at him, and he'd *never* done that before. "You can't tell," he said. "You can never tell what the Bird will do." Then he called one of the butchers over and introduced him to Mickey. Mickey guessed he was fifteen years old. "Say hello to Bird's main man," he said to the butcher. And then to Mickey: "This is my nephew Tony."

Tony nodded, and Mickey nodded back. Bird hugged the kid's head, a sullen cold-looking kid, and Mickey watched to see if Bird had picked up any bloodstains on the yellow shirt. "He don't talk much," Bird said, "but this little fucker can cut meat." Then he called his other butcher, who was colored. Mickey knew

Bird had one working for him, but he didn't expect to be introduced. Mickey shook hands with him too. He went back to work, the nephew stayed.

Bird said, "Tony, take the meat out of Mick's truck and cut it for him, all right? Do a nice job, don't sneeze on it or nothin', okay?" Bird laughed and squeezed.

When Bird had finished squeezing him, the nephew climbed in Mickey's truck. It shook as the boy moved the meat to the door. Then he jumped out, put one of the sides of beef over his shoulder, and carried it to his table. "Fourteen years old," Bird said, "strong as a fuckin' bull. Kid's twice as strong as we was. . . ."

Mickey smiled. By the time he was fourteen years old, he could work all day, with anybody. His old man had won a twenty-dollar bill once in Waycross, Georgia, betting he could lift a fat man off the floor of a truck stop there. He could still see the fat man's face and remember his name. Giachetti. He weighed 480 pounds and lay with his arms against his sides, flat and wet, not to offer any handholds, and Mickey had grabbed him behind the neck and by the belt and got him off the floor anyway. The fat man cried from one end of the diner to the other that he'd been cheated, like there was official rules to picking fat people up, and in the end he'd thrown the twenty on the floor and left. It was the first time somebody hated him because of what he was, and it stuck with him. He thought of Jeanie's sisters then. The way things was going, it was a miracle Giachetti hadn't showed up at the house with a suitcase, to move in until the funeral.

Bird's nephew sharpened a knife. The blade was a foot and a half long, and flashed in the light. The light came from two bulbs hanging cockeyed over the table from black cords that had been taped six or seven places. Now that he looked, Mickey saw one of them was wrapped in Band-Aids. When the knife was sharpened, the nephew began to cut. He never considered the meat, he just cut. He had a quick, practiced motion—you could almost see Leon with his razor—and a look on his face that he'd seen everything on the planet. If he'd opened up a cow's ass and found pearls, his eyes would have stayed the way they were—flat as a foot of snow.

Bird sat down in a school desk built for somebody four foot tall. The warehouse had been leased to the school district before Bird and Sophie, and there was all kinds of shit around that they'd left. For instance, there was a box of books on South America Mickey sometimes noticed on the way in. He'd of taken one of those home to read, except right on the cover it said "Seventh to Ninth Grades." He already did more explaining than he cared to, and he wasn't about to open that can of worms.

Bird sat with his arms on the little desk, his elbows hanging over the sides touching his knees, which were even with the top. He pointed to another desk the same size and told Mickey to have a seat. Mickey shook his head. "I'd need a fuckin' corkscrew to get out," he said.

There were four boxes of advanced algebra books stacked against a support beam, and Mickey took one down and sat on it. He'd picked a book out of those boxes once, thought at first it might of been about Germany. Nobody had to worry about him bringing home no advanced algebra.

"I ain't going to worry about no more shit, Mick," Bird said. "I made up my mind. It's going to be like the old Bird, doin' business." Mickey didn't know what business he was talking about. Bird laughed. "You think I'm crazy? The mind is a powerful tool, Mick. I found out the secret. I'm goin' back to the way I was, I ain't nervous now. . . ."

Mickey said, "Bird, you was always nervous."

"The secret," he said, tapping his head, "the secret is I don't give a fuck. That horse is going to come in tomorrow, and if they don't want me doin' business in Philly, I'll go somewheres else and do business. They don't own the world, Mick. Fuck, they don't even own Miami. Somebody else owns that. Sophie's friends all moved down there anyway."

Bird was bouncing his feet on his toes, holding onto the desk top, like the teacher wouldn't let him go piss.

"This horse is a nice horse," Mickey said, "and she's in with a bunch of shit, but it's still a horse, Bird. Little bitty ankles, ugly teeth, shits in balls . . ."

"She's a lock," Bird said.

"There ain't nothin' that weighs half a ton with little bitty ankles that's a lock," Mickey said. Bird winked at him again, like it was a joke between them. His nephew had finished with the first side of beef. He'd packed it in cardboard boxes, carried them back to the truck. The colored boy was faster, and he was working on the meat they'd taken off the semi.

"You don't understand," Bird said. "I don't give a fuck. Just like that horse don't give a fuck. She don't know and I don't care, that's what makes it a lock." He looked at Mickey again. "You don't see it, Mick?"

Mickey shook his head. "What are you going to do if she don't run? What if they scratch her?" But he could see Bird wasn't hearing him. Hell, maybe he wasn't hearing Bird.

"The reason I'm tellin' you," Bird said, "is you're my man, Mick. You helped me out, and now I'm tryin' to help you, mentally. But if you don't wanna lissen, it's on you. I can see things so clear, you know? Like you wonder how you didn't see them before."

Mickey nodded toward the semi they'd stolen. "They're going to want their truck back," he said. "At least take them the truck."

"Yeah, you got to settle accounts," Bird said. "But my friends come first. When we get straightened out in Miami, you always got a place, Mick. You know, if you got to disappear for a while. Right now . . ." He shrugged and looked around the warehouse. "All I can do right now is hide you here. They can't touch us, Mick." And he began to laugh again.

Mickey had heard that Indians were afraid to kill white men if they were crazy, but he didn't think the people who were running things now were. "You can't see it," Bird said. "Mick, I swear on my mother's grave, it's so clear. . . ."

As he said that, the band saws stopped and the lights went

out. For five seconds the place was dead still and solitary black. Then Mickey could hear Bird breathing through his teeth. Tony and the colored boy hadn't moved, like they were waiting for the people who ran things now to come in with flashlights and shotguns. Bird was breathing louder. Mickey couldn't see his face, but he knew it was awful. Ever since he'd walked into his house yesterday and found Jeanie crying, he'd been *knowing* shit.

He got up off the box. Nobody said a word. A door opened toward the front, and there was a flashlight. "Arthur?" she said. "Arthur, the electric went out again. . . ."

Bird's breathing got choppy. "We're over here, Mrs. Capezio," Mickey said.

"Is that you, Mickey? I didn't know you was here."

"Yeah, we're all over here in the dark. Right, Bird?" Bird didn't say anything. So he said, "We're all over here," again, and the old woman found them with the light.

"It's the whole block," she said, coming toward them. "Same as before. Arthur?" He didn't answer.

Tony the nephew said, "Hey, how long is it going to be? I can't do nothin over here without light."

"You hush," the old woman said and came the rest of the way to Mickey and Bird. When she put the flashlight on Bird's face, Mickey saw it was frozen. She said, "You hush," softer now. She handed the flashlight to Mickey and pulled Bird's head into the lap of her dress, and patted the back of his head. It was still dark, so Mickey didn't have to find something to do with his eyes.

In about five minutes the old woman said, "You hush," again, and Bird did. His breathing smoothed out, and a minute later he stood up, smoothing his hair, wiping at his forehead with the backs of his hands. "Jesus, Mick, I don't know," he said.

"It's nothin'," Mickey said. "Nobody knows what they're doin'. Get yourself a beer. I gotta go back to the house, see about the funeral, but I'll come back and drink one with you."

"The funeral?" Bird said. "Shit, I forgot. My brains ain't payin' attention to me. How's Jeanie doin'?"

"She's with her sisters," Mickey said.

"That's good," Bird said. "You don't appreciate your family, then somethin' like this happens, right? She takin' it all right, though?"

Bird seemed normal again. He wasn't frozen up and he wasn't hugging anybody. He seemed like somebody you could talk to. "Actually, she's got some idea somethin' else happened out there," Mickey said. "I don't know where it come from, but there it is."

"Let's get outta here," Bird said. He took the flashlight from Mickey and led them all out into the flower shop. Aunt Sophie, Mickey and Tony. The colored boy said he'd as soon wait in there. They walked through the shop and out the front door, and it wasn't until they were outside that Mickey got a look at Bird's face.

He made up a rule of life: don't ever say somethin's normal until you can see their face.

If Bird's eyeballs had puckered and whistled "The Battle Hymn of the Republic," he couldn't of looked crazier than he did then. Shaking and scared and pissed and worried all at the same time, and no focus to any of it. He held onto himself as much as he could and said, "I'll be okay in a minute. I just got to remember how to get back."

Mrs. Capezio took his sleeve. "Where you want to go, Arthur?" she said.

He talked to himself. "I don't give a fuck, I don't give a fuck. . . ." She looked at him and frowned. "You got a nice home, Arthur," she said. "You got no reason to talk like that."

He held onto himself as much as he could. "I can't remember now," he said.

Mickey said, "I shouldn't of worried you about Jeanie."

Bird began to breathe through his teeth again. "I'll find out about that for you," he said. "I swear to Jesus. I tried to cut your meat but the electric went off. . . ."

Mickey said, "You can't do nothin' about the electricity."

Bird put his hand on Mickey's arm. "I'll find out about Leon for you," he said. He allowed his aunt to put an arm around his waist and walk him across the street toward their house. "I'll do that, Mick," he said. "You got my word."

Mickey said, "Don't worry about Jeanie, she's a little funny in the head right now. It happens. . . ." He wanted to tell him to stay out of the business about Leon, but it mattered to him to say he would help. Mickey watched him follow the old woman into the house, and he thought it would be a long time before Bird could help anybody.

Aunt Sophie tried to put him to bed, but Bird went into the bathroom instead. He brushed his teeth and changed shirts and spit on his shoes and wiped them off with a towel from a motel in Phoenix, Arizona. Where was Arizona? Who gave a fuck?

That was more like it.

He stood up straight and looked at himself in the mirror. He oiled his hair and tucked it in behind his ears, and he could feel it snug against his head, like a cap. Aunt Sophie knocked on the door with a water bottle. "You feelin' better, Arthur?"

"Fine," he said. "I'm goin' out for a little while, Doll. Be back in a couple of hours."

"Arthur," she said, "you oughta rest. You didn't look too good."

He opened the door and showed her he was handsome again. She put her hands on her hips.

"You looked worse," she admitted. She liked oily-haired men. He leaned over and kissed her cheek, and she squeezed the back of his arm. Bird went out the front door and found the new Cadillac parked against the curb. Nothing down, the first payment—$448—due June 15. They'd give him two weeks, so he'd have the car till July. If they came earlier, who gave a fuck?

He got in and hit the buttons until all the windows were rolled down. He drove fifty miles an hour all the way to Snyder and his hair never moved. He made a right turn, then double-parked beside a heavier, darker Cadillac in front of Vinnie's Italian Bakery. He walked past the girl at the counter, feeling strong, and went right to the office and knocked on the door. Vinnie would be there, he was always there this time of day. If he wasn't, who gave a fuck about that either?

Vinnie answered the door himself, even though there were a couple of his nephews in the room with him to do that. He was pissed off at his nephews. He said, "Yeah?"

Bird stepped inside. Vinnie had known Arthur Capezio forty years, but it wasn't friendly enough between them to come in uninvited. One of his nephews moved toward Arthur, but Vinnie shook his head. He didn't want nothin' from his nephews. "What is it?" he said.

Bird sat down on a chair beside the window where he could keep an eye on the Cadillac. He said, "Vinnie, I got a favor to ask."

Vinnie said, "You don't mind if I sit down. . . ." Everybody had a favor to ask, nobody had time to show a little respect. Vinnie Ribbocini had been like Angelo's right hand, but since the new people started running things, that didn't count no more. Actually, they wasn't new. They'd always been there, but nobody noticed. They was muscle or go-fers mostly. Sons and nephews of men with brains and experience and balls, who'd used that to come into the business, but nobody ever took them serious. Angelo didn't—to him they was like children, in a hurry for everything, always pushin' to get into the shit business—and look what it got him. And now Vinnie's own nephews, tellin' him he ought to go along, that it looked bad 'cause he wouldn't kiss ass. The new people had discovered respect, and they was in a hurry for that too.

"Lissen," he said to Bird, "I know things is dryin' up for you right now. You don't have to come pushin' in here like some fuckin' punk kid to tell me that. I'm in the middle of business here, where's your fuckin' manners?"

Bird shook his head. "It ain't that, Vinnie."

"And where's my fuckin' truck? I throw you a bone, you gonna keep my truck to show you appreciate it?"

Bird explained. He said the electric went out so he couldn't unload it. "I got a favor to ask," he said again. Vinnie threw open his arms. "There was a problem down at Holy Redeemer," he said, "buildin' a new hospital or somethin', and this guy got killed. Leon Hubbard. Nice boy. And the boy's mother married a guy who works for me. A good guy, and his old lady's goin' crazy 'cause they ain't tellin' her what happened."

"So what?"

"So maybe you could send a couple guys over and find out. I don't mean do nothin', just to find out. Bounce somebody around a little bit so they'll talk to you."

"Then what?" Vinnie said.

"Then nothin'. Then I tell the guy, and he can tell his wife or do what he wants with it."

Vinnie scratched the bottom part of his left ear. The bottom part was all he had left on that side. The truth was, he didn't know what was going to happen one day to the next, just like the old men he knew who been around forever, and walked around now talkin' about Angelo like he was still alive. Vinnie didn't particularly like Arthur—at the bottom he was weak—but he didn't have nothin' against him either. "And that's all?" he said. "There's no problem over there, just a couple of guys to push around?" It was straightforward and easy, the way things used to be.

"That's it," Bird said.

Vinnie shrugged. "When do I get my truck back?"

Peets knew Old Lucy wasn't coming to work, but he kept looking for him. That was how he first spotted the men across the street. There were two of them—Jews or Italians, he could never tell which was which—sitting in a black Thunderbird with a roof that looked like rippled water. The Thunderbird was parked on the side street in the no-parking zone at the end of the block, where buses stopped.

Peets saw them about three-thirty, and then he noticed them again just before four. One had sunglasses and one of them didn't. Outside of that, you couldn't tell them apart. Peets didn't wonder what they were doing, he was thinking about Old Lucy and the seconds he'd sat in the cherry picker watching while Leon was flashing his razor in front of the old man's face.

He thought about it, and he still didn't know why he hadn't moved when he could. It was like something you watched because you couldn't do nothing about it. Something that had to be played out because the time had come.

He threw that out. In one way it had to happen, but it didn't have to be there, with Old Lucy. The old man came to work on time, he did his job. Peets owed him his nine dollars an hour, he owed him a place to do his work. He went over it again, how it had looked, trying to decide when he should of gotten off his ass and done something.

At four o'clock he let the crew go, but Old Lucy was still on his mind. He cleaned up by himself. First the cement mixer, then he covered the cement sacks, then he covered the cinder block. Anything you didn't cover in the city was gone in the morning.

He went to a pile of scaffolding they'd delivered that morning and stacked it. There was a reason to everything. When he couldn't find it, he stacked scaffolding or books or pennies, or he'd make beds the Marine way, or line up everything in the refrigerator by colors. And after he'd put order to something else, whatever he was trying to figure out seemed to fall into order too.

He worked half an hour after the crew left, straightening up. And when there wasn't anything left to straighten, he began to shovel a load of sand out of the pickup, so he could use the truck in the morning. He was standing in the pickup bed when he heard the doors slam, almost together.

The men came across the street, one of them walking straight to the truck and the other one going around the fence to the front of the hospital, and then coming toward him from behind. The one who had come straight looked around, in no hurry at all, like he was checking the work. "You the boss?" he said.

Peets did not care for the question. He picked up a shovel of sand and tossed it in the pile near the man's feet. The man stepped back, checked his pants and shoes. Peets had only seen pants like that on television, on Spanish dancers. The other one was at the side of the truck. "I'm the only one here," Peets said.

The one in back of him said, "That's a fact." Peets waited.

"The thing is," said the one who had come straight, "somebody got kilt here yesterday, and there is some feeling that it didn't happen the way the cops said." Peets stared at the man and held onto the shovel. "We was wondering," he said, "if you was here when it happened."

Peets kept his eyes on the one in front and thought about the one in back. "This guy who got it, he was an important guy. He was important to important people, and they don't think it oughta happened at all, and then not to tell the truth . . ."

Peets said, "He always said he was important," and threw another shovel of sand on the pile on the ground. The man moved back this time. He held out his hands.

"We can do this the easy way or the hard way," he said. While he said that, the other one fit his fingers into a set of artificial knuckles. He closed the fist, opened it, closed it again. The knuckles stuck out maybe a quarter inch. The one in front of Peets said, "What's it going to be, home boy?"

It was rush hour now. There was blocked intersections and bus smoke and a steady line of nurses and assorted white uniforms coming out of Holy Redeemer Hospital. And nobody looking. Peets had a sudden vision of these two going to visit Old Lucy. He said, "It happened the way I said to the police, and you Jew boys can do it any damn way you want—hard or easy—and it don't matter to me."

The one behind him screamed, "Jew boys!" and punched the side of the truck with the artificial knuckles.

The one in front called him off. "Whatta you want to do this for?" he asked Peets. "We didn't insult you, right?" And while he said that, the other one climbed into the truck bed behind Peets and pushed him once in the back.

"Let's go somewhere we can talk," he said.

Peets turned around and stood over the man that wanted to talk. He felt the back of the truck drop when the other one got on behind him. The one who had pushed him threw the hand with the artificial knuckles at Peets' face, and caught the top of his forehead. When Peets looked, there was a piece of wrinkled-up skin hanging from the metal. The one behind him put an arm around his neck and tried to choke him. Peets kept his eyes on the one with the knuckles. His head burned, and the one trying to choke him said, "Hit him, Ronnie. Fuckin' hit him."

Peets felt an old calm settle in, he noticed the blood dropping around his boots—not a lot of it, about like the drops you get right before a heavy rain. He noticed a man across the street watching. The one with the knuckles had a peculiar look on his face, but he steadied himself and turned to throw another punch.

Peets reached out and smothered his hand, and then found his face, and then, with the same broad motion you might use to shape an eye cavity in clay, he pushed into the corner of the socket and took the man's left eye out. The man screamed again, a truer scream than when Peets had called him a Jew. He grabbed for the eye and bent over, trying to somehow take it all back, and now it was sprinkling blood around his feet too.

And the calm passed and something was loose in Peets.

The man holding his neck had froze, Peets guessed he'd seen the eyeball. Peets reached behind him and grabbed the waist of the man's pants. It wasn't easy because they were tight. The only sounds were the traffic and Peets' own breathing. He caught another look at the man across the street. He was sitting on a fire hydrant now, watching.

Peets pulled the one in back off his feet. He felt him give up the hold on his neck. He turned back to him then, thinking again that it was Old Lucy they were after, and picked him up by the jaw and the pants and held him over his head. The man's hand found Peets' face, and Peets bit his thumb. He'd spent years in a dojo, he could fight judo or karate, even box a little, but in the end it always came down to biting fingers.

Fighting was fighting. Twelve years of bowing and walking around wrapped in a tablecloth and you still ended up biting fingers. He threw the body now, from the bed of the truck to the ground. One of the legs attached to it hit the rear gate of the truck, twisted and came to rest bridged to the little pile of sand Peets had shoveled out of the truck.

The leg looked broken, but Peets jumped down and made sure. Then he looked across the street at the man on the fire hydrant. The man looked back. He stood up, slowly, nodded, clapped five or six times and then headed east down the street.

Philadelphia.

A MEADOW
IN THE
CITY

Shellburn brought her home from the Pen and Pencil Club. He only went there when he needed somebody to take home. Sometime after one in the morning, somebody would come in. A photographer sometimes, or a copy editor. Somebody.

He'd been drinking vodka and orange juice all night long. She came in with a couple of people he didn't like—he didn't like anybody that came into a bar laughing—and stood next to him. Shellburn never drank sitting down. "You're Richard Shellburn," she said. He thought she might be a city hall reporter for one of the radio stations.

"Yes, I am," he said.

"I thought you'd look older."

"I thought you would too," he said. She smiled at him and laughed, and didn't have an idea what he was talking about.

"Can I buy you a drink?" she said. He told her it was screwdrivers and she made a face. A cute face. She looked about twenty-two to Shellburn, which meant she was probably thirty. "I can't stand vodka," she said, and moved away from the men she'd come in with.

Shellburn nodded. "You might just as well shoot it into your veins," he said.

"Why is that?" she said. He shrugged. "Oh, you mean you might just as well put it in your veins. . . ." She was standing closer to him now. She was wearing a Temple University sweat shirt and blue jeans with the word "Chic" written over the back pocket. Oh, yes, she'd shown him her ass.

"Do you go to Temple University?" he said. He killed the screwdriver in his hand and took another one. There was a line of them on the bar. Shellburn bought them six at a time because the bartender got busy this time of night, and because he liked the way it sounded, ordering half a dozen.

"I graduated," she said, "in journalism. I'm freelance now, sports mostly. . . ." He looked at her closer. "Sports," she said. Then, "You don't approve of women in the locker room?"

He thought about that half a minute, and then he said, "Who was Yahama Bahama?" She smiled and leaned against his leg. She picked up one of his screwdrivers and finished it before she put it down. He guessed it was how the women's movement bought you a drink.

"Is that a name for your penis?" she said. "Jesus, everybody's got a name for their penis. . . ."

They finished the vodka and orange juice and he took her back to his apartment. She didn't believe him when he told her Yahama Bahama had been a middleweight fighter. She sat next to him in the car with one arm in back of his shoulder, and the other one draped across his stomach so her hand rested in his lap. She was a pretty girl, but she wasn't troubled enough to be much of a piece of ass.

He parked the car on the sidewalk in front of his building, and before they got out she pushed her hand up into the crotch of

124

his pants, and then kissed him on the cheek. It seemed like a misunderstanding.

He lived on the second floor, behind a steel door that unlocked in three places. The windows looked out across the Delaware River to Camden, New Jersey, and the view was the first thing she noticed. Then she went to the only table in the place, and sat down on the chair in front of it—the only chair in the place—and looked at the old typewriter sitting on the table. "So this is where you do it," she said. Her fingers touched the keys, but she didn't press any of them.

The apartment had three main rooms and two of them were empty. The room they were in had the table and the chair and the typewriter and a mattress in the corner. There was a phone on the floor next to the mattress, and a black-and-white television set on a bookshelf in the corner. "Sometimes I do it there," he said.

She said, "Sometime could I watch you write a column?"

"Sometime," he said. He turned on the television set and took her away from his table. He didn't like people touching his typewriter. He didn't like touching it himself. She went with him to the mattress and unbuttoned his shirt. She didn't seem to notice his body, which was white and moley and had inverted nipples. It was nothing like the bodies she saw in the locker room, he knew that.

And as he thought that, it began to come to him who this girl was. She'd spent two weeks in the Phillies' locker room, if he remembered it right, and then written a story for *Velvet* magazine describing the different sizes and shapes of every penis on the starting rotation. She unbuckled his belt, pinching his skin there, and then unfastened his pants. He sat on the mattress, thinking of the players' wives who had formed a barricade in front of the locker room to keep her out and said on television that nobody was going to see their husbands' private parts but them and Danny Ozark.

The sports reporter was smiling.

She pulled his pants down around his knees, then fought his

125

shoes off and pulled the pants over his feet. He was wearing sky-blue, leafy underpants that were two feet long. He wondered if she had ever seen Jim Palmer, who was a pitcher for the Baltimore Orioles, in his underwear. Jim Palmer posed in underwear for *Newsweek* magazine.

She took the pants back to the table and folded them over the back of the chair, and then put her own clothes on top of his. She was wearing a pair of red panties under the jeans—panties the size of the ones Jim Palmer wore in *Newsweek* magazine—and nothing under the sweat shirt. She was slim, and tan for early May. And she had high-beam tits.

She folded into the mattress and reached into his shorts for his poor, drunk dick. She found it, smiled—whatever it was behind that smile, he didn't like it— and began to rub it up and down, absently, while she looked at the typewriter.

"Could you always write?" she said. "I mean, did you always want to be a writer?" He pictured her asking Pete Rose if he always wanted to be a baseball player. She let go of his dick and cupped his balls. "Hmmmm?"

Shellburn barely noticed. He was getting sleepy now. If he didn't fuck this graduate of Temple University Sportswriters' School in the next ten minutes, it wouldn't happen in eternity.

"As a boy I wanted to shave things," he said.

She pulled on his dick and smiled. "You're kinky?" And then she bent over without being asked and put old Yahama in her mouth. He couldn't feel it at all, but there wasn't much else she could be doing down there. There was a cool sensation when she came up for air. "You had a lot of those screwdrivers," she said.

"Eighteen," he said. "But you drank two of them. That's why I can't get it up. You drank two of my screwdrivers."

"Relax," she said, "tell me about shaving . . ." and she began rubbing him again.

"If that relaxes any more," he said, meaning his dick, "we got a problem with brain death." She giggled and looked back toward his typewriter.

126

"Do you work every morning?" she said. "Is there a time you do it, or do you wait for an inspiration?"

"The family had two dogs," he said. "A mongrel and a sheepdog. I was never allowed near the sheepdog with a razor."

She looked around the room. "It doesn't look like there's much here to inspire a writer." He looked around with her.

The place was empty, but he couldn't think of anything he wanted to put in it. It was a place to sleep. Shellburn could sleep anywhere there was a television on. There was nothing he saw outside that belonged there with him. No painting, no furniture, no plant. As a matter of fact, he was thinking of getting rid of the table.

He had moved to this place after his separation, and what was in the room was what he'd brought with him. That was six years ago in September, and all he'd added were two locks on the door. The woman he'd married was twenty years younger than he was. Stevey. Her father owned furniture stores in Camden and North Philly, where he sold bedroom suites to blacks and Puerto Ricans who couldn't afford them and who, on an average, would make two payments and quit. Then her father would hire other blacks and Puerto Ricans to repossess the bedroom suites and he would sell them again. Her father was a rich man and a big employer of minority Americans. He had a letter thanking him from President Richard Nixon. He resented having them around all the time, though, and used his money to keep his daughter as far away from that part of the world as he could.

So Shellburn's wife had grown up in private schools, taking dance lessons and violin lessons and tennis lessons and art lessons. She had gone to the Moore School of Art, and some of the teachers there thought she had a talent.

Then she'd gone to Paris and learned to resent America.

That was the kind of woman Shellburn had married. He'd met her at some women's club where he'd given a talk. He was getting $500 then. She liked him right away, and thought they made an interesting couple—this great, rough-talking, common man's writer, who spoke better to the city than any man alive, and the young artist, who would paint things that spoke to no one but herself. She liked the cultural juxtaposition. Those were the words she used, "cultural juxtaposition."

He smiled, thinking of her motives. He could smile at her, but he never asked himself who would marry somebody like that.

The freelancer from Temple was encouraged by the smile. She got closer to Shellburn and pecked at his cheek and pulled at his dick. "Tell me something about writing," she said. "Tell me a trick."

Shellburn shook his head, and the motion staggered him. "It's like shaving," he said. "You bleed worse than it hurts."

Shellburn's marriage had lasted sixteen months, counting the time in the lawyer's offices. It had taken her three months for it to set in that she really had married beneath herself, and the juxtaposition lost its novelty about a week after that. Shellburn hadn't done anything to save it, and that had brought out the violent edge of cultural juxtaposition.

He was used to watching things happen, and he watched this. "Do whatever you want to," he'd said, and she'd thrown a mason jar at his head. She'd bought forty of them for drinking glasses—five different sizes, eight glasses each size—and before the papers were signed she broke everything but the little juice glasses, which would bounce off the walls with impunity. Shellburn liked the little glasses for their toughness, but she took them with her when they split up.

She took the glasses and the silverware and every stick of furniture in the house. She got the Audi and the rugs and the Nautilus machine she'd bought him for their first Christmas together. She took everything and then sold it and went to Europe, back to Paris to forget. She would have taken the television, but to sell that somebody would've had to know she had one.

"I don't get it," said the girl from Temple. Her hand was still on his penis but it had stopped moving. He looked down at his stomach and his penis and her hand. Stevey would have wanted to paint it, a still life, and it would have come out looking like

Venetian blinds. "Why do you have to bleed?" the girl from Temple said.

Shellburn had a brief thought that he was paralyzed, but he moved his legs and saw he was only numb.

"I think you ought to get a word processor," the girl was saying. He closed his eyes and time drifted, and then Stevey and the freelancer from Temple University had each other's voices, and when he woke up, Stevey had caught him in the cheek with a mason jar and was saying. "Oh, no, you don't." Only it was the girl from Temple.

She had taken off her panties, he could see that. She had also pulled his head up out of his pillow and he was staring now at her crotch, about half a foot away. He realized she had slapped him awake and she was sitting on his chest.

"I have needs too," she said.

"A talking cunt," he said, "oh, no . . ."

She rode up his chest, and Shellburn let her push his face into her pubic hair. "There," she said, "that's better. . . ." And Shellburn smiled and went to sleep.

Shellburn could sleep anywhere there was a television on.

The phone rang just as Donahue introduced his first pervert, so it was a few minutes after nine o'clock. The freelancer from Temple was sleeping on the side of the mattress near the wall, but the phone didn't wake her up. He studied the line of her back a minute and then picked up the receiver.

"Richard?" It was Gertruda, calling for T. D. Davis. T. D. answered his own phone, but he never made his own calls. Gertruda put Shellburn on hold, and he studied the girl next to him on the mattress. He pulled the sheet down with his toe to look at her ass. He realized he was still drunk.

"Richard, good morning," T. D. said. He always sounded surprised to get you on the phone. "What you doin'?"

Shellburn said, "I'm lying here with a jaybird-naked-ass girl graduate of the Temple University School of Journalism."

"Good. How was she?"

"If you let me off the phone, I'll try to find out for you," Shellburn said. T. D. laughed, the girl reached down in her sleep and pulled the sheet back up over her bottom. Shellburn did not take either of those things for a good sign.

"Richard," T. D. said, "I need a favor. We ran a story yesterday, some boy killed on a construction job, and somehow we got it all dicked up. I'm finding out now who. But the thing is, you know, this boy was a veteran and supported his mother. I think she's crippled or something, and he was one of those unofficial neighborhood leaders we count on in this city. . . ."

Shellburn held the phone away from his ear and looked at it. T. D.'s voice got farther away, like Shellburn had gone into a coma. He waited until it stopped and put the phone back against his ear. "You follow me, Richard?"

Shellburn said, "She's got my dick in her mouth, T. D. Is this important?"

"What I was thinking," T. D. said, "was that instead of sending one of these damn kids down there and get it wrong again, why don't I ask Richard Shellburn to head over there and write me a column about this boy? Get it done right."

Shellburn said, "Because he's getting blown."

"Be good for you to stretch your legs anyway," T. D. said.

Shellburn looked at his legs. Bone-thin, almost hairless. Old man legs. "I had a couple things I had to look at today," he said. He didn't want to find out about Leon Hubbard, he already knew. He could sit down right now at the table and write it in twenty minutes, off what Davis had just told him. "I could send Billy over there, I guess. . . ."

T. D. said, "Maybe you could go yourself. You know, get some of that description in there. Bibles, pictures of the dead boy, grieving mother. Things only Richard Shellburn would see."

He picked up a sock off the floor and put it in his mouth. "I can't talk now, T. D. I'm eatin' pussy." And then he broke the connection with his finger.

He looked again at the girl on the mattress. She was stirring, now that he thought about it she was probably already awake. Shellburn called Billy for the address and phone number of Leon Hubbard's widowed mother.

He wrote the phone number in the dust on the floor beside the mattress. He found a crayon in the bathroom—how long had that been there?—and copied the numbers onto a piece of typing paper. The freelancer from Temple University got off the mattress and stormed past him into the bathroom. He thought she was mad, but then he heard her throwing up. Then she opened the door six inches and asked for her purse.

He passed it through the crack. A little later the toilet flushed, the water went on and off, and a couple of times the toilet flushed again. He heard her open his medicine cabinet. There wasn't anything in there but pills. Valium, aspirin, shit from when he was sick. There were pills six years old in there.

A minute later the medicine cabinet shut and she came out wearing a towel and some lipstick. She gave him a quick kiss on the cheek but didn't grab his peter—now there was a word he hadn't thought of in a while—and she fell back into the mattress and smiled.

"Come back to bed," she said. He looked at her breasts and her butt and her legs and her mouth with the fresh lipstick. She had all the parts you could ask for, but something was missing for Shellburn. Once you could fuck somebody, then you were left with whether you wanted to. Shellburn remembered when those two things went together.

"I've got to be somewhere," he said.

"Can I come along?"

"Not this time."

"Remember, you promised I could watch you write a column."

"Sometime," he said. And he thought, *Right after I suck off a German shepherd on Broad Street.* He took a shower, shaved and put on clean clothes. When he came out she was still lying on the mattress. Her eyes were closed and she was breathing in steady, deep sighs that blew her hair where it crossed in front of

131

her mouth. He looked at her and thought of how empty her life was.

He opened the door quietly and let himself out, and he was half into the hallway when she said something that reached out like two-inch fingernails and grabbed his stomach from the inside. She said, "You know, I was just thinking what a really terrific magazine piece you'd make. . . ."

Shellburn got into the Continental and lay his head against the adjustable steering wheel. She was still up there, in his apartment, probably making notes. All he'd said was, "Lock up when you leave," and then he'd closed the door before she could sit up and get a look at him.

The digital clock in the dashboard built a fragile 10:28 out of straight green lines. Cars were in the street, honking. It was dirty and busy, and he thought about the house in God's Pocket where they wanted him to go. The place would be narrow and small and dark. The windows would be closed and the mother would be sitting in a dark dress on the couch, so he wouldn't be able to see her until his eyes adjusted, and when she spoke it would be so soft he'd have to ask her what she'd said, over and over.

There would be relatives around, big guys, and an argument. Old brothers against young brothers, maybe. Shellburn felt a line of sweat break out at his hairline, and he was suddenly weak. He started the car to get the air conditioning on, noticed his hands shaking.

He pulled into the street and headed for Lombard Street, where he turned west and took it all the way to Twenty-fifth. He could go north on Twenty-fifth and be inside the house in three minutes. The clock said 10:50, and Shellburn stopped at Twenty-fifth Street, then went past it, crossed the river on the South Street Bridge and got on the Expressway South.

He drove out past the refineries and the airport, and then got on I-95. He began to feel better. He took the Continental up to eighty—in that car you couldn't tell eighty from forty—and put the radio on. He would take care of the house in God's Pocket when he got back, or it would take care of itself.

He hit a button and rolled the window down a few inches, and then turned the radio up to cover the noise. The radio had been set to WWDB-FM talk radio. Listeners called in to report their feelings about Mayor Green and abortions—speaking of the mayor—and capital punishment.

The subject of the day, however, was a week-old wolf-pack killing, in which eight or ten black kids stomped an eighteen-year-old freshman at the University of Pennsylvania to death on Chestnut Street at five o'clock in the afternoon to steal his wallet. Some of the callers were for it and some were against it. Six of them reported that most black crime was directed against other blacks, four callers said there wasn't anything else for inner-city children to do and predicted a long, hot summer.

On the other side, a lot of people wanted public executions, and there were stories about things that had happened to elderly parents. They said getting old made you a target in the city.

Shellburn drove past Wilmington and found 213 South. The land changed, and the voices from the city faded and broke with static. A woman called in and began to cry. She was drunk, he thought. He wondered if she was as drunk as he was. The vodka was coming out of his skin now, and he turned the air conditioner off because the air on the sweat was chilling him.

"I'm sorry," the woman on the radio said, "I'm all alone. . . ." He closed his eyes and could see her, she was one of his people too. "But the thing I want to say . . ."

The man who answered the calls and told the people what he thought said, "Madam, is it possible you have been imbibing this morning? You sound like you need to sleep it off."

"I'm not drunk," the woman said, and Shellburn could see her straightening in her chair. "Please, what I wanted to say . . ." Shellburn crossed the little bridge over the Bohemia River, made a right turn over another, smaller bridge.

"We've got people waiting, madam. . . ."

"Let her finish," Shellburn said. The man who answered the

calls and told the people what he thought had read the week-old account of the wolf-pack killing from the *Daily Times*. That was how people got on the subject of public executions, and things that happened to their mothers, and the lack of job opportunities for inner-city youth, and how Frank Rizzo had tried to genocide them anyway. Genocide was a big word on the street this year. And in the middle of all the words on the street, it seemed to Shellburn that the man on the radio had somehow stumbled across the real thing—a drunk old woman who wanted to make her statement before she slid off into the other side, where she knew nobody would listen.

The man on the radio was cutting her off. "Please," she said again. The man on the radio sighed.

"All right, madam, say it. We've got people waiting."

She gathered herself. "Thank you," she said. "What I wanted to say . . ." Shellburn felt himself tense. "What I wanted to say was . . ." Then, "I can't remember now."

Shellburn came to a dirt road that looked like a tunnel hidden in trees. He followed it up and down two hills, and then around a long left-hand turn. Then there was one more hill, and at the top of that the trees disappeared and the land opened up and it was like the first day of the world. He parked at the side of the road. From there, he could see the Bohemia, and the cove where it emptied into the Elk River and ran into the Chesapeake Bay. It was a quarter mile from the road to the water, a long, sloping meadow that ended in a hundred feet of thick trees. Beyond that was the cove, a mile and half around the lip.

There were a few sails on the water, and beyond them, two or three miles, was another meadow like Shellburn's on the other side. There were horses over there, sometimes cattle, and in the morning you could see deer on both sides.

Shellburn got out of the car and walked fifty yards into the meadow. That was where the house was going to be. The ground rolled there and began its long, easy drop to the water. From there you could look out a window and watch the storms coming in over the water. Or you could watch the geese coming in, so thick sometimes they could have been a storm too.

He'd bought the meadow two months before he'd married Stevey, and never told her. He'd been forty-five years old, and he'd had a picture of the place in his head a long time. The picture had a house in it, a family.

At the time, of course, Stevey was planning a life around the impact their cultural juxtaposition would have on Center City society, it never came up that he had a picture in his head of her pregnant and isolated, living on a hill in Maryland overlooking the Chesapeake Bay.

He didn't know how long he'd had the picture, he thought it must have been there a long time before he knew what it was—like that feeling you've forgotten something—because when he saw it, he *recognized* it. He'd bought twenty-one acres for $85,000, everything he had, and instead of worrying about the money—Shellburn always worried about money—he took the perfect fit of the price and his bank account for a sign.

And he'd never even told her. They were married in a 230-year-old church and moved into a townhouse in Society Hill, where the front door was four feet from the street, and where she watered one skinny-ass little tree growing out of a hole in the sidewalk next to a fire hydrant.

And when it was over a few months later—over except for the lawyers—he would get himself drunk and lonely at some Center City bar and wake up in the morning, parked where he was now. He wouldn't remember driving down, and he'd sit there in the early sun, watching the water birds come in like storms.

He walked farther into the meadow, watching where he put his feet. There were holes in the ground, covered with dried grass, and there were rabbit nests.

He'd thought about selling the property. A year after he'd bought it a developer had offered him $140,000, and he knew then he ought to take the money before he wrapped himself around a truck some night trying to get there. He knew he ought to take the money because he'd never build a house there. He'd gone past that turn.

He didn't sell the meadow. Not for $140,000, not for the

quarter million they'd offered him last year. Not after the marriage ended, not after he'd nearly died in the hospital.

He had a picture in his head, and in the picture he was safe all the time.

He came to the bottom of the meadow, and climbed over a barbed-wire fence that separated it from the woods. A long time ago the land had been a cow pasture. He began to sweat again, and he felt shaky and sick and poisoned. He stopped for a moment and it passed.

The last hundred feet to the water was grown over with thick underbrush, and everything that grew there had thorns or stickers and was four times as wiry as it looked. Shellburn walked carefully, lifting his feet straight up and down, pushing the briers down and away with his hands, then stepping on them to get past. The briers rose with his feet and then clung to his pants legs and made tearing sounds as he made his way through. When that happened, something in him always wanted to run.

But he was slow and steady, and pointed for the water. Then he ducked under the lower branches of an oak tree and was there. The tree was 150 years old, so thick you couldn't get your arms around it. You might as well try to hug your house. The mouth of the tree took the last six feet of ground before the bank dropped down to the beach. Shellburn used a branch to ease himself down onto the round, gray rocks that were the floor there. Then he looked back at the bank where the tide had eaten the ground from underneath the old oak and had left half its root system hanging in the air.

The tree was tilted about thirty degrees toward the water, holding on. Shellburn hadn't noticed it until after the heart attack, when he was thirty degrees toward the water himself.

He admired the tree until his breathing got easier. The wind off the water was cool, and he walked north until the beach changed from rocks to sand, and then found a place to sit where the bank fit his back and held his head, and it was no work or pain to look out over his cove. He closed his eyes and the picture was still there—he could feel it the same way he could feel the cove—and for a long time what he was and what he might have been were as close as Shellburn could ever get them.

And it was late afternoon before he knocked on Jeanie Scarpato's door in God's Pocket.

Mickey got up early while the house was still quiet. He didn't want her to see him in Leon's bed again. When he'd cleaned up and gone downstairs, though, Jeanie and her sisters were sitting in the kitchen, drinking coffee and working over a new box of donuts. There was a beer can on the sink, where he'd left it when he'd come in last night. He'd had maybe a six-pack to help him sleep.

He walked in there with the beer can and the sisters and patted Jeanie on the shoulder. She reached up and touched his hand, for just a second, and then let her hand fall back into her lap. Like it was a pain there that came and went before it mattered.

"You all right this morning, Jeanie? You sleep all right?"

The sisters gave each other the now-famous look over the table. "Jeanie?"

"It just seems like it's been so long," she said. He could barely hear her. "Like it happened two years ago and it's still going on."

"It'll start going fast again," he said. "As soon as it's taken care of and we did what we could." And it was like saying it to an empty room. It sounded like that too, like he was telling it to himself, so he'd believe it.

He looked at the curve of her head, and how the hair seemed to get blonder where it touched her skin, and for the first time he thought he might not be able to get her back. Not even after the sisters moved out and Leon was in the ground. And then for a few seconds, he couldn't breathe.

He took the truck around to half a dozen regular stops and only got rid of half of the meat that Bird's nephew had cut before the electricity went out. If he didn't find somebody with a restaurant, he was going to lose most of it. He'd have to get rid of it before it went bad, one way or the other. Anywhere meat went bad, it never smelled the same. He should of been pissed at Bird—anybody with eyes could see he couldn't handle that kind of a load—but when he thought about Bird, all he could see was the old woman leading him home. He'd keep the meat seven days if the truck stayed cold. Seven days, and then he'd take it over to the Women's S.P.C.A. Or maybe he'd find somebody in Jersey.

He made his stops and then he went to the bank, and began thinking about the horse. There was $868 in his account. He took it in fifties, all except what couldn't go into fifties. The teller's name was Miss Olby, and she was plainly inconvenienced.

Back in the truck, he reached up under the seat and found McKenna's bag. He put the fifties on top of the money from the Hollywood and the Uptown, and it wouldn't fit into his pocket. He went back.

The bank had velvet ropes in the lobby, with the idea that you were supposed to stand in line between the ropes until it was your turn to see a teller. The way you knew when a teller was available was that she would turn on a light over her cage. Which is all to say it was not Mickey's idea to go back to Miss Olby to turn the rest of the money into fifties too. But when he got to the front of the line, her light went on and he put the stacked bills in front of her and asked for twenty-eight more fifty-dollar bills.

He had seen people take house floods better. She sighed, she checked her drawer, and then she had to get up off her stool, and go clear to the next cage for more fifties. "Usually we don't do this," she said.

He wondered if it was some kind of sign he should leave the money alone, that something would go wrong at Keystone. He decided it couldn't be, though. If you waited for a friendly bank teller to get your money out, the banks would have it forever.

He found Bird dressed in a suit with somebody else's shoulders, sitting behind the wheel of the yellow Cadillac in front of the flower shop. Mickey parked the truck inside and said hello to Aunt Sophie, who picked him a carnation off the counter and asked him to keep an eye on Bird.

Bird had the car running and the air conditioner on. The windows were open, the radio was playing, and he was sitting there in the middle of it, staring at the racing form. Mickey slid into the front seat and looked to see what keeping an eye on him was going to take. "How you doin'?" he said.

Bird handed the form to Mickey, dropped the car into gear and drove sixty miles an hour down South Street, slamming over potholes. Mickey put his eyes behind the racing form so he wouldn't have to see it coming when they died.

Bird got on I-95 at Girard and drove up through North Philadelphia, and then out past the Northeast. To get an idea how big Philadelphia was, all you had to do was go to the Northeast and try to find a street sign. Going to the Northeast was like going to the hospital, you forget all the little things they do to you, you forget how slow time moves until you're there again.

The road was six lanes—three each way—divided by a concrete wall. Bird slowed down to forty miles an hour and drove all the way to the Street Road exit in the general area of the middle lane. About halfway there he said, "I took care of that matter for you, Mickey."

Mickey looked at him, waited. "You remember," Bird said, "that matter at Holy Redeemer with Leon."

"I remember."

"Right. I got some people lookin' into that right now. I ought to have somethin' for you to tell Jeanie by the time we go home, if you want." He gave Mickey a smile straight from Byberry.

Bird did the driveway into Keystone at sixty miles an hour. He threw the Cadillac into Park still going around thirty and stopped one yard short of a kid in a red vest and a black tie who, with the confidence of youth, obviously thought he was in control of the valet parking traffic. The Cadillac would have stopped on top of the boy, but in the end he'd run. The car made the last noise you hear before somebody you live with tosses their cookies. Bird got out, handed the kid in the red vest a five-dollar bill and then bought a program, all in one thought. "Be careful of it," Bird said to the kid, "it's new."

They took the escalator up to the reserved seats, which Bird paid for. Then Bird bought a couple of large beers in paper cups and they sat down to wait. It was a wait Mickey wouldn't have minded at another track. At another track he would have gone down to the paddock and looked at horses or trainers, sometimes you could see something that would tell you what was going on inside the horse. That was the only kind of spooky shit Mickey didn't mind thinking. Something about Keystone, though, made you hate to move.

Bird spread the racing form over the seats in front of him and studied the seventh race. The two women sitting in those seats turned around and looked at Mickey in a way he was getting used to. Bird read the racing form the same way rich kids arranged cocaine in lines on their mirrors, scared shitless that something was going to blow away from him.

"It's the same as it was last night," Mickey said. Bird didn't hear him. His finger was following a race that the only other New York horse in the race had run a year ago, as a two-year-old. Mickey had seen the race and thrown it out. He was the kind of handicapper who could throw a race out and not think about it again. Bird wasn't.

"I don't like this other filly, Mick," he said. He slid the form over to Mickey, keeping his finger on the race that worried him. "She's come down a long ways in class."

Mickey said, "Yes, she did."

Bird went over it again, that race and a couple of others. The filly hadn't run in half a year. "I don't like her," he said again. "She'd got a decent workout last week. . . ."

Mickey shrugged. "Put her on the bottom of an exacta," he said. He opened his own form and looked over the fifth race. Then he got up, bet a ten on a fourteen-year-old horse named Lexington Park, got a couple more beers and watched the race on a television set. He'd bet the same ten dollars on the same horse in Chicago a long time ago, and he'd won then and he almost won now. This time, though, the favorite got him in the last couple of strides.

Mickey sat down beside Bird. "That's somethin', you know it?" he said. Bird looked up from his racing form and the seventh race.

"What?"

"That old horse went out and almost stole that race," Mickey said. He pointed out to the track, where they were bringing the old gelding back, his neck and mouth foaming. You could see the heat coming off his back. Bird looked for half a second, then put his nose back in the seventh race.

"This horse," he said finally, "this horse can beat Turned Leaf."

Mickey said, "Your nerves are eatin' your brain, Bird. Lookit, you got a couple beers sittin' on the floor. Drink a beer, relax, give yourself a chance. . . ."

Bird looked at the beers, then at Mickey. "I took care of that matter for you at the hospital," he said.

"Yeah, thanks," Mickey said.

"I talked to downtown," he said. "They listen to me, Mick. You oughta listen to me too. The filly can beat Turned Leaf."

Mickey said, "You remember what we saw up in New York? You remember about sewin' up her pussy? I ain't tellin' you what to do, Bird, but if she runs at all, there's nothin' in this fuckin' dog kennel that's going to catch her." Bird took a roll of money out of his pocket and began to count it, right there in his seat. "What the fuck are you doin' now?"

Bird said, "It's the other filly, Mick."

Mickey said, "How much you got there?"

Bird shrugged. "Seven, eight thou, I don't know. Whatever I could get my hands on. You know how things been." Mickey watched the sixth race thinking about Aunt Sophie. She'd asked him to keep an eye on Arthur. He didn't know if that meant to take his money away before he could lose it or not. He didn't know how he'd do that in the middle of the reserved section of the clubhouse either.

The tote board flashed up the seventh race and Turned Leaf, the two horse, opened at eight to one.

"Three to one," Bird said. "They made her the second favorite in the program, and all these fuckin' cannibals never would of seen her are going to bet her down. You wait and see. . . ."

Mickey looked at the board and Bird's filly—the six—was three to one. "C'mon, Bird, I'm responsible," Mickey said. "I told Sophie I'd keep an eye on you."

Bird said, "Responsible? There's nobody responsible for each other."

Mickey leaned back in his seat and watched the board a few minutes, then he stood up to bet. "Be right back," he said. He went to the fifty-dollar window and put the stack of fifties on the counter. "Two win, forty-five times," he said. The man behind the window was smoking a cigar. He sighed and punched up the tickets and never looked up. Mickey thought he had a future as a bank teller if he wanted it.

He put the tickets in the pocket where his money had been and bought himself a watery Pepsi-Cola. He took a swallow and checked the cup, wondering what kind of people Jeanie's family was to drink that kind of shit night and day.

When he got back to the seats, Bird was gone and there was a jockey change on Turned Leaf. They'd put a Colombian named Charles Suarte on her, and Mickey didn't like the looks of that at all. Bird had left two beers on the floor and his racing form on his seat, and the smell of hair oil up and down the aisle. When he came back, he was carrying three inches of tickets, most of them exactas with the New York filly on top. "Not the whole eight thousand," Mickey said.

Bird sat down next to him, picked one of the beers up off the floor and took a long drink. "It turned out I had a little more," he said. He split the tickets into two piles—exactas and win tickets—and put one pile in the left pocket of his suit coat and one pile in the right pocket. Then he patted the pockets. "George ain't never going to say no to Bird again," he said. George was the automatic twenty-four-hour bank teller at Girard Bank.

"You're fuckin' crazy," Mickey said.

Bird nodded. His filly went to five to one, Turned Leaf stayed where she was. Mickey closed his eyes and waited. There wasn't anything he could do about it now. Not about horses or jockeys or people, alive or dead. It was out of his hands.

A few minutes later, just after they'd announced one minute to post, he heard Bird say, "No, no . . . Fuck." He opened his eyes and looked at the board, and somebody had dumped enough late money on the six horse to drop her to five to two. "The fuckin' cannibals," Bird said. Down on the track they were loading the gate. The two men pushed them in, one at a time. Horses didn't like the starting gate, neither did jockeys. That's where you got killed.

"Cannibals," Bird said again. That was what he called anybody that knew less about the horses than he did, but it wasn't ignorance behind that kind of late money, it was the opposite. Mickey had a feeling that seemed to continue from the moment that morning when he'd looked down at Jeanie's hair and the curve of her head and thought maybe he'd lost her. It was part of the same thing.

The race was only six furlongs, which was a good thing for the Colombian. He couldn't have held her much longer. He put Turned Leaf on the outside and pulled her head that way all the way around. And she ran anyway, looking sideways. She came six wide around the last turn, fifteen lengths behind, and still closed so hard that the Colombian had to stand up to keep her from finishing second.

Mickey watched the finish standing up, without moving, and then he sat down. "They ought to break his legs," he said, not to anybody in particular. "That spic couldn't of been plainer about it if he'd of nailed her dick to the starting gate." He noticed Bird then. He'd taken the exactas out of the side of his coat and begun to separate the winning tickets from the others. All of the exactas had the six horse on top, so everything in the other pocket would be a win on the six.

"I tried to tell you, Mick," he said. "It was a lock. . . ." The prices came up on the board then. Bird's filly paid seven dollars

143

to win, and the exactas, six-one, was $54.60. Bird sorted his tickets. "Sometimes you just know," he said. "Sometimes you're so sure it ain't real."

Mickey didn't say anything. He took the tickets out of his own pocket and dropped them on the floor, that was how easy you got left behind. "You notice that race my filly run in New York?" Bird said.

"Yes, I seen it," Mickey said.

"I figure they wouldn't of kept her out this long if they wasn't going to bring her back ready. I figured they had her ready to run that same race again. . . ." Mickey closed his eyes.

Bird was talking and sorting, Mickey was imagining what he would say to Smilin' Jack. There must of been people in the neighborhood before that died and the families didn't have the money to cover it. He'd ask him for a couple of weeks, a month to get him his cash. Bird was still sorting. He must of had eighty ten-dollar exactas that said six-one.

The ones that had the six over some other horse he was flipping into the air, one at a time, watching them blow in the wind and drop into the seats around him. A few of them dropped on Mickey, one landed in his chair. "When I get like this I ain't real. . . ."

Mickey went with Bird to cash the tickets. It came to just over $32,000. Bird divided the money and put half of it into one side of the suit coat and half of it into the other side. "You ready to go?" he said.

Bird gave the kid he'd almost killed on the way in a twenty to get the car, and then drove out of the parking lot at thirty miles an hour, just like somebody normal. On the way back to I-95 he said, "What was that job Monday? Seven hundred?"

Mickey shook his head. "It's old business, Bird. I took the meat." It was one thing to lose your ass, it was something else to have your friends feeling sorry for you.

"Seven hundred, right?" Bird reached into one of his coat pockets and pulled out about two pounds of hundred-dollar bills and handed them to Mickey. "Take seven of them," he said. "Take ten, for the interest."

Mickey gave them back. "Keep your money, Bird," he said. "I took the meat."

"Fuck meat," he said. "Look, I got maybe thirty thou here. I got to give six back, which I borrowed, the rest is clear. I'm goin' to Miami. They got trailer parks down there, you can buy one of them things for what, twelve, thirteen thou? That's what Sophie wants, to live in one of them trailer parks with her buddies, grow some shit in the yard."

Mickey said, "You borrowed six and bet the wrong horse? What were you going to tell them if you lost?"

Bird said, "Five. You gotta give six for five, the fucks, but I been tryin' to tell you. It couldn't happen. Now take your grand and gimme my money back." Mickey took seven hundred-dollar bills and put the rest back in Bird's pocket.

"I'll give you the meat," he said.

"Fuck meat," Bird said. "You always gotta be movin' it in or out or sideways, so fuck it. They can't touch you when you don't give a fuck." They drove with the traffic then, neither one of them saying anything until Bird turned off the Interstate into South Philadelphia.

"I think I'm done now," Bird said. "I think I'm used up in Philly. These new people takin' everything, they don't own Miami. The people that own Miami know what their business is about."

Vinnie Ribbocini was sitting behind his desk with a glass of milk and a package of Oreo cookies when they came in, without knocking, and stood one on each side of the door staring at him.

Vinnie knew one of them. The new people had him overlooking his business. His name was Sally. "So what do you want, comin' in here like this?" he said. "You want to put smack in the jelly donuts, what is it?"

The one he knew came across the room to the desk. The other one stayed where he was. He had that look like he had them fuckin' little earphones on, that you couldn't hear what everybody else could hear. He was standing with his feet wide apart and his coat open. The shooter. Vinnie laughed out loud. The one he knew reached across the desk and slapped him across the face.

The slap spun him around in his chair. "I oughta fuckin' kill you right here," the man said. Vinnie straightened himself and stared at him. He promised to kill him for that. "Before Angelo got wasted," he said, "if I spit in your face, you'd a asked if it was all right to wipe it off." Sally slapped him again.

This time the old man saw it coming and moved with the hand. His cookies sprayed into the wall, the milk stayed where it was. He picked it up and took a drink. His hands were shaking, and he was ashamed. The left side of his nose was bleeding down into his mustache, and he dabbed at it with a Kleenex he took out of a box on the side of the desk that hadn't been disturbed.

"You set me up," Sally said.

The old man laughed at him. "If I set you up," he said, "you'd be where you belong."

Sally said, "I sent my brother-in-law on that job yesterday. Him and another guy just as good. I sent him over there with two eyeballs, Vinnie, and when they find him he's walkin' around Broad Street holdin' one of them in his hands." He grabbed the old man's shirt and pulled him across the desk. "You told me it wasn't no problem."

The blood filled his mustache and began to drip on the desk. He stared right into Sally's eyes.

"The other guy, they got his ass in the hospital, tied to the ceiling in six places on account of his back's broke and his leg's broke, and they can't give him no painkiller because they don't know if his fuckin' head's broke too."

He let go of the old man and straightened his clothes. Vinnie used another Kleenex to clean the spots off the desk. "So?"

"So you said it wasn't no problem, Vinnie. And I sent my brother-in-law over there with another guy, just as good, and they run into a fuckin' gorilla. I mean a real fuckin' gorilla. What's that make me look like?"

The old man saw that they hadn't noticed him shaking, and Sally's voice began to change, like he wanted to talk now. If they'd seen he was afraid, they'd of beat him half to death before they wanted to talk.

"So shoot the gorilla," the old man said. His nose began to swell, he could feel it. It had been broken before and he knew better than to blow his nose, but he did it anyway.

"It ain't him we want," Sally said. "We ain't got no business with him, never did. Not until you asked us to go to the hospital."

"So shoot me," he said.

Sally shook his head and sat down on the corner of the desk. Blowing his nose had pushed some of the blood up into the cavities under the old man's eyes, and they were swelling now, cutting off his vision. "To tell you the truth, that crossed our mind," Sally said. "Comin' over here, me and Mike talked that over, right, Mike?" Mike smiled, distracted, almost polite. He'd be the one to do it, if that's what it came to.

"My sister calls me up and says they found Ronnie walkin' around carryin' one of his eyeballs, it crosses my mind to come over here and cut your head off. She's real upset, screamin' all over the neighborhood that nobody can get away with that. You know how they are. So I promise her I'll take care of it, but, like I said, on the way over, me and Mike talked it over, and we figure it don't have to be you. I mean, somebody told you it was no problem and you told us. So it's him. . . ."

Vinnie saw his nephews was working both sides—they'd talked to these two—and he shook his head. The reason these two wouldn't cut off his head, they was afraid. The old man was the one Angelo had listened to. Angelo loved him. They might kill him, but they wouldn't cut his head off. Scarin' was one thing, but you didn't want nobody scared and pissed at the same time. That would be bad for everybody.

"I done business with this guy since before the Japs bombed Pearl Harbor," he said.

"He fucked up," Sally said. "Somebody's got to make this good."

"So shoot the gorilla," he said again.

Sally said, "We ain't goin' near that motherfucker." The old man laughed at them again, and Sally slapped him. His eyes had swollen almost shut now, so he didn't see it coming and it knocked him out of his seat. Then there were hands on his collar, lifting him back up. "It's him, or it's you and him," Sally said. The old man could smell his breath, and his legs were shaking like the palsy.

And he saw what they would do, and gave them the address. Sally wrote it down and then, without another word, they walked out the door. The old man heard them get into their car outside. He turned toward the window, but his eyes were almost shut and he couldn't see. The door to his office opened, and he heard the girl who worked behind the bakery counter. She came in and made a noise like she'd found a kitten. "Oh . . ."

He sat up straight and faced the voice. "Lock up the store and go home, child," he said.

She said, "Oh, Mr. Ribbocini . . ."

"Go home," he said. And for a few minutes he listened to the sounds of the cash register and the window blinds and then the front door being closed and locked. He was still shaking, but he wasn't scared.

"I shouldn'ta gave you up, Arthuro," he said out loud. "But we're all dead now, so it don't matter, and I need to see these monkey cunts dead too. Humor an old man on this. . . ."

Shellburn stopped at a bar near the Wilmington airport and bought a six-pack of Schmidt's. There was a phone booth outside, a few yards from the highway, and he opened one of the beers before he dialed the number in God's Pocket. He deposited seven quarters, a dime and a nickel and got a busy signal. So he went over uninvited, which would have seemed like bad manners to him if he hadn't been who he was.

He found a place to park the Continental on the sidewalk just outside a dark, wet-looking hole in the block called the Hollywood Bar. There was a faded rainbow painted across the win-

148

dow. The six-pack of beer was working, smoothing him out, and he went inside to use the bathroom so he wouldn't have to ask Leon Hubbard's mother if he could use hers.

There were a couple of old women drinking rock nips at one end of the bar, a couple of old men drinking the same thing at the other end. Shellburn got the idea they were married. They watched him come in. There was a wasted rummy in a neck brace, standing by himself in the middle, talking to the bartender. The bartender was tired of listening and looked played out when he brought Shellburn his can of Schmidt's from the cooler.

When he said "Schmidt's," one or two of the men had looked at him again. They drank Rolling Rock or Ortlieb's at the Hollywood. Shellburn drank half the beer and went into the bathroom. The toilet was cracked and leaking and rotting out the floor, and when he stepped inside, the wood gave underneath his feet.

There was a mirror in the towel machine and a bare orange light bulb over the sink. Standing on his toes, Shellburn could see the top half of his head. He patted down his hair and saw that his eyes were a sunset over Key West. Reds, pinks, lovely. He tucked his shirt into his pants and brushed some of the dust from Maryland off his shoes, and then went back out and finished the beer.

"Is that Leon Hubbard's house across the street?" he said.

The bartender cocked his head, to see who was asking. Then he said, "You aren't Richard Shellburn, are you?" Shellburn nodded, the bartender reached across to shake hands. "I knew it," he said. "I read you every day. You look different from your picture, but I knew it was you."

"Is that the Hubbard place?" he asked.

"Scarpato," the bartender said. "The mother's remarried. Jeanie Scarpato."

Shellburn looked at the narrow brick row house across the street. The windows were all covered, like nobody lived there anymore. "How's she taking it?" he said.

The bartender shrugged. "He was the only child," he said. Shellburn had another beer, then put a five-dollar bill on the bar and walked outside. They watched him cross the street and knock on the door. Then the door opened, and a few seconds later he went inside. One of the old women said, "Richard Shellburn is the only one ever come down here, to the Pocket."

Ray shook his head. "Adlai Stevenson was right on this spot," he said.

"Well, I never voted for him," the woman said. "I like Ike."

"Dwight David Eisenhower had the third-lowest I.Q. of any U.S. President since Grover Cleveland," he said. Then they ordered more Rolling Rock beer and watched the street so they would know how long he was in there with Jeanie Scarpato before he came out.

Shellburn knocked on the door and waited to see the grief-stricken mother, so he could put her red eyes and shaky hands and her tear-stained cheeks in the newspaper, along with the harsh, naked light in the bathroom of the Hollywood Bar, where Leon Hubbard drank. And then she opened the door and Shellburn was struck stone dumb. "Mrs. Scarpato?" He heard his voice but he didn't seem to be the one talking.

"Yes?" It wasn't that she was the most beautiful woman he'd ever seen. She was pretty, but it took him a few seconds to see that.

"I'm Richard Shellburn, *Daily Times*." She opened the door for him and smiled. He curled around that smile like he was paper on fire.

"Thank you very much for coming," she said. He followed her into the living room, where two darker, older women were sitting on the couch, drinking hot chocolate. "You don't know how good it is to talk to somebody that understands. . . ."

"I understand," he said.

The women sized him up, heavy and suspicious. Jeanie Scarpato offered him a chair and then sat down near him on a footstool, hugging her knees, looking up. It wasn't that she was beautiful, it was like he'd looked into her face and found a perfect fit. She looked like the other half of whatever piece he'd been broken off of.

She had eyes that were harmless and couldn't make up their mind. And her hair was soft and touched the hollows of her cheeks and neck, and he could see the edges of her ears poking through farther back. And he wanted to touch the hollows too.

He cleared his throat. "I was very sorry to hear about your son," he said. The bottom rim of her eyes went dewy and teared over. She wiped at the tears and he noticed her hands. Great hands, they just *fit* her.

"Thank you," she said.

The women stood up and cleared the cups off the coffee table. The bigger one said, "We've got to go now, hon, run some errands. . . ." Showing themselves a little sweeter for the newspapers, and a minute later they both went out the front door.

She was talking, something about Leon. "It didn't happen like they said, Mr. Shellburn. I know Leon, he was my boy."

"I know," he said, "I know. . . ."

She was looking down at her hands now, as still and white and fancy as Sunday gloves you might find in a trunk in the attic, and before Shellburn had realized he was doing it, he had reached down and picked them up, and was holding them against his cheek.

Richard Shellburn had knocked on the door in the middle of what was about to be a scene. Joyce had just said everybody had their crosses to bear, like Leon was already old news, and then there he was to save her. He looked older than she expected, but friendlier than his picture. "You don't know how much good it does to talk to somebody that understands," she'd said, for her sisters.

"We're going to go home and do some errands," Joyce said. She and Joanie waited, and when Jeanie didn't answer, they left her there in the living room with Richard Shellburn. She noticed he was sweating. He smelled like he'd been drinking. "Something is wrong about what happened to Leon," she started. "I don't know how I know, but it didn't happen like they said."

He was looking down, she was looking up. Vulnerable. He liked her.

"It isn't money," she said. "Ever since it happened, everybody says, sue the hospital, sue the construction company, but I need this cleared up for myself." She stopped to see if he was following her. It was hard to say, but then he said, "I know, I know . . ." and then he got her hands. He'd held them against his cheek and closed his eyes. She waited him out, and in a minute he sighed and let go.

He took a note pad out of the inside pocket of his coat and found a soft-tip pen in another pocket, and asked about Leon. "What kind of a boy was he?" he said.

Jeanie was glad to see the note pad. There was a moment, while he was holding her hands against his cheek, that the thought had crossed her mind that it might only be somebody who looked like Richard Shellburn. And not even that much.

"He was mechanical," she said. "Even though his father died when he was a month old, so he never had the kind of help in those things that most boys get. Do you have children, Mr. Shellburn?" She saw he was writing, and it made her feel satisfied, in a way, to think she would be down on paper someplace.

"No," he said, "I'm not married."

"Leon's father was killed on duty," she said. "He was a Philadelphia police officer, and we had been married eleven months. I didn't know what I was going to do. . . ." She stopped herself. This was about Leon now. He was looking up at her, waiting. "Anyway," she said, "I did what I could. He was always a sickly child, which was why he never got very big, the doctors said. There were big people on both sides of the family. . . ."

"I noticed your aunts," he said.

She left them aunts. "Yes. Well, he was like other children, I suppose, except small for his age. And he never liked anybody else around the house, you know. My friends. He never brought any of his little friends by either, even when he got older. He had a girl friend, a lovely girl, but we never met her. She's a flight attendant for U.S. Air."

Shellburn was writing words on his pad, sometimes looking at the pad, sometimes looking at her. "Is this helping?" she said. He smiled at her, and she thought he might hold her hands again. He seemed so sad about it.

"And he went into the service, but he didn't stay in long. They sent him to Korea, I know that, but he got discharged for his nerves." He looked up. "That's how I know something happened," she said. "Leon wasn't anybody to have things fall on his head. He used to check the street before he went out the door, he was always looking around behind him, over his head, getting up and looking out the window."

Shellburn said, "He was a bricklayer, first class?"

"It was a month and a half," she said, "I don't know. But he was mechanical. He would have picked it up fast, if he wanted to. Anything Leon wanted to, he could pick it up fast. . . .

"He never finished school, though. With Leon, nothing was ever quite finished. Every time you thought you got close to understanding him, there was still something he held back. Do you know what I mean? You could never say this or that was Leon, not all the way."

She was quiet for a minute, looking at Shellburn's pad, wondering how it would all look written down. "Since he died," she said, "I get the feeling I didn't know him that well. It makes it lonelier, in a way, but things were beginning to straighten out. He had a lovely girl friend. . . ."

She saw Shellburn looking around the living room then, and then he spotted Leon's picture on the table beside the sofa. It wasn't the handsomest picture she had of him, but it was the one she liked to look at. He was sitting almost sideways from the camera, wearing a suit and a narrow black tie, smiling like he didn't have a care in the world.

"That one makes his ears look bigger than they were," she said. She stood up and brought him the picture. "There's others around. He had nice, even features." And saying that, she thought of her own.

He gave her the picture back. "Did he live here, with you?"

She said, "With me and my husband." Then, "Would you like to see his room?" He followed her up the stairs. He walked heavier than he was, she thought, like he was tired. She opened the door to Leon's room.

Shellburn said, "Did he have a cat?" She shook her head, and then she noticed the smell too.

"Leon didn't care for animals," she said. "Even when he was a little boy, he was always frightened of dogs and cats. I used to wish we could of lived in the country and had a few animals around so he could of gotten used to them. I think the country air would have been better for him. There's so many his age that already died of cancer, from right here in the neighborhood. It must be the air from the refineries, but then, people have to have jobs. . . ."

She was about to repeat the whole argument over the refineries that was argued every time somebody from the Pocket got cancer, but then she noticed that Richard Shellburn had stopped whatever he was doing and was standing beside Leon's unmade bed, staring at her. He'd completely changed channels.

"Mr. Shellburn?" she said. He didn't move. He had the exact complexion of a moth, and he was tired and sad at the same time. Mostly he looked sad. "Mr. Shellburn?" She reached out and touched his arm, and he sat down on the bed. And then he got her hands again, just like he had downstairs, and she let him have them. He looked so sad. He held her hands against his cheek, and began talking about a place by the water.

"I just came from there," he said, "this afternoon. There's a cove where the river empties into the bay, and a meadow above it. I've had it a long time, and nobody knows."

She sat down on the bed next to him. He let go of one of her hands, held onto the other one. She wasn't sure if this had something to do with Leon or not. "I go there at night sometimes," he said. "I drink too much and wake up there in the morning, with the birds coming in and things growing everywhere you look."

He was looking at her now to see if she was following his drift, and she gave him that too. "I know," she said.

154

"You do, don't you?" he said. And he let go of her hand and put his arms around her neck and pulled her into him. He was as soft as her sisters, and she could smell the alcohol in his skin. And it made her happy to sit there with him. Richard Shellburn, holding onto her for comfort. She had been with most kinds of men, but nobody ever acted like this. She didn't expect many did.

She put her hand down, as much for balance as anything else, and it rested on his leg, just above the knee. She smelled the alcohol and cats, and then they were lying back, and he was showing her the fall of the land by the water with his hand. "The house was going to be on the hill," he said, "where you could wake up in the morning and see the whole picture."

"I know," she said.

"I was just there this morning," he said. And then he held her a long time, lying on Leon's bed, and didn't say anything else. She felt him relax, and then sometime later she felt him pull himself together. Little movements in his shoulders and arms. Not muscles. He didn't have muscles the way Mickey did, and he didn't rub her with his dick or try to get his hands up under her skirt or in her blouse. He had an erection, she could see that, but he never tried anything. She thought it was part of how sad he was.

They'd been on the bed half an hour when she felt him moving, and then he sat up and blew air out of his mouth and felt his whiskers, and seemed to forget for a moment that she was there. It happened suddenly, and the skin where she had been against him felt cool and empty. She sat up and put one of her hands on his leg again. "You seem so sad," she said.

He blew again and stood up. His notebook was on the floor next to the bed, and he picked that up and began looking at the pages on top, flipping back through five or six of them. "I don't know what I can do yet," he said, like it was all connected to Leon after all. And then she heard the front door open downstairs, and Mickey walking into the house.

He called up the stairs. "Jeanie?" he said. "You up there?"

Richard Shellburn ran a hand through his hair and straightened his shirt. She walked to the top of the stairs and looked down. Mickey was filthy. "I'm up here with Richard Shellburn," she said.

She surprised herself, how natural that sounded.

Bird left the Cadillac outside the front window of the flower shop and walked in with his long, thin arm around Mickey's neck, and dropped all the money in his pockets on the counter, beside Aunt Sophie's eyeglasses. She'd left them there while she boxed corsages. The schools were having their dances this weekend, and it was busy.

She looked at the money, then she looked at Mickey to see if Bird had stuck up a Purolator truck to get it. Mickey smiled at her and pulled himself loose from Bird. "He go wacko?" she said.

Bird pulled the old lady toward him and kissed her head and her cheeks and her nose, leaving wet marks everywhere he went.

"Sometimes it works," Mickey told her.

Bird said, "I tried to get Mick to come with me on this horse, but he wouldn't listen."

"Nobody listens to crazy men," she said.

Bird hugged her again and said, "But they oughta. You listen to some of those old bums walkin' around on the street, talking to themself. They get like that, they *can see* somethin'." He picked up some of the money and held it in front of the old woman's face. "What do you see?" he said.

"That's very nice," she said.

"We're goin' to Florida," Bird said. "We're going to get out of here while all these people are fightin' each other over who does business. We'll get suntans."

"You going to leave your business, Arthur?" she said.

"We'll let Tony run it," he said. "I don't care. . . ."

"You be better off giving it to the nigger," she said. "Tony don't care about the business."

"Then we'll give it to the nigger," he said. The old woman began to smile. Arthur could be so funny. . . .

Mickey had to see Smilin' Jack. It was getting dark, and he didn't want to do it after Jack started to drink. "I'll see you tomorrow," he said, but Bird stopped him on the way back to the warehouse.

He stopped him and shook his hand, and embarrassed him. "You always got a place," he said. "No matter what happens, you always got a place to stay. You're like my own family."

The old woman told Arthur to pick up his money off the counter so she could finish her work, and then she walked Mickey back through the flowers to the door that led to the warehouse. She kissed him on the cheek and said, "You looked after Arthur good, Mickey. That's a nice boy, not to let him do nothin' crazy."

She turned on the lights in the warehouse and he walked through the meat cooler, and then out past the truck Bird hadn't given back, and got in his own truck. He didn't bother to check the load, it wasn't going to be his truck long enough to worry about.

The neon light was still on in the window at Moran's Funeral Home. Mickey found Jack in the viewing room, leaning against a dark pink casket and its contents, an old woman wearing a fluffy sort of dress that just missed matching the color of the box. Jack had loosened his tie and his shoelaces and was drinking a can of Rolling Rock, and he hadn't heard the front door when Mickey came in.

"Jack?"

He jumped away from the casket and spilled the beer down the front of his suit. "Jesus, God," he said, "you scared the piss outta me." He wiped at the beer, then noticed some of it had spilled over the woman in the box. He forgot about himself and took care of her. He wiped at it with his hand and then blew on it and then wiped at it with the handkerchief from his suit coat pocket. "You think this is going to stain?" he said.

Mickey looked at the woman closer. "I don't think so," he said.

"This shit's organdy," Jack said. "Fuckin' water stains organdy. . . ." Mickey waited while Jack worked on the dress. "You want to know the way this business is?" he said. "Right now, if the family walked in here, they'd think I was feelin' her up." Jack stood back and took another drink of the beer. "You suppose people are going to smell this shit on her?"

Mickey shrugged. "At an Irish funeral?" Jack thought it over and calmed down. He looked at the spots on the woman's dress from different angles, then he got down into the casket and blew on it again.

Mickey was waiting for the right moment to bring up the problem with Leon's funeral, but he saw there wasn't going to be one. "Jack," he said, "I got a problem with the money."

Smilin' Jack stopped blowing on the old woman's chest and came out of the casket as stiff as the old woman herself. He turned around and picked up his beer, which he'd put on the rim of the casket while he blew on her. "That's too bad," he said.

"It's nothin' permanent," Mickey said. "I was thinkin', if we could have the service, I could pay you in a couple weeks, a month tops. If I don't have it by then, I'd sell the truck. You know, it was just a bad time for it to happen."

Smilin' Jack finished the beer. "How come it's a bad time?" he said. "How much money you got?"

"Seven hundred."

Smilin' Jack threw the empty can into the wall over the casket. "What about the fuckin' money from the Hollywood?" he said. "There was more than seven hundred they collected there."

Mickey said, "Things happen. You'll get your money, but I got to have this funeral on time, and it's got to be right. The mahogany box, everything. Jeanie's all fucked up over this."

Jack said, "That's nothin' to me. It's your fuckin' woman and your fuckin' body unless I get paid." He was shouting.

Mickey closed his eyes. "Don't get hysterical," he said. "You ain't an old woman, and I don't want my business on the street."

"You ain't got no fuckin' business," Jack said. He was still shouting. "What you got is somethin' on the side, right? No, you bet a game. That's it, you bet a fuckin' game. . . ."

"What I did is nothin' to do with you," Mickey said. "What you got to worry about is makin' sure everything is right on Saturday. You'll get your money." He stood up and moved closer to him. Smilin' Jack relaxed and smiled the smile that sucker-punched Mole Ferrell.

"Sure, Mick," he said. Mickey saw Jack was going to hit him. He wondered how many beers he'd had, fixing up the old woman in the casket. "Sure," he said.

Mickey said, "Jack, put it out of your head. . . ."

Which Smilin' Jack took to mean Mickey was scared. He said, "What? What are you talkin' about?" He smiled again, then focused on Mickey's nose and then aimed a right hand that the old woman in the box would have ducked. Smilin' Jack followed the fist, stumbled, the word "motherfucker" stumbling out too, and Mickey grabbed his collar underneath his ear and kept him from falling. Then he straightened him up and slapped him across the face, harder than he meant to.

"This ain't the time to panic," he said. "You'll get paid in two weeks, a month at the outside." He held him and said, "You understand me, Jack?"

Jack's face was red and his eyes were watering and surprised. He shook his head. "Jesus," he said. "I don't know what's wrong with me. Me and the old man ain't been gettin' along, I don't know. Hey, let me get us a beer."

Mickey sat down and waited. He heard Jack bumping into things in back, opening doors, cleaning himself up. In five minutes he was back, holding a couple of cans of cold beer. "Yo, Mick," he said, "I was wrong. I don't know what's got into me. . . ." He touched Mickey's beer with his own, and they drank a long toast.

After that there wasn't much to say. "I'm sorry, Mick," Jack said.

Mickey said, "I just didn't want none of this on the street. Jeanie's all fucked up."

"Yo, we'll take care of it, don't worry about the money. . . ."

Mickey said, "I said you'll have it in two weeks, a month tops." Smilin' Jack leaned toward him and they touched beer cans again.

"You and me got no arguments, Mick," he said.

When the beer was gone, Smilin' Jack took Mickey to the side door, which opened to Lombard Street. "I hope you don't mind going out the side," he said. "I'm locked up in front."

Mickey said, "I don't mind nothin'." Jack opened the door and the light from inside threw their shadows across a square cement step, eight feet on a side. There was a railing around three sides of the step, and the fourth side, to the right as he went out the door, led to a ramp, wide enough to handle a coffin.

Jack said, "I got to get the light fixed out here."

Mickey said, "I don't mind," and stepped out the door. On the way out he had the feeling Jack was getting ready to sucker him again. But he walked past and nothing happened. The air was cooler than it had been when he'd gone in half an hour before, and it was beginning to mist. "It's gettin' cold," he said.

Jack said, "Yeah, it's a cold world," and shut the door. There was no handle on the outside. Mickey heard him on the other side, locking up. He put his hand on the railing and walked down the ramp. The railing was cold and wet, and he let go of it to shake the water off his hand, and that was when he stepped on Leon's leg and bounced the rest of the way to the sidewalk.

He knew it was Leon before he looked, he knew it before he hit the sidewalk. He tucked himself in as he fell, and if he hadn't grabbed the railing and snapped his elbow out of its socket, all he would have had for damages would have been his ear, which felt like it was floating in a pan of hot boiling water.

He sat up, holding the ear, and made himself breathe slow and even. He could hear his pulse in the ear and feel the elbow swelling. He moved his legs, one at a time, then his neck. Nothing else was hurt. The mist turned into a light rain.

He stood up and felt for the body. It was lying across the width of the ramp, face up, the arms folded across the chest. He started to slip and caught himself, his hand across Leon's face. He went from there down the front of his shirt and found his belt. He turned the body over and used the belt to lift him up off the ground. The body was stiff and awkward, the arms stayed close to the chest. There was an alley halfway between Twenty-sixth and Twenty-seventh, and Mickey took him there. He held the body as high as he could, but it was heavy and the head skipped on the sidewalk. He could not get rid of the feeling that there was something left in there.

He dropped Leon face down a few yards into the alley and flexed the hand he had used to carry him. The elbow on the other side was beginnng to hurt him more now, but he had torn it out before and knew what to expect. The ear was a surprise. That was on fire.

He turned the body over and then lifted it by the collar until it was almost standing against the wall. He heard cats farther back in the alley. He remembered Leon telling him he and his friends hunted cats when they were growing up. They'd used softball bats. He left Leon in the alley and went for the truck.

On the way, he stopped at the ramp and found a place where the railing was waist-high from the sidewalk. He pressed his chest into the railing, then reached through it with his good right arm, through and down, and touched his left hand. Without stopping or thinking it over, he lifted the hand slowly until the forearm was touching the rail. He was sweating now, hot and cold at the same time. He gave himself five seconds—not enough time for the pain to gather itself—and then lifted his left shoulder slow and steady against the railing, and at the same time he used his right hand to run his left hand over, until the palm was up. Finally, there was a popping noise in the joint, and the pain changed, took on a heat and steadied, and Mickey lowered his hand, slowly, and stepped away from the rail.

He put his hand in his pants pocket to protect the elbow and walked around the corner. It was eight o'clock, but in the rain the street was empty. In the rain, it could have been midnight.

Without stopping or thinking it over, he backed the truck into the mouth of the alley and left the engine running and the turn signals on. Leon had fallen and was lying next to the wall. The turn signals blinked yellow, and Mickey picked him up—clumsy now, working with only one hand—and dragged him toward the truck. Putting the elbow back together had left him weak, and he dragged the body, holding onto the collar, a length of his step at a time.

The truck lights blinked on and off Leon's face, orange and black, until it looked like he was crawling. It looked like that, and then it looked like somebody was taking flash pictures of Mickey disposing of the body. He dragged Leon to the truck and left him on the ground while he opened the door. There was a small light inside that ran off the generator. The sides of beef Bird had given him were still laid out in gauze wrapping over the back axle. He climbed in and moved two of them farther back. As he bent over, his elbow moved and settled, but he kept working, without stopping or thinking it over. He knew not to give it a chance to all gather up on him. He listened to the sound of his own breathing and felt his pulse in his ear.

It took a long time to make a place for Leon. He didn't know how long, it felt like half the night. Then he climbed out and picked Leon up one-handed, by the front of his shirt, until he was almost standing again, then leaned him back onto the floor of the truck. He got back in and dragged him to the spot he had cleared over the axle, between four sides of Kansas prime beef. He straightened Leon's hair—he didn't know why, but it seemed right—and then, after he'd looked at it a minute longer, he moved the hands so they looked a little neater on his chest.

Then he drove the two blocks to his house, put the truck in the garage, plugged in the generator, and locked the door. Before he walked in the house he tucked in his shirt and brushed off his pants. Then, without stopping or thinking it over, he went in and called for Jeanie.

He'd thought the place was empty at first, then somebody was moving upstairs. "Jeanie?" he said. And she came to the head of the stairs, and from her face he could see that he looked worse than he thought he did. He was about to tell her that it wasn't nothing, but she said something first.

She said, "I'm up here with Richard Shellburn," like that was the name of something that was supposed to be upstairs. A minute later the reporter was standing behind her, red-eyed and wrinkled, all out of focus. "He wanted to see Leon's room," she said. Her voice sounded weak; he thought she'd seen his arm. It was still swelling, and there was more heat in it all the time. But she came down the stairs without looking at it. In fact, without looking at him.

"Richard Shellburn," she said. "This is my husband."

Mickey didn't offer to shake hands. Shellburn was older than he looked in his picture. Older and grayer and messier. And afraid. Richard Shellburn wore that like a sandwich board. He was patting himself down now, looking for something.

He found it in his coat pocket, a reporter's notebook. He took it out and checked the top pages. Shellburn said, "I think that's all we need for now ..." and put the notebook back. Too fast. Jeanie walked him to the front door, and Mickey saw them looking at each other before he left. "There may be something that comes up," he said. "We may have to call you again."

Jeanie said, "Please do. This is all I've got to do." And she thanked him for coming. Mickey watched them from the bottom of the stairs, on the spot he'd been standing when Jeanie told him she was up there with Richard Shellburn.

She took the reporter's hand in both of hers and thanked him again. "If there's anything we can do ..." Then Shellburn nodded at Mickey without exactly looking at him, and stepped out the door. Jeanie watched him cross the street and get into a car, and then she turned back into her own house.

He was going to tell her there was a problem with the arrangements as soon as he got in the house. He didn't know how he was going to tell her, except he was going to do it without stopping or thinking it over, but then it was too late because Jeanie gave him one of those smiles she used for priests she

163

didn't know, and walked past him without even noticing his ear.

She sat down in the middle of the sofa, then dropped her head into one of the cushions and pulled her feet up and closed her eyes. "Jeanie?" he said, but she settled deeper into the couch, farther from him.

Mickey went upstairs and looked in the bathroom mirror. She should of noticed the ear. It was skinned, top to bottom, and torn about half an inch where it connected to his jaw. The blood from the tear had run in a thin path straight down his neck into his shirt. He found some alcohol in the cabinet, thrown in there a long time ago and hidden by years of accumulated makeup and perfume and shit for glossy hair.

When Jeanie was through using something, she didn't throw it away. She just quit using it.

He soaked a Kleenex in alcohol and cleaned the ear, starting with the edge and working in into all the ridges and nests in there. Then, slowly, he pulled his left hand out of his pocket. He unbuttoned his shirt and let it fall off the damaged arm. The inside of the elbow was dark red and turning blue, about half as big again as it had been the last time he'd seen it. When he leaned to turn on the bath water, the elbow moved, and the pain, now there was time for it, took him over. He closed his eyes and bent over the arm and thought of Leon in the truck, and Jeanie up here in the room with Richard Shellburn.

And now there was time, he let himself feel it. And then he was throwing up, wet-eyed and shaking, again and again, a long time after his stomach had given up the beer he'd drunk with Jack Moran. When it stopped he stood up, and stepped into the bath. He found some of her bubble bath on the edge of the tub and poured that over the water. The water was hot, and he was tired every way there was to be tired.

He lay down and the water took the weight out of his elbow, out of his chest. He closed his eyes and held on. It wouldn't be the same for her after it was all over, he knew that. She would wake up in the mornings different, and maybe she would look at him again, and maybe she wouldn't. He held on. He wanted to go downstairs where she was sleeping and give her something, or just be in the same room with her. He opened his eyes, and it was all weak. The bathroom looked different, he couldn't say how. The truck had looked different at first after old Daniel was gone too.

He wanted to give her something so bad it made him weak, and he saw that took away the thing she'd wanted him for.

And then there were two quick knocks and the door opened—before he had a chance—and Jeanie walked one step into the bathroom and stopped cold, staring at the bathtub where he was lying up to his chin in bubbles, crying like a baby.

She never said a word. She just turned around and walked out, and closed the door behind her.

It wasn't that she'd traded in her husband for Richard Shellburn. It was more like he'd deserted her. That was a good word for it. Deserted. Ever since what happened to Leon, Mickey wasn't there anymore. He never got near her. He was out in his truck or he was drinking. She'd told him something had happened to Leon, and he'd gone to deliver meat. It was more like he didn't know what to do than he didn't care, but it amounted to the same thing.

There was a time when his awkward way around her was nice—after all the others it was sweet, a man like a boy—but when she'd finally needed him for something, he'd been afraid to get near it. It wasn't just finding out what happened to Leon, but that would have done for starters.

She woke up on the couch, thinking about that. It was dark outside and she didn't know how long she'd been asleep. Her sisters hadn't come back, the house was quiet. Mickey was probably across the street at the Hollywood. It didn't seem to matter, he'd taken himself out of it. She thought of Richard Shellburn again and the strange way he'd held her. It was as new remembering it as when it happened. She wondered if the place in Maryland was real, he'd seemed so sad. . . .

She got up, wanting to look at herself in a mirror. She

wanted to see what Richard Shellburn had seen. And so she'd walked up the stairs to the bathroom, knocked—why hadn't he said he was in there?—and then walked in on him, like that. She might as well of found him dressed in nylons and high heels. The bathroom smelled like vomit, and she got out before she threw up too.

She got out and went down the stairs, and the phone rang. She had a feeling it was Richard Shellburn, and put something for him in her voice. "Hello?"

"Jeanie?" It wasn't the columnist, but it was somebody drunk.

"Yes."

"Lemme tell you some advice. Go ask your husband where Leon is."

She said, "Who is this?" It sounded like Jack Moran. "Jack?"

There was a pause at the other end, the sound of a beer opening. "I ain' sayin' who this is, but just do yourself one favor. Ask your husband where the body is." And then he hung up.

"Ask your husband where the body is."

It had that old, comfortable feel of tragedy. Leon was supposed to be at Jack Moran's, at least that's who had his suit. Then she remembered the cop. Eisenhower, like the president. He'd looked at her too. He was quieter about it than Richard Shellburn, but he liked her. She thought maybe Eisenhower had taken Leon somewhere to test him. The cops hadn't wanted to, but he said he'd look into it again. He hadn't wanted to, but he was the kind who would do what he said.

Yes, Eisenhower had taken Leon for tests. She didn't know why Jack Moran would be calling her up at this time of night to tell her something like that, except Jack Moran was an ugly drunk. She wanted to tell Mickey—no, she wanted to tell Richard Shellburn.

When she had to, Jeanie could be adjustable.

She heard the toilet flush, and then the sound of his footsteps, going into Leon's room. The phone rang again. "Did you

166

ask him?" She hung it up, then put the receiver under a pillow. It was quiet upstairs, and she went into the kitchen and made herself a cup of hot chocolate.

She wondered how it was Richard Shellburn had noticed her, with all the girls there were in Center City. Just their clothes made her feel too far behind to ever catch up, and made her not want to go there anymore.

Somehow, though, he'd looked past all of them and found his way to her house. And he'd laid down with her on a bed and held her, and told her about another place. She remembered the way he'd been and knew she was the only one he would tell.

She liked that. She liked it a ways better than walking in the bathroom and finding her husband—who'd never even say it if he had a headache before—crying in the bathtub. The hot chocolate made her sleepy, but she stayed in the kitchen. She didn't want to go upstairs.

She hadn't thought about Shellburn's looks. She guessed his face was handsome once, but he was beyond that now. He seemed so sad. He was older than Mickey, and his back and arms weren't hard, but Richard Shellburn was from some other place where that didn't have nothing to do with it. She'd been with most kinds of men; some of them gone to seed, but there was a difference between that and somebody who never had muscles. She reminded herself then that she hadn't traded in Mickey for the columnist. He'd deserted.

She fixed another cup of hot chocolate and sat for an hour in the kitchen, thinking about them, and then Joyce came in the door, carrying a sack of groceries, and Jeanie realized that it had been an hour and she hadn't thought about Leon once. She thought maybe she was making an adjustment.

She slept alone and woke up rested, the first time since Leon died. Joanie had moved back to her own house, Joyce had slept on the couch. The door connecting Leon's bedroom to the bathroom was open when she got up, and Mickey was gone.

She took a long bath, paying attention to her waist and her legs and her arms. She had skin like a girl. No family resemblances at all. She imagined how she would look to Richard Shellburn.

She stayed in the tub until the water turned cool, and then wrapped herself in a beach towel Mickey had bought her in Atlantic City. Then she did her eyes, using lighter shades than yesterday. Without knowing it, she painted herself happier. She began to hum. She brushed out her hair, watching how it fell over the line of her shoulders—a girl's hair, blowing on the beach at Atlantic City—and then she noticed a ball of Kleenex the size of a fist lying in the wastebasket, covered with dried blood. She had to look twice to see what it was.

Everything stopped. She dropped the brush in the sink and went into her bedroom, and put on the same underwear and dress she had worn the day before. There was something inside her—as ugly as a ball of dried blood—and it hadn't gone away. She'd thought it was gone, but it was there, and it frightened her.

She went downstairs and found Joyce in the kitchen eating waffles. "Mickey left early," her sister said. "It wasn't even light. Didn't say where he was going. . . ."

Jeanie sat down beside the telephone and dialed the number Eisenhower had left. The man who answered the phone was the one who'd called Monday and said Leon was dead.

"This is Mrs. Scarpato," she said. "Leon Hubbard's mother, and last night I received a phone call about my son."

"Slow down, slow down," he said. "You said your name was what?"

"This is Jeanie Scarpato. My son was Leon Hubbard."

"Oh," he said, "Mrs. Hubbard."

She looked at her sister and shook her head. "Last night I got a call about my son, that I should ask my husband where the body was."

The policeman said, "Do you have reason to believe your son has been harmed in some way?"

"This is Mrs. Scarpato," she said. "You talked to me Monday, on the telephone, and told me that my son Leon had been killed in a construction accident."

"Oh, the dead son. You should of said so. I thought it was somebody else. You know, we get a lot of calls come through AID and it helps if the complainant identifies themself."

She said, "Is Mr. Eisenhower coming in?"

He said, "*Officer* Eisenhower has been reassigned back to detectives."

She said, "Could you tell me if he had my son taken somewhere for tests?"

"Tests?" he said.

"To tell how he died," she said. She heard her voice shaking. "There was some question of how my son died. . . ."

"Well, I don't think he would of took him anywhere," he said. She could just see him looking under his desk. "If it was a homicide, the M.E. might still have him, but we don't take the bodies, ma'am. We're the investigative arm, and if there was some reason to take a body somewhere for tests, I can assure you Officer Eisenhower would of told me."

She left her number for Eisenhower and hung up the phone. It was inside her, ugly as dried blood, and she was afraid of it. She thought it must have been there every day of her life, a plug in some smooth surface inside her, and then Leon had died and pulled it loose, and let the light in behind it. In the light, all the familiar footings inside her turned out to be ledges. In the light, she could see the long drops, and it made her afraid even to breathe.

"Mickey seemed different this morning," Joyce was saying. "Like he was sorry now for how he acted." She fit the last piece of waffle into her mouth. "They're always sorry when it's too late." She put her fork across the plate and put the plate in the sink and ran cold water over it.

When she turned away from the sink, she saw Jeanie was getting ready to cry. "You've got to get used to it," she said.

"You don't know what it is," Jeanie said.

Her sister said, "You're not the only one ever had something

169

happened. At least it was a good, clean thing. He didn't get cancer and suffer all summer, like some of them from this neighborhood. Think how terrible that would of been."

Jeanie said, "I don't need to borrow grief from nobody." And then Joyce was putting on her coat, and deserting her too.

4

A NEWSPAPER ROMANCE

They came for Arthur early in the morning. Sophie recognized one of them from Monday morning. He was the man who had gone with Arthur and Mickey to steal the truck in New Jersey. He was wearing a very smart coat, although it would have looked better with a tie.

It was her habit to cut a carnation for Arthur's friends when they came to visit, but there was something about this man— even Monday there had been something—that you didn't want to pin a flower on him. He was quiet, but he wasn't shy. She liked shy men, now that she was older, but she hadn't ever liked men without manners.

It was Thursday morning, before the children started walking past the window on their way to school. The schools made the boys wear ties and the girls all had uniforms, different colors for different schools. She liked watching them on the way to school, except the ones who smoked. She did not think girls ought to be smoking cigarettes in Catholic school uniforms.

They came in, the man from Monday morning and another man, who was younger—just a baby, really—and bigger. She liked his haircut. She admired the size of their shoulders and backs and arms. They had been watching the shop, she knew because they came in right after Arthur. He was normal again when he came in, his hair combed nice, and he'd put on a nice smell. She thought any woman would be lucky to have Arthur when he was normal. He'd leaned over the counter to kiss her, and then gone into the back to take care of his business. He'd said, "Get your suntan lotion packed, Sophie, we're goin' to Disney World."

Nobody could make her smile like Arthur. He was in back two minutes when they came for him. The one from Monday morning came in first and looked from side to side, paying as much attention to her as the flower arrangements. The younger one came in behind and locked the front door. "Where is he?" said the one from Monday morning.

The younger one pulled the shade over the long window that ran the length of the door, and she stared at them in the darkened room and understood they were going to kill Arthur.

The one from Monday morning walked around the counter and knocked seventy corsage boxes off a card table in back. "You ought to be ashamed," she said. "This is how you do your business? Scaring old women?"

He pushed her out of the way and looked behind the curtain that hid the cashbox under the counter. "You going to steal my money too?" she said. "You going to do your filth and steal twenty dollars from an old woman too? Like the niggers?" Aunt Sophie did not think the men needed to know there was $30,000 in there.

The one from Monday morning said, "He's in back," and came around the counter. The younger one had already taken

172

the gun out of his belt, and now the one from Monday morning took his out too. It was a fancy gun with a wooden handle and a barrel that was so long and black it seemed a second behind the rest when he brought it around. He didn't need a barrel like that to kill Arthur.

The younger one said, "You want me to go around to the back?" The other one thought it over.

"Yeah," he said, "he can't run, but what the fuck? Take the back to make sure."

The old woman spoke to the one who was still a baby. She said, "You're so young, why would you want to hurt an old woman and her nephew?" He put the gun back in his pants and unbuttoned his coat. "Arthur takes care of me," she said. "If you hurt him, you might as well kill me too. Without him, who's going to take care of me?"

The young one went out the front door. She watched until the shade had stopped moving. "He's so young for this business," she said.

The man from Monday morning looked at her, for the first time. "If I was you, I'd shut my mouth," he said. "We can leave as much behind as we want to here."

She said, "He's hardly more than a baby."

The man from Monday morning said, "You keep that in mind, old woman." He looked at his watch, giving the other one time to get in back. "You just keep that in mind."

She saw he was getting ready to go into the back for Arthur now. "He never hurt you," she said. "He ain't in nobody's way. He'll do anything you want. Please, Arthur ain't no trouble, you don't have to do this. . . ."

The man from Monday looked at his watch again. It hadn't been very long, it couldn't be time yet. He pointed the gun at the old woman's face, but she never thought he meant to shoot her. "Remember what I said, missus. We're comin' back out this way in a minute."

She crossed herself, and he saw she was leaving it up to God. He turned his back, satisfied with that, and stepped toward the door to the meat locker. She saw him take the safety off, and noticed how relaxed he held the gun, like it was part of his hand.

And she reached through the curtain and found her own gun—a fifty-year-old revolver her husband had given her the first year they were married. It had never been fired. The man from Monday morning was at the door now, and she pointed the gun at the back of his head. The gun must have been about his age, and it seemed to her that it must have been there all that time, waiting for him. Like God had made one, and then the other to correct the mistake.

She held the gun in both hands and pulled at the trigger. Her husband had taught her to shoot, but it was a long, long time ago, she couldn't even remember where they went to practice, so she just pulled. It wasn't up to her anyway. It was moving by itself now, after all those quiet years, to meet him.

The noise when it went off shattered the glass door to the refrigerated box where she kept her roses. She thought it was the noise. The man from Monday morning turned around—he was ten feet from the roses—and his gun was coming back for her. She knew it was him, even though he didn't look the same. His eyes were bigger, for one thing. She wished she'd been wearing her glasses when they'd come in, and she wished the gun wasn't so loud.

Her ears were ringing. She couldn't hear herself shout to Arthur to run for his life.

The man from Monday morning must have thought she was talking to him because his gun stopped, and he took a step sideways, like he was going for the front door.

She jerked the trigger again, and the second shot caught him in the neck, right below the chin. She was sure. It threw him back into the wall, and she had to remind herself now who it was, because he didn't look anything like he had. And then he fired his own gun and blew out the other door to the flower box. She'd have to get the roses out of there right away.

Then Arthur came through the door, wacko again. He

stopped in the doorway and saw the man on the floor, and the blood sprayed all over the wall. And she thought from his face that he was going to lecture her that this was no way to run the business.

But he said, "Sophie, I swear I never thought it would come to nothin' like this," and then he began to shake. She took his hand and moved him out of the way.

"Just a minute, Arthur," she said. And then the door slammed open again and the young one came through with his big shoulders and his nice haircut and his baby face, and she shot him in the nose. The noise hung in the air with the smoke. "This one is so young," she said to Arthur. "Barely a baby."

But Arthur didn't seem to hear her. He was shaking and buggy-eyed, and then he went over and began to kick the man from Monday morning in the face. Screaming, "This is my family! You fuckin' hear me? My family. You fuck . . . you fuck . . . you fuck . . ." And every time he said that word, which she did not like used in her shop, he kicked the man in the face again. He did that until he was out of breath and sweating and his pants was all messed up with blood where he'd missed with his shoe.

When he quieted down, she said, "Go change your pants, Arthur. The police is coming."

He said, "I swear to Christ, Sophie, I didn't know nothin' like this was going to happen." He shook his head, looking at the mess on the floor, and she took him by the hand again and led him out the front door.

"Go change your pants," she said. "You got blood all over them, and the police is coming. You don't want nobody takin' pictures of you like that." But he stood in the doorway, looking back at the floor, shaking. She could feel it in his hand, and when she touched the back of his neck, she could feel it there too.

"Arthur," she said, "we ain't got time to go wacko. Not now." And she pushed him gently out the door and watched him to make sure he could still find the house. Then she picked up the phone and called the operator, and asked her to call the police and tell them two men had just tried to rob her flower shop. And then she went into the closet and found her broom and a dust-pan, and began sweeping up the pieces of glass.

The phone woke him up again Thursday morning, and he focused on it with one eye, as evil as he could make it, but it wouldn't stop. It rang seventeen times before he picked it up. Gertruda. "Mr. Davis wants to see you, Richard," she said.

Shellburn said, "I can't get my other eye open."

He'd gone from Leon Hubbard's house to a bar in Center City where, at eleven o'clock, he'd called the paper to say he wouldn't be writing for Thursday. He said he had some loose ends to tie up. He'd forgotten that and called again at two, and said he had the flu.

Gertruda said, "Mr. Davis wants to see you at ten-thirty. He was sure that's what time he wanted to see you."

Shellburn said, "Did it sound sexual?"

"Ten-thirty," she said, and hung up. He lay back in the pillow and closed his eye and thought about Jeanie Scarpato. When he'd been younger, Shellburn thought he understood temporary insanity. He would read those words together and think of the things he had done and the lies he had told, trying to get into somebody's pants. He knew what it was to give himself up for twenty minutes of a woman's time.

Twenty minutes. And then in the mornings he'd wake up with a woman he didn't know, and try to explain to her who he really was. And that was even crazier than the rest of it because, even if he could have done that, nobody wanted to hear it then.

And he would read how a garbage man had gone home and shot his wife and her mother and two neighbors, and he thought he understood how the garbage man might have felt, standing in front of a judge and jury trying to explain that it wasn't really him who'd done that, trying to explain who he really was.

Shellburn thought he understood that much of it, but he never understood the shooting. He wondered if that came up out of the same hole as going pussy-crazy. He followed those cases all the way through trial, looking for similarities.

Shortly after his marriage, he quit going pussy-crazy. He

didn't give it up, but he quit giving himself up. He thought about Jeanie Scarpato again and what had happened at her house. It wasn't like pussy-crazy, but there was something in that bedroom he wanted that bad.

He reached over his head for another pillow, thinking of the way she looked, and hugged it against his chest. It was soft and cool and fit him perfectly. Was it that easy?

He lay like that for an hour, and then his thoughts moved from God's Pocket to T. D. Davis and he got up, feeling better than he expected to, and took a shower. He stood under the water, wondering if T. D. Davis wanted him to write better or to quit. He didn't know if T. D. liked having him around.

For twenty years Shellburn had made his reputation reading strangers. He could walk into a neighborhood bar or a hospital room for half an hour and know who everybody was. Some of it, of course, was experience. Cops lied to you, firemen told you the truth. Lawyers were always full of shit. But there was more to it than that. Shellburn could pick up what people were to each other, and the balances that connected them, and that was where he looked to see who they were.

He was good at that in a bar full of strangers, but the older he got, the more he realized he couldn't do it with the people he knew.

The closer Shellburn got to anybody, the less he could read them. He didn't know, for instance, if Billy Deebol liked him or pretended to, or what Gertruda was thinking when she called him in the morning for T. D. Or what T. D. wanted from him. Shellburn had made his reputation reading people he didn't know, and he kept it to himself that he couldn't read the ones he did know. There was nobody close enough to tell that to anyway.

Maybe Jeanie Scarpato.

He dried himself in front of a steamed mirror and wrapped himself up to the armpits in the towel before he cleared a patch of the mirror to take a look. His eyes were red and he needed a shave, but Shellburn thought his color was better. He'd been gray a lot lately.

He came out of the bathroom, trailing water footprints,

thinking about calling her. It was just ten o'clock, though, and he decided to wait. He wasn't sure what to say yet, anyway. He dressed sitting on the mattress. Socks, shirt and pants. He had to lie down to get the pants on. He was still sweating from the shower, and the clothes stuck to his skin.

He stood up and went to the table where he'd thrown his pants over the typewriter when he'd come in last night. He got his wallet out of the back pocket, some folding money out of the front pocket. The change fell on the floor, quarters and dimes scattered over the room in a way that might have resembled the beginning of the universe. It wasn't ten o'clock in the morning, and he'd already discovered the big bang. The only question that mattered then was when the cleaning lady came in and swept it all up.

"Yes, I am still drunk," he said out loud.

He pulled into the office parking lot right at ten-thirty. The elevator was slow, so he was ten minutes late walking into T. D. Davis's office. He wasn't worried about the ten minutes, he wasn't worried about Davis. He was only slightly worried about Jeanie Scarpato's husband. He'd watched them together for two minutes, and that was more time than he'd needed. She looked right through him, and he looked at her like there was nothing else in the room.

A long ways down the road, he would feel bad about Mickey Scarpato.

He knocked once on the door before he went in. T. D. Davis was sitting beneath the torn picture of himself and Jackie Robinson. He had a copy of the *Daily Times* on the desk in front of him, opened to page 2.

Shellburn sat down without being invited to and looked across the desk. T. D. sighed. "I thought you was headin' over to God's Pocket," he said, "write us a column about that boy got killed in the accident."

"It needs more time," Shellburn said.

T. D. said, "I didn't see your column on page 2 today. I opened the paper and we got some goddamn picture of this girl

178

had her teeth wired together in Omaha to lose weight." Shellburn waited. "That ain't my idea of what our readers want to see on page 2 of the newspaper, Richard." Shellburn leaned forward to look at the girl in Omaha. She was smiling.

"Not over breakfast," he said.

"Have you been feelin' all right?" Davis said. "I looked at page 2 today and started to think there's been a lot of days you been missin'. Our readers count on you. They buy the paper for it, some of them, and then they turn to page 2 and see this fat girl in Nebraska smiling at them with a bunch of scum and shit stuck to her teeth." T. D. looked at the picture again.

"So I had Brookie look back over the last year, and you know, you missed forty-two days, not countin' vacations, Christmas and personal leave. I heard that and thought I better ask if you been feelin' all right, because if you haven't, then we got to get you to a doctor."

Shellburn said, "It just needs a little more time. There's some loose ends to tie up."

T. D. cut him off. "It's a daily job," he said. "Every day, 365 days a year. There ain't nothin' matters less than what you did yesterday."

Shellburn saw T. D. was coming to it now. "I been thinkin' about it, hoss," he said, "and the idea hit me that maybe we ought to bring in another columnist, you know, somebody to take the load off." T. D. watched him. "I don't mean like you, I was thinkin' maybe we ought to get us a woman columnist anyway."

Shellburn smiled at him.

"A lot of papers are doin' it," T. D. said. "Forty-five percent of our readership is women, and maybe we ought to give them something to read too. You know, from one of their own. Pussy diseases, rape clubs, like that. Even when you're workin', you don't speak to our average female reader."

"You going to run pussy disease on page 2?" Shellburn said.

T. D. shrugged. "It's been done," he said. "There's that girl

179

up in Boston does real well. We could run hers when you was sick, or we could take turns."

Shellburn said, "Did you find one yet?"

T. D. shook his head. "It ain't decided yet, hoss. I just thought I'd bring it up, you know, let you think it over." He leaned closer now, making a show of looking at Shellburn's face. "You sure you ain't sick? You don't look worth a shit."

Shellburn said, "I never been better."

"If you get sick, you ought to see somebody," T. D. said. "Ain't nobody gettin' any younger, and you've had the heart problem already. I don't want the *Daily Times* killin' you. That's partly why I was thinkin' about this female thing."

"Whatever you think," Shellburn said.

"There's one other thing," he said. "If it was a drinkin' problem . . ."

Shellburn shook his head. "No."

"Well, if it was, you know, we sent people up to Live 'n' Grin before to dry out. We could do it for you too. If that's what it turned out to be, it wouldn't have to be no public announcement."

"It's just loose ends," Shellburn said. He stood up, nodded at T. D., and headed out the door. When he got to Gertruda's desk, he turned around and said, "I told you and told you, T. D., I don't take it up the ass."

T. D. Davis sat still for fifteen minutes, looking at the chair on the other side of his desk. People didn't change, he knew that. Richard Shellburn was scared of dying and scared of having people find out where he lived and scared of losing his job. T. D. had seen him in the hospital after the heart attack, he'd gone in and talked to him for two minutes when he was scared back to his momma, and nothing Shellburn ever did would change that between them.

He sat and looked at the chair. *Something* had changed, though. He'd run it all by him, and Shellburn never blinked. Maybe he didn't believe him. T. D. remembered Jimmy White then, and those two-hundred-mile-an-hour eyes coming into the office behind the chain saw.

It was a long time afterward that he figured out that Jimmy White hadn't changed, he'd just never paid enough attention to who he was. He sat and looked at the empty chair and wondered if he'd paid enough attention to Richard Shellburn.

The first stop, Mickey had to make himself open it up. He parked in the alley behind the Two Street Tar and Feathers, a bar that didn't do a lot of business with colored people, and he'd gotten out of the cab, walked around to the back of the truck, and just stood there with the garbage, looking at the handles that opened the back end up.

He'd waited there until a couple of kids came by carrying one of those forty-pound radios, and stood at the mouth of the alley watching him. White kids, walking around on a school day with a radio like that. Mickey said, "How come you're not in school?"

The one holding the radio said, "We graduated." He might of been eleven. The neighborhood didn't need colored people, they was growing their own.

Mickey knew enough about kids not to tell them to go away. He said, "Lemme see your radio," and began to walk toward them. When he was ten feet away, they ran. They stopped once, half a block away, and called him a motherfucker. Mickey went back to the truck and made himself swing one of the back doors open. Leon was right where he'd left him.

His arms were folded over his chest, and there was some dirt on his suit. His face looked as sweet as an angel, only nicked a few places. Mickey stepped over him getting into the back, trying not to look, and then stepped over him again getting out. He couldn't get it out of his head that there was something left inside the body. He was carrying two ten-pound packages of steaks when he noticed the dirt on Leon's suit again and, against his will, he got a picture of Jeanie coming across the body and seeing that he hadn't even kept it clean. So he put the meat down and wiped at the trousers and coat. The dirt didn't brush off, but it did seem to spread out, and after a couple of minutes the coat looked the same all over, and Mickey picked up his meat, got out and shut the door, and it was that same relief as when the doc is finished examining your prostate.

The next stop was four blocks deeper into South Philadelphia, and there was no alley. He double-parked in front of the bar and climbed in and out without looking at Leon's face. It wasn't like a load of meat, but he thought he was getting used to it.

Mickey made six regular stops, put a little over $250 in his pocket, and then he started across the bridge to Jersey to talk to a couple of restaurants about the sides of beef.

He was halfway across when WFIL, country in the city, left off on Hank Williams, Jr., for a news bulletin. He reached for the button to find another station—there was enough news around without going out of your way looking for it—when he heard it was the flower shop.

"Details are still sketchy," the lady said, "but police are investigating two killings in a Philadelphia flower shop this morning that are believed to be mob-related. The two men were apparently killed in what was described by neighbors as a wild shootout about six-thirty this morning in the God's Pocket section of the city. Dead are Salvatore Cappi, forty-four, of Snyder Avenue in South Philadelphia, and William Tolli, twenty-four, of the Northeast. According to police, both men had been associates of local organized crime, belonging to the faction formerly headed by Phillip 'Chicken Man' Testa, who was killed last year in a bomb blast at his home. Police are talking to the owner of the shop—seventy-four-year-old Sophia Capezio—and her son, Arthur 'Bird' Capezio, fifty, who, according to police, is also a known associate of organized crime, but no arrest warrants have yet been issued. . . ."

Then the woman read the same history of Philadelphia's organized crime violence that they always read after somebody got shot, told who got found in a garbage sack and who got shot in his car and who got found with his dick and a wad of twenty-dollar bills in his mouth. Only they never mentioned it was a dick, they always said he'd been mutilated. Mickey heard the woman say mutilated and wondered if she knew what that meant.

He didn't think so. He thought somebody wrote it for her and she read it. He couldn't imagine a woman talking about something like that if she knew what it was.

He felt sad about Bird. As soon as he heard God's Pocket, he knew Bird was dead. Even if he got two of them this time—he wondered how that was possible, the way he'd been lately—they'd be coming for him. He thought about the $30,000 Bird made at Keystone, and how he'd said he was taking Aunt Sophie to Florida. But there wasn't anywhere in Florida for him now. Or if there was, Bird would never find it.

Mickey moved the tuner over to 1060, looking for KYW all-news radio. He knew a bartender in Queen's Village who sat around all day listening to KYW, the same news over and over. Twice a month he broke out in hives. He found the station just as they were finishing up the story. ". . . The seventy-four-year-old woman, who police say fired the fatal shots, has not been charged."

Well, it was a fucked-up world. He thought of Aunt Sophie and how strong her hands were for an old woman, and was sadder than he had been for Bird. She and Bird might get out of the city, but that was putting it off. It seemed like all any of them could do now—himself included—was put it off. It was an accident where they all were, but that wasn't nothing anybody wanted to hear. He wished he could tell that to Jeanie. Just say, "Lookit, if Leon doesn't get killed, none of this shit would of happened."

He wished he could tell her it wasn't his fault that he didn't look the same to her anymore. Somehow, though, the more it went on, the more it was his fault.

He drove past Camden into Cherry Hill to a place he knew just off the highway. The guys that owned it were brothers. One you couldn't talk to, the other one you could. The brothers never talked to each other.

The brother you could talk to was named Nicholas, and he

worked from noon to six. The brother you couldn't talk to was Stanley, and he came in at seven o'clock at night, when they opened for dinner, and ran things until closing. They left an hour between shifts, so they wouldn't have to look at each other. The place was called Brothers.

Mickey rang the bell in front, and Nicholas came to the door. He was short and bald and fat, and anytime you got near him you could hear him breathing. Mickey knew him from Garden State. Bird introduced him one afternoon and told him how he and his brother worked their business.

Mickey said, "Hey, Nick, you got a minute?"

Nicholas took his time, deciding. "I'm here," he said. "What do you want?" When the brothers divided up the business, they decided Stanley ought to run things at night, when the customers came in, because he had the clothes for it. Nicholas, though, had the personality.

"I got some meat," Mickey said. "I thought maybe you could use some meat."

Nicholas shook his head. "No," he said. "How much you got?"

"Seven sides, Kansas choice beef."

Nicholas shook his head. "No," he said. He was still standing on the other side of the door. "How much you want?"

Mickey shrugged. "A thousand," he said. "I ain't got time to fuck around with this." Nicholas opened the door and came out.

"You got it with you?" he said.

"Yeah. Lemme get you a side to take a look."

Nicholas said, "I can look at it in the truck."

"I got some other shit in there," Mickey said. Nicholas gave him a long look.

"I don't care what you got in your truck," he said. "I don't see nothin' but meat when I'm lookin' at meat."

Mickey said, "Let me pull one down and show it to you."

"Fuck it," Nicholas said. "I don't think I want in this." He started back into the restaurant and Mickey stopped him.

"All right," he said, "take a look. It's good beef, but the thing is . . ."

184

"I don't see nothin' but what I'm lookin' at," Nicholas said. "Anything else is your own business. I don't want to see it, I don't want to know about it." Mickey opened the door to the back end of the truck. He climbed in and then he turned around and gave Nicholas a hand up. The truck dropped under the new weight, and then the fat man was standing right next to him and Mickey couldn't hear him breathing.

His air came out all at once. "Look," Mickey said, "I'm just doin' a guy a favor. Don't pay no attention to that, it's nothing."

Nicholas said, "It's a fuckin' body." He leaned over and touched a leg, then moved up and touched the hand. "It's cold," he said.

"It's a refrigerated truck," Mickey said. "What do you think?" He knew he'd made a mistake. "What do you say, Nick? Can you take this off my hands, or what?" It was dark in the truck, but Mickey could see his face change. "The meat," he said. "I'm talkin' about the meat. Forget that."

The fat man touched the lapels of Leon's suit. "It's a cheap suit," he said. "What happened to him?"

"He died," Mickey said. "It's just doin' somebody a favor."

"What kind of a favor is that?" he said. "You takin' him out for some fresh air?" The fat man was touching Leon's shirt now. "I don't like this," he said. Then he stood up, without looking at the meat, and climbed out of the truck, sitting down first and then dropping the few inches to the ground. Mickey got down behind him.

"You can't go carryin' a stiff around in the back of a truck," Nicholas said. "You put me in a bad position. Because of you, I'm an assessory now."

Mickey said, "You ain't nothin' because you didn't see nothin' but the meat back there. It's dark in there, and all you did was look at the meat before you bought it."

Nicholas shook his head. "No," he said. "I ain't takin' that kind of meat. Who knows what sickness it could of got, ridin' back there with a human body?"

"Nicholas," he said, "the body's clean. It got cleaned up before I put it back there."

The fat man shook his head. "No," he said. "Shit, I'm already an assessory if I don't call the cops. They find the body back there and trace the meat, the first thing you know, the papers will be sayin' we're fuckin' cannibals over here. Can you see my point? You see what that kind of shit does to business?" He shook his head, walking away from the truck. "No," he said, "if you was to *give* me the beef, I still don't need that kind of trouble."

Mickey said, "All right. You was the one who wanted to see what was back there."

"I didn't want to see that," he said. He wiped the hand he'd touched Leon with against his pants, then smelled it. "I didn't want to see it, I didn't see it. I don't know nothin' about it, and you didn't come by today and knock on the door."

Mickey nodded. "There's one thing," he said. "You was the one who got back in there, nobody made you, and a couple of weeks go by and nothin' happens, I don't want to go into my stops and hear stories."

Nicholas held up his hands. "You think I'm going to tell this?"

He took the meat two other places in Jersey, but nobody wanted to see it. The place he knew in Moorestown, the man said, "I don't want nothin' to do with anything that don't come with receipts. I don't know who nobody is anymore." He drove from there to Berlin, and in Berlin they wouldn't even talk to him. By the time he got to Berlin, he knew it wasn't going to work.

All the way there and back, the story about the shootout at the flower shop was on the news. First they had the two guys dead, then they had one of them dead and one of them critical, and then they said Aunt Sophie had been hospitalized, and then they said there was two dead and Aunt Sophie was in police custody. They kept breaking into the show to say what they'd said before was wrong.

Finally he turned the radio off. It didn't matter where they had Bird and Aunt Sophie. For some people, there wasn't anyplace to go. He decided he'd sell the truck tomorrow, he knew a place in South Philly where they'd buy it. He wouldn't get what it was worth, but there'd be enough to put Leon in the ground. He thought he might go back to work for Dow Chemical, or he might catch on with Mayflower.

He thought about truck-stop whores and truck-stop coffee. Drinking eight cups of it, listening to the same shit he'd heard the day before, and the day before that; staying there because it was cold outside, or because sometimes you get tired of being alone in the cab. Or spooked. At night, you could forget where you were going, or why you were going there, or what you were pulling. Sometimes at night, you started to feel like there wasn't nothing connecting you to nothing else.

He remembered, for the fiftieth time that day, how she'd looked at the newspaper reporter when they'd come down from Leon's room. He wasn't nothing special. Mickey could see that, but she couldn't. People who were famous looked different to her. They shined. She'd told him that after she'd seen Tim McCarver buying clothes on Chestnut Street. She said he wasn't as big as she'd expected, but once she saw who it was he seemed to shine, like there was more light on him than anybody else.

Mickey had said, "Who is Tim McCarver?" It turned out he played baseball. For a while after that, she watched the Phillies' games on television. And anybody who'd come in, she'd tell them about seeing Tim McCarver buying clothes on Chestnut Street.

"At first," she'd say, "you wouldn't notice him, because he isn't as big as you think, but then he smiled and you've never seen nicer features, and he just seemed to . . . shine all over. He's much handsomer in person. . . ."

Every time she told it, he got better, which Mickey guessed had something to do with how famous people got famous in the first place. Richard Shellburn, of course, wasn't any Tim McCarver to look at. He was soft and sick-looking, and depressed. Mickey knew enough about Jeanie to guess she'd turned it around, though, made it into something artistic. He thought about Shellburn and was surprised to feel himself getting mad.

He'd took it for granted from the beginning that there wasn't any reason Jeanie picked him to marry. And for the last four days, watching her turn away, he took it for granted there wasn't any reason for that either. At least if there was, it was decided apart from anything he did. It'd scared him and worried him and had him thinking shit that grown men don't think, but it didn't make him mad. It was like getting mad at the weather.

But now he thought about it, why couldn't Shellburn stay in Center City to hunt pussy? There was every kind of woman in the world in Center City, and somebody famous could find one of his own. What was he doing, coming into his house to take what he had?

Of course, it wasn't really his house. He'd moved in with Jeanie and the kid. Maybe that's how Leon had seen him, somebody coming in to take what was his.

He drove the White Horse Pike all the way from Berlin back to Philly, content to stop at the lights and watch the afternoon traffic. He began to look at it different. It was only four days since Leon died, in a couple of weeks who could say what would happen? And if she ran off with the reporter, he might find somebody else. He'd got confidence living with her. Not enough to know what to say, like in a bar when there was two hundred hard dicks walking around trying to pick up women, but if he met somebody, maybe at a party . . . He thought of how that might go, but he was doing Jeanie all over again.

There was a hitchhiker on the highway just past the entrance to the high-speed line. She was young and round-faced, homely as an Idaho potato, and she had a guitar. Mickey pulled the truck into the right lane and then off the road. He looked in his rearview mirror, and when she didn't move he backed up to where she was.

Her hair was tied into an old-fashioned ponytail, and she watched until he had stopped before she moved toward the truck. To be that skinny, she had to be using a needle. She opened the door but didn't try to get in. "How far you going?" she said.

He said, "Philadelphia."

She nodded, looking over the truck like she was thinking of buying it. She had two earrings on each side, and the holes she'd drilled to hold them were red and infected-looking. Her fingernails were bit to hell, and the skin that puffed up over the top looked infected too.

"What part of Philly?" she said.

"South Philly," he said. "Where you goin'?"

"I don't know," she said. "New York."

He said, "Well, I can take you as far as Philly. You might catch a ride up 295, but I ain't got all day." Mickey didn't like people driving by thinking he was trying to pick up this skinny girl.

She looked at the cab and then she looked at him. She said, "I think I'll wait for somebody goin' farther than Philly." And then, before he could say anything else—not that he had anything else to say—she slammed the door and walked back to the place she had been before and stuck out her thumb.

He wondered what it was about him she didn't like. It wasn't the truck, if she didn't like trucks she wouldn't of opened the door. He watched the mirror for a break in the traffic, embarrassed, wanting to get away from her. The traffic was steady, though, and he sat there two minutes. Once she turned around, and when she saw he was still there she picked her guitar up and walked twenty yards farther away.

There wouldn't be nothing after Jeanie but what he paid for.

The front door was locked when he got home, and he went through his keys twice before he found the right one, thinking somewhere in the back of his head that she'd taken it away.

The house was empty, he closed the door and stepped in. He turned on the television and walked from the living room to the kitchen and got himself a Schmidt's and a cheese sandwich. The place was all right while he moved, but as soon as he stood still it felt like he'd broke in.

On the television they were showing pictures of the flower shop. There was a pool of blood just outside the door, broken glass. They brought the bodies out in green bags. Then they showed old pictures of Angelo Bruno, open-mouthed against the car window after they'd shot the back of his head off. And then Chickie Narducci, lying in the street next to his Buick, hit seven times and not even covered with a blanket, just lying out there while the kids and neighbors and reporters stood on the sidewalk and looked. And then they showed a snapshot of Chicken Man Testa, and then the front of his house after they blew it up.

Television loved blood on the sidewalk. The people that decided what went on the air, they were the same ones who'd stand out in the cold for an hour and a half looking at Chickie Narducci's body.

Mickey sat down. He put his sandwich in his lap and drank the beer. On the news, they said Aunt Sophie had been released and was not expected to be charged.

He took the phone off the table and put it in his lap, next to the sandwich, and called Smilin' Jack. Jack said, "Moran's Funeral Home," in that voice he used for business.

"Jack, this is Mickey."

"Oh?"

"Can we still do it Saturday? I'll have the money by tomorrow."

Jack Moran said, "How you going to get the money?"

"That's my business," he said. "I'm askin' if you can still do it Saturday. The mahogany box, everything."

"I got to have the money twenty-four hours in advance," he said.

Mickey said, "All right, I'll drop Leon off tonight. . . ."

"No," he said, "I don't want to see none of you again until after I see the money. Fool me once, shame on you. Fool me twice, shame on me."

"I never fooled you," Mickey said.

"You come into my place and slapped me around," he said. "You try to get over on me like I was some jerk-off. What the fuck did you expect?"

"Tomorrow afternoon," Mickey said. "One o'clock, maybe two," and he hung up. Then he ate his sandwich and waited for

Jeanie to come home, so he could tell her it was going to be all right.

He had called at noon and said they needed to talk. "Have you found something out?" she said. He said yes, but the way he said it, she knew it wasn't about Leon.

"I'll pick you up," he said. And she said yes.

Jeanie stood in front of the closet half an hour, pulling things out, putting them back. She took a skirt and two blouses with her into the bathroom and hung them from the towel rack, where she could look at them and make up her mind while she was in the tub. One of the blouses was a flat red, the other one was white. When she got out, the white one went back in the closet. She put on her makeup slowly, considering her eyes and the color of her skin as if she was seeing it all for the first time. She put perfume under her arms and in the creases beneath her breasts. She dressed and touched the line of her blouse from the side of her breast to her waist. It was the right blouse. He knocked on the door just as she got downstairs.

Richard Shellburn was moving better than he had last night. His hair was combed and his shirt was ironed. He didn't look as sad with his hair combed. He started the car and said, "Do you know who T. D. Davis is?"

She'd thought it was something to do with Leon at first.

"T. D. Davis is the kind that never comes right at you," he said. "When he wants you to know something bad, he goes around the edges and leaves you to find it in the middle."

She waited then for him to tell her something bad about Leon, but then he was talking about rape clubs and lady columnists. They'd driven out past the airport before she figured out that he was talking about somebody at the newspaper.

Twenty minutes later they were out of the airport traffic and riding south on I-95. He was still talking to her like she worked at the *Daily Times* and knew the people he knew. And something else too. He was talking like there was already something between them, like he'd decided to just skip two months. She didn't know that she liked that.

"Where are we going?" she said. He smiled at her then and reached across the seat to touch her hand. He had a soft hand, wet and heavy. She guessed it didn't make much difference what his hand felt like, because she put her other hand on top of his and squeezed. She was trusting something, she didn't know exactly what. Her sisters had moved out of the house now, Mickey might as well be on Easter Island.

"I wanted to show you the place," he said.

Half an hour later, they went past a sign that said Maryland welcomed safe drivers. He hadn't moved his hand an inch. They were on a two-lane road now, following a green tractor at fifteen miles an hour around curves and up and down hills. She had no idea what direction they were pointed.

"When I was little," she said, "my father used to take us to the shore in August. I never knew how he found his way, and I used to think if it wasn't for him, we'd never get back." She looked out the window. Cows, weeds, daisies. Brick farmhouses. "It all looks the same, doesn't it?" she said. "If you woke up out here alone, you'd never get back."

Shellburn moved his hand then, back to the steering wheel. "You wouldn't want to," he said.

They came to a bridge. The tractor crossed it and went straight. Shellburn turned right, onto a little dirt road on the other side. They rode beside a river for a few hundred yards. There were sailboats on the water and people sitting in them wearing sweaters and white hats. Jeanie thought of herself in a sailboat, then the trees got between them and the river and she thought about waking up lost in the country.

Shellburn covered her hand again. "Almost there," he said. She suddenly felt happy, and she wanted to tell him something true. It didn't matter what.

She said, "When you told me about this, I didn't know if it was real." He looked at her, but he didn't move his hand. "I thought it might of been something you made up. I mean, sometimes I still pretend I'm a dancer. I went to New York to study when I was younger, and sometimes I pretend I stayed there and got famous, and that's where I am."

Which was all a lie, except about wondering if the place was real. Jeanie Scarpato only pretended things that could happen, like her sisters dying. He put his arm around her shoulder then and pulled her closer. She fit herself into his side.

They went around more curves and then over one last hill, and then she saw the place he'd told her about. There were sailboats out on the water here too. It was all the way he'd said it, but she'd liked it better when it was a story.

"It's beautiful," she said.

He sat there with his arm around her looking out the window. Then he got out of the car. "C'mon," he said, "I'll show you where we'll put the house."

At least two months, he'd skipped. But she took his hand and slid over his seat, and came legs first out of the Continental. He took a blanket out of the trunk, then a straw basket. The price tag was still on the basket. She took his arm and went with him toward the water. The ground was soft, and the grass was deeper than it looked, and tougher. It caught at her feet, and once she stumbled. He walked beside her, limping and smiling, and by the time they'd gone fifty yards he'd broken a sweat.

Then he stopped, moved a few yards to the left, and pointed out over the trees and water.

"Right here," he said, breathing hard. "The living room goes right here." He looked at her, and she tried to think of something to say.

"It's a good view," she said.

He spread the blanket over the ground and put the basket in the middle of it and himself next to the basket. She sat down on the other side. He was wearing a tie and pants that hung off his legs like old skin.

"Sometimes it's like that for me too," he said. "I think about this place, and I'm not sure if it's real." He opened the basket and pulled out a bottle of French wine. The kind with a cork. Then he looked back into the basket, moving bottles, until he found the corkscrew. She saw three or four more bottles and a bag of potato chips. Paper cups. The tag on the basket said $9.95, and over that, Crown Liquors.

He sat pretzel-legged on the blanket with the bottle in one of the holes where his legs crossed, and pressed into it with the corkscrew. His hands shook, and she looked out over the water again and pictured herself in a sailboat and a white hat.

When she looked back at him, he'd taken the top of the cork out and pushed the rest down into the wine, where it floated in pieces on top. He took the stack of paper cups out then and filled two of them with the wine, handed one of them to her. She sipped at it, straining the bits of cork with her teeth, and by the time she took the cup away from her lips he was refilling his glass. "How would you like to wake up in the morning here?" he said.

"I wouldn't know where I was," she said. He laughed and touched her hand, and then he drank everything in his cup and filled it again. Somewhere off to the side she saw something move in the trees. "There's something over there," she said.

He rolled over on his elbow and looked. "Probably a deer," he said, and when he rolled back he put his hand on her ankle and then smoothed the skin on the back side of her calf. She saw the movement again, but when she turned to look, nothing was there.

"You don't have bears, do you?"

"Bears?" he said. "Jesus, wouldn't that be great?" He poured himself another cup of wine and freshened hers. This time she threw it down with him, mostly thinking about bears. "I'm fifty-three years old," he said after a while.

She said, "You don't look that old."

He said, "I'm fifty-three years old, and a whole city loves me." He laughed and she laughed with him. "Every day when I go to work there's letters from people who love me," he said. "People I never met. They want me to come to dinner or go out drinking or visit them in the Poconos."

"Do you go?" she said.

He shook his head. "Golf," he said. "They want me to play golf." He lay back on the blanket, resting the cup on his chest. "Sometimes I think I ought to take one of them up on it," he said. "Just bring a suitcase over and move in." As he spoke he found her leg with his hand again, moved it from her ankle up her calf. She had the feeling that he'd moved in on her, now that he mentioned it.

"How long do you think it would take to get tired of having a celebrity around?" he said.

"I don't know," she said. His hand had come up over the top of her knee, bringing the skirt with it. The skirt fell into her lap, Richard Shellburn was looking at the sky. She took a long drink of her wine and then brushed the hair back off his forehead. She left her hand there and said, "It's hard to believe it was only Monday Leon was alive."

He looked then and saw her legs were bare. "Time is a bad bastard," he said. "There's nothing else that works against you like time. It goes slow when you're where you don't belong and fast when you're comfortable. Are you comfortable here?"

"I think so," she said.

"And then, no matter what you're doing, there's another kind of time, keeping track. But it isn't to tell how far you've gone. It's to make sure you can't get any of it back."

Something moved again, farther up in the trees. A glimpse of brown, and then Richard Shellburn moved again. His hand slid from her knee all the way up her leg and stopped with one finger resting against her underwear. "Let me tell you about your husband," he said. She didn't want to hear Richard Shellburn tell her about Mickey, not with his hand on her pants. She wasn't sure she wanted to be with Richard Shellburn at all, but she was lost in this, and trusting something.

"Your husband," he said, "can put an air conditioner in the wall by himself, or pick up an engine block."

That was true, but she didn't say anything because she didn't want to get herself in any deeper. "And he sits in that bar across the street from your house, every night for two hours, talking with his pals, and when he comes home he doesn't say jack-shit." While he talked, she felt his finger slide under the elastic, and then he was touching her clitoris. Not moving, just touching it. She wasn't sure Mickey knew it was there.

"He can take the air conditioner apart and put it back together," he said, "because he knows all the parts. That's what he understands, air conditioners and engine blocks."

He slid the finger down her clitoris and found her lips, and circled them once just inside the rim. She knew she was wet. He took the hand out of her pants and sat up. Then he filled their cups, touched his to hers, and drank throwing his head back, throwing something away. And she threw hers away too. He pulled her down, on her back, and she let him. She saw a cloud pass over the sun, and then his face was over hers, so close then that it could have been Mickey or Tom Hubbard, or any of the ones in between, and then his hand was back between her legs, with more purpose now, and she was trusting. She was trusting him to take her back after he was finished.

She felt him push inside her and closed her eyes, and then couldn't open them, because he was all over her eyelids, kissing her. He had a nice touch, though. He moved in and out slower than Mickey, like he had a reason for it besides happening to be there, and he wasn't in a hurry to get somewhere else.

A few minutes later he pulled her hand down between them. She thought he wanted her to hold his balls, but when she reached for them he stopped her. He pulled himself off her chest, far enough for her to see his face, and put her hand on her clitoris. "What?" she said.

"You know what," he said. She could feel his cock and his eyes, and she began to move her finger. She closed her eyes again. It wasn't something she wanted to see. It moved her, though, farther away from Mickey, from Leon. She was trusting.

She felt him begin to tighten just as she came. And when he yelled, she thought at first it was just the way writers made love.

• • •

196

Shellburn had gone from T. D.'s office to the fourteenth floor and called her from there. Then he went to a liquor store just across the bridge in Camden, New Jersey, and bought four bottles of sixteen-dollar wine—which was the best wine they had in Camden—along with some cups and potato chips and the basket. He saw the basket and knew it was going to be perfect.

He came back across the bridge and picked her up. The daylight didn't spoil her looks. Some women got out in the sun and looked so healthy, in two minutes they had you thinking what you'd done to your liver. Jeanie wasn't like that, and he drove out past the airport toward Maryland, explaining about his job. That's how he told her who he was.

He took it a step at a time, and she understood. Sometimes she didn't say anything for ten and fifteen minutes at a time, and he liked that. She was putting it together. And he liked it when she told him in the car that she wasn't sure the place in Maryland was really a place in Maryland, and not something he'd made up. It was something he'd made up, until he'd seen it.

They came over the last hill and saw the cove, and she didn't say anything at first, just put it together, and when she spoke, it was simple and perfect. "It's beautiful," she said. He thought he would like to write a column that ended just that way. *"It's beautiful," she said.* He couldn't think what the story would be about.

And she went with him into the field, not pushing him, not having to be pushed. She had no motives. She showed him her legs—dancer's legs—and he slid his finger up under her panties, and the hair was soft and pressed flat against her, no tangles as his finger went through it. And she never pushed him, or had to be pushed. It was like she'd expected him.

He pulled her panties off one foot. Pale blue panties with little white edges, ruffled. Panties like that didn't come wrapped together in threes at J. C. Penney. He'd seen the bill that came to his wife one month from Nan Duskin. He thought of Jeanie living in the place she did, with the kind of husband she had, spending that kind of money on panties, and it broke his heart. Shellburn was touched by her underwear.

He pulled his own down with his trousers, until he felt the cool air on his bottom, and then settled on top of her and pushed his way inside her, taking an inch, giving back an inch, taking an inch and a half. He moved slowly and kissed her eyes and her lips and her ears.

She got wetter as it went on, and each time he pulled out of her the air touched his dick and cooled it, and it would feel that much warmer when he went back in.

And then he pulled back off her and put her hand on her clitoris, trying to hold her eyes with his. She'd closed her eyes, though, and her mouth had opened. A thin line of spit went from her front teeth to her lower lip, and she had begun to breathe harder, and as he watched that happen, his own breath came harder, and she rode up into him, meeting him, and then just as she began to shudder, the collie sneezed in his ass.

It took a few seconds to realize what it was. He hadn't seen it when Jeanie said something was moving in the trees, and he hadn't heard it come up behind him, even though it was wearing a choke collar and tags for rabies inoculations. There was, when he thought back on it, one warm blow of air, and then a lick—it was as much a question as a lick—that touched him dead in the crack of the ass. He jumped—he may have screamed—and came completely out of Jeanie Scarpato, and then rolled over onto his back, holding onto his bottom like he'd been shot. The collie dropped to its elbows and made that noise they make when they want to play. He was black-and-white and square, and there was mud hanging from the clumps of matted hair hanging off his edges, and leaves and Jesus knew what kind of other shit hanging from the mud.

"Get out of here," Shellburn said. Jeanie was sitting up, reaching for her blue-and-white lace panties. The dog ran close to the ground, doing a tight figure eight that ended where it had started, back in front of them. He had a head like a Concorde jet, and his mouth was bubbling out on both sides. Shellburn said, "Go on, boy," but the dog had seen the cup on the blanket next to him, and he took a step closer to put his nose inside it.

198

Shellburn let him. Jeanie had her pants back on and was edging away, making no sudden moves. "He won't hurt you," Shellburn said.

"He must be lost," she said.

He tried to protect the afternoon. "No, there's a farmhouse half a mile over that hill. . . ." He pointed over her shoulder, away from the water. He didn't want her thinking about anything lost. The collie liked what was in the cup. Shellburn watched him splash little drops of it up on his muzzle and his head while he drank. "He's probably just out having a look around."

"I thought he bit you," she said.

When the dog had finished the cup, Shellburn filled it again, and found new ones for himself and Jeanie, and filled them too. She took the drink but kept an eye on the dog. Shellburn reached out and patted the collie's narrow head. Then he saw the uncomfortable way Jeanie was sitting, and he patted her too.

"There'll be plenty of other times," he said.

He leaned over to kiss her cheek, and his trousers dropped off his hips to his knees. The collie looked up from his wine. Shellburn pulled his pants back up and fastened the belt. The dog went back to his cup.

Jeanie said, "I think I better get back," and the afternoon was out of step.

"It's my fault," he said, not wanting her to blame the place.

"It's a bad time," she said. "There's too much left to do at home."

Shellburn poured the collie a last round and collected the basket and the blanket. She straightened herself and he admired the flat drop of her stomach and the way her blouse clung to her sides. He thought of how warm she'd felt, but she was all business now. On the way to the car he stopped at the top of the hill and looked out over the cove. "You're right," he said, "it is beautiful," but she'd already opened the car door and was getting in.

The trip back was like the trip down, except when she didn't talk he worried about what she was thinking. She sat still in her seat looking out the window, and about halfway back Shellburn had the feeling it might be hard to talk her into coming back.

Mickey woke up when she slammed the car door. It was dark outside. He sat up in the chair, she came in the front door. He heard the car going up the street. A heavy car.

She jumped when she saw him. "It's going to be all right," he said. She didn't know what he was talking about.

"Leon's back at Jack Moran's," he said. "We'll have the funeral Saturday afternoon." He saw he was going too fast. "The services. We'll get it all over Saturday." She stumbled kicking off her shoes, he stood where he was. "It's going to be all right," he said.

She smiled at him and started up the stairs. He followed her, keeping the same distance. "That reporter ain't going to help nothin'," he said. "When he gets what he wants, he'll forget about you."

She stopped on the steps and turned around. He thought for a second that she was going to tell him that Richard Shellburn cared about the common man, but she just stood there looking. "It's going to be all right," he said. She went the rest of the way upstairs and into the bathroom. He heard the bath water running, and then it was quiet. It was quiet a long time.

When the phone woke him up, he was in the chair again. He didn't remember sitting down. There was a blanket over him, and a different kind of quiet upstairs. She was asleep, but she'd come down and covered him with a blanket. He got to the phone on the fourth ring, and from there he could see into the kitchen where there was a clock on the wall. It was two-thirty.

"Yeah?"

"Mick? It's Bird." He was whispering.

"Where are you?"

"I'm home," Bird said, "and Sophie's packin'. Askin' do I need what color socks. You should of seen it, Mick."

"I heard about it," Mickey said. "How the fuck did she get them?"

200

"I don't know," Bird said. "When I got out there the one asshole was already in pieces. It was the guy went with us to Jersey Monday."

"Yeah."

"Well, when I got there he was already down. I didn't even know she kept that fuckin' thing loaded. They was hollowpoints, too. They had to be. I got there, she moves me out of the way and points it at the door and waits, and sure as shit, a minute later this other guy comes runnin' through and she blows a piece of his head off. A major piece."

"What the fuck?" Mickey said. "They goin' to whack the whole world?"

"I don't know," Bird said. "With these people, they could whack babies for cryin'. We're leavin' in a couple minutes, I ain't going to make it easy for them. Me and Sophie are gettin' in the Cadillac and headin' south."

"Where?"

"Don't tell nobody this, make them find us."

"What do you think?" Mickey said. "I'm going to give you up?"

"I mean nobody. Not even Jeanie. We're goin' down to Palatka, Florida, which nobody ever heard of. They got a trailer park there, a bunch of old people like Sophie. A river. Did you know the St. Johns River is one of only two rivers in the country that flows north? It's very interesting."

"What the fuck are you talkin' about?"

"If that don't work out," Bird said, "we can try Miami, get lost down there in the Jews and the Cubans. Whatever, we gotta get out of here. I ain't going to help 'em." Mickey thought of Bird in Florida, coming out of the trailer in the morning to watch a river flow north.

"Did they say anything?"

"They didn't get much of a chance," Bird said. The connection went quiet then, while they thought of waiting it out in Florida. Then Bird said, "Lissen to me, Mick. If you need a place to stay, you can always come to Palatka."

"Good," he said.

"Only don't sneak up on Sophie. She's probably up there puttin' notches in the handle right now. Jesus, Mick, you should of seen her."

"And the people, they didn't say nothin'?"

Then Bird was talking to Aunt Sophie about what sweaters he wanted her to pack. "The last trip she took, she come to America," he said when he was talking to Mickey again. "No, Soph, I don't need no red pants. . . . Hey, Mick, I got to go."

And then the connection went dead, too fast, before Mickey agreed to it, and he sat in the living room looking at the phone. And the house seemed emptier than it had before.

He slept in Leon's room again. He got up at nine, Jeanie was still asleep, buried in a pile of pillows and blond hair. He brushed his teeth and washed his face and waited until he was downstairs to put his shoes on. The next time she saw him, he wanted it all done.

He drove by the flower shop on the way to Little Eddie's Automotive Emporium. He could still see flowers through the window, but the whole place had been roped off by the police, and there were barricades all around the front that said CRIME SCENE—DO NOT ENTER. There were cops inside. The first thing cops did after a shoot was see how many guys they could get in the room where it happened, and they stayed until they got another room somewhere else.

The Cadillac was gone, Bird and Sophie with it. The cops would be going through their place across the street soon, trying to find them. Palatka. Mickey shook his head, thinking Bird must have found it in one of the geography books lying around the warehouse.

"One of only two rivers in the country that runs north. It's very interesting."

The cops would be back in the warehouse now, trying to put his business together. Mickey wasn't worried that Bird kept records, but he had to get rid of the meat today anyway. He'd thought of one other restaurant, over by the Italian Market, where he knew a bar manager, and planned to stop there after he made the deal for the truck. If they didn't want it there, he'd give it to somebody old.

Little Eddie's Automotive Emporium sat in a gap between two lines of row houses near Third Street and Emily. He had thirty-five cars on the lot and one colored man that was supposed to keep them all shiny. His office was eight feet square, and there was a deer head on one wall and a deer's ass on the other. Little Eddie was close to eight feet square himself. Between deer parts was a sign that said 1/3 DOWN and above that one that said BUYERS ARE LIARS. People who knew them both from the old neighborhood said Little Eddie was funnier than Joey Bishop, and could of been that famous if he'd got a break.

Mickey left the truck on the street where he could see it and went in. "Hey, Mick," Eddie said, "you come to sell me your truck?" Whenever somebody bought a new car, Little Eddie would try to buy it from them for four hundred dollars. That was one of the ways he was humorous. He'd seen Mickey's truck the week he bought it, at a bar where he was making a delivery. "Lemme buy that truck off you," he'd said. "What's somethin' like that worth?"

The truck was $19,000, but Mickey didn't tell him. "I'll give you four hundred, right now," he'd said, and the whole bar laughed. Every time he saw Mickey after that, he asked about the truck. He'd say, "You takin' care of my truck?" Every single time.

Mickey looked around the office now, smiling. "Yeah," he said. "I need to get rid of it."

Little Eddie's face changed. "What's wrong with it?" he said.

"Nothin'. It's a temporary financial problem." Eddie stood halfway up and looked past Mickey to the street.

"What'd you pay for that?" he said. Mickey pulled out the bill of sale. Eddie whistled. "They seen you comin', didn't they?"

Mickey didn't mind. "What can you do?" he said.

Little Eddie shook his head and looked troubled. He lit a cigarette and said, "I don't know where I'd get rid of somethin' like that, Mick. It's specialized, and what I got here is a young-couples/singles–oriented operation."

Mickey shrugged. Everybody he knew, they changed when they did business. Bird had told him once that it didn't mean nothing, it's what business was. Mickey never saw why you couldn't be one way all the time. If you changed, then something was wrong one place or the other, maybe both.

"What can you do?" he said.

Little Eddie looked out the window again. "There's nothin' wrong with it?"

"It's got eight thousand miles," Mickey said. "I changed the oil twice already, kept it in the garage. Here, start it." He handed Little Eddie his keys, three pounds of them, holding onto the one that would start the truck. Little Eddie got out of his chair and went to the door. He had a layer of loose fat like a bear that was always a little behind whatever he did. He called the colored man, who was running an electric buffer over a six-year-old Camaro. His name was Stretch.

Eddie watched him put the buffer down and start toward the office. "That is the slowest nigger God ever put on the face of the earth," he said. "Sometimes I think he made the rest of them faster than us to make up for him." Mickey didn't like the way Little Eddie said "nigger." Some people could say it careless, like it was just a word—which it was—and some people made it an insult.

"He can start it," Mickey said, "but I don't want him takin' it out." Something crossed Little Eddie's face. "I got some stuff in the back," Mickey said.

Little Eddie gave the keys to Stretch, talked to him a minute, and then closed the door. He sat back down behind his desk. Mickey saw his chair was a couch somebody had sawed in half. "I'll tell you the truth," Eddie said, "this is a motherfucker, this business. Sometimes I wonder what the fuck am I doin' here. The nigger's makin' more money than me, and he can't keep up. The cars look like shit. The kids come in, they know I ain't going to get into any fuckin' car for a test ride, so they say they want to see this car or that car, and you got to let them look, right? How are you going to sell somethin' if you don't let nobody see it?

"So you give them the keys and they're gone for half the day, and when they bring it back it's got French fries and beer cans all over the floor, they burned half the oil out of the engine. You know what I mean here? Somebody's always tryin' to get over on you."

Outside, the colored man started the truck.

Little Eddie opened a desk drawer and found his truck book. "What's that, an eighty-two?" he said.

"Yeah, it's six months old." Little Eddie ran his finger down a list of trucks.

"I had this idea," Eddie said, "to open up at night. Maybe seven, eight o'clock, after the sun goes down. Cars look better when the sun goes down. You don't have to keep tellin' the nigger he missed this or that, 'cause most of it you can't see at night anyway. What do you think?"

Mickey said, "What's the book say?"

"I might be able to get rid of it for you," he said. "I'd have to make a couple of calls, you know. If it's all right, I might get you seven and a half, eight. . . ." He shook his head. "It's a bad time of year. Business stinks in spring, Mick. Everybody's thinkin' about pussy. I'm tellin' you the truth."

Outside, Stretch was revving the engine. Mickey was sitting with his back to the window, watching Little Eddie, so he didn't see it when the truck pulled out in front of a SEPTA bus and started north up Third Street. Little Eddie was talking about doing his business at night again, and suddenly Mickey noticed the sound of the engine was gone. He turned in his chair to see if Stretch was finished.

Little Eddie said, "He's just takin' it around the block once, make sure everything works." Mickey was on his feet, moving toward the door. "Hey, he'll be back in a minute. . . ."

He ran out the door and looked up Third Street. The truck was a block ahead, stopped in front of the bus. Little Eddie came out of the office. He said, "I can't buy no truck without takin' it out for a drive, Mickey. You know that. . . ."

Mickey started after it. It'd been fifteen or twenty years since he ran anywhere but to keep something from falling, and then only if there was somebody underneath it. Running hadn't felt dignified ever since he started working for himself, and he'd started that when he was a boy. It was something he'd never thought about much, and then one year every time you looked out the window, there was some guy forty-seven years old, in new sneakers and a faggot-colored headband, moving up the street half a mile an hour with this glazed look on his face.

Mickey Scarpato was never swept up in the jogging craze. Jeanie, back when it was all right to talk to him, had said once that he was scared to be trendy.

He hadn't run for fifteen or twenty years, and he'd forgot what it was like. Toward the end of the first block it began to come back to him. There was a jolt every time his foot hit the cement. It went right to his head. His arms were tight and uncomfortable and every five steps there was something to get out of the way of. A school kid, a dog, a garbage can. There were uneven places in the sidewalk.

He was closing in on the truck. It was still sitting at the stop sign, in front of the bus, but just as he got there the traffic began to move again, and then he was running in a cloud of diesel smoke, and the truck was out a block in front of him again. He could see the bus driver's face in his mirror, smiling. He must of thought Mickey was trying to get on.

He kept running, dodging kids and garbage cans, people watching him from their steps. The jolts when his feet hit the cement had changed. They weren't getting to his head now, they all stopped in his chest. Two blocks, and it already hurt to breathe.

The truck was still a block ahead of him. Stretch had his arm hanging straight down from the window, and Mickey could see his head moving up and down with the radio. A block farther—between Tasket and Moore—they were throwing a family out into the street. A woman was crying, holding a five- or six-year-old child, and two men were putting her furniture on the sidewalk, trying not to look at her as they worked.

Mickey was watching Stretch bebopping in the window of his truck and didn't notice the woman and her furniture until he was almost on top of her. He hit a chair, missed a chair, jumped over a television set. Then he had to step on a bed, to keep from falling, and on the other side of it there was a sofa with cigarette burns in the cushions. He stepped on that too, and the woman began to cry "Stop" over and over. He didn't know who she meant, but he knew how she felt.

Jumping the television set killed half of what he had left. He thought of Jeanie and what was in the back of the truck, and pushed himself up the street. He thought of Stretch going into a parking lot somewhere and opening it up. The woman with the furniture was still crying.

He moved into the street. There was less to run into there. His lungs seemed to be cramping up. They wouldn't hold what they would before, anyway. He wondered if he had that glazed look yet that he'd seen on joggers.

The streets went by. Reed, Wharton, Federal. There was a stoplight at Washington, and that's where Stretch saw him. He'd glanced into the outside mirror, and then he'd turned around and looked out the window. Mickey was soaked with sweat, his eyes were burning, his hands were balled into fists. He wanted to tell him, "I ain't mad, I'm runnin'," but Stretch ran the red light to get away.

Mickey passed the bus and crossed Washington. The people inside looked down at him, smiling. It took seventy-five cents and a window seat to look down on him then, but it could of been anybody else. It was just a matter of when it was your turn. He was closed off now from the noises of the street, all he could hear was his own noises. And they sounded like a choir, singing, "On the road again . . ." Just those words, over and over. He could not make them sing the rest of the song.

Stretch stopped at Carpenter and put his head out the window again. He was in back of a tow truck now, and Mickey closed the distance again. At Christian he was a half a block away, at Catherine a hundred yards. When the truck stopped at Fitzwater, he could almost touch it. The street began to sway. Mickey saw Stretch blowing the horn at the tow truck, looking back like he was cornered. Not panicked, just beat and ready to give up. Then the tow truck moved and Mickey stumbled.

He didn't try to stop the fall, he'd lost the feeling in his legs anyway. He covered his head with his arms and rolled. The street was softer than it looked. He hit something hard—there was a crash and a shattering sound, almost like glass breaking—and then he stopped.

He didn't try to move, he didn't even open his eyes. He lay in the street, and the voices were singing "Oh, Jeanie . . ." over and over, instead of "On the road again."

A minute passed, nobody came. He opened his eyes and saw that he was lying against a tire. The traffic had stopped. He sat up, looking around. The tire was bald and it belonged to an old Ford station wagon. He grabbed a door handle and pulled himself up. His legs were trembling, he still couldn't breathe and he felt sick to his stomach.

There was a kid in the station wagon, sitting in a car seat in the back. He was a cute kid, four or five years old, blond. He looked at Mickey for half a minute and began to scream.

Someplace else there was screaming too. The knees of his pants were torn and he'd scraped the skin off his elbow, the same one he'd separated falling over Leon. Alive, Leon was a pain in the ass; dead, he was killing him. There was another scream up ahead.

Mickey stood up straight enough to see over the traffic, which was stopped now. He'd thought at first they'd stopped for him, but when he saw he wasn't run over or dying, he knew that didn't make sense. He saw his truck then. It took a minute to recognize it because he'd never looked at it from underneath before. It was lying on its side on Fitzwater Street. People were closing in on it from all over. The back was caved in and there was a bus stopped near it on the sidewalk, pointed almost the same direction. The corner of the bus where the side met the front was folded in on itself and flat. One of the truck tires was still moving.

He took a step and almost fell. His legs were on their own. He tried again, holding onto parked cars, and made his way fifty or sixty feet closer to the accident.

He was that far when he saw the back door of the truck had come open in the accident. People were passing him from behind, trying to get closer. He moved a step at a time. Sides of beef were scattered all over the street. People were dragging them into their houses, trying to get them into their cars. There was a fist-fight starting over by the bus. "This is my motherfuckin' meat," one of them said. The other one said, "I got here the same time as you," and threw a right hand from nine feet away.

Mickey watched them circle each other, and the meat, neither one of them letting the other one get closer to it. They threw jabs and right hands, but they never got close enough to land. "Motherfucker, you're going to get killed," one of them said.

Mickey felt himself coming back. His breathing smoothed out, it looked like he wasn't going to throw up. He heard sirens, a long way off, and honking from the direction he had come. He hit the front of his thighs, trying to get them to stop shaking.

He took a few more steps forward, until he was standing in the intersection. From there, he could see all of it. He could see fights starting in two other places, he could see old Stretch sitting against a wall across the street, bleeding from the head, staring at a circle of people—mostly kids—right in front of him. The screaming was coming from there.

Mickey took a step, and just then a girl who had been standing in the circle broke out, covering her mouth with her hand, and ran up the sidewalk. The circle broke and then mended, but in the second that took, Mickey saw what was inside it.

One of them said, "Where the fuck did he think he was, in a suit like that?"

It took the police about fifteen minutes to come, and by the time they did the only meat left on the street was Leon. They came in three cars and pushed people away from the body, and then one of them, a little one with a clipboard, walked around the circle of people, asking if anybody had seen which vehicle had hit the victim, or knew who he was. He looked like one of the cops come by to see Jeanie.

Nobody knew nobody that wore clothes like that. The bus driver said he wasn't talking to nobody until he'd talked to his union rep, and Stretch was too dazed to talk. The little cop looked around and then walked right to the corner where Mickey was standing, until he was close enough so Mickey could read his name tag. ARBUCKLE. He looked like an Arbuckle.

The police put a blanket over the body, but nobody moved it, even after the wagon showed up. The blanket was blue and yellow, and Mickey could see the words "Bull's-eye" sewed into one side. A horse blanket. He thought of Jeanie again, finding out all the places that body had been, and then he turned around and walked the mile and a half back to Little Eddie's Automotive Emporium.

Little Eddie knew trouble when he saw it. He was sitting outside on a Mustang, watching Mickey come the last block, smiling like he had a mouth full of broken glass. Mickey sat down next to him on the car.

"Where's the truck?" Little Eddie said.

"Wrecked," Mickey said.

Little Eddie nodded. "Where's Stretch?"

"Hospital, I guess."

Little Eddie gave him the broken-glass smile again, thinking maybe Mickey had put him there. "That's the last one I ever hire," he said. Then, "You got insurance?" Mickey stared at him. "Use my phone, if you want to call the company."

Mickey looked at his elbow. It was a mess. "I told you," he said, "you could start it, but I said don't take it nowhere."

Little Eddie put out his hands. "Look, what can I do? In this business, everybody in the world's tryin' to get over on you. I got to try before I buy. . . ."

"You said seven and a half," Mickey said. "Let's go inside, I'll sign over the title."

"I can't buy somethin' wrecked," Little Eddie said. "I'd like to help you out, Mickey, but I got a business to run, what's left of one."

Mickey said. "You already bought it." He stood up and started for the office. Little Eddie followed him, breathing hard, sweating. Mickey signed over the title. "You better make it eight," he said. "You said seven and a half or eight, and you're probably going to get eleven, twelve out of your insurance."

"That takes a long time," Eddie said. "Time is money. I got to put out seven and a half for two, three months, that costs me." He opened the top drawer of his desk and pulled out a checkbook.

"Eight," Mickey said.

"Plus, the insurance company is going to raise up my rates," Little Eddie said. "You know you don't get over on the insurance company. They'll get their seven and a half back out of me, and Christ knows what they'll want for Stretch."

Mickey stared at him. "Seven and a half?" Little Eddie said.

Mickey said, "I don't care," and Little Eddie wrote the numbers. He handed him the check and put the title back in the drawer with the checkbook.

"Tell you the truth," he said, "you had me for eight, Mick, if you wanted to be a prick about it. . . ."

Mickey got a bus to Broad Street and cashed the check. He took it all in hundreds, The teller looked him over, torn and bloody, and made him wait while she called Little Eddie. She put the phone back in the cradle and handed it over, seventy-five one-hundred-dollar bills. Against her better judgment.

He caught a cab back to the Pocket. Cab rates in Philly stayed even with Locust Street pussy. One went up, the other went up. The chances of catching a social disease was about the same too. On the way there he squeezed his legs, trying to get some feeling back into them. The trouble wasn't that they didn't have any feeling when he squeezed them, though, it was that they went numb when he used them. "Fuck it," he said.

The cabdriver turned around. "The Pocket, right?" he said. The cab let him out in front of Moran's Funeral Home, the bill was seven dollars. "I can't take no hundred," the driver said.

"It just come out of the bank," Mickey said.

The driver shook his head. "I don't have that kinda change. The fuckin' places I drive to, they ain't even sent in missionaries yet."

Mickey went through his pockets and found a ten. "Keep it," he said. He crawled out of the cab on dead legs and walked through the gate to see Smilin' Jack.

The waiting room was empty again. Mickey walked into the back, past the viewing room and the display room and the office. He heard yelling upstairs. "This is my fuckin' business now. You had yours. . . ." Then, "What the fuck do you want?"

The voice got louder, and then the door to the stairs opened and Jack was standing in the hallway, a yard away, red-faced, looking eight directions at once. "Mick," he said. "I didn't hear you come in."

"It's cause you were yellin' at your father," he said.

Jack looked back up the stairway and shook his head. "I hope they put me outta my misery before that happens," he said. "How you been?"

"I been all right," Mickey said.

Jack said, "Lissen, I'm sorry about the misunderstanding. You know, I got problems too. Nobody realizes that. They think because you're a professional, you don't got problems."

"I realize you got problems," Mickey said.

"Hey, bygones are bygones, right? That's the whole principle of the business." He closed the door to upstairs, and that was bygones too. "C'mon in the office," he said. "You want a beer?"

Mickey shook his head. Smilin' Jack sat down at his desk and noticed Mickey's clothes. "What happened to you?" he said. "You okay?"

Mickey took the roll of hundred-dollar bills out of his pocket and counted sixty of them on the desk. It was dead quiet in the office. He pushed the money across the desk and left it for

Jack Moran to pick up. He didn't want to hand it to him and touch his skin. In his whole life Mickey'd never disrespected old Daniel. "Six thousand," Mickey said. "That's for the mahogany box and the funeral and everything else, right?"

Smilin' Jack picked up the stack of bills and counted them, using a little sponge on his desk to wet his thumb. When he finished, he straightened up the stack. "Where is the deceased?" he said.

Mickey rubbed his elbow. "They got him at the morgue again," he said. He told them there'd been another accident. Smilin' Jack nodded like it was something happened all the time.

"When it rains it pours," he said.

"Yeah, well they got him down there, but they probably don't know who he is," Mickey said. "He wasn't carrying no identification." Jack scratched his head. Mickey said, "Can we still take care of it tomorrow? I want to get it over."

"I don't know," Jack said. "This never come up before. Let me call down there and find out." He reached for the phone, and Mickey stood up. "Sit down, I can tell you in a minute," Jack said.

"I'll give you a call tonight," Mickey said. He didn't want to be in the room when Jack called about Leon. He just wanted to get the boy in the ground. Even if Jeanie was gone, he wanted to get the boy buried. He wanted to be past Leon, so he could look up and not see him there waiting for him anymore.

The paramedic was a thirty-seven-year-old Vietnam veteran named Michael Cooper who took tranquilizers to get through the morning and sleeping pills to get through the night. He smoked a little dope to kill the time in between, which is what he'd been doing when the call came in to go to Third and Fitzwater. He'd gone over in the ambulance, hanging out the window to feel the wind pressing on his face. "I get off on the weather," he said to the driver.

The driver looked at him without answering.

"You take this shit too serious," he said to the driver, who was twenty-three years old. "When you been around it enough, you see it don't mean nothin'." The driver looked straight ahead. "You weren't in Nam, were you?" Michael Cooper said. "No, you're too young. Man, when you've seen some dude's supposed to be running things eating cinnamon rolls next to a stack of bodies, you know you ain't supposed to take it serious."

The driver said, "I get sick to my fuckin' stomach, listenin' to this Nam shit. Nam-this, Nam-that, seem like every fuckin' time I turn around, there's some motherfucker tellin' me about Nam like there ain't nobody else ever done nothin'." He spit out his window.

Cooper smiled at him. "You got a lot of anger, bro," he said.

The driver said, "Fuck," and Cooper stuck his head back out the window and watched people on the street turning to look as they went past. Two blocks from the accident the traffic stopped dead. The driver pulled up onto the sidewalk and drove half a block farther, but there were cars parked there too, so Cooper got out and ran. The sidewalk seemed to float up to his feet.

By the time he got to the corner, the police were pushing back the crowd. One of the cops had a clipboard. Cooper asked him, "What we got, man?"

"Where the fuck have you guys been?" the cop said. The cop didn't wait for an answer. "There's one against the wall over there," he said, pointing to a thin black man sitting on the sidewalk, holding a cloth against his head, "and there's one on the street. I think he's dead."

Cooper walked through the accident, smelling the street, noticing the texture of the road, the patterns of the windows against the brick houses. He didn't look at the body until he was next to it, and then he only looked a little while.

He touched the hands and the skin on the cheek. The cheek was smooth and cold, and there was powder on his fingers where he'd touched it. Cooper walked away from the body and threw up into the drain on the corner. He'd seen dead people, stacks of them, but he never went to funerals. You saw them like that, dressed up and drained and filled and powdered, you had to consider it. If you didn't walk away from it when it happened, you were stuck with it.

"You'll get used to it." It was the cop again, snuck up behind him, smiling. ARBUCKLE the name tag said. "The first few, it bothered me too," he said. "I never threw up like you did, but it takes a while."

Cooper's eyes watered and his nose stung. "He's dead, right?" the cop said. "I thought he was dead, but it ain't official until you say it."

"He's dead," Cooper said. And then he walked over to the black man sitting against the wall to look at his head.

Arbuckle stood near the vomit, waiting for somebody to show it to. Somebody who was a cop. Too bad Eisenhower took the day off, he'd of loved it. A kid doctor who couldn't stand to see nobody dead. He thought Eisenhower would have loved it, but with him you could never be sure. He wasn't always what the stories about him said. Arbuckle never said it, but he was glad they'd put through Eisenhower's transfer back to detectives. He hoped his new partner would be somebody you could count on to be one way.

He waited by the vomit awhile, and when nobody came by he went back into the crowd to look for witnesses again. It took an hour to clean up the mess. Wreckers, ambulances, sweeping the glass. The doctor had gone into a bar halfway down the block. Arbuckle made a note of that, but there wasn't much else to write down. Nobody would admit they'd seen it.

He stayed until the truck was towed, asking questions and drawing pictures that showed where it was and where the bus was, and where the body was lying in the street. He thought about drawing a little pool of vomit, but you couldn't count on everybody having a sense of humor.

When it was finished, Arbuckle went back to the station house and made a phone call to the city room of the *Daily Times* and asked for assistant city editor Brookie Sutherland. Brookie Sutherland had told him anytime he had something to give him a call.

Arbuckle didn't know why Brookie Sutherland liked to talk

to him personally, but whenever he called with something, Sutherland put his name in the paper. The regular police reporter never did that. "This is Arbuckle," he said when Brookie Sutherland picked up the phone.

"Hey, buddy, how are you?" Arbuckle winced. His greatest fear was that his phone was bugged, and someday his friends would hear a newspaperman calling him buddy.

"Look, I got a little accident here," he said. "One fatal, one hospitalized. I thought you might be interested." Arbuckle always called everything "little" when he talked to Brookie Sutherland.

"Just a minute." He heard him load his typewriter. "Okay, shoot."

Arbuckle cupped his hand over the receiver and read him the times and places off his accident report. "We don't got a name on the DOA yet," he said. "Wasn't carrying no ID."

Brookie Sutherland said, "Is that it?"

Arbuckle felt disappointed. He never knew what the *Daily Times* would like and what they wouldn't. He thought for a minute, and then told him about the doctor who threw up. He started that by saying, "Well, there was one human interest story. . . ."

Brookie Sutherland thanked the cop and hung up. There was a new girl on tryout, and they'd put her on Friday nights to see how she did. A timid-looking girl, always wore white blouses with a scarf around the neck, skirts that were too long. He wasn't sure, but he thought she was pretty. You couldn't tell about that until a girl had been around awhile and the office had a chance to form an opinion. "That dumb sonofabitch," Brookie said, loud enough so she looked up from her desk.

He smiled at her. "Cops," he said. "I got one calling that wants to give me a human interest story about vomit." Brookie Sutherland could see she didn't understand. "I got the weirdest sources in the city," he said.

"It sounds like it," she said. He couldn't tell if she liked him or not. He thought he might ask her out for a drink after work.

"Check with the medical examiner's office," he said, "and

see if you can get me an ID on some guy who got killed in a traffic accident at Third and Fitzwater this afternoon, will you?"

Then he put a fresh piece of paper in his typewriter and prepared a memo on Peter Byrne's having blown a fatal-accident-in-South-Philadelphia story. He wrote, "Tried twice to reach Byrne, but per usual, he was out of office." He hadn't called, but he didn't have to. Byrne was at Hammer's Bar drinking with his buddies, the cops. To Brookie Sutherland, the way Peter Byrne got his stories was unprofessional.

The memo was three paragraphs long, and he signed it at the end and then made two copies. One went to T. D., one to the managing editor. He kept the original for his own file on Peter Byrne.

Half an hour later the new girl had the name. "It's Leon Hubbard," she said, "but it's kind of strange . . ."

Brookie Sutherland held up his hand and smiled. "The first thing you learn," he said, "is that every accident is strange."

She said, "But this guy . . ."

Brookie Sutherland stopped her again with his hand. "The news hole on Saturday is this big." He made a bird's beak with his thumb and first finger. "All we got room for on Saturday is the name, the time, the place. If he wanted space, he should of waited till Monday. Unless the President gets shot, there's no room on Saturday."

"All right," she said.

"The guy wasn't the President," he said. She shook her head. "Then all we want is the name, the time, the place. Gimme two paragraphs, okay? And put the cop in. Charles Arbuckle, AID. You got to throw the bears a peanut to keep them interested."

"Okay," she said, "two graphs." But Brookie Sutherland wasn't listening. She typed her code into the VDT machine, slugged the story HUBBARD, and began to write:

ONE MAN WAS DEAD AND ANOTHER INJURED AFTER A BUS/TRUCK COLLISION YESTERDAY IN SOUTH PHILA-DELPHIA. ACCIDENT INVESTIGATION DIVISION OFFI-

CER CHARLES ARBUCKLE, WHO INVESTIGATED THE AC-
CIDENT, IDENTIFIED THE DEAD MAN AS LEON HUB-
BARD, OF TWENTY-FIFTH STREET IN THE GOD'S
POCKET SECTION OF THE CITY.

POLICE SAID NO CHARGES HAVE BEEN FILED IN THE AC-
CIDENT.

She finished the story, checked it for mistakes, and then pressed a key on the keyboard to file it in the system's memory.

The key she punched blinked on and off for about half a minute, and then a note came up on the screen. DUPLICATE SLUG. She looked over at the desk and thought about trying to tell Brookie Sutherland again, but she decided it might make him mad. She changed the slug to LEONH and this time the system took it.

"It's in there," she said. Sutherland looked up and smiled.

"Good," he said. "See? There isn't really much to do Friday night, unless they shoot the President. Hey, why don't we have a drink after work?"

She looked at him like she didn't understand. "I'm married," she said.

He smiled and turned red. "Oh. I didn't mean like that. I just meant as colleagues. . . ." And then he was looking through some papers on his desk, still smiling and still red, and she knew he'd never be nice to her again as long as she was there.

Mickey called Smilin' Jack right at five o'clock from a phone booth in Center City. He didn't want to see Jeanie until he could tell her about the funeral, one way or the other.

"Jack," he said, "it's Mickey."

"Hey, Mick, how are you?"

"I'm fine," he said. He left it there for the undertaker to pick up.

"I called down to the medical examiner," Jack said. "It's lucky there's a guy I know down there. I told him what happened, that you was just bringin' the body over for me when the

218

accident happened, and he took care of the red tape." Mickey waited. "So we do it tomorrow," Jack said. "Tomorrow afternoon, I got somethin' else in the morning."

"What time?"

"Three o'clock? It ain't going to be nothin' fancy. Just a nice, quiet little service here. Dignified. Some flowers, we got a minister will say a few things over the casket, cost you a fifty. And then we'll all drive out to Edgewood in Delaware County and bury him there. That sound all right?"

"That's it?"

"Right. The same way we was going to do it before. The details don't make much difference in the long run, as long as you get him in the ground dignified."

"I paid for the mahogany box, Jack."

"Right, right. I didn't mean nothin' was different. I just meant, you know, in the excitement a lot of the details don't get noticed."

"Okay," he said.

"And Mick," he said, "I want to apologize for what happened, you know? I mean, it don't do nobody any good to have it all over the neighborhood."

Mickey hung up and called home. The phone rang eight times and nobody answered. He wondered if she was with the newspaper reporter again.

Eisenhower woke up at seven in the morning, thinking of his brother diving off the roof of the Holiday Inn. It felt like he'd been dreaming about it every night since it happened. Even when he was working, it was off somewhere in the back of his mind, working too. Even when he was having himself a piece of ass, it was working. Especially when he was having himself a piece of ass.

He'd quit drinking the night it happened. He knew without trying it wouldn't be any fun without How-Awful! And that's what Calamity Eisenhower had always gotten drunk for. Fun. His brother was different.

Sober, they were the same. How-Awful! was crazy, Calamity was crazy, and anything mean they did was never on purpose. But from the first night they'd sat out under the bleachers at Franklin Field, twenty-five years ago, drinking a half-pint of vodka each, the juice had always dropped his brother's pitch. What did they call that—a minor key? It was in the pitch, it was in his eyes.

And all the crazy-ass, crying-funny things they'd done drunk together, that sad key was always there in How-Awful! And the older they got, the more it showed. But he never let it settle inside him and turn him ugly. He'd shoot up a bar, or drive a car into the Delaware River, but he never let it take him over. It was inside him, though, and for as long as Calamity lived he'd never believe his brother didn't know the swimming pool in Arizona was empty.

He lay in bed a few minutes, trying to bury himself in the pillow, but once he'd started thinking about Arizona he knew it was all over for sleep. His leg was bothering him anyway.

He got out of bed and put on a pair of shorts and a sweat shirt and tennis shoes. He brushed his teeth and splashed some water on his face and then walked into his living room, where an eighty-pound Everlast heavy bag was hanging from a beam in the ceiling. He wrapped his hands carefully and put them inside a pair of eight-ounce gloves and beat on the bag for twenty straight minutes.

Until he was sweating and tired and he'd quit thinking about his leg. He slipped off the gloves and untied the wraps and hung them in the bathroom. Hand wraps smelled worse than anything in sports. He pulled some cheese and ham out of the refrigerator and put them into a hamburger bun, and sat down at the kitchen table to eat breakfast. Then he realized he didn't have anything to read, so he limped downstairs and across the street and bought a Saturday *Daily Times*.

He put the paper next to the sandwich and opened a carton of milk. He turned the first couple of pages, looking for something he wanted to read, and was about to turn the newspaper over and look at the sports section when he noticed the story,

220

down in the corner of page 6. At first he thought it was some kind of mistake the paper made, running an old story twice, and then he thought it might of been two Leon Hubbards.

But not on Twenty-fifth Street in the Pocket, it wasn't. He read it again, a traffic accident at Third and Fitzwater. AID Officer Charles Arbuckle.

He'd underestimated him. The body was dead five days, and Arbuckle had called the newspaper and told them he had a traffic victim. He decided not to think about how Leon Hubbard got to Third and Fitzwater, he'd save that for later. For now, he just concentrated on Chuck Arbuckle and his phone calls to the *Daily Times*. "You poor, dumb fuck," he said.

And then he began to laugh, out loud, a way he couldn't stop if he wanted to. Crazy-ass, crying-funny laughing, until his chest hurt, until all he could think of was what a shame it was that How-Awful! wasn't there to see it too. Crying-funny laughing.

It was almost over now. That was the first thing Mickey thought when he hung up on Smilin' Jack, that this time tomorrow he could rest. And after the phone rang eight times at his house, he hung up and thought it again.

He took two hours to walk back to the Pocket, stopping in every bar on the way. When he got there his house was dark, and he'd had enough of empty rooms.

His legs were feeling better, he wouldn't have minded walking another hour or two, but there wasn't anyplace to go. He thought about checking Bird's place, but he didn't want to look at that now. He stood on the sidewalk outside the house for a minute, thinking it over, and then he crossed the street and went into the Hollywood.

McKenna was behind the bar, running up and down, killing an argument that would not stay dead at one end of the bar, pouring straight shots and beer to forty or fifty people. Some of the customers he was nice to, and some of them he had to keep in line. Mickey wondered how he kept it straight from night to night, who was who. At the end where the argument was, everybody was drunk and staking claims, and jumping claims. In a while they'd get mad and punch holes in the bathroom wall. It was possible they'd punch each other.

Mickey went to the end away from the argument, away from the kids. McKenna brought him a Schmidt's and a glass, and even though he was in a hurry he took the time to ask about the funeral.

"Tomorrow afternoon," Mickey said, "if you wouldn't mind lettin' people know."

"That's good," McKenna said. "Saturday's a good day."

"It's just a small service, up at Jack's." McKenna nodded. Mickey felt somebody wedge into the spot next to him, hurting his elbow, and then he smelled something wet and awful. He turned to look, and it was Ray and his neck brace.

McKenna held his nose. "Awful, ain't it?"

Ray spit on the floor, stepped on the spot like he was putting out a cigarette. "I can't take this off," he said to Mickey. "If I take this off, I could aggravate the injury."

Mickey sucked on his beer. "Don't want to do that," he said.

"It doesn't smell bad," Ray told him. "Can you smell it? It's medicinal, like a hospital, McKenna wants me to take it off because of his criminal liability. . . ."

McKenna said, "It's a medicinal smell, like you cut off your fuckin' lizard for a necklace."

Ray said, "Mickey doesn't think it's so bad."

"How do you know that?" McKenna said.

"He's still standing here, isn't he?"

McKenna said, "Yeah, but he's grievin'. You can't expect him to smell right." McKenna reached into the box and brought out another Schmidt's. Then he went to the other end of the bar to kill the argument again.

Ray leaned closer to Mickey. "A shame about the boy," he said. He shook his head. The brace was stained at the edge where it met his neck. Mickey nodded, pulling away. There was a whole class of people that couldn't talk to you when they were drinking without putting their mouth right up next to your face.

"The whole neighborhood was sorry," Ray said. He was spitting too. "But there's no way anyone can entirely sympathize with you. It's like being black. You can feel for them, but you can't ever really understand what it is."

The woman on the other side of him yelled to McKenna. "Ray's talkin' about the niggers again." Ray was the only person in God's Pocket who liked colored people, and every time he opened his mouth about them in the Hollywood it was trouble. McKenna left the argument and came back to Mickey's end of the bar.

He put a finger in Ray's face and said, "I told you before, no talkin' about niggers."

Ray ran his hands over the neck brace, reminding him. "It's a free country," he said. "We still have the First Amendment. Some of the people in here tonight fought for freedom of speech."

McKenna leaned closer. "If you bring patriotic into it, you're flagged," he said. "You start talkin' about niggers and America in here tonight, I swear you won't get another drink till winter. You understand?"

For an answer, Ray pointed to his shot glass, which McKenna filled with Old Hickory, locally brewed bourbon whiskey. Ray put his fingers around it and picked up where he'd been. A long time ago Ray had got used to being told to shut up. "What I was saying was, nobody can feel what you feel. They didn't live with the boy, they can't know what it's like."

Mickey said, "That's the truth."

"And they didn't live with Jeanie. They look at it from the outside and say this or that, but it's just talk."

Mickey looked at him. "What's just talk?"

Ray shook his head. "Doesn't matter, because they aren't there. They don't live in your house, they haven't walked a mile in your shoes."

Mickey said, "Every fuckin' time you begin to say some-

223

thin', Ray, you throw in somethin' like walkin' in other people's shoes. That's why everybody thinks you're full of shit."

"It doesn't matter what *everybody* thinks," Ray said. "I was educated at the University of Pennsylvania. Do you see anybody else educated in this bar?" Ray looked down the bar, then in back of him. "There's nobody here who went further than twelfth grade," he said.

"Not me," Mickey said. "I quit when I was fourteen."

Ray nodded his head. "But you're an intelligent man," he said.

"What are they sayin'?"

Ray said, "Nothing. It's nothing. Everybody in this neighborhood quit thinking at the end of the Korean War. The ones that didn't quit thinking got out." Mickey started to say something but Ray stopped him. "You want to know why I didn't get out," he said. "The truth is, I don't know. Maybe I like being the only educated man in the Hollywood Bar. Maybe . . ."

"What I want to know," Mickey said, "is what everybody's sayin' about this."

Ray shook his head. "To what purpose? They can't understand, it's like trying to understand being black. . . ." He'd dropped his voice to say that last part.

Mickey said, "Because I wanna know. Because how somethin' looks to everybody else is sometimes how it really looks."

"There are no absolutes," Ray said.

Mickey found himself leaning into Ray's face to talk, ignoring the smell. "Have you ever noticed them old sayings?" he said. "Like, It takes one to know one, and, It's the early bird that gets the worm? And, Nothin' is for nothin'?"

Ray nodded. "Clichés," he said. "They have replaced thought."

Mickey said, "Yeah, well, everybody says things like that, but when you sit down and think about it, they're always true. That's why everybody says them. Lemme tell you another one. Whistlin' past the graveyard. You ever think about that, what it really is?"

224

"The average American has substituted clichés for thought," Ray said.

Mickey pulled away from Ray's face and drank the second Schmidt's. "Tell me what they're sayin' about me and Jeanie," he said.

Ray closed his eyes, putting it together. He drank the shot of whiskey he'd been holding and tugged at his neck brace. "That she's fucking Richard Shellburn," he said. "And she's got you sleeping on the couch."

"She ain't fuckin' Richard Shellburn," he said.

Ray shrugged. "It's not what I think," he said, "it's what they're saying." Mickey looked around the bar to see who it was looking in his windows at night.

"She ain't fuckin' nobody," he said again.

He'd seen the way she looked at him, but she wouldn't do that. He would of felt it, just being around her. Of course, he hadn't been around her. Not since the morning Leon had got himself killed. "She ain't," he said.

For the first time since Mickey knew him, Ray didn't have a thing to say. "What, did she go somewhere with him today?" Mickey said. "She's got some idea that Leon got killed different than the cops said, that's all. He's just helpin' her."

McKenna had heard some of that, and he was back down in front of them again. "What the fuck are you startin' now, Ray?" he said.

Ray pointed to his shot glass. "We were just talking," he said.

"I heard what you said," McKenna said. He was staring at Ray, Ray was looking at his shot glass. "The fuckin' funeral's to-morrow afternoon, and you're talkin' shit like that."

"I didn't say anything that everybody else in here didn't say first," Ray said, and he looked back at the bartender to see how far he wanted to take it. McKenna got Mickey another Schmidt's out of the cooler.

"Don't listen to nothin' he said, Mick," McKenna said. Mickey picked up the beer and drank most of it. "Fuckin' people talk about everything." McKenna poured Ray another shot and one for himself and put another beer in front of Mickey. "Forget about it," he said.

Half an hour later, Ray threw down the shot and looked around. "You want to know the real reason I never left?" he said. He was drunk enough so some of the words were slurring now, and the thoughts slid into each other too. "The real reason?"

Mickey stared at his hands. He was wishing Jeanie would get home. He wanted to be around her tonight, to see where it stood, but he didn't want to go home and wait. He'd had enough of empty rooms.

Ray reached over and took the shot McKenna had left for himself on the bar, putting his own shot glass where the full one had been. "The real reason," he said, "is forgiveness." Mickey looked up from his hands. "I want to be forgiven," Ray said. One of his eyes had crossed, and the spit had collected in the corner of his mouth and was running down his chin.

"Don't worry about what you said," Mickey said. "It's just talk."

Ray shook his head. "You can't forgive me," he said. "You're an intelligent man, but you don't know anything here. I grew up with these people. They've seen me lying in puke and I've seen them lying in puke."

"I seen you lyin' in puke, Ray," Mickey said.

Ray shook his head. "Everybody here has stolen something from somebody else. Or when they were kids they set somebody's house on fire, or they ran away when they should have stayed and fought. They've stolen from each other and they've lent money to the people they took it from. You're an intelligent man, but everybody here's seen everybody else naked. They know who's scared to fight and who cheats at cards and who slaps his kids around. And no matter what anybody does, we're still here, and whatever we are is what we are." His head was beginning to fall, a couple of inches at a time, and then he'd catch it.

"And no matter what I am, they've got to forgive me, because I'm no worse than anybody else, I'm just different. The only thing they can't forgive is leaving the neighborhood." As he said that, Ray folded his arms on the bar, making himself a pillow, and then dropped his head, neck brace and all, from a foot above the bar, and went to sleep where he landed. He looked so peaceful.

Mickey finished his beer, thinking about it. When McKenna came back and went through the formality of trying to wake Ray up, Mickey got another one, and then another one. About eleven o'clock he looked out the window and the lights in the house were on, and when he looked again at one, she had gone to bed. He thought about what Ray had said, and he wanted to be forgiven too. Not by the neighborhood—Ray was right, they didn't know anything about each other, him and God's Pocket—it was Jeanie he wanted to forgive him. He didn't know what for.

McKenna gave last call at two and turned on the lights, and for a minute everything stopped. Mickey saw that Ray was attached by a line of spit to a puddle he'd made on the bar. And he saw the rest of them too, frozen in the light. Pale, soft faces, missing teeth, mascara run all down the girls' cheeks. A fat girl sitting six feet away—how long had she been there?—crying into a glass full of wilted cherries.

People who would never leave God's Pocket, who couldn't. "Drink up," McKenna said.

Somebody yelled, "Yo, turn off the fuckin' lights."

McKenna went back to the wall and dimmed the lights. "Drink up," he said again. And they did. They'd seen each other in the light once, and that was enough. They finished their drinks and left the bar in twos and threes, back to row houses and hangovers, and the mornings to get through.

Mickey watched them leave, drunk as he'd been since he was a kid, and he knew in that moment exactly what Ray had been talking about, only he'd said forgiveness when he meant love.

Mickey could see how you could get them mixed up.

And he could see he'd never shown Jeanie enough of who he

was. That's why she thought everything was his fault. He finished the beer in front of him and helped McKenna get Ray over to a booth. They tried slapping him awake, but when McKenna pulled up his eyelids, all there was was white, so they dragged him across the floor and laid him out in the booth. It was a hard fact that nobody alive could wake up Ray when his eyeballs went white.

He left his change on the bar for McKenna and crossed the street, and there was something moving around inside his head that turned out to be an idea. Tonight he was going to wake her up and let her see him. He didn't trust himself to wait till morning. By morning, he'd pull back. He didn't know what he would say, but he was going to give her something to forgive, or love.

He went through the house and checked the garage even though there was nothing in it, and decided what he would tell her as he was walking up the stairs.

Richard Shellburn had told her at ten-thirty in the morning that he loved her. He said, "Let me pick you up."

Jeanie said, "I'm not sure, Richard. There's so much going on right now. The funeral, my husband ..." It was the first time she called him Richard, she hadn't known what to call him before.

He said, "I love you."

She said, "Thank you."

"Let me pick you up," he said. It didn't seem to matter what she said, it never changed him.

She said, "I could meet you somewhere."

"Bookbinders," he said. She met him there for lunch, and the owner had come over to the table to shake hands with Richard and make sure the food was all right. It reminded her of New York, and the way things could have been all along. When Richard had introduced her, the owner had taken her hand and said, "You're very beautiful to be with somebody like this ugly guy." And they all laughed like it was funny, and she liked that.

And after he'd brought them a drink and left, Richard looked at her and said, "He's right." And she was special again, the way she was supposed to be.

They left her car in the parking lot and took the Continental to Rittenhouse Square. The doorman at the Barclay opened her door and helped her out, and a kid in a bow tie and a dark red jacket parked the car. She'd never been to the Barclay before. He held her arm at the elbow and took her into the bar. They had Scotch there, and then he ordered champagne when they got to the room. It was on the sixteenth floor. She looked out the window at Rittenhouse Square, and there were a hundred people down there walking dogs—nice, little ones you could pick up and put in your purse. He came up behind her with a glass of champagne, putting his arm around her to deliver it. When she took the glass, the hand moved to her stomach.

"I love you," he said. She was still looking out at the square, so it wasn't as uncomfortable as if they'd been face to face. "From the minute I saw you," he said, "I loved you." It turned her cold.

She knew that was how writers wrote, so in a way it didn't surprise her that's how they were in person, but it turned her cold. He kissed her on the back of the neck and she let him. If there was a place to stop in all this, it was gone. His hand moved up to her breast, and then back down her stomach to her legs. She wished she was in the park, holding one of those dogs on a leash. One of the little ones that couldn't pull you off your feet. He kissed her again, and it ran a shiver up the back of her head. He did have a nice touch.

Then he moved between her and the window and said it again. "I love you." She was looking at the floor, but he took her chin in his hand and brought her eyes up into his face. "I love you," he said. If he was going to do something, why didn't he just do it?

She didn't know why she didn't want to look at him. She didn't know why she began blinking tears. "I'm sorry," she said.

He put his arms around her neck and held her next to his

ear. She could feel his hand and his hair and the edge of the champagne glass. "It's too much all at once," he said.

And that was true, and at the bottom it was all empty. When Tom died, it had been enough. The looks at the cemetery, the things she overheard. *"So beautiful, and with that poor sick little baby . . ."* It took his place. And there was a way people treated her afterward, there was always a consideration.

Jeanie Scarpato depended on that consideration, and accepted it naturally in a way that made it pleasurable to offer.

On the day Leon died, there was no time to think of him at all. For that day, it was only the loss, the neighbors coming by with hams and salads, her sisters' shoulders. But somewhere in the time since, she had come to the bottom of it, and at the bottom it was empty.

She'd tried to turn them away from her toward what happened to Leon, to tell them he hadn't died in an accident, but it wasn't set up for that. They listened, and then they patted her hand or her shoulder, or they hugged her, or told her it would be all right.

And it wasn't set up for her to refuse that, because empty as it was, it's the way it had always been, and she couldn't give it up.

She stayed in Richard Shellburn's arms five minutes without moving. Then he let go of her and got them both another glass of champagne. She took it like medicine.

The room was quiet. Even with both of them there the air never seemed to move. That's how you could tell an expensive hotel. "I don't think I belong here either," she said. She sat down on a small couch facing the bed and wiped at her eyes. He sat down on the bed and watched her.

"You want to take care of Leon first," he said. "And your husband."

She shook her head. "I don't know," she said. "Everything happened at once, Mickey's somebody different. . . ." She felt him staring at her.

He stood up and walked to the window. "It's not the right time," he said. He stood there awhile and then he said, "It's better than a dog sneezing in your ass, though."

She smiled at that and put her head against the arm of the sofa. She felt tired and a little dizzy. He said, "Why don't you lie on the bed?"

She said, "I've got to leave soon." He pulled the champagne bottle out of the ice bucket and walked back to the window. He seemed ordinary to her now. She closed her eyes, and a little later she heard him talking on the phone. A few minutes after that, somebody came to the door with more champagne. She wasn't asleep and she wasn't awake, nothing was all the way anymore.

When she opened her eyes again, the room was dark. She was thirsty and cold. "What time is it?" she said. He was in the room, she knew he was in the room.

He said, "You were tired." She sat up and looked around. He was over on the bed, sitting cross-legged in the dark, staring at her. There were two empty bottles of champagne on the bed with him, and he took a drink out of another one in his hand.

She went into the bathroom and turned on all the switches on the wall. Light, sunlamp, a fan. She brushed her hair and washed out her mouth with a little bottle of Lavoris the hotel left with the soap and shampoo. Her shirt looked like she'd pulled it out from under the front seat of the car.

She tucked it into her pants and then began to fix her face. A little lipstick, some color for her cheeks. It wasn't anything artificial she did with makeup. She didn't use it to cover anything up, she let it bring her out. It had been like that as long as she could remember.

When she came out, Shellburn was still sitting cross-legged on the bed. "Is it all right if I turn on the lights?" she said. She heard what might have been a laugh.

"No, leave them off," he said.

"Are you mad?"

"I love you," he said.

"I can take a cab back to my car," she said.

"All right." He sounded calm to her, and for a second she wondered if it was all just trying to get himself a piece of ass. She put a knee and a hand on the bed and kissed him on the cheek. One of the bottles rolled over her fingers.

"Call me," she said. All the way down the hall, she wondered why she'd said that. She thought she might of felt sorry for him. The doorman looked at her different than he had when she'd been with Richard Shellburn, it was like they were both the same now. He got her a cab, though, and held the door. When she climbed in he said, "There you go."

"Thank you," she said.

"Another day, another dollar," he said, and he closed the door before she could be sure what he meant. The cab smelled like somebody lived in it, and she told the driver she wanted to go to Bookbinders. A block from the hotel the driver suddenly turned around and said, "I don't change nothin' bigger than a ten."

"All right."

"I had this fare when I first come on," he said, "tried to give me a hundred. You believe that, a hundred?" She smiled but she didn't answer. She had problems of her own.

Mickey wasn't at home. She let herself in and got out of her clothes and into a robe. She was still cold from the hotel room, and she made a cup of hot chocolate, thinking of herself floating someplace between Mickey and Richard, waiting for one or the other to do something to save her and Leon. It felt like everybody she'd ever known had missed the point.

Did Richard Shellburn think she was the kind to walk into a hotel room, with Leon still waiting to be buried, and tell him she loved him too? All in all, she'd rather of been raped.

She thought of Mickey throwing off the sheets, tearing her nightgown, pinning her to the bed. Yes, she'd seen him pick up the air conditioner, as high as his head, and fit it into the wall. She saw him lift up the back end of Mole Ferrell's Toyota when the jack slipped and it fell on him—you could of understood it if it had been Mole Ferrell that got killed on the job, he was born for injury. But Mickey had never picked her up, he was afraid to be forceful.

232

And afraid to be soft. He didn't have a nice touch, like Richard. She finished the hot chocolate and went upstairs and lay on top of the bed. She imagined Mickey coming up the stairs. She got back up and put on a yellow nightgown—trying for a few seconds to remember if she'd ever heard of anybody else who only liked one color—and then she stood in front of the mirror half an hour, moving the part in her hair, lightening her eyes and then brushing mascara into her lashes until they looked too heavy to open.

When she'd finished, the effect was a fifteen-year-old girl trying to look thirty. It wasn't anything she made up, it was inside her and she'd just let it come out. She lay in bed two hours, waiting for him to come home. About two o'clock she heard the noises on the street and knew McKenna was closing. Mickey must have been the last one out, though, because it was another fifteen or twenty minutes before she heard him downstairs.

She spread her hair out over the pillow and pulled the bedding down so that he would see the curve of her waist to her hip under the sheet. She heard him coming up the stairs and closed her eyes, and waited for him to look into the room and see she was helpless.

She could tell from his steps that he was drunk. Sober, he was as light on his feet as Leon. He climbed the stairs, not even trying to be quiet. She lay with her hair spread over the pillow and her eyes closed. He came down the hall and stopped in the doorway.

She heard his breathing, and then he was moving again, toward the bed, and a step before he got to her she opened her eyes and jumped. "Oh, Mickey," she said. "It's you. . . ."

He sat down next to her on the bed. Her eyes got bigger. "What are you . . ." She let that die. "Oh, no," she said, "no . . ."

He reached over and touched her arm. It wasn't rough and it wasn't gentle. He said, "Jeanie, we got to talk."

She closed her eyes. "Oh, no," she said. He noticed the fear had gone out of her voice and thought that at least was a start.

233

"I got to tell you what happened today," he said. She closed her eyes. "Don't go to sleep," he said. "We got to talk."

"It's late," she said. He turned on the light next to the bed, and it hurt her eyes. "In the morning," she said.

He shook his head. "In the morning I'll change my mind," he said, "and this whole fuckin' thing will be right where it was."

She said, "At least turn off the light."

"I got to see you when I say it," he said, "so I can tell how you're takin' it." He looked at his hands a couple of minutes and then he began to say things. "This morning I took the truck down to sell it."

She looked at him. "Why'd you do that?"

"I didn't have the money to bury Leon," he said. "I had the money, but it wasn't enough to do it right. Fuck, what do I know about it? The only family I had was Daniel, and there wasn't nobody else there to worry about when I buried him, so I just did it." She was looking at him now suspicious, like she expected it all along. He decided not to mention Turned Leaf.

"Anyway," he said, "I took the truck down to Little Eddie's, but the guy he's got workin' for him took it out and wrecked it. He hit a bus, I don't know how bad the guy's hurt, but they took him to the hospital." He stopped and looked at the ceiling. "His name is Stretch," he said.

She didn't say anything, but she was paying attention. At least she knew he was there. "Anyway, see, Bird's been havin' troubles of his own, and now he's out of business. You see what I'm talkin' about? The truck don't matter, let me put your mind to rest about that." He wasn't telling it right. It was supposed to be about him.

"How much do you need?" she said.

He shook his head. "I don't need money. Little Eddie bought himself a truck as soon as Stretch hit the bus." He looked at the ceiling again to tell her the next part.

"Anyway," he said, "Leon was in the truck."

234

"What?"

"Leon was *with* the truck," he said, correcting himself. "He was in the back."

"With the meat?"

"Take it easy," he said. "I kept him separate, the meat never touched him. I took care of him, kept him clean. . . ." He wished now he'd turned off the light when she'd wanted him to. "Anyway," he said.

"Stop saying anyway," she said.

"Right. So Stretch ran into the bus, and the truck tipped over in the middle of the street."

"No," she said.

"Yeah," he said. "And the back door flew open, and Leon fell out." It wasn't supposed to be coming out like this, and he could see she wasn't understanding his side of it. It wasn't about him at all. He said, "See, Jack Moran wouldn't bury him until he had the cash."

"He's been riding around in the back of that truck all the time?" she said. "Mickey, he was just a baby." He thought of the way Leon had looked at the medical examiner's, like an angel.

"I didn't want to mention it," he said. "I knew it'd upset you."

"Where is he now?" she said. She sat up like she was going to put on a coat and go pick him up. He saw that she would need a coat, that nightgown must of been made for the summer.

"He's at Jack's," he said. "It's all settled now. The cops picked him up, but Jack knew somebody at the morgue got him out in time for the funeral."

She lay back down and turned away. "Turn off the light, Mickey," she said. He turned off the light and sat on the edge of the bed waiting for her breathing to even out. He didn't want to leave until she was asleep. He didn't want to feel like he was running away.

He'd thought telling her what happened to Leon would make her see him. He sat in the dark, trying to remember how that was supposed to connect. He'd begun to wonder if she was asleep when she suddenly spoke to him again. "Do people know what happened?" she asked.

"Jack knows," he said, "but I didn't tell nobody in the neighborhood. Or your sisters . . ." Who did she mean?

"Jack Moran?" she said.

"Yeah, he had to know. But he ain't anxious to have it all over the neighborhood that he threw Leon out the door because he didn't have cash in hand to bury him. That makes him look bad."

"Threw him out the door?" she said. He could have screwed a bolt through his forehead.

"Yeah, well, not exactly threw. He put him outside. I tried to get him back in, but Jack'd locked the doors. He'd been drinkin', and you know how he gets when he's like that."

"Out on the street?" He reached over to pat her shoulder and stopped his hand just before it touched her, not knowing what she might do. He knew her better than this when he didn't know her.

"He wasn't there long," he said. "Only a couple minutes before I found him, and then I got him right in the truck." He waited a little bit, but Jeanie didn't say anything else. After a while she picked up the pillow and put it over her head. He saw she didn't want to talk and went back downstairs and fell asleep on the couch.

In the morning, Mickey couldn't walk. The couch was a foot shorter than he was, so he'd slept with his legs bent about like a frog's, at least that's how they were when he woke up. He tried to straighten them out, and the shot of pain caught him up short before they'd moved an inch. He sat up on the couch and looked at his legs, expecting they'd be purple and hard. They looked like his legs. He rubbed them, up and down from his knees to his shorts, and every place he touched hurt, but not like it did when he tried to move them.

He thought of the way he would look at the funeral—the way he would look to Jeanie at the funeral—and pushed himself off the couch. His legs were still bent, but not as bad. He closed his eyes and straightened them. It took a minute, a minute and a half, and then before he opened his eyes, he lost his balance and stumbled.

He caught the fall, but his legs had moved a new way, and it felt like he was breaking guitar strings in there. He stood up straight again, this time the pain lost some of its edges. He didn't know if it was because he was getting used to it, or because he'd done it before and the strings were already broke. Maybe that's what getting used to something was, running out of strings to break.

It was quiet upstairs. He moved from the couch to a chair to the table with the telephone, keeping most of his weight on his arms. The table was next to the staircase, and he used both hands on the banister to pull himself up. At the top of the stairs, he found out he could walk without hurting himself if he kept his steps six inches long.

He went into the bathroom that way and filled the tub with hot water. He got in, butt first, and then pulled his legs in after him. He lay in the tub while it filled, squeezing his legs, working the elbow, trying to remember how much walking you have to do at a funeral.

The water was up over his chest before he realized he had to stand up to turn it off. He tried it with his toes, but that was new guitar strings breaking all over again. He put a hand on each side of the tub and pushed up, and as he did that the phone rang. She picked it up as he got his feet under him, and when he turned off the water he could hear her talking.

It was one of the sisters, he could tell from her voice. "I'm all right," she said, "how are you?" There was a pause. "Are you sure?" There was another pause, this one was longer. "I wasn't trying to say you couldn't read. . . . No, I'm just tired. I've carried it all alone. . . . Of course you and Joanie helped, I didn't mean you didn't help, but there's things you can't know about until it happens. . . ."

He eased himself back into the tub while she said goodbye,

and the phone rang again before he'd found a comfortable position. This time he couldn't hear what she said. She must have moved, he thought. Then he thought of Richard Shellburn and the muscles in his legs tensed, and he hadn't run out of strings to break yet.

A minute later she opened the bathroom door and looked at him. "Everybody knows," she said.

"What?" he said.

"It was in the *Daily Times*," she said. "About the accident. Only they said Leon got killed again."

He said, "Why'd they say that?"

She shook her head. "Everybody in the neighborhood, my sisters, everybody that's coming to the funeral is going to know."

"It ain't so bad, Jeanie," he said. "We didn't do nothin' bad. It's nothin' to be ashamed of, runnin' into a money problem."

"I have to live in this neighborhood," she said. And the way she said that, he didn't. She went downstairs then, and when he got dressed and went down there too, she came back up. They passed in the living room without a word.

He thought of McKenna's stories about his fights with his wife, but that was always over getting drunk or staying out all night. McKenna had something he'd done to get her over, and when his wife was over it, it was all right again. Mickey was trying to get Jeanie over who he was.

He thought of the newspaper reporter again and tried to see where he came into it. Mickey knew from the last five days how it was when all you had for ambition was for time to pass, but Shellburn had been doing it a long time. He thought maybe that's what getting old alone did to you. He thought maybe he'd find out for himself before it was over.

Of course, Jeanie liked famous things—she talked about New York City, and the whole place sounded like the inside of a store window—but he didn't know how she could look at Shellburn and not see he was losing ground every day, that he might as well of had lung cancer. And that all he wanted from her was comfort while it ended.

238

· · ·

It turned out three o'clock was too late for a funeral. If you had it at nine or ten in the morning, people got out of bed, put on their neckties and had to hurry to get there on time. Three o'clock, though, meant they got out of bed in the morning, put on their neckties and then had five or six hours of Saturday to kill before the service.

It wasn't that funerals didn't call for drinking, but the time for that was the night before, or later, after it was over. Or both. You could grieve with a hangover, probably better than you could sober, but nothing that came out of a bottle was any good before they started saying the words. It made things come up that might of been left alone.

They had the service in the viewing room. By the time Mickey and Jeanie came in, a few minutes before three, every chair in the place had somebody sitting in it, except for the front row, which was saved for members of the family. He held her at the elbow as they walked down the aisle, in front of her sisters and their husbands, her eyes fastened ahead on the closed coffin sitting underneath the cross. Mickey thought of the old woman in the organdy dress that had been there the night he slapped Smilin' Jack, he thought that most of the people in the room would end up in that same spot. Not for their funerals—the funerals would be at church—but this is where they'd get primed.

The room had that same stale smell as the Hollywood. It never occurred to him before that the smell belonged to the people as much as the bar.

He guided her down to the front seats, five feet from the box, and they sat down just as the minister came out and began to talk about Leon. He said he didn't know him, but the Lord did. And the Lord had His reasons.

Mickey looked straight ahead and Jeanie buried her face in a handkerchief. He felt her shaking but he didn't know what to do about it. She hadn't spoken to him since that morning in the bathtub.

Once or twice, the minister stopped and looked toward the back of the room, where people were coming in from the bathroom across the hall. He'd never been in God's Pocket before, but he seemed to know he was losing his hold and hurried the last part. Then he hurried off the podium and stood with Mickey and Jeanie and Smilin' Jack on the front steps of the funeral parlor, shaking hands with the people who had come to say goodbye to Leon. He even shook hands in a hurry.

The people shook hands with Jeanie first, the ladies kissed her on the cheek, then they shook hands with the minister, and then with Smilin' Jack, and then with Mickey. The ladies told Jeanie they were sorry for her troubles—Mickey could hear himself included as part of them—and they told Smilin' Jack and the minister it was a very good service. Ray said it was the best since Caveman Rafferty's—a local middleweight who was beaten to death one Saturday afternoon twelve years ago on national television. Caveman was born and raised in the Pocket, and it was still common knowledge that there were five people in the neighborhood who could beat him in a fight. It was an argument who they were, but there were five of them. Everybody agreed on that.

Nobody had much to say to Mickey. Some of the kids from the Hollywood and the Uptown even stared at him, like there might be trouble later. Everybody'd read the *Daily Times*, or heard about it. Mickey stared back. Whatever happened between him and Jeanie, it wasn't going to be a bunch of kids from the bar that caused it.

It didn't turn out to be the kids that made the trouble anyway. Mickey and Jeanie and Jack and the minister had been shaking hands out on the funeral parlor steps about ten minutes, the casket had come out and been loaded into Jack's eleven-year-old Cadillac hearse, and then Mole Ferrell had stepped out of the door, looking lost. Mole had been sitting near the front, so he was one of the last in line at the bathroom after the minister had finished. He came out, rolling and dizzy, and shook hands with Jeanie and Mickey. He smelled stronger than anybody but

Ray. "Leon was always a good boy," he told them. "I remember when he had his paper route. . . ."

Mickey hadn't known Leon ever had a paper route. He thought he must of fucked it up terrible or Jeanie would of told him about it. She was always looking to mention his good points, up to and including dressing himself, and when things got slow—as they tended to do when you were looking for Leon's good points—she could sit in front of the television news, listening to all the crimes the colored people had done to each other in North Philadelphia that night, and count it to his side that he hadn't shot who they had.

She'd shake her head and say, "Can you *imagine* how you'd feel if your child did something like that?"

"A lot of paper boys just throw the paper any which way," Mole Ferrell was saying, "but Leon always put it in the door. He was a good boy." As Mole Ferrell spoke, his eyes went big and out of focus, and he seemed to be seeing it again. Mole had been hit in the head a lot and was famous for moving around in time.

He glanced at Jack as he talked, and then looked at him again. Jack was smiling his funeral director's smile, and when Mole Ferrell looked at him, he remembered the night when Jack smiled that smile and then sucker-punched him. Or maybe it was that night again.

Whichever, one minute Mole was looking at Jeanie, saying how important it was to know your *Daily Times* would be in the same place every morning, and the next minute he screamed, "All right, motherfucker," and hit Jack Moran dead in the middle of the face. The punch came halfway across the entranceway to the funeral parlor and knocked Jack off the steps. Mole Ferrell was big and slow and did not struggle when the minister grabbed him around the waist. "Please, sir," the minister said, "remember where you are." Of course, it was the minister who'd never been in God's Pocket before.

Smilin' Jack lay flat on the ground for a few seconds, and then he sat up, covering his nose with his hand. Blood leaked

241

through the fingers. He sat up and stared at Mole Ferrell, who was still wearing the minister around his waist, staring back.

Jeanie had stopped crying. Mickey noticed that, and when Jack moved his hand, he noticed that his nose had been moved an inch off center. "This man is drunk," said the minister.

Mole looked down at the top of Jack's head, then at Mickey, then at Jeanie. Changing gears. "He always left it right in the door," Mole said. "Leon was a good boy."

Then he said, "Father, I got to go." He pried himself out of the minister's arms, shook hands with Mickey again, and then walked through the little white gate and headed back down the street toward the Hollywood.

Smilin' Jack's housekeeper had heard the noise and came out the door just as Mole Ferrell was leaving. Jack was still on the ground, and he'd thrown his head back, trying to get the bleeding to stop. She knelt next to him and began wiping at his face with her apron. "Mr. Moran," she said, "what is happened to you now?"

Jack let himself be cleaned up. She handled his face gently, shaking her head like he was her own child, and when most of the blood was gone, she ran her finger along the bridge of his nose until she found the place where the cartilage separated. "Oh, dear," she said, "you all busted up, ain't you?"

Smilin' Jack didn't answer. When she took her finger off his nose, he stood up, still looking at the sky, and headed back into the funeral parlor. The housekeeper tried to take his arm but he pulled away. Mickey opened the door for him and Jack walked in, bleeding. Jack closed the door behind him, in his housekeeper's face. She seemed to notice the blood on her hands then, and they all waited on the front steps and didn't know what to do. Fifteen or twenty people were standing on the sidewalk when it happened, and they hadn't moved either.

"Dear Jesus," the housekeeper said, "three o'clock Saturday ain't the time for no funeral." She folded her arms to hide her hands. The coffin was in the hearse, the hearse was still running. They stood on the steps and waited.

In a few minutes they heard Jack upstairs, arguing with the

old man. They stood on the steps in their best clothes and listened. Mickey said, "You want to go back to the house and wait?" Jeanie didn't answer him. She was looking over at the hearse now.

Upstairs it got louder. Mickey wished he had somebody to talk to. The housekeeper smiled at him, a sweet old gold-tooth smile full of apologies. It was her family, and it wasn't. "He shouldn't talk that way to his father," Mickey said, looking up there.

The old woman shook her head. "It don't matter," she said. "The old gentleman, he don't hear none of it. He just sit there in the wheelchair."

Mickey looked at her to make sure he'd understood. "The old man's deaf?"

She smiled at him and shook her head. "He don't know morning from night," she said.

It was getting dark before they got back from the cemetery. They'd waited at the funeral home an hour, and then Jack Moran had come out wearing a clean shirt. He'd stuffed cotton into both sides of his nose, but he hadn't changed suits, and Jeanie saw the bloodstains in the material.

He'd come out looking angry and gone to the hearse without apologizing. She and Mickey and the minister got into the Cadillac behind it, and her sisters followed that in Joanie's Ford wagon. At the grave they put the coffin under a tent, and the minister read from the Bible. *"To everything there is a season. ..."*

She had to admit it was a beautiful coffin.

Mickey looked straight ahead, the sisters stood together, apart from the others. Jack Moran's nose was bleeding again. She saw they were all tired of Leon now, they wanted to get it over. She thought she wanted to get it over too, but when the service had ended, she couldn't leave him there alone. The minister had tried to talk to her. "There's nothing more you can do now, Jeanie," he'd said.

"A few minutes," she'd said. And she'd stood out there

243

under the tent for an hour, because she couldn't stand to leave him alone. Finally Mickey had come close to her, touched her arm.

"They're closin' the cemetery," he'd said.

And she'd pulled away from him, and walked alone back to the Cadillac. She didn't want to be near him, or her sisters. She didn't want to be near anybody she knew. She turned to the window and stared outside the whole trip back.

At the house, Mickey had wanted to talk, but she'd gone upstairs, into the bathroom, and stared at her face in the mirror. Stared a long time, until it felt like a trance. It was like that at the graveyard too, standing beside the coffin. Time didn't come into it anymore. After a while, she washed her face, and then she began putting on makeup again, slowly, without a plan. She put it on that way to see what she would be when it was finished.

Sometime later the phone rang, eight or nine times. Mickey must have gone out. She picked it up and waited.

"Jeanie?"

"Hello," she said. It was Richard Shellburn.

"Is it finished?"

She said, "Why does everybody want it to be finished? He was mine, not anybody else's."

"I'll pick you up tomorrow," he said. "We can have lunch and talk. If you want to, we could take a drive out to the place."

"I don't know," she said.

"That's the reason to do it," he said. "I'll pick you up."

"No," she said. "Not yet." Not ever, she thought.

"Let's go to the place," he said. "It'll do you good, just to be out in the fresh air."

"It's not my place," she said.

"It will be," he said. "I'll pick you up." She let the line go quiet for a minute. "You don't have a place of your own," he said.

"I know it," she said. He was saying something else when she hung up. Then she went back to the mirror and darkened her lips and lightened her cheeks, and after a few minutes it came to her that she didn't know what she looked like anymore.

She closed her eyes to clear her head and saw the casket. Sitting under the tent at the cemetery, and she saw herself standing next to it. She saw the black dress and her hair, but she couldn't see her face. She could see Leon's though, she could see him awake, curled over on his side somewhere in the box. Awake and blinking. It was a beautiful casket, but it was too big for him.

And when she opened her eyes and saw herself in the mirror, she was surprised—for the half-second she could see it—how bad this had hurt her. She thought it must be like a car accident, when you couldn't tell for yourself how bad you were hurt. Your body lied to you at first, you had to wait and see.

Then she couldn't even remember where she'd seen the damage in her face. She studied herself a long time and then washed off the makeup, and began her face over again, without a plan, to see if it would be happy again when she finished.

DEAD ISSUES

Sunday afternoon Old Lucy thought they'd finally come to get him. He was sitting in his chair by the window, looking out across the street when he heard the police cars. Minnie Devine was at church. The noise they made wasn't a siren anymore, it was a panic noise.

It started out a long ways away, and then got closer, like a heart attack. There was two of them, then three, maybe more. Lucien was glad Minnie wasn't here to see it, he'd worried her enough, not eating. He came to the table, but he couldn't eat. He felt too tired.

He thought maybe he ought to get dressed, but he guessed they'd tell him what to wear. The noise got louder, until it seemed to be coming from the kitchen. He felt himself trembling.

He'd never been in jail before, never even been in the hospital. "Well, boy," he said out loud, "it's all comin' to settle now."

In the week since he'd killed Leon Hubbard, Lucien had come to think of the boy and himself in it together. The last couple of days, he'd found himself talking to him, guiding him through what was happening. He felt friendly toward him, and when he thought of him that way it took the pressure off what he'd did.

He got up out of the chair, feeling heavy and tired, and pulled his jacket off the hat tree. He thought it would be cold where they'd put him. He put the jacket on and stepped out the front door, wearing his slippers. He didn't want them coming into Minnie's house to get him.

He stepped outside, and one of the police cars came around the corner, making that panicky sound that seemed to match his heart. He thought they'd made a mistake when they went past him, but there was another car right behind, and it went past too. And then a third one. And then the children from the neighborhood was all running and skating toward Broad Street, where the police had finally stopped.

It came to him that it was the Korean. The Muslims had finally settled with him. He sat down on the steps and waited. The children would be back soon and tell him what happened. It was likely they shot him in the night.

The Korean would have been asleep in the doorway, they wouldn't of even had to get out of the car, just slow down, roll down the window, and shoot. The Korean might never of even woke up. That's the way Koreans was.

He shook his head, thinking about it. There was things that God meant to happen, he believed that. But there was also things wasn't decided until they came around, and the Korean had gave up his family and his house to wait for them. He thought again that the Muslims probably come for him at night. That's the way they was.

He wondered how long the Korean had been sitting there before somebody noticed he was dead, and how many people noticed it before somebody called the police. It didn't make no sense, sittin' there waitin' for them to kill him. It didn't make no sense that the Korean didn't have a plan of his own. Everybody dies, he thought, it's all settled in the end, but it's no sense in waitin' for them to come by in the night.

A few minutes later, one of the children came back from the Korean's direction. She was a wild girl, never paid no attention to her mother. Lucien knew everybody in the neighborhood from listening to Minnie over the last week. Thirteen, fourteen years old, she already been pregnant. "Clorese," he said, "what all them police doin'?"

She had a pinch of chewing tobacco under her lip and a scar from her nose to her ear, and she looked him over like he was For Sale. "They offed one of them Ko-reans," she said.

"When they did it?" he said.

"I mind my own bi'niss," she said.

"That's what I heard," he said. She shrugged and began to walk away. "The police be askin' questions?" he said. He wondered what he'd say if the police asked him.

"You askin' all the questions," she said. "All they doin' is cleanin' him up off the sidewalk." She shrugged. "He didn't give no fuck if he died. They's some people around like that." Lucien saw that she meant him. "I mind my own bi'niss," she said.

He sat on the steps, and in fifteen or twenty minutes an ambulance came around the corner, screaming like there was something left to do, and it stopped up where the police cars was. There was still a crowd, but it didn't have a bloody spirit. He could tell that from where he was. It was just a Korean.

He thought of the boy again, and the way the blade had felt up under his chin. He worked his whole life, nobody ever tried to take nothin' away from him before. At least they never tried where he couldn't get around it. So he'd picked up the pipe, and the feeling when he'd hit him had went all the way down to his shoulder, solid as a bag of cement. "It wasn't all your fault, boy," he said. "You was takin' more than you knew."

He looked down the street, trying to see if Channel 6 had the

Action Cam live on the scene, but it was too far to tell. He saw them carrying something from the street to the ambulance, though. He guessed it was the Korean. Then the ambulance left, and the people hung around the spot.

They was still there when Minnie Devine come back from church. She was wearing a light blue hat with webbing that come down over her face. "How was the services?" he said.

She said, "Reverend asked for you, said was you sick."

"What'd you say?"

"I said you was out of sorts."

"What'd he say?"

"He said Jesus was good for that." She noticed then he was sitting outside in his slippers. "Lucien, what come over you now?"

"I heard the noise," he said, "and there wasn't no time to get dressed." She made a face, but she didn't say anything. He looked back down the street, where she had come from. "Did you see the police carry him off?"

"I seen it," she said. "I couldn't do nothin' but seen it, all the children they got runnin' around blockin' things up. Nobody goin' to church no more. . . ." She looked at him.

"They must of finally shot him in the night," Lucien said. It wasn't like him to think so much about other people's business. He guessed that's what happened when you quit work and didn't have no business of your own.

She shook her head. "Ain't nobody shot that Korean," she said. She started up the steps past him, but he reached out and touched her hand. She saw he didn't understand. "They didn't do nothin' to him," she said. "He died by hisself."

She went past him into the house, hung up her coat and hat, and put her church Bible away in the drawer where she kept it. She went into the kitchen and began to fix a chicken for dinner. "He just died by hisself?" he said, close behind her.

The voice startled her, but she answered without turning around. "All by hisself," she said. "I believe that's what he wanted."

"They ain't nobody wants to die sittin' in a doorway," he said.

"Then what else was he doin' there, Lucien?" she said. And when he didn't answer, she went back to fixing the chicken.

Shellburn sat dead still.

She'd hung up on him. She'd said the place in Maryland wasn't hers, he'd said it could be, and he'd felt her moving away then, even before she'd hung up. The more he thought about it, the worse it seemed. He went over it again, getting so lost in it that when the phone rang he thought he was saved. Only it wasn't Jeanie. "Richard? It's Billy."

Shellburn sighed.

"Is it a bad time? I can get back to you later." Billy was always worried that it was the wrong time. The boy must have been born premature. "I got a call from T. D. is why I'm calling you."

"What'd he want?" Shellburn said.

"You," he said. "He wanted to know if you'd seen the *Daily Times*."

"I've seen it every day for twenty years," Shellburn said. "It's beautiful, tell him."

"It's the God's Pocket thing," Billy said. "We got your construction worker dying again. Tuesday we wrote he was killed on a construction job and today we got him dying in a traffic accident at Third and Fitzwater. He says you could of prevented the whole thing. . . ."

Shellburn said, "He's trying to blame me?" He shook his head in the empty room.

"The way he sounded, he was getting heat from somewhere," Billy said. "And you know if he's getting heat, he's going to hand it to somebody else. They already fired some girl only been there a week."

Shellburn said, "That sounds right."

"What he said was, the neighborhood's losing its faith in the *Daily Times*," Billy said.

250

Shellburn laughed out loud. "Fuck, what does it say?" Billy Deebol read it to him and waited.

"You want me to read it again?" he said. Shellburn hadn't said anything, he was putting it together with Jeanie on the phone.

"Once is enough," he said.

"T. D. wanted you to call him," Billy said. "He says he wants you to go out there and straighten it out, like you were supposed to do."

"Fuck T. D.," Shellburn said, and saying that, a column began to come to him, in a shape. He bought a paper at the bar where he ate dinner—four beers and an egg sandwich—and then he drove over to the office. The whole place was empty on Saturday night, quiet. He sat down in front of his typewriter and thought of ways to start it. Thinking of Jeanie reading it, thinking of T. D. reading it. He was breaking his hardest rule: you don't let anybody else into it. If you did, it always showed. The only person you could imagine reading it was yourself, and if it didn't make you cringe, then you could go ahead and write it.

The truest thing in the world was that you showed who you were writing a column. He said that at his lectures, and they always took that to mean politics or how you feel about the death penalty. Which had nothing to do with it. There were as many dick shrivelers that wanted to ban nuclear sites and love the brother as there were that wanted to bomb Russia. It was almost incidental, what you had for issues. But how you saw things, how physical things went into your eyes and what your brain took and what it threw back, that told who you were.

"*Until the coming of New Journalism,*" he wrote, "*you only got to die once in this city, even if you came from God's Pocket.*" He read that over a couple of times, then changed "coming" to "advent."

"*There was a time,*" he wrote, "*when a 24-year-old working man could die once, have the event noticed in his local newspaper and then move on to his reward, without the complications of an*

251

additional death." He read it back, out loud, and decided the tone was right. You had to hard-boil dying, unless it was a cat.

"*On Saturday, the* Daily Times *changed all that. We had help, of course. Someplace in this city is a policeman who cannot tell an accident victim from a five-day-old corpse, someplace there is a SEPTA bus driver who doesn't stop for red lights. Everywhere, in fact, there are SEPTA bus drivers who don't stop for red lights.*

"*But it took the* Daily Times *to turn what happened to Leon Hubbard into a multiple death. And to turn his death into a nightmare for all the people from God's Pocket who loved him.*

"*For his mother, his friends, his co-workers.*" Shellburn thought about throwing Mickey Scarpato in there, and then decided against it.

"*The first death, according to police, happened when part of a crane came loose and hit Leon Hubbard in the back of the head. The* Daily Times *reported that incident on page 16 of last Tuesday's editions in a two-paragraph story.*

"*It was reported incorrectly but then, Leon Hubbard wasn't important. If he had been, surely one of the New Journalists would have written at some length about what Leon Hubbard had for breakfast, what he was about the moment it happened.*"

Shellburn stopped again and thought about T. D. Davis.

"*There are people at the* Daily Times *who aren't going to like this,*" he wrote. "*Some of them are the New Journalists themselves, who dislike facts, and some of them, I suppose, are the people who brought the New Journalists to Philadelphia from places like Florida. It would be hard for me to care less what they like.*

"*There isn't a New Journalist in this city worth a hair on Leon Hubbard's head or of any man who works for a living who knows what it is to get up every morning and sweat for his money.*

"*Leon Hubbard lived in a row house on 25th Street in God's Pocket—small, dirty-faced, neat as a pin inside. And Leon Hubbard was like the other working people in God's Pocket. Dirty-faced, uneducated, neat as a pin inside.*"

Shellburn read it again, weighing T. D. Davis and Jeanie Scarpato in the sentences.

"The workingmen of God's Pocket are simple men. They work, they follow the Phillies and the Eagles, they marry and have children who inhabit the Pocket, often in the homes of their mothers and fathers. They drink at the Hollywood Bar or the Uptown Bar, small, dirty-faced little places deep in the city, and they argue there about things they don't understand. Politics, race, religion.

"But they understand their lives—as much as anyone can—and their deaths. And in the end they die, like everybody else, leaving their families and their houses and their legends. Sometimes they die old, but more often it's a heart attack at 52, or cirrhosis at 47, or cancer. The refineries where they work poison them, and poison their children. And sometimes, like Leon Hubbard, they die at 24, when part of a crane comes loose and caves in the back of their head.

"And there is a dignity in that. A dirty-faced dignity that the New Journalists will never understand. Because they have never been dirty-faced, they have never had to work for a living. The air they breathed growing up didn't have poison in it, their fathers didn't die from bad livers or hearts at 50 years old. Their fathers put them through journalism school.

"Of course, I have no idea what they teach in journalism school these days, but it's not the lessons of God's Pocket. And so maybe it's not their fault—the New Journalists'—that a death in that world doesn't matter to them. That a 24-year-old man who supported his mother and his neighborhood is dead.

"And maybe it isn't their fault that it matters so little that they get the age wrong, or miss the street where the dirty-faced little house was. Maybe, it isn't their fault that they care so little they can report the same man dying two different times in the same week.

"But it's someone's fault. Someone gave the New Journalists their VDT machines, someone brought them to Philadelphia, someone gave them the space in this newspaper to write. Someone armed them and turned them loose, and the victims pile up quietly all over Philadelphia, and in the forgotten editions of this newspaper.

"And the victims sit quietly in God's Pocket and a hundred other neighborhoods like it in this city, and they take it. They are *afraid and ignorant. They are being used like guinea pigs in an experiment in child journalism, and none of them is doing a thing about it.*

"None of them cares enough to come down here and shake somebody by the throat, none of them cares enough to say, 'You can't insult me.' Leon Hubbard might have done that, I don't know. But I know we owe him an apology, and all the people who knew him and loved him and worked with him. And I know that if we stop listening to Leon Hubbard's story, and all the stories like it in the neighborhoods of this city, eventually the neighborhoods will stop listening to ours."

Shellburn typed a "-30-" at the bottom of the page, and then put his feet up on the desk to read what he had written. He smiled, thinking of the phone calls Monday morning, thinking of the crybaby New Journalists writing their defenses in columns that they would submit for the Op-Ed page, and that would never be run. He thought of Jeanie Scarpato and stopped smiling.

He wondered if she would understand the chance he was taking, going against his own paper for her. She was confused now, he knew that from the telephone call.

She was confused, and it would have been better to wait a week, but in a week she might have moved so far away from him that it wouldn't matter what he wrote. And in a week, Leon Hubbard would be old news, unless the New Journalists hauled him out and had him killed again.

He stapled the column together, went downstairs to the city room and put it in the night managing editor's mailbox instead of Billy's. He didn't want anybody softening it up. He checked his own mail then, about twenty letters, half that many messages. One of them from Yahama Bahama. He pictured her for a minute. Pretty hair, perfect teeth, legs, everything. It didn't do a thing. The best he ever liked his wife, Shellburn never stopped looking for other women.

That was what Jeanie Scarpato had done to him. That and the column lying in the night managing editor's mailbox spoke how much he could feel. He had an impulse to call her then, but he pushed it back.

"Let her read the column," he said out loud, "let her see what you've done for her."

T. D. Davis was watching television.

The Jap golfer was lining up a putt of less than one foot on the eighteenth hole of a course someplace in North Carolina. The announcers were whispering. "Keith?"

"Yes, Don."

"Keith, I think you could say this is the most important eight inches in this young man from Japan's life." The camera was behind the golfer, and from that angle the sun caught the blade of his putter. From that angle, it looked like the Japanese golfer could have been pissing into the cup. He stood over his ball ten seconds, then fifteen, too long. He stood up and backed off.

"It's definitely the most important eight inches in his life," Keith said, "and I think he realizes that more than anybody."

A moment before the phone rang, T. D. sat up in his chair to study the golfer from Japan. T. D. had seen the signs earlier, on a three-footer at the fifteenth. He was trying so hard now to concentrate that he'd gone past it. He'd turned the microscope a little past things and now he couldn't get them focused again.

The Japanese golfer walked away from the putt for another look. T. D. smiled. The Japanese people, of course, were famous for trying hard. That's why the handles didn't fall off their car doors, but T. D. could see this one was out of control. He'd lost a stroke at the fifteenth, another one at the sixteenth, and now he needed this little eight-inch putt to hold off Tom Watson, who had played the back nine in thirty-two. Watson, the greatest player in golf, was standing on the edge of the green, watching. The Jap knew he was there.

The lie might have been a little downhill, not enough to make any difference, unless the Japanese let it. He walked back and stood over the putt again. Ten seconds, fifteen. Too long. He tapped the ball and it rolled past the hole on the left side.

The phone rang just as the television camera got close to the

Japanese golfer's face—half apology, half terror. T. D. wondered if there was a club in his bag for cutting open his stomach. T. D. had been raised underprivileged in a country where they liked to say anybody could grow up to be President, but now he'd made himself a place, and the spirit behind that belief was the single most repulsive thing he could think of. T. D. liked the old order. Watson, Nicklaus, Palmer. He picked up the phone, watching the crowd and the golfers head back to the fifteenth hole to begin a sudden-death playoff.

"T. D. Davis," he said. T. D. always answered his own phone, he kept a listed number in the phone book.

It was Brookie Sutherland. "T. D., I just got into the office," he said.

"Fine."

"Yessir. Anyway, I got in and Shellburn's column was in my mailbox, like when Billy Deebol's on vacation—you know, Shellburn won't use the VDTs himself. . . ."

"I know."

"Well, I was going to keyboard the column, and then I happened to notice what it was about, and I thought you'd want to know."

T. D. Davis said, "Dead mummers . . ."

"Well, no," Brookie Sutherland said. "It's about somebody getting killed in South Philadelphia, and then it libels the paper. You want me to read part of it?"

The television station had gone to commercial while Tommy Watson and the Japanese were headed back to the fifteenth. "The paper can't libel the paper," T. D. said.

Brookie Sutherland began to read. "*Someone gave the New Journalists their VDT machines, someone brought them to Philadelphia, someone gave them the space in this newspaper to write. Someone armed them and turned them loose, and the victims pile up quietly all over Philadelphia, and in the forgotten editions of this newspaper.*"

He read the part about the readers being guinea pigs and not having enough balls to come down to the paper and choke somebody, too. When he'd finished, the line was quiet. T. D. Davis had the feeling that Sutherland was out of breath. "You want me to read the rest of it?"

Back on television, the Japanese and Tom Watson had arrived at the fifteenth tee. The hole was a dogleg left, and the approach to the green was over a peanut-shaped pond the color of paper money. Watson played first, since the Japanese had bogeyed the last hole. He used a three wood and drove the ball 250 yards straight out into the bend of the fairway.

"I guess you better," T. D. said.

While Brookie Sutherland read the column, the Japanese hooked his drive into the trees on the left, punched out with a seven iron, and then dropped his ball into the middle of the peanut-shaped pond, trying to make up for the stroke he lost in the trees. Watson had stood with his caddie in the middle of the fairway and watched it happen. The thing T. D. liked about caddies was that they knew they were caddies, and even if they thought they were as good as Tom Watson, there was always that sixty-pound bag to haul around to remind them what they were.

On the phone, Brookie Sutherland was at the part about the guinea pigs again. On the television, the camera was back in close on the Japanese golfer's face. He looked like—oh, like he might have just lost the feeling in his legs. "Keith," one of the announcers said, "I think his face tells the whole story."

T. D. Davis studied the look. Shock and loss, the misunderstanding the Japanese golfer had had about where he fit into things. Davis studied him until it almost could have been Richard Shellburn.

Brookie Sutherland was finished. "What do you want me to do?" he said.

T. D. didn't let his feeling into his voice. "What you're supposed to do," he said. "Keyboard it for Monday's paper." And then, before Brookie Sutherland could thank him for his time or offer to mow the lawn or suck his dick, T. D. Davis hung up.

• • •

Monday morning T. D. came into the office at exactly eight-thirty. He said good morning to Brookie Sutherland and Gertruda and then went into his office and read the column for himself.

The papers hit the street forty-five minutes later, and by eleven o'clock the city was screaming like the delivery trucks were out running over pet dogs. People didn't like Richard Shellburn calling them dirty-faced and ignorant. There were about twenty calls from the Pocket, maybe thirty others from places like it. T. D. could hear the tone of their voices shade when they realized who they'd got on the phone.

He told them all the same thing, that he didn't tell Richard Shellburn what to write. A woman said, "Doesn't anybody look it over before you go ahead and put it in?" and he'd said, "Just for spelling. Richard Shellburn is the most-loved columnist in this town, and we like to think it was his own judgment got him there."

A man from God's Pocket said, "Well, if he wasn't over here gettin' in Leon's mother's pants all the time, he might of noticed everybody here ain't dirty."

T. D. had Gertruda keep track of the calls, and when it hit thirty he had her try to call Shellburn. Gertruda said she'd let the phone ring five minutes. "Then call Billy Deebol," he said. "Have Billy run over there and wake him up."

Billy knocked on the door just as the noon news started. Shellburn had been out of bed long enough to collect his newspaper and find a cold beer in the refrigerator. He'd moved the typewriter off the table for room to read the paper and had just settled down to it when he heard the taps on the door. "Richard? It's Billy. . . ."

Shellburn got up and slid the bolts in the door, and Billy was standing there in his suit and a new haircut, apologizing for knocking on his door. "You want to come in?" he said.

Billy shook his head. "I only got a minute," he said. "T. D. is trying to get ahold of you."

"I disconnected the phone," Shellburn said.

"I can tell T. D. you weren't here if you want me to. They're pissing through the phones at the office. I think they had thirty calls the first hour."

Shellburn said, "Anybody come down there to strangle T. D. yet?"

Billy shook his head. "I don't think they're pissed at him. At least not from what he said. From what he said, it's you." Shellburn stopped smiling. "That's what he told me. . . ."

Shellburn closed his eyes and tried to see if that could be true. "What for? I'm the one on their side."

"I thought you'd took the day off," Billy said, "when there wasn't a column in my mailbox." Shellburn could see he was holding back.

"We've been friends a long time," Shellburn said.

Billy nodded. "All right. I can see how maybe they might of taken it wrong today. I mean, they might of missed the point."

Shellburn went back over to the table and picked up the paper and began to read the column out loud. Billy stopped him when he called them dirty-faced. "That right there," he said. "And the part about not understanding their religion. . . ."

He dropped the paper on the table. "Nobody understands their religion," he said, "that was the point." Then he remembered Billy had six kids, and saw that he should have explained it. You couldn't do that later, after it was in the paper. "How many calls?"

Billy shrugged. "Thirty or forty," he said.

"And nobody's pissed at him?"

"Just for lettin' you write it."

Shellburn noticed that Billy was standing in the doorway. "C'mon in," he said. "It's all right."

It was the first time Billy had ever been inside. He sat down in the chair and looked at the table, not wanting to seem nosy.

"You want a beer?"

"All right."

Shellburn got two beers out of the refrigerator, gave one to

Billy and then sat down on the mattress, holding one in each hand. "You know what I was talking about, don't you?"

"Yes," he said.

Shellburn said, "It was about people. Good people and bad people."

"Maybe you shouldn't of called them dirty-faced," Billy said. "That might of been where the misunderstanding was."

"It's a compliment," Shellburn said. "They work for a living, they get dirty."

"That's dirty hands," Billy said. "Dirty-faced is you don't take a bath." Shellburn thought that over. Billy sipped at his beer and looked at the table.

"You been over there yet?" Shellburn said. "The Pocket?"

Billy shook his head. "I've been going over Judge Kalquist's trial records," he said. "I thought maybe I could get that finished this week."

"The patterns," Shellburn said, "that's what we're looking for, the patterns."

"The patterns aren't clean-cut," Billy said. "Not to nail his ass with. . . ."

Shellburn didn't seem to be listening. "It's never clean, is it?" he said.

"The little stories are clean," Billy said. "Dead-dog stories, the bums at Christmas . . ."

"No matter what you do," Shellburn said, "you never get to the bottom. No matter how deep you go. How long we been working on Kalquist, three weeks?"

Billy nodded, not pointing out that he was the one who'd been doing the work. "Three or four," he said.

"And after all that time, going through trial transcripts and sentences, we don't have anything but patterns."

Billy Deebol was getting more uncomfortable by the minute. "I'm not sure we got a clean pattern, Richard," he said.

"Dead dogs," Shellburn said. "The reason dead dogs are clean is because they can't tell you you're wrong. Same way with the bums." Billy noticed Shellburn was a minute or two behind the conversation, but sometimes he got like that. "If you could talk to a dead dog, you think he'd tell you he was devoted and cute and that's it? If you got down to it, what it was like to be a dog, it might turn out that he deserved to get run over." He shook his head. "There's nothing clean, Billy. Nobody ever told the whole truth yet."

Billy sipped his beer. "You want me to tell T. D. you weren't home?" he said.

Shellburn nodded. "Yeah, I'll get to him later this afternoon. And keep after Kalquist, will you, Billy? All we need is the pattern."

Billy finished his beer and stood up. The room smelled stale and old, and in a way he hated to leave Shellburn there alone. In another way, it was what Shellburn wanted. "I'll tell him you weren't home," he said.

"You and I've been friends a long time," Shellburn said. Billy Deebol blushed. This time he'd said it for no reason except to say it. "We got to keep looking for something clean." Billy headed for the door.

"You still want me to go down to God's Pocket?"

"Maybe you better," Shellburn said. "Down to the Hollywood and buy a couple of rounds." He stood up, unsure of his balance, and found his pants on the floor. "Here, you need some money?"

"No, I got money."

Shellburn dropped the pants back on the floor. "Yeah, just do that, and I'll take care of everything," he said. "In the end, it won't mean anything. In two weeks, it'll be forgotten. You want a beer to take with you?"

Billy Deebol took the beer and left. Shellburn locked the door behind him, got another beer for himself and sat down on the mattress near the phone and thought about looking for something clean. He plugged in the phone and called her number, but nobody answered. He let it ring fifteen times, then he disconnected his phone again.

There was a six-pack left in the refrigerator. When that was gone, he'd call T. D. and then get back to thinking about something clean.

It turned out there were two six-packs in the refrigerator. Shellburn sat on the mattress and drank them. He'd been drunk when he'd gone to bed and half-drunk when he woke up, and somewhere around the fifth beer, he knew he was drunk again. He felt cheated. There was no building up to it, no thinking, no irony, no visions of people he had known. Suddenly, he was just drunk.

He put seven beers on top of that and then went back to sleep. When he woke up again, Channel 6 Action News had just plugged in for the evening report, anchorman Jim Garner was looking at him in that fatherly way he had, draining the day of its stories. Shellburn had been told that in the world of television, the people who read news were called talent. He wasn't sure he believed that, but he hoped it was true.

He remembered T. D. then, and that he had to see him. He shaved and took a long, hot shower. He couldn't make up his mind. One minute Jeanie was gone forever, the next minute he had her living with him in Maryland. One minute he'd beat the New Journalists, the next minute they'd beat him. He had Kalquist, and he didn't. He felt like he was the only one left, he felt like he spoke for millions. He did wish he had another beer, though. He was sure of that.

He put on a coat and a tie and after-shave lotion, spent fifteen minutes finding the car, and then drove right to the newspaper.

When Shellburn came in, Billy Deebol was in T. D.'s office, sitting in a chair that T. D. had moved off the Oriental carpet, holding a handkerchief full of ice against his mouth. There was a splash of blood down the front of his shirt that crossed his tie and ended at the end of his sleeve. The sleeve was ripped from the cuff to the shoulder. T. D. was sipping a cup of tea.

"They didn't like your column out in the neighborhoods,"

T. D. said. Shellburn pried Billy's hand away from his mouth. A front tooth and the one next to it were sheared right down to the gum, the lips were cut where teeth had gone through them.

"You ought to get that stitched," Shellburn said.

"He went over to where you ought to have been in the first place," T. D. said.

Shellburn said to Billy, "How'd it happen?"

Billy shrugged. "I bought a round of drinks, and one of them hit me in the face. Then another one picked up a beer bottle and hit me in the mouth. I saw that one, but there wasn't anything to do."

"You wrote the column," T. D. said, "and sent Billy-boy out to fix it."

Billy shook his head. "That wasn't it," he said.

T. D. said, "That's what happened."

Billy said, "It wasn't on purpose."

"How'd you get out?" Shellburn said.

"They pushed me out," Billy said. "After they'd hit me with the beer bottle, that was all they wanted me for." He looked up at Shellburn. "I know it wasn't on purpose," he said. Shellburn had to remind himself that Billy was thirty-seven years old. He looked maybe seventeen now, like he'd just seen what was out there for the first time. Shellburn pushed the ice and the handkerchief back, gently, to his mouth. He had a soft touch.

"You ought to go down to the emergency room now," he said, "get some stitches." Billy nodded. Shellburn was trying to remember what they'd said earlier, about nothing was ever clean. He was wondering if this wasn't close to it, what he was feeling now. More than wanting the woman, or the place in Maryland.

"There was 134 calls today," T. D. said, over the teacup. "You should of been here to answer them, Richard."

Shellburn said, "I'll take care of it now."

"I ain't tellin' you to go down there," T. D. said. "I'm not sayin' you ought to go. . . ." He looked at Billy, to make sure he'd witnessed that, and the look he got back reminded him of somebody a long time ago, in New York. Billy Deebol would need watching.

Billy pulled the ice away from his mouth to talk. Part of the lip followed it half an inch, and then unstuck itself and began to bleed. "Stay away from there, Richard," he said. "They aren't listening right now, and there's too many of them to talk to anyway."

Shellburn smiled at him. He seemed like such a kid. "They aren't going to do anything to me," he said.

Billy shook his head. "That ain't the Germantown Woman's Association you can make a speech to," he said. "Who you are doesn't count down there now." He looked from Richard to T. D. Davis, and Davis saw that expression again, and thought of Jimmy White coming into his office with a chain saw.

"You probably ought not to go down there," T. D. said. "Let it cool off. . . ." But Shellburn was already going out the door. He almost seemed happy.

Mickey was sitting in a booth with Ray when Shellburn came in. Ray was getting ready to pass out. The kids at the bar had beat up somebody from the newspaper earlier, they were still bragging about who did what. Mickey had moved over to the booth because he didn't want to hear it.

Not that anybody was talking to him anyway. Ever since the funeral, things had changed. It was like he'd done something worse than anybody ever did before. Even McKenna wasn't the same to him. Mickey spent most of his time at the bar, and slept on the couch or in the Monte Carlo. And Ray had started to make sense to him. In fact, it worried him that he might be going that way himself. He might of got comfortable with it, being an outcast.

Shellburn stopped at the door, looked around, squinting, and then found himself a stool somewhere near the middle of the room. The whole bar went quiet, and Mickey smiled at that. "Give me a beer," Shellburn said.

McKenna put his arm on the bar and leaned toward the reporter. "Mr. Shellburn, nothin' personal, but I think I better ask you to leave, for your own good."

Shellburn looked left and right, then in back of him. Then he looked at the bartender and shrugged. "Schmidt's," he said. He had some balls, Mickey gave him that. More balls than the fighters and stompers of the Hollywood Bar.

Mickey had never appreciated Shellburn's intentions with his wife, but he'd quit blaming him. It was like when the pipes froze and they came and dug up the street in front of your house. You don't blame somebody for looking in your hole.

He knew by now that her idea of things was an Esther Williams movie. *Million-Dollar Mermaid*. She was the kind that could smile underwater. And she could be nice to you, and fuck you and marry you, but the camera was always rolling.

"What the fuck you writin' about us in the paper for?" somebody said. "What's it your bi'niss what we do?"

Somebody else said, "Who the fuck you callin' guineas? You ain't even from here, makin' us look like assholes. . . ."

Then half the bar was shouting at Shellburn, but the ones next to him, the ones he could see, were quiet. It was always the scaredest ones that you had to watch. The kid sitting next to him at the bar—a fat kid with a wide pink-and-white face—got up, nodded at Shellburn, almost friendly, and walked out the door.

Mickey noticed Shellburn seemed to be turning gray. "I didn't make you assholes," Shellburn said to the bar. "I said the opposite."

Mickey closed his eyes. Explaining was the worst thing you could do when it was all against you.

"We ain't that simple," one of them said, and then they all seemed to drink at once.

Shellburn looked at the bartender again. "Schmidt's," he said. McKenna sighed and gave him a beer. "Let's everybody calm down," he said.

"Fuck calm down," one of them said. "What the fuck's he doin' down here now?" Shellburn sat over his beer, like it was

265

none of his business. They all came off their stools then, and when Shellburn turned around to face them he was flushed and sweating. Mickey never saw anybody change colors so fast.

"I came down here because somebody hit my friend in the face with a beer bottle," Shellburn said. "It's a misunderstanding. . . ." Then the door opened and the fat kid with the pink-and-white face came back in, carrying a bat. He came in and stopped by the door, and then a dozen more of them came in. Some of them had crowbars, and some of them had reinforcement steel off construction sites. They'd put tape around the bottom for handles. They stood at the end of the bar and waited, and before long there were at least twenty. Bats, crowbars, steel. Babies, most of them not old enough to drink, all watching each other to see what to do.

"This is my city," Shellburn said.

"The motherfucker come down here to get fucked up," the fat kid said. He was holding the bat in both hands, close enough to the door to be the first one out in case Shellburn was carrying. Mickey saw Shellburn trying to find who it was talking, trying to find somebody to talk to him. It was the wrong time for that.

The others moved closer and Shellburn turned to McKenna. Mickey saw the look on McKenna's face then, like Shellburn wasn't even there. "Take it outside, Dick," he said to the fat boy.

The fat boy said, "He come down here, McKenna. It's his own fault. He come down here to get fucked up."

Shellburn stood up, the ones closest to him moved away. "I came down here because somebody got hurt," he said.

"Fuck him up," the fat boy said.

Mickey looked across the table at Ray, whose head was beginning to drop. "What the fuck?" he said. "Over something he *wrote*?"

Ray shook his head. "Nothing to do with it," he said, and then he crossed his arms for a pillow and went to sleep.

McKenna didn't want to see it either. When Mickey looked again, Shellburn was trying to tell him something was wrong. "I'm sick," he said, and, shiny with sweat, he bent at the waist and choked. A thin line of yellow spit was all that came out. McKenna walked away.

The fat boy said, "Ain't as sick as you going to get."

McKenna pointed at him. "Take it outside," he said again, and then three or four of them had Shellburn by the back of the collar and they pulled him outside. Mickey saw Shellburn's eyes were closed and that he didn't fight it. Ray began to snore.

Mickey got out of the booth, and on the way out he looked at McKenna and said, "What the fuck's wrong with you?"

"You ain't from here," he said.

He went through the door and pushed through the circle around Shellburn. Nobody pushed back. What it came to, he thought, was they'd had a reporter to beat up earlier and the ones that missed out wanted this one.

He found Shellburn in the middle of the circle. His eyes were still shut tight and he seemed to have some kind of spasms. The kid holding onto his collar let go and backed away. "What the fuck?" Mickey said. "What are you going to do out here, thirty of you against one old man? For somethin' in the newspaper?"

"It ain't your fuckin' business, Mickey," one of them said. "You ain't from here either, so stay the fuck out of it." It was the fat boy talking, but Mickey couldn't find his face.

"I don't give a fuck," Mickey said. "Not this . . ." He moved a step toward them, they moved back. He turned back toward Shellburn to tell him to get in his car and leave, but when the reporter opened his eyes, Mickey could see something was wrong, that he was losing track of it. And then Shellburn smiled at him and said, "It's all light and dark." Still trying to explain.

Something in that spooked Mickey, but before he could ask Shellburn what he was talking about, the reporter was falling backwards, into the window of the bar. The glass held and Shellburn fell to the sidewalk, and once he was down, there wasn't anything that could help him.

One of them kicked him in the head, and when Mickey pushed him away the others went at him with the bats and iron.

Four or five times he pulled them away from the reporter, but as soon as he stopped one, somebody else took his place working on Shellburn's head. They hit him fifty or sixty times before Mickey gave up.

He left them out there with what they'd done and went back in the bar. McKenna shook his head. "I'm closed," he said.

Mickey walked back to the booth where Ray was sleeping and sat down. He finished his beer, wondering what it was worth, belonging somewhere, if it ended up like this. He thought it must of been worth something, or he wouldn't of felt so bad leaving it.

By the time he got back outside, the street was as empty as three o'clock in the morning. A wedge of light went from the window to the sidewalk, Shellburn was under that, lying against the wall, something dark on the ground beneath a rainbow, painted a long time ago across the window of the Hollywood Bar.

The police came by early the next morning, and the three mornings after that. One named Eisenhower had been there before, after Leon died. He took Mickey outside and said, "I heard you were the one that knocked him down."

Mickey said, "Where'd you hear that?"

Eisenhower shrugged. "If I was you, I could understand that, knocking him down. I know you didn't have nothing to do with kicking his head in. That's kids."

"McKenna tell you it was me?" Eisenhower shrugged again. It had to be McKenna, of course. He was the only one talked to the police, because they could shut him down. And the name he'd given up was Mickey's, because he wasn't from the neighborhood.

"Well," Mickey said, "I don't know nothin' about it."

Eisenhower said, "Sooner or later, somebody's going to tell it, give everybody up. That's the way the place is."

"Yes it is," Mickey said.

"When it happens, it'll rain shit in God's Pocket. That wasn't some bum got beat to death in the middle of the street, it was Richard Shellburn. We got the *Daily Times*, the New York

Times, CBS, ABC, UPI and Jesus knows who else calling every day, wanting to know what's happening about Richard Shellburn. He ain't going to go away."

The second time Eisenhower came, Mickey noticed Jeanie looking at him. The next morning, he saw Eisenhower was looking back. He heard her tell him, "My first husband was a police officer."

Later that day, a couple of the neighborhood kids stopped him in the street. He didn't know if they had been at the Hollywood that night or not. "Yo, Mick," one of them said, "we want you to know we 'preciate you not talkin' to the cops. You stood up, like you was part of the Pocket."

"Don't include me in nothin' about the Pocket," he said. He walked through them, and when he was about a block past, he heard them back there, shouting.

"Yo, Mick. Who's fuckin' your wife now?"

Four days after Shellburn got killed, Mickey walked into the house and found Eisenhower sitting next to her on the couch, drinking hot chocolate. The cop jumped when he came in the door, Jeanie never even looked to see who it was. "I just dropped over to tell you it turned out Shellburn had a heart attack," Eisenhower said, "would of died anyway. I don't know if that changes things. . . ."

Mickey said, "It don't have nothin' to do with me either way."

The next morning he packed his things and caught the Amtrak for Palatka, Florida. He was surprised it all fit in the same two cloth bags he'd brought it in with when he moved in. It seemed like being married and living in a house, somehow there ought to of been more.

Peets heard the news about Richard Shellburn on the truck radio. It was a little after six o'clock in the morning, and he was already at work. He couldn't sleep in the morning since his wife left.

He didn't know why it bothered him in the morning,

he went to sleep easy enough at night, but sometime around four-thirty or five he'd miss her weight—or her heat, or something—there on the other side of the bed, and that would wake him up.

He should of gone to the hospital after the fight, he knew it then. Something depended on her thinking he couldn't get hurt, and the one with the knuckles had half scalped him. But he'd tied his shirt around his head like a cleaning lady and gone home, thinking there was some things you couldn't hide. "Dear God, Peets," she'd said. And he knew just from the sound of it that things had changed.

She'd taken him to her hospital to get his lid sewed back on, she'd made him dinner afterward. And the next day when he got home, she'd left him a note with a phone number, in case he couldn't find his socks. "I need some time to get over this," it said.

So he woke up early and made breakfast and then he went to work an hour and a half early. There wasn't much to do until the others showed up, but it was comfortable there, and it wasn't comfortable at home. Sometimes he'd pick up the beer bottles somebody was leaving there every night, more often he'd just sit in his truck and listen to the morning news.

This morning the news was that Richard Shellburn'd had a heart attack the night they found him lying on the sidewalk with his head beat in. A spokesman for the district attorney's office said, "The development of this new evidence, of course, immeasurably complicates the potential prosecution."

Peets shook his head. "It's a lot of that going around," he said. The radio repeated the story every eight minutes, but they'd been picking over Shellburn's bones all week. In between, they gave the weather and the helicopter traffic report.

About quarter to seven, the C bus stopped at the corner, and Old Lucy got off.

Peets was looking in his rearview mirror at the time, checking skirts, more out of habit than anything, and he turned around in his seat to be sure. The old man stepped off the bus and walked slowly into the site. He put his lunch pail against the wall where he ate and then crouched dead still near the cherry picker to wait.

Peets left him alone fifteen minutes. If the old man didn't want some time alone, he wouldn't of come an hour early. Finally, though, he turned off the radio and got out of the truck. He slammed the door so the old man would know he was there.

Old Lucy stayed where he was. He didn't turn his head or stand up. Peets crouched down beside him. "Mornin', Lucy," he said.

"Peets."

"Radio says we got a good day to work." Old Lucy didn't say anything. "You been all right?" Peets said. "I thought of comin' over to your place, but, you know, you don't want to go buttin' in."

"I got it settled," the old man said.

Peets nodded. "Sometimes it can take a while," he said.

"Took that boy his whole life," Lucy said. Peets let that alone, and after a while the old man said, "But it do settle. Ain't nothin' so bad or so good you can do that it don't settle, and in the end you became what you been." He was looking down the wall he'd started, at the work that had been done since he left. It was the most Peets had ever heard him say at one time.

Peets started to put his arm around Lucy's shoulder, but he patted him once on the back instead. "I'm glad you come back," he said. He said it and then he pulled away from it. "I mean, lookit that wall. I can't get no work done here alone, Lucy."

"I can see that," Lucy said. Then he looked at Peets and didn't try to hide what the settling had done to him. "I might be old now," he said.

Peets stood up on bad hinges. He said, "I might be headed that way myself." And in a few minutes they walked over and uncovered the cement bags, so they could get back to building the new wing of Holy Redeemer Hospital.

· · ·

Mickey woke up, and the air was warm and still, and it smelled like the glue they used to stick the place together. Bird had bought the mobile home used, for $12,000, and he and Sophie paid the man forty dollars a month for the space in the lot. Most of the spaces were sixty dollars, but theirs was on the far end, away from the recreation center and the site of the proposed swimming pool. One side of the mobile home backed up to the woods, and every morning after Sophie and her new friends had finished worrying over tornadoes and their flowers, she and Bird went back into the trees and practiced shooting the pistol.

It was Bird who insisted on it. He'd set up bottles and cans in a clearing back there, and they'd take turns shooting. "I don't say nothin'," he'd tell Mickey, " 'cause I don't want to scare her, but, you know, they're comin'. And we got to be ready, right?" Then he'd ask if it was all right to go practice now. Mickey would say it was all right.

And Bird would smile and take her out into the woods, and she smiled and went with him, and they depended on Mickey like he was their father.

The mobile home had three bedrooms. Mickey's was in the back, the air conditioner was in front, and it was that still, warm air that woke him up every morning. Sometimes he woke up thinking about Jeanie, and sometimes, like this morning, it was the reporter. What had he said? "It's all light and dark"?

He got out of bed with a headache and listened. He heard them outside. He put on a pair of pants and went into the bathroom and brushed his teeth. Bird had put tape around the handles of all the toothbrushes and written each of their names on the tape. "Yo, Mick," he'd said. "I got an idea. What if I write everybody's names on their toothbrush? Would that be all right?"

Sometimes they walked into the woods together, past the clearing scattered with broken glass and shell casings, all the way to the river. It was wide and muddy and slow, and it flowed north. "See, what'd I tell you, Mick?" Bird had said. "See, what d'ya think?"

It took a while to get used to how Bird and Sophie was away from Philly. They clung to him like something that floated after the boat sank. He didn't pull away from it, though. He guessed his own boat had sank too.

He brushed his hair and laid his toothbrush next to Sophie's on the sink. Then he went back in his room and found the yellow alligator T-shirt Mickey and Sophie gave him the first night he was there. He put it on and went out the door. "Watch your step," Sophie said.

The first step out was a yard down, and they always told each other to be careful. Mickey even noticed himself saying it. She and Bird were sitting in lawn chairs on the little piece of grass that went with the trailer lot. Sophie was in the shade, holding a water can over her flowers. Bird had taken off his shirt and put his face into a three-sided sun reflector. He said good morning without opening his eyes. Mickey smiled at them. There was some people shouldn't take off their shirts in public.

Sophie said, "You want some breakfast, Mickey?"

He shook his head. "I can't even think about food, this time of the morning," he said.

Bird folded the sun reflector and sat up, sweating. He looked at his watch awhile. "We better go practice," he said. "You want to come along, Mick?"

"I think I'll just read the paper."

"You don't mind if we go?"

"No, it's all right," he said. "Just be careful."

Aunt Sophie picked up a big straw purse off the table and looked inside. Then she reached in and got the gun, and then a box of shells. "Lemme carry those for you," Bird said, and she gave him the shells. She leaned over and kissed Mickey on the cheek and then the two of them walked off into the woods. She carried the gun behind her back, the way young girls in the movies carried their hands when they flirted. Bird waded through the weeds like a sunburned heron. Sometimes, when Sophie was with her new girl friends, Mickey and Bird talked. "We got to be ready, when they come," Bird would say.

Mickey never knew what to tell him. They might come and they might not. In the old days, you wouldn't of had to wonder. "Bird," he'd said, "I can't live off you and Sophie forever. I got to get a job, start somethin'. . . ."

"You'll be here when they come," Bird said. "You'll know what to do."

He sat down in the chair Bird and Sophie had bought for him and picked up the Gainesville *Sun*. It was different from the *Daily Times*, calmer. He wondered what he would do if they came. It wouldn't make much difference, of course, they wouldn't come in stupid like at the flower shop. If they came at all.

He'd give it another month, or two.

It was quiet awhile, and then he heard the shots a long ways off, spaced minutes apart, breaking the quiet Florida morning like unexpected reminders of the people he'd loved.

They were out there in the woods most of an hour, Bird and Sophie, shooting at bottles.

FEBRUARY 5, 1983
TIMBER LAKE
CECIL, NEW JERSEY